Portia of the Pacific Trilogy

Includes:

Chinawoman's Chance

The Spiritualist Murders

The Stockton Insane Asylum Murder

James Musgrave

ISBN: 1943457379
ISBN-13: 978-1943457373

Contents

Interactive and Multimedia Enhanced eBooks

EMRE Publishing is now selling completely "enhanced" versions of its books, including the first two mysteries in this trilogy, through the unique Embellisher Multimedia Stream platform. Simply register inside the eReader to have access to the variety of titles. They contain relevant historical videos, music, interactive content, and a complete audiobook edition in many of the great titles.

Visit https://emrepublishing.com/new_embellisher-ereader/ to see what's available. In addition, if you are also an author or one who sells online, you may want to take Professor Musgrave's free online course, "Developing Your Digital Marketing Platform" (https://payhip.com/b/j3Xs). Besides eBooks, you will learn how to sell other tangible goods and services, as well as digital podcasts, courses, and a variety of video products.

Chinawoman's Chance

"Whereas, in the opinion of the Government of the United States, the coming of Chinese laborers to this country endangers the good order of certain localities within the territory thereof. (Sec.1)" *Chinese Exclusion Act*, 1882.

CHAPTER 1: FLAYED

Jenny Lind City Hall, Police Department, Detectives Office, Kearny Street, San Francisco. February 12, 1884.

"I tell you, Captain, she was flayed like a dressed deer. Clean down to the bone."

Detective Sergeant Eduard Vanderheiden, or "Dutch" as his peers called him, was a tall, thin, bald, and agitated man with thick, auburn mustaches that curled on the ends like charmed snakes and flaming red chin whiskers. He also had a constant wink in his right eye. This nervous tic would often garner Dutch a drunken swing from a jealous husband's fist if he were seated within arm's reach of the Dutchman's chin. At age forty-nine, Dutch was never afraid to gawk at a pretty lady. That was his problem.

Captain of Detectives, Isaiah Lees, sat, manning the telegraph machine that connected each of the three San Francisco districts. Lees wore a brown frock coat and vest with checkered pants and spit-shined Oxfords. His face had the jowly redness of his fifty-four years, his hazel eyes were deep-set, and his brow was almost always in a contemplative frown. His graying goatee and full head of curly-brown hair were well groomed. His one affectation was to wear a cape whenever he was on a case, and, as a result, many of the beat cops referred to him as "Sherlock." Captain Lees, after all, was born in England.

"Now that makes sense. Tongs use very sharp hatchets to enforce their will. I would wager she was probably keeping money from her handler, or else it was retribution for some other financial transaction. If twenty years in Chinatown taught me anything, it's taught me, money is the reason for everything." Lees stood up.

The First District of the San Francisco Police Department, with its station house at First and Mission Streets in Happy Valley, extended from California Street to Rincon Point. There was also a little lock-up or "calaboose" located in the First District station house. The Second District, with its station housed at City Hall at Pacific and Kearny, where Captain Lees and Detective Vanderheiden were now, was inside the former Jenny Lind Hotel, and it embraced the main business district. The Third District, with a station on Ohio Street, covered the area from Pacific Avenue north to North Beach.

Whenever a major crime was committed, the uniformed officer would send a message back to the Detectives' Office on Kearny, the Second District, and a detective would be dispatched to the scene. After the arrest, detectives took offenders to the main jail on Kearny.

"But she weren't no Tong girl. She was working at 814 Sacramento, next-door to the rooming house. A white working girl. You know, most of the Tongs got their Chinawomen working over on Sullivan's Alley or Bartlett's." Vanderheiden pointed to a location on a large map hanging on the wall in back of the telegraph machine.

"Those white girls sometimes work alone. Who's at the crime scene? It might become dangerous." Lees picked up his holstered Colt .45 and buckled it around his waist. He felt for his Bowie knife behind his vest and attached his captain's badge to his cape, which was draped over the back of the swivel chair.

"Cameron was first on scene. Oh, and don't be surprised if Cook shows up. Cameron knows to notify the Chinatown Squad when there's a ruckus. This ain't no ruckus, but we know Tongs can start a war over much less." Dutch winked at Lees. He followed the captain out the door, and they rode the elevator from the third-floor office down to the street.

Inside the elevator, Lees scowled up at the taller detective, whom he had known for twenty years on the force. They had both been beat policemen after the Civil War and earned their detective appointments through hard work and many arrests.

"Jesse Brown Cook and his band of holy rollers don't understand how it is now that they passed the Exclusion Act. These Asiatics had no rights to begin with, and now that they can't get over here by boat, the competition between these men has escalated. I'm not surprised by this murder, and there will probably be a Chinaman behind it. But kid Cook gets his marching orders from Sheriff Connolly," Lees said.

"I seen Connolly call out the health team to fumigate every blasted gambling parlor, opium den, and hooker house in Chinatown. The mayor blames the chinks for every outbreak of typhus, malaria, and plague. But Connolly will poison the Chinatown rooms when the white kids in San Francisco so much as get the measles!" Dutch punched into the air with his fist.

Lees smiled. "You know how the excrement rolls downhill? Leland Stanford, the pope of the bluebloods, says the Chinese are inferior humans. He never liked it when the coolies defended themselves against the Irish workers who attacked them while working on Stanford's railroad. And Stanford testified to Congress to get the Exclusion Act passed. He hand-picked Connolly, the Irishman, and Connolly picked Cook, the holy joe. The three of them think they're saving Christian America from the Yellow Peril. America's not supposed to exclude. It's supposed to include. Everybody!"

"Okay, Captain, I know where you stand. You're preachin' to the choir here. Just don't lose your temper with the kid the way you did last week when they fumigated the room where the baby was."

"That baby died, Dutch! All because of Cook and his band of holy rollers. But Cook was just the proximate cause. The underlying cause is men who think they're better just because they're rich, white and Christian." Lees returned the scowl to his brow, and they both stepped out into the chilly night air of San Francisco.

Detectives Lees and Vanderheiden walked the four blocks down Kearny to Chinatown. Once a crime scene was secured, they knew there was no rush. Unless suspects were reported on the scene, the methodical process of criminal detection would be usually slow and arduous. Witnesses, if any, needed to be interviewed. Evidence, if any, needed to be collected and classified. And, of course, the journalists were always there to provide a circus atmosphere.

Captain Lees had always enjoyed working the Chinatown beat.

Sailing from his home in Lancashire, England in 1848, he was an eighteen-year-old immigrant looking for adventure. When he landed in San Francisco aboard the Mary Francis on December 20, the Gold Rush had just begun. He worked as a laborer and engineer until he was drawn to the profession of law and order by performing a citizen's arrest when he saw a man stabbed for $300. He was hired by the newly established police department in 1854 and was promoted to captain four years later.

Now, as Captain of Detectives, Lees understood the social realities of being an immigrant in a strange land. Even though England was not China, he still believed the same fear and insecurities existed inside the men who came here to seek their fortunes.

Captain Lees had advanced in his chosen profession because he read a lot, and he was, like all good detectives, a student of human nature. He understood that humans joined groups to protect themselves from perceived threats to their livelihood or their person.

In a strange way, Lees himself had joined the police department because he felt threatened by the burgeoning greed of San Francisco during the Gold Rush. He witnessed men behaving like monsters. Raiding gold mining claims, killing the owners or stealing their gold—or both. When the railroad construction began, he saw how the owners, like Stanford, would speak out of both sides of their mouths.

On the one hand, they told the ruling class what they wanted to hear that America should be kept white. On the other hand, if they wanted to maximize their profits, the way Stanford did, they turned around and imported Chinese workers from Guangdong Province in southern China.

Lees knew these rich bastards were sly, however, in that they contracted with the governing Manchu in China, who forced the men in their country to become indentured servants. These immigrants had to wear the Manchu pajamas and distinctive queue pigtails and swear their allegiance to their rulers back home.

Lees wondered if Stanford or any of the other rich men ever thought about what life would be like if they had to forsake their civil rights, give up their families, and travel inside overcrowded steamships to a new world where they were accepted only by the greedy businessmen who would then run their lives and determine their fortunes? These Chinese had no human rights to vote, to organize, to marry, to testify in court or to even socialize with their superiors outside these Chinatowns.

Lees knew history. The first Americans were British subjects fleeing the Crown's persecution of their religion and their strange ideas about independence and freedom. They became indentured to profiteering "companies" in England who sent them to the New World under contract. Why couldn't men like Stanford see that these Chinese men were the same indentured citizens as their forebears had been? How was Buddhism any stranger than being a Quaker or a Catholic? Money! That's what changed their tune.

According to Lees, who was a pragmatic realist, most of the ills of a society and its persecution of minorities, could be traced to the unholy quest for profit at the expense of others. It had always been this way, and it was continuing in his beautiful San Francisco to this very day.

Chinatown's twelve blocks of crowded wooden and brick houses, businesses, temples, family associations, rooming houses for the bachelor majority, opium dens, and gambling halls were home to more than 22,000 people. Even though the population had fallen after the 1882 Exclusion Law was passed, the atmosphere was still bustling and noisy, with brightly colored lanterns, three-cornered yellow silk pennants denoting restaurants, calligraphy on sign boards, flowing costumes, hair in queues and the sound of Cantonese dialects being spoken in the alleyways and outdoor markets. In this familiar neighborhood, Lees and Vanderheiden knew, the immigrants found the security and solidarity to survive the racial and economic oppression of greater San Francisco.

As they came up to the crime scene at 814 Sacramento, it was exactly 8 PM, and Lees saw that Cameron had roped off the front of the small door leading into the one-room apartment. Next-door, at the two-story rooming house, he could see several white women hanging their heads out of room windows, and they smiled and waved down at him and his partner as they ducked under the rope and shook hands with Officer James Cameron who was standing on the front step.

"Jimmy! You come up and see me after you're done, you hear?" One of the women yelled down, and Cameron's face reddened.

"Don't mind those wenches, Captain," said Cameron. "They get a toot on with that opium, and you can never tell what they'll come out with."

"I know, Jimmy," said Lees. "Got anything for us?"

"No, when I arrived, there was just the body on the bed inside. One of the girls next-door knew where I was on my beat, and she come running up and told me about hearing a scream inside this little bungalow. You'll see exactly what I saw when I entered. Of course, I didn't touch a thing, but there was no visible weapon anywhere in plain sight. Only her gruesome corpse lying on that threadbare cot. No furniture. Just that bed and a small bedside table with a gas lamp. I tell you, Cap, I got sick to my stomach. I never seen nothing so horrible in me life."

"Do we know the murdered woman's name?" Dutch asked.

"Yes, it's Mary McCarthy. She used to live at the Methodist Mission for Wayward Women, but I guess she decided to ditch the straight and narrow and try to make some money on her own. Don't know if she had a handler, but it don't seem like it. I asked a few of the girls next-door, and they said they never seen no men, besides Johnny boys, escorting her to or from the apartment. As you know, clients come inside. Pimps escort their dollies around town and are usually dressed like peacocks."

Captain Lees opened the red door, and it squealed on its hinges. He stepped through, and the two other men followed him. The single gas lantern was glowing on a small table next to the cot. Lees motioned toward the lamp.

"Hold it over the body, Dutch. I want to inspect her," he said.

The tall detective gently grasped the bronze lantern by its semicircular guards and held it up over the cot. The bright light shone down on what was left of Mary McCarthy, woman of the streets. In the corner of the room, the sound of what must have been a rat scurrying into a hole made Lees swallow hard.

Lees immediately saw that the face of the victim had not been harmed. In fact, he could still see the rouged cheeks and red lipstick, and Mary's green eyes stared at him accusingly beneath heavy blue eyeshadow and dark brown eyebrows. Her reddish-brown hair was piled high and fastened with ribbons and a silver seahorse comb. However, beginning at the nape, there began a horrific display the likes of which

Lees had never seen before on man or beast.

Dutch's description of a deer flaying was hardly an acceptable comparison. The pulling from the outer epidermal layers was just the beginning. After removing the skin, the slayer had then removed all of the muscles, tendons, and intestines from the poor woman's corpse, until all that was left lying on the cot was the skeletal remains of a once lovely, nineteen-year-old orphan by the Christian name of Mary McCarthy.

Lees' eyes roved over the body like two searchlights. He stopped when he saw something exposed in the pelvic region, between the woman's legs. "Bag," he said, and Officer Cameron quickly took out a small paper sack, from a cloth container around his waist, and handed it to his superior. Lees bent down, reached out, and extracted a piece of thin lamb's skin from the orifice, and he gently dropped it into the bag. "Mark it as number 1, Jimmy," the Captain told the young officer.

"Looks like one of them new Sheiks. They sell for twenty-five cents apiece in the *Examiner*. Advertised as married women's friends. Ha! That Comstock Law's making a lot of rich businessmen," said Dutch, chuckling.

"I guess she had a customer before this happened. Something about him made her want to use protection." said Lees. "But there's hardly any splatter on the floor, walls or even on the cot. How did this butcher do it? And, more importantly, what did he do it with?"

"Maybe he was a butcher—a real one, Captain. We should investigate all the butcher shops in Chinatown. Maybe a Tong hatchet done this, but I think you hit the nail on the head. Only a butcher would know how to keep the blood from running like a river all over the place." Dutch shook his head.

"Yes, I think that's a good proposition. First, we'll run through my Rogues' Gallery of photographs to see if any butchers are there who've committed crimes. Then we'll go to the butchers without a record of criminal behavior." Captain Lees motioned for Dutch to put the gas lantern back on the little bedside table.

Outside, the Chinatown Squad wagon was pulling onto Sacramento with its loudly obnoxious siren and clatter of horses' hooves. Detectives Vanderheiden and Lees looked at each other and raised their eyebrows.

"Kid Cook," Captain Lees said.

"He will be cooking up something for certain," Dutch replied.

The door opened, and a tall, dapper, twenty-four-year-old sergeant entered, followed by three of his men. With a black-brush mustache, wide-set, piercing brown eyes and a commanding demeanor, he immediately took up position in the center of the small room. His blue uniform was ironed and spotless, and there was a yellow insignia of an Asian tiger stitched on his hat's crown.

"Gentlemen! I see you've secured the scene quite well, but now we can enjoin the real suspects. I'll question Little Pete and Big Jim. They have most likely punished this lass for overstepping her bounds. You fellows know how these hi-binders feel about freelancers. Without getting protection money, they can become quite monstrous."

Captain Lees let out an audible sigh. "Jesse, my lad, you know as well as I that Fong Jing Tong and Chin Ten Sing are old men now. They haven't been active since the 1860s, and I would imagine they would readily confess to an assassination plot on Chester A. Arthur himself at this point in time. They are both senile, my good man."

"I can see you don't understand the ways of these pagan idolaters, Captain Lees. They worship their ancestors, and they always obey their wise elders. Sheriff Connolly has placed me in charge because I've studied their ways, and I've become quite proficient at weeding out the bad ones."

"At the grand old age of twenty-four, you've been able to cast a wide net of noxious fumes. I know. . ." Lees began, but Dutch grabbed his arm.

"Captain, I think we need to get back to the station and look over those photographs."

"All right, Detectives. We'll be keeping you informed. If I get a confession, I'll certainly let you know." Cook stepped over to the bed and looked down at the victim. "Oh, my! Would you look at that. Did you know, Captain, their Buddhist and Taoist religions require that corpse bones be shipped back to China for proper burial? Indeed. They also believe that the skin emits evil spirits, and so they will never handle a dead body until it's been stripped of the evil outer flesh. Our Christian coroners have been given that foul duty."

"I know all about the religious practices of the Chinese, my dear

Cook. And those Christian coroners get paid handsomely for their work. If you look closely, however, you'll see that this woman is not a Chinawoman. I'm not saying there might not be a Chinese connection here, but as it stands right now, I'm open to any suspect—Chinese or other races." Lees opened the front door. "Good night, gentlemen," he said, and he stepped out onto the front step. Dutch followed him.

Outside, the local newspapermen were awaiting them. They had the new dry plate cameras, and they were busy taking photographs of the scene and interviewing possible witnesses on the street. Now Lees and Vanderheiden were part of their picture-taking. One young man Lees knew as Boscombe, from the San Francisco Examiner, wearing a blue suit and matching derby, stepped forward, pen and paper tablet in hand.

"Any suspects, Captain? Find a weapon? How long has she been dead? Can we also get inside to get a photo of the body?"

Lees was surprised by the young reporter's last question. "Also? We have not allowed any person to come inside this crime scene, Boscombe. You know the rules. Nobody allowed in until we've gathered all evidence and questioned all possible witnesses."

"But there was a reporter inside earlier. I passed him on my way here. His name is Kwong. George Kwong. He's a reporter for *The Oriental*. He told me he got a picture of the white prostitute who was killed on Sacramento. His smile was wider than a Cheshire Cat's. When I got here, your man already had the rope up."

Lees knew that name. Kwong. Yes, that was the name of the leader of the Sam Yup Company, Andrew Kwong. Andrew also owned part interest in *The Oriental*, so that would explain how his son, George, got the job. Kwong was one of the Christian converts who got money from the Methodist Church to publish the only newspaper allowed in Chinatown. As the leader of the businessmen's company, he was probably the wealthiest Chinaman in San Francisco.

"As to your first three questions, Boscombe, no, no, and we won't know until the coroner gets here." Lees stepped past the gathered reporters, who were shouting out questions to him, which he ignored. From experience, Lees knew that no matter how he would answer the questions put to him, they would, most of the time, get transformed into something outrageous, to attract readership for their papers. Besides,

Cook would certainly give them enough nonsense to fill their papers for weeks.

"I can see the headlines already, Dutch. INNOCENT CAUCASIAN DAMSEL MUTILATED BY BARBAROUS CHINESE RELIGIOUS CULT, or some such balderdash." Lees spat into the gutter. "However, I do want to meet with the Six Companies' leaders to investigate what they know about this murder—especially Andrew Kwong and his son, George. How did George get wind of this murder before anybody else? Why would that Christian rag want to promote the killing of a white woman?"

All around them, the noise of the Chinatown streets permeated the evening's glow, as the wispy fog began to creep across the pavement ahead, like the premonition of some curse beginning to cast its spell over the entire City by the Bay.

All of Chinatown and soon, most likely, most of Guangdong Province would be aware of the murder investigation. Kid Cook had taken it upon himself to arrest fourteen of the leaders of the Tongs. He had taken them to Sheriff Connolly's station, so Captain Lees was not informed until one of his detectives, Danny Carey, was over there because his best informer, Li Wong, had been arrested, and he discovered Wong was locked inside the jail on Kearny Street.

Lees knew the only thing really separating the Tongs and street justice was the sheriff's department. San Francisco had decades of vigilante law before the department was formed, and blood vengeance was still in the hearts of many citizens, as a holdover from the frontier and Gold Rush days.

Lees had learned to work with both the good and bad members of Chinatown. To the sheriff's department, however, the Tongs were always the bad men, never to be trusted

Lees knew better. There were Tongs he could work with to keep the overall peace, and they were much more valuable to him outside than they were locked-up. He also believed it was a better use of his time to follow the leads he had already uncovered in this case, especially the one that pointed to George Kwong, the son of Andrew Kwong, head of the Sam Yup Company. However, Captain Lees knew there was no such thing as cornering a man of his reputation. It would cause an immediate response from the entire community.

Therefore, Lees was going to arrange a meeting with all of the Six Companies' leaders at one time so that suspicions would not be raised. If and when he procured enough evidence to make an accusation or arrest, all of the leaders would be informed so that possible violence might be averted. Of course, Kid Cook and his arrests of Tong leaders had already placed all of Chinatown on high alert, and this was not good for Lees and his investigation. Again, it seemed, Lees was fighting is inner foe: the conflict between his police department and that of the freewheeling and unrestrained Sheriff's Department that provided the captain with more obstacles than they provided assistance.

Once back at the Office of Detectives on Kearny, Captain Lees told Detective Vanderheiden to arrange the meeting with the leaders of the Six Companies in the morning. Before retiring to his apartment on Montgomery Street, Lees did a thorough search through his photographic records of arrested and convicted felons.

There were seven who had listed their occupation as "butcher," but none of them had a sexual assault or other such conviction. Two were arrested for larceny, one for assault, and four for drunken vagrancy. Only one was Chinese. Lees decided to delegate the questioning of these seven to one of his detectives, of which there were five, not including him and his partner. Perry O'Brien would probably be the best candidate, as he was not working on a case presently.

As Isaiah Lees leaned back in his chair with his feet on the desk, he thought about what questions he would ask of these leaders, and he remembered yet another connection to the victim. Mary McCarthy had previously been a member of the Methodist Mission for Wayward Women. He knew the woman, Rachel Benedict, the appointed head of that mission. She would need to be interviewed as well.

Finally, he also realized, Andrew Kwong received the money for his newspaper, *The Oriental*, from the Methodist Church in San Francisco. With those dots connected, the Kwongs became even more suspect. Was there perhaps some rivalry between father and son, which had caused one of them to murder young Mary McCarthy?

Lees knew he needed to find out who had visited McCarthy the evening of her murder. Was it one of the Kwongs or some other member of the Six Companies? Did McCarthy perhaps begin to blackmail one of her clients? She was, after all, a freelance whore.

Of course, at this stage of the investigation, this client might have been anybody, and his hunch that this person was connected to Chinatown might be wrong. One thing was certain. The inscrutable way the Chinese could keep what white men called a "poker face," would be an added difficulty when he questioned them all at their meeting.

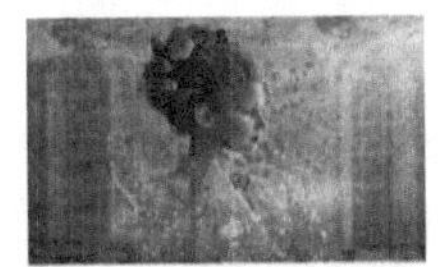

CHAPTER 2: PORTIA OF THE PACIFIC

Baldwin Hotel, California Street, San Francisco, February 13, 1884.

Clara Shortridge Foltz, age thirty-five and mother of five, was visiting her lover, Charles Gunn, age twenty-nine and a bachelor, when she was kidnapped by four Chinese men. Mrs. Foltz had met Mr. Gunn four years earlier, when she was serving as the first woman appointed Clerk of the California State Assembly in Sacramento. She had noticed the rather short but handsome young man with a full black beard standing in the front of the audience, smiling at her, as she spoke about women's suffrage to the mostly approving, mostly female gathering.

Minutes before the men in black silk pajamas broke into the room, Charles was listening to his lover tell him about the strange occurrence she had experienced the night before, around Portsmouth Square, near Jackson Street, in Chinatown. "I saw a man in the alleyway, and he was standing in the shadows leering at me. I was quite frightened, as I saw a flash of what I could have sworn was a blade of some kind in his right hand."

Mr. Gunn was immediately compassionate, and he put his arm around her waist as they stood together near the door. Charles had often heard Clara bemoan her condition as a woman left with five children, and he thought she sounded too unromantic most of the time. In fact, to the young politician, she sounded like Abraham Lincoln at Gettysburg, even when they were making love. Charles knew it was time for her to go back to her lonely room on Montgomery Street, and he was feeling sad.

"What did you do?" Gunn inquired, his voice a bit tired after their earlier lovemaking.

"I ran out of there, of course. I suppose I should have reported it to some policeman, but it was dark, and I knew this fellow had escaped. I saw him run off down the alleyway. Besides, just because he had a knife didn't mean he was up to no good."

"No, I suppose you're correct. You were wise to stay out of

harm's way, my dearest," Charles said, giving his love another peck on her rosy cheek.

It was then that the four men burst through the door and confronted them both. One of the Chinese had a hatchet in his hand, and he waved it dangerously around. Charles, who was unarmed, attempted to stop the men from stealing his woman from the hotel room by shouting at the top of his voice to attract attention, but these men quickly formed an ingenious human arrow, with one man in front and three behind. They lifted his lover above them so that she was resting upon their hands in a vertical position, and they stormed out of the room, down the stairs, and out into the noisy hubbub of California Street.

Some passersby momentarily stopped and watched the strange procession, a woman in a fancy blue dress being carried by small but wiry men dressed in what looked like black pajamas. However, the Chinese were so fast and so efficient at dodging and weaving through the crowd that they were soon running down a side alley and out of sight. After running after them for a block, poor Mr. Gunn was finally out-maneuvered by the quick turns and adroit dodges, and he was thus left in the dust, standing on the sidewalk, waving his fist in anger.

***

All that Clara Foltz could think of as she was being whisked down the alley, headed toward Chinatown, was that her youngest daughter, eight-year-old Virginia, would have loved riding up in the air on the hands of four men. Clara herself was not unpleased with the experience, as these men were so competent at carrying her that she felt no discomfort. Somehow, after giving birth to five children beginning at age sixteen, in the rural wilds of Indiana and Iowa, this experience did not seem dangerous at all.

Even though Clara, a free love advocate, had procured the latest contraceptive, a gold wishbone stem pessary, an intra-cervical device, she was terrified about being raped. As long as she did not panic, and kept her wits, she believed she might even be able to talk her way out and survive this "bump in the road," as her grandmother used to call life's little adversities, such as tornados, dangers of childbirth with no doctors, and the attack from wild Indians on the plains.

As her entourage was clambering down the stairs inside a Chinatown building, however, the bumps became a bit much, granted, but the room into which they ultimately took her was quite large and filled with beautiful Asian decorations. Paper lanterns of almost every shape and size were lit, and, as they lifted her and let her slide—feet first—to the floor, she saw a row of stern-faced Chinese males staring back at her from behind a rectangular wood table of about twelve to fourteen feet in length and three feet high.

Perhaps her body was not going to be plundered for sexual gratification. However, she did believe all the anti-Chinese rhetoric, and she surmised that these men in front of her were in direct communications with the warlike Manchu profiteers back home. Again, she remembered the dark figure in the alleyway the night before and his huge, flashing blade. She shivered.

Mrs. Foltz often spoke in defense of Denis Kearney's Workingmen's political party, which was established in response to high unemployment and was in sympathy with the nation-wide railroad strike of 1877. This labor unrest, caused by the jobs taken by these Chinese, had even led to the infamous riots of that same year.

Clara had read about how the crowd back then had become agitated against these Chinese immigrants and went on a rampage that lasted three nights. The white men—mostly Irish immigrants--killed several Chinese, destroyed Chinese laundries, and raided the wharves of the Pacific Mail Steamship Company, which transported these dreadful Chinese to America to take jobs away from others.

But now, Clara observed six much different Chinese men sitting behind the long table, and all but one wore the silk robes, round hats, wispy facial hair and long queues down their backs. They looked the same as the men she had seen so often in the newspapers, both in photographs, and exaggerated in the political cartoons of the editorial pages. Only one man was wearing a western suit, with white shirtsleeves and tie, and he was seated in the center position. He began to address her in well-spoken English.

"I am very sorry for your rude transport, Madame Foltz. You see, we have been rushed into taking rather extreme measures. Let me introduce you to my compatriots, from your far left, and continuing down the line, we have Li Youchin of the See Yup Company, Wong Suh Woo of the Ning Yuen Company, and my name is Andrew Kwong of the Sam Yup Company."

Her host turned toward the gentlemen on his left and continued, "Next, we have Yueng Sheng of the Yeung Wo Company, Al Soo-Hoo of the Hop Wo Company, and Stephen K. Fong of the Hip Kat Company." Each one of the men bowed deeply as he was introduced.

"Thank you for your introductions, gentlemen, but as you are certainly aware, you are presently classified as kidnappers under the law. I suggest you explain the grave importance of this imposition upon my personal freedom and safety, as I cannot guarantee I will not prosecute you all when this is over." Clara was surprised that her voice sounded clear and confident. She may well have been addressing the California Supreme Court, if it weren't for those four rather ominous henchmen and escorts, who were still standing closely around her.

"I am happy to hear you mention the law, Madame Foltz. The main reason you have been brought here, under less than auspicious circumstances, is to retain you as our attorney. Fourteen members of our community have been arrested, and we have no means to defend them. I attended the trial you prosecuted in December 1880. I was impressed by your argument to the jury of all men about the guilt of the accused, Mr. Wheeler. You told them that you believed Mr. Wheeler's defense was not acceptable because he was trying to blame the victim, the sister of his wife, with whom he was having a love affair. He said he killed her and stuffed her body inside a trunk because she had asked him to do so. The victim was, Wheeler's attorney said, too embarrassed because a rival lover had found out about her relations with Wheeler, and she wanted to die."

Clara smiled, and she was relieved these men were not aware of her prejudices. She remembered the case well, as she and her female attorney friend, Laura deForce Gordon, were the first women ever to prosecute a murder case in a court of law. The publicity surrounding the case was good for her practice, even though the same basic prejudices existed at the time and would contine.

Many men believed that women could never argue to an all-male jury because they would "seduce them" with their wiles and feminine emotions. The prejudices she knew so well continued because of the legally established concept that a woman was a child, incapable of adult reason, and when she married, her civil rights merged into the protective custody of her overlord and master, her husband.

Oh. Yes, Clara knew personally about such "protective" husbands. Her Civil War veteran husband, Jeremiah Foltz, had abandoned her and her five children for a young woman in San Jose. To protect herself from society's harsh judgement against "sinful, abandoned women," she lied. She told everyone that her husband had died, and she was now a widow. At every turn, it seemed, Clara had to fight the male establishment to pursue her calling.

"Madame Foltz? Did you hear me?"

Andrew Kwong was talking to her. Clara cleared her throat.

"Yes, I did win that case, even though it was adjudicated a mistrial because of another attorney who brought forth unacceptable evidence. However, I might add, the Defendant Wheeler was later retried and was hanged."

"And justice was served," said Kwong.

"Justice can be a cruel mistress, Mr. Kwong, as you and your fellows know so well. I must admit, I have been aware for some time about the way your people and other indigent poor are treated in our courts. I have even been working with others to propose a possible new office of the public defender, paid by the state, to address this flagrant imbalance in representation." She pointed at the American flag in the corner.

"Our Constitution's Fourteenth Amendment does say, after all, 'equal justice under the law,' but it applies only to persons born here. I believe it should apply to any person who is lawfully living and employed here because he or she must answer to the same laws that natural born citizens must obey. I must admit, however, that I have a certain personal prejudice about you and your people. Are you not part of the problem in our society instead of being part of the solution? Your business treaties are between your rulers, the Manchu, and our federal government, are they not? How can you demand your rights in our local courts?"

Clara wanted to be honest with these men. After all, she had never really explored their side of the immigration and civil rights issues. She wanted to know more about them. It was actually the first time she had voiced their side of the argument out loud, and the logic of it actually sounded very good to her.

After Andrew Kwong had translated what she said to his fellows at the table, they talked amongst themselves for quite some time. Finally, Mr. Kwong spoke for them.

"We believe you will help us because we are in a similar predicament as your other minorities, the Negro and the aborigine. We are also very like your majority, the female population. It is true, we are bound by our Manchu leaders back home because they negotiated the treaty which binds us in most of our contracts for employment in America. They are, as you said about your husbands, our lord and master. However, we, unlike you, must serve two masters. Not only are we bound by the contractual arrangement which we did not negotiate, we are also bound by your criminal and administrative justice systems, which we did not democratically approve. Therefore, can you wonder why we have needed to circumvent both masters to survive in America and have any future chance to assimilate into your society?"

Kwong straightened his necktie. "I have converted to Christianity in the Methodist faith and learned English, but I am not any closer to citizenship than my Buddhist and Taoist friends. Perhaps, I can mingle with the whites a bit more easily, but my civil rights are still forbidden. I have read about your Suffrage Movement. I understand you often take steps that are forbidden to you by the law, such as birth control and pressing the authorities for equal employment. You have forced the hand of the California legislature to permit women to be employed in the legal profession, have you not?"

"Why, yes, I and my sisters have accomplished this. We also argued successfully so that women can attend Hastings Law School. But I have not been able to attend because I must work to support my five children and my parents. I am still proud to see other women attend, however. Are you suggesting you and your brethren want the rights of American citizens? Do you hope to become citizens?"

Andrew Kwong answered quickly, "Yes. We would like to marry the female of our choice and have children. Why can't we be ordained citizens, even without a birthright? If we promise to uphold all the laws in these United States, then we should be granted citizenship, no?"

Clara was becoming more interested in the plight of her captors. Their argument equating to her cause of women's suffrage was a good one. How many years have women been virtual slaves to their master husbands simply because the American laws forbid women the right to vote and to enter into contracts on their own behalf? These poor Chinese have faced a similar dilemma.

"I like your argument. What is it you want me to do for you? How much are you willing to pay?"

Clara was a good negotiator. She knew the law of politics also. She had argued and spoken out for Republicans, Labor Independents, and Democrats. Usually, she was attracted by the party's specific stand on Women's Suffrage, but money had also often swayed her. She believed leaders in America were the ones willing to take a risk and speak out about issues that affected the population. Most followers were gladly willing to allow these leaders to speak for them, although sometimes it was to their detriment.

"Simply stated, we want you to argue for us in San Francisco criminal courts. Right now, fourteen men are being held without bail in your jail on Kearny Street. Tomorrow, we are being visited by Captain of Detectives, Isaiah Lees. He is investigating the murder of a Caucasian prostitute named Mary McCarthy. She was killed inside one of our apartments in Chinatown. The fourteen Tongs who were arrested are suspects, and I would assume Captain Lees will be looking for more. We want you here to represent us. We are willing to pay you the sum of one hundred dollars per hour for your representation." Andrew Kwong looked to his right and left, and the other men nodded their approval.

One hundred dollars per hour. Clara had never been offered so much money by anybody. Once, a wealthy dentist paid her to travel to the state legislature to get a bill passed which would allow him a refund of the money he had bequeathed the University of California. She had to fight him, tooth and nail, for every cent he paid her, and she ultimately had to take him to court to win a small judgement. That fiasco had taken up thousands of hours of her time and effort, living frugally on bread and cheese, and sleeping in the halls of the Sacramento Congress.

"Gentlemen. You shall have your representation. What time should I be here tomorrow?"

"Please be here before Captain Lees arrives at one in the afternoon," said Andrew Kwong.

"I will be here at noon. I have a lot of questions of my own to ask. The intrigue is just beginning, I expect. You can also be assured, gentlemen, that once Clara Shortridge Foltz is on your side, she becomes a tenacious tigress protecting her young."

When Mr. Kwong translated what she said, every Company leader at the table smiled, and Clara was pleased.

***

Clara had no escorts for her return to her lonely residence on Montgomery Street. She had moved into the small apartment after the dentist and his wife, with whom she had been residing while doing his bidding, cast her out. She used the money from her judgement against him to rent her new place, wherein she also had her business office as well as her bed.

Her parents, Telitha and Elias Shortridge, still lived in San Jose with her five children. The goal she had was to make enough money to be able to move her family to San Francisco, but since the economy had taken a downturn, she thought that was probably not possible. But now, surprisingly, she was again invigorated with the prospect of making enough from the Chinese Companies to afford the move.

Clara had learned the law while working for a judge, Richard Warren, who was a friend of her father, from the time when her father practiced law. He merely sat her down inside his library and told her to study "the codes," as he called them, as well as the old books he had when he attended law school. Clara had poured over the rules and laws about contracts, criminal law, civil law, wills, torts, and compensation. Her father had early on recognized his daughter's gift for argument and her almost photographic memory.

But it was Clara's belief in herself and her abilities that gifted her with the initiative and drive needed to pass the bar on her first attempt. Even though she had not sat in a college classroom for more than one hour, she was able to become an attorney in California, something many men were never able to do.

If it were simply a matter of passing the bar, Clara's feat might not have been so noteworthy. However, she, along with her close friend and fellow attorney, Laura de Force Gordon, successfully argued with the California State Legislature to pass the ordinances which made it legal for women to pursue the profession of law, or any other profession, and to attend law school.

Although Clara wished she had the time and the money to attend law school, she now realized she had to put her mind and legal talents to work at providing the best possible defense for her new clients in Chinatown. What came to her first, as she walked along the breezy sidewalks of San Francisco, deeply inhaling the cool air, was the fact that she would need a different translator.

Even though Mr. Andrew Kwong seemed quite polite and educated, she knew his inevitable alliance would always be with his comrades. Therefore, he could not be trusted to always give her the truth. Clara realized she needed somebody to work with her who would not be biased. She knew of one Chinese who spoke perfect English, and who had successfully worked in a profession, albeit illegal, that was in direct conflict with the men.

Her name was Ah Toy, former prostitute and Madam, and the only Chinese woman to make it out of the confines of Chinatown and become a wealthy entrepreneur. Clara had successfully assisted her in suing a Tong leader who was trying to extort payment from her for his protection. When the 1854 Anti-Prostitution Law, aimed at the Chinese and not others, and the California Supreme Court decision in *People v. Hall*, which prevented Chinese from testifying in court, were established, Ah Toy retired from her brothel business. She began investing in real estate and took up residence in Santa Clara and San Jose.

However, Clara knew, Ah Toy was presently visiting San Francisco and living in the giant Mark Hopkins Mansion up on Nob Hill, the highest point in San Francisco. Mark Hopkins had been one of the “Big Four” owners of the Central Pacific Railroad, along with Leland Stanford, Collis P. Huntington, and Charles Crocker.

Mr. Hopkins had died in 1878, so his wife and first cousin, Mary, was left with the property. She was a great lover of art and sculpture, so when Mrs. Sherwood Hopkins, age sixty-six, saw the many Chinese art objects that Ah Toy owned, she arranged for this meeting to buy some from her. Mary was not the typical “snob” on Nob Hill, so doing business with a former brothel madam did not faze her one bit. Besides, most of her husband’s fortune could be traced to the employment of cheap Chinese male labor, so Mrs. Hopkins was impressed by this attractive Chinese woman’s success and determination.

Clara took the cable car, even though inventor Hallidie’s wire rope did not assuage her fear. She held onto the seat in front of her for dear life, as she heard the groan of this rope being stretched while her clanging car mounted the steep incline on California Street toward One Nob Hill. The looming presence of the Victorian giant on the hill cast a shadow over her as she stepped down from the steps. To Clara, who spent most of her life in wood cabins on the Iowa plains, or crowded city apartments, it was quite monstrous. She had read that they painted all of the redwood to resemble stones.

This was the gaudiest mansion in all of San Francisco. It took up the entire block, and it was one mass of cupolas, turrets, and flying buttresses. Clara supposed there were also gargoyles hiding in the rafters somewhere leering down at her. There were dozens of balconies and bay windows, and if the mansion were white, it would have looked like one of those sugar confection castles seen in a Nob Hill bakery shop window. Instead, it was a very depressing gray-black.

As Clara walked up to the main gate, she saw the private security guard house. When a man armed with a Winchester rifle slung over his shoulder stepped out of the shadows, he startled her. "Madame? Who do you wish to visit?"

She supposed the guard was there because of the railroad labor strikes that were going on. When she looked closer at him, she smiled. He was wearing a gray-black uniform, including a ridiculous-looking British Bobby hat with a black plume sticking out of the top. "I'm here to see Miss Ah Toy. I believe she's a guest of Mrs. Hopkins."

"And, who are you? I need to communicate your identity up to the house."

"Clara Shortridge Foltz, Esquire. I don't think Miss Ah Toy is expecting me, but if you can contact her, I am certain she will vouch for our friendship."

The guard stepped back inside the guard house and returned momentarily.

"You may go up, Mrs. Foltz. Miss Ah Toy will be expecting you. Just tell the butler, Hannigan. He'll answer the door."

As Clara walked inside the gardens, she could look out over the hill. The entire City of San Francisco lay at her feet, and she understood why the wealthy wanted to be so high above everything. It gave one a God-like perspective. However, as she walked up the steps leading to the front entrance, the darkly ominous presence of the giant house cast a spell over her.

After raising the large brass ball knocker and letting it fall against the redwood, the door was immediately opened, and a short, thin and red-haired man dressed in black tails and a ribbon necktie, stood before her. "Mrs. Foltz?" She nodded. "Please follow me. I'll be escorting you to Miss Ah Toy's room on the second floor."

The inside of the house was also dark, and she almost wanted to grab onto the butler's tails so she wouldn't get lost, but her eyes gradually became accustomed to the shadows. He took the stairs on the left, but before following him, she briefly looked down another gas lit flight of stairs in front of her. She could see that it led to the main drawing room below, and there were various paintings hanging on the walls, with two rows of benches for viewing the artwork.

The butler opened the door, and her old friend stood there to greet her. "Portia of the Pacific! My knight in shining armor! How are you, my dear friend?"

Clara knew not to hug the woman, as she was a reserved Chinawoman, raised in the old Chinese traditions. However, her speech was never reserved, as one would assume of a former "woman of disrepute." She was as tall as Clara, about five feet nine, and she had a respectful, sideward glance that made her brown eyes glisten when she raised her head to look at you.

The attorney also knew Ah Toy's clothing would be flamboyantly colorful and fantastic, and it was. She wore a long black silk dress called a *cheongsam* that extended down to cover her bound feet, and its front was adorned with an Asiatic, golden dragon, holding in its mouth an American eagle. The poor bird was obviously trying, quite unsuccessfully, to escape. Clara felt pristine and underdressed in her royal blue dress, with a slight bustle in the rear, that buttoned up to her neck in the front.

They sat together on the red couch with violet grapes adorning the pattern. Ah Toy's raven hair still shined, but it was graying at her temples, and there were white strands throughout the crown and down her pigtail. She was now fifty-six-years-old, but she had few wrinkles, and her wide smile and dazzling white teeth could still captivate.

"Carrie, how is your most wonderful family? I trust they are healthy, and your children are attending the best schools."

Clara had never introduced Ah Toy to her family, but she had often told the Chinawoman stories about what they were doing. Ah Toy was one of the few people Clara allowed to call her "Carrie," her given name at birth in Indiana. Family given names were very important to the Chinese.

Ah Toy had begun her career as a seductress on her voyage to San Francisco from Hong Kong. Her husband had died on the trip, so she took up with the captain and become his mistress. When she landed in San Francisco, she had enough money to start her own harlotry business.

"Yes, my family is well. They are all staying in San Jose until I can save enough to move them to San Francisco. That is actually one of the reasons I have come. I now believe I might be able to make enough money to be with my family again." Clara leaned forward and grasped Ah Toy's hands. She searched her friend's face for a reaction.

"How wonderful! Please, tell me the details."

"I need an interpreter for a new job. Believe it or not, I am now employed by the Six Companies of Chinatown. They are paying me one hundred dollars per hour to represent them in their legal problems." Clara didn't know how this news would affect her friend, but she wasn't surprised when Ah Toy rose to the challenge immediately.

"Of course, you do! I know those slant-eyed monkeys like the wallet inside a sailor's bellbottoms. I have a lot of time on my hands these days. Mrs. Hopkins is oh-so-slow to choose her art! I want some excitement, and now you have appeared. What will we be working on?" Ah Toy's brown eyes glowed.

"I am sorry, but I really don't have any very specific information at this point. The only facts of which I am aware concern a murder of a white prostitute who was killed inside one of the Companies' whore houses. Fourteen Tongs have been arrested already, and the Captain of Detectives, Isaiah Lees, will be meeting to question the leaders of the Six Companies tomorrow at one in the afternoon. Andrew Kwong, the English-speaking leader of my employers, was the only person I had to trust as a translator. That's why I've come to you."

"I know Andy Kwong. He has business interests all over the spectrum. Don't let him fool you, Carrie. He profits from all the sin trade. He just converted to Christianity to trick the white authorities. That newspaper, *The Oriental*, is a propaganda mouth of the Methodist Church. He runs that so he can run his whore houses, opium dens, and gambling parlors. He has his son, George, do most of the reporting."

"You see? That is why I need you as my interpreter. You not only speak the language, but you also have inside knowledge of the community. However, they are my clients, so my profession requires me to do my best to represent their interests." Clara stood up. "Can you meet me tomorrow at noon in the basement of the Tin How Temple? I can pay you for your trouble."

Ah Toy stood up and raised her right hand. "Stop! I will be there, but I don't need your money. I am an independently wealthy dowager, Carrie. When Mrs. Hopkins buys my artwork, I will have even more money. I am doing this because I love you, and I want some excitement in my life again."

Clara was surprised when Ah Toy walked toward her, in her bound, mincing gait, and grasped her by the shoulders with both hands. "I missed you, my friend. You are one of the few women who never judged me because of my profession, and I want to thank you for that. I also thank you for including me in your new adventure."

"I know you will help me make the right choices. Even after what you told me about Mr. Kwong, I still believe he was sincere about wanting his people to have the right to become American citizens. That would include you, of course, my dear friend." Clara reached up and squeezed Ah Toy's hands.

"Hannigan!" Ah Toy yelled. "They have a pneumatic telephone to call the staff, but I prefer using my lungs." She smiled at Clara. "Besides, this redwood house is like one big echo chamber. Americans claim to be Materialists, and yet when they have beautiful materials, like the redwood used in this building, they want to cover it up and make it dark and sad." "Be well, my friend," Clara said, and she walked to the front door. "I'll see you tomorrow afternoon."

"*Míng tiān jiàn*," Ah Toy said.

"Which means?" Clara asked.

"See you tomorrow."

CHAPTER 3: THE MEETING AT THE JOSS HOUSE

Tin How Temple, Waverly Place, Chinatown, San Francisco, February 14, 1884.

Captain Isaiah Lees liked to pursue a case in an orderly fashion. When he entered the temple on Waverly, accompanied by Detective Vanderheiden, he had his day of investigations all planned. First, he would interview the leaders of the Six Companies, then he was going to visit Rachel Benedict, head of the Methodist Mission for Wayward Women in Chinatown, and, finally, he wanted to visit the Mayor, Washington Bartlett, to plead with him to call off the Chinatown Squad arrests of Tongs.

Lees knew that if these Tong leaders were not released, there could soon be a war, which would not look good for the city's reputation.

Also, the Tongs acted as protectors of some in Chinatown who could not fight for themselves. Without their "security force in place," the population of Chinatown felt fearful, and they would react like a giant tortoise, withdrawing into its shell.

Tin How Temple was dedicated to the worship of the Goddess Mazu. She was believed to be able to protect China's seafarers as well as Chinese who were living away from home. Captain Lees saw that the Chinese head of the temple, Guan Shi Yin, was performing a prayer and spirit medium ceremony in front of the temple. Lees knew the Chinese got very superstitious whenever something bad happened in the community.

The woman, dressed in an elaborate gold and silk robe and headdress, was the medium to receive Mazu's messages, and she was in a deep trance, shuffling around on the sidewalk. The black beads on the ends of a string, fastened to her headdress, were bouncing in front of her eyes as she nodded and shook her head. She was mumbling something in Chinese, and Guan Shi Yin, dressed in what looked like gold pajamas, was translating for her to the audience. There were about two hundred men in the audience, and they were clasping their hands in prayer and reciting something back to the medium, perhaps questions for Mazu or some form of thanksgiving.

"Think praying to Mazu will help get their Tong gangsters out of the hooskal, boss?" Dutch pushed through the crowd in front of Lees to get to the front door of the temple.

"Probably works as well as when you pray to the porcelain goddess after a drunk," Lees told him, making a mental note to question Guan Shi Yin. If the Tin How Temple was anything like Christian churches, he knew, there were a lot of sinners who went there to find a way to be forgiven. There were also religious fanatics, who had begun to believe God was telling them to do things. Either way, Lees knew, the Mazu curator would know if there was anybody saying anything about the murder.

***

Clara sat with her interpreter, Ah Toy, at a side desk that Andrew Kwong had set-up for them. Kwong had told her that he wanted an appearance of formal strength shown to the Captain of Detectives when he asked his questions. The six members of the Companies sat behind their usual Clan table in front of which Clara had been brought the day before.

When Lees and Vanderheiden entered, Clara heard loud chanting coming from outside until the door was closed behind them. The two detectives seemed at first befuddled by the formal arrangement of seating, and they didn't know where to stand. Andrew Kwong pointed to a rostrum in the center of the room.

"Please, gentlemen, you may use that witness stand to ask your questions. It has a flat top for you to place your notebook." Lees glanced about and Clara thought he probably thought he was being tricked into intimidation by the group, but he didn't mind. He strolled over to the witness stand, and he took out his notepad from the inside of his gray cape and placed it on the flat top. He then turned to Dutch. "You have a pencil, Detective Vanderheiden?"

"Here you are, Captain," the taller man said, handing his superior a yellow pencil from his breast pocket.

"Now. Let's get down to the facts we know about this murder, and then I will begin my questioning. I don't think we need introductions, Andrew, but I would like to know the identities of those two attractive ladies seated on your left," Lees smiled, nodding at Clara and Ah Toy.

Clara thought that Captain Lees appeared quite a bit different than the police she had worked with when trying her only criminal case, *The People v. Wheeler*, in 1879. He looked a lot less formal, with his frock coat, cape, and checkered pants. His voice also had the hint of a British accent.

"I can introduce myself, Mr. Kwong. Captain, my name is Clara Shortridge Foltz, attorney-at-law, and this is my assistant and translator, Ah Toy. I have been retained to represent the interests of the Six Companies, and this will include advising them on their rights regarding your questions, if I may be so bold. Fourteen citizens of Chinatown have already been arrested by San Francisco sheriffs, so you can imagine why Mr. Kwong and his partners are concerned."

"Thank you, Counselor. It's an honor to meet you. However, as it is my duty to investigate a murder, which took place within one of the residences of your clients, my questions will relate to finding a possible murderer. I understand your concern for the welfare of the men who were arrested, but right now it is of no concern to me other than they might be possible suspects. At this point, anyone within reason is a suspect. The sheriff's department is in charge of their incarceration, and I suggest you take it up with them. Right now, I must find the killer or killers. Does that explain my purpose to your satisfaction?"

Clara felt like Lees was trying to handle her with kid gloves. She wondered if he knew her by name or reputation. "Yes, I will certainly contact Sheriff Connolly about their release. You may proceed with your questions." Clara believed her courtroom demeanor would assist her, as this policeman was obviously ignorant in the finer points of the law.

"Gentlemen, who owns the residence at 814 Sacramento?" Clara thought Lees wanted to narrow the search right away. If he could limit the range of suspects, it would improve his chances at finding clues as to possible connections with the victim.

"That is one of my properties, Captain," Andrew Kwong answered. "I rented it to Miss McCarthy when she came to my office and told me she had graduated from Mrs. Benedict's Methodist school.

She wanted to find employment, but she did not have the resources to pay rent for a place outside Chinatown. I am a Methodist, so I was sympathetic to her plight. I rented the apartment to her at five dollars per week."

"Were you aware that she was not looking for legal employment? In fact, she was working as an independent prostitute inside your residence, and had escaped Mrs. Benedict's home, not graduated." Clara studied Lees who watched the faces of all six of the men. She glanced at her clients as well. None, including Kwong, showed any emotion.

"I object. The rental agreement Mr. Kwong uses is legal and straightforward. It has a clause that stipulates that the renter can be evicted if she or he is discovered to be committing illegal acts on the premises. If he knew of this prostitute's activities, then she would have been immediately evicted." Clara responded as if she were talking to a judge.

"This is not a courtroom," Lees pointed out. "As you must be aware, Mrs. Foltz, laws are written mostly to protect the wealthy. In this instance, your clients. The reality of a cold-blooded and heinous murder, however, makes me a realist. For example, let us say there is a law against spitting on the sidewalk. It was written to protect the health and well-being of persons who use that sidewalk. However, this law is quite meaningless until an enforcer chooses to make the abstract words real by giving a citation to a violator. Excuse my vulgarity, but expectorant can flow like a river all over our sidewalks, but until a policeman acts, there is no law."

Lees walked over to stand in front of Clara and Ah Toy's table.

"I am one of those policemen who is trying to enforce the law against the willful and premeditated spitting on another person's life. In this instance, Mrs. Foltz, we are talking about a person who would not only kill this nineteen-year-old Miss McCarthy but who would then proceed to strip her body's skin and internal organs from her skeleton, leaving her unfit for a Christian Methodist burial."

Clara felt momentarily stunned. She hadn't heard the crime described in quite such details. Still, she tried to hide her surprise.

"Must you be so descriptive, Captain? You may proceed." Clara looked over at Ah Toy and raised her eyebrows.

"No, Captain, I was not aware that she was a prostitute. If I knew, then I would never have rented her the residence." Andrew Kwong turned right and then left, getting nods from his five colleagues.

"We all know who handles your dirty business, and many of them were arrested by the sheriff. You need to pay your bribes with more regularity." Lees wanted to get a rise out of them, and he could see by their reaction that he did.

"Our Tongs were arrested because there was a murder in Chinatown. My people become guilty before any evidence has been gathered. What kind of justice is that?"

Kwong's neck grew red.

"I agree," Lees said. "The Chinatown Squad wants to make a name for itself at your expense. I, however, want the truth." Clara felt surprised. This detective, indeed, wasn't like others she'd known. "Have any of your men ever had anything to do with Miss McCarthy?"

"Despite what you may think, Captain, the Six Companies does not maintain constant communications with our Tongs. We contract with them to keep our community safe. What they do on their own is not our concern."

"It should be, if what they do is run your gambling, prostitution, and opium interests." Lees crossed his arms across his chest. "But, never mind. What I want from you is access to all of Chinatown. I want you to communicate to your people that there is a murder investigation going on. I would also like to have your new lawyer and her translator accompany me. That way, you can be certain I won't step on anybody's toes."

"Of course. I will tell my people today, and you can begin starting tomorrow. Mrs. Foltz and Miss Ah Toy? Please arrange your schedules so you can accompany the good Captain."

Clara and Ah Toy nodded.

Lees stepped over to stand in front of Andrew Kwong.

"Before I leave, I would like to ask you and your son, George, a few questions privately, Mr. Kwong." Lees knew this was the time he could get into the real possibility of clues. The newspaper reporter had seen George going out of McCarthy's place on Sacramento shortly after, or possibly even before, she was murdered. The other members of the Six Companies were window dressing.

The elder Kwong spoke to one of the Six Companies directors in Chinese, asking him to contact his son, George, and tell him to come to the temple basement immediately. When the room was emptied of the others, except Clara and Ah Toy, Andrew Kwong let out a sigh.

"I knew it would come to this. You suspect me because I am the wealthiest person in my community, and I also have assimilated into your society to the greatest degree. Murder, however, does not assist me if I wish to ingratiate myself further and become an American citizen."

Clara realized this was her chance to put Lees on the spot. She turned, eyes riveted upon Captain Lees.

"Are you accusing my client of murder?" Clara sat up straight in her chair. "Nobody is accusing anybody of murder until enough evidence is collected to prove such accusations beyond a reasonable doubt. This is the law, is it not, Mrs. Foltz? I am simply asking questions at this stage in my investigation."

"Very well. Just remember. If I believe my client's best interests would be harmed by answering one of your questions, then I will advise him not to respond." Clara looked over at Mr. Kwong until he nodded his head in agreement.

"Indeed. However, I would point out that if he doesn't respond to important questions, such as the one I am now going to ask, he will become even more suspect."

"I understand," Clara said.

"Mr. Kwong, where were you on the evening of February 12, between the hours of six and eight?"

Clara nodded at Andrew Kwong to give him permission to answer, but she was wondering if Captain Lees suspected something more than just the usual alibi responses.

"I was at home. My wife can vouch for my presence as well as my two servants. I retired that evening at ten, after going over some of the proofs for the next day's distribution of *The Oriental*."

George Kwong entered the temple basement. He was a tall young man of twenty-two, and his raven hair was slicked back and parted, in the Western tradition, and his conservative brown frock coat, white shirt, and necktie completed his business attire. His deep-set brown eyes moved over the faces of the others and stopped on his father's grim scowl.

"Father? You wanted to see me? What's all this about?"

"This is Captain Lees of the San Francisco Police Department and his assistant, Detective Vanderheiden. And these are the two women I told you about who are representing the Six Companies. The Captain wanted to ask us some questions about the murder of that prostitute on Sacramento two nights ago."

"I'm going to ask you the same question I asked your father. Where were you on the evening of February 12, between the hours of six and eight?" Lees knew what he would ask next if the response was what he thought it would be.

"I was at the paper finishing the galley proofs for the next issue." The young man didn't look at Lees. Instead, he kept staring at his father.

"I am afraid that won't suffice," Lees said, shaking his head. "You see, I have an eyewitness who says he saw you leaving the scene of the murder at approximately a quarter after seven. In fact, he told me you bragged to him about getting a photograph of the victim inside her apartment."

Lees studied the man. Clara could see perspiration begin to form on the young man's upper lip and forehead. She wondered why he was so nervous. Was it Lees' presence or did he have something to hide?

Andrew Kwong began to speak to his son in rapid Cantonese.

Ah Toy whispered the translation to Clara. "He's telling him not to answer any more questions. His duck is in the deep fryer. A Chinese expression."

Clara felt a sinking feeling in her stomach. Was she representing guilty men? She pushed the thought aside. She thought of her family. Clara had a job to do—for them.

"Excuse me, Captain. My client will not answer any more of your questions until you bring forth evidence of this alleged meeting," Clara said.

"I will be getting this testimony. I was simply giving Mr. Kwong an opportunity to be honest. The truth will come out, one way or another."

"Very well. Ah Toy and I will meet you here tomorrow morning at nine to go around with you on your detective hunt. If you would be so kind, please bring an affidavit from your witness about my client's whereabouts on the night of the murder."

"Thank you, Mrs. Foltz. I will bring such proof with me, and I look forward to showing you how a detective works at the street level."

Clara and Ah Toy were allowed to leave the room first. Clara was baffled by the captain's desire to have her go with him on his rounds. Perhaps, he just wanted to distract her. He seemed to be highly suspicious of Mr. Kwong and his son, George. She knew she was a novice when it came to detection and "sleuthing," as they called it. This Lees seemed a nice enough sort, so she believed she could learn a lot from him, even though he was on the other side. She liked his expression about murder. The taking of a human life is all that *should* be considered important. That's exactly the way she saw events when she was in the courtroom, so she thought well of this police captain who believed the same thing at the enforcement level.

***

After telling Andrew and George Kwong that they should not leave San Francisco until the murderer was found, Lees and Vanderheiden left the temple basement to go to their next interview. Lees believed the Kwongs were his prime suspects, so he wanted them close by.

Rachel Benedict was the Head Mistress at the Methodist Home for Wayward Women located in St. Louis Alley off Jackson Street. This was where the prostitute slave auctions were held when the girls of 10-16 were brought there by the Tongs to be displayed like prime cuts of meat and sold to the highest bidders.

Lees knew that Miss Benedict had purchased some of her "students" at these auctions, even though the church usually didn't have the money to do such things. He was going to ask her about this, along with more pertinent questions about the victim.

Miss Benedict's "school" was a converted bordello. It had a sloping, red tiled roof, with windows filled with colored glass images of different scenes from the Bible. Once inside, Lees could smell the odors of an abode that kept a clean and meditative sanctuary for young women who wanted to escape from the wildly carnal life that lay just outside, only a few doors down. Bath salts, lye soap, and rose fragrances combined to nip at his nostrils in a pleasant way.

Inside the main room, where the prostitutes were usually seated, waiting for their customers, was now filled with six Chinese ladies and one Caucasian, lounging in comfortable stuffed chairs, reading books taken from the wide assortment of bookcases that stretched along the walls on three sides. This was obviously the room now serving as a library.

Captain Lees asked the one girl who was white and wore a long yellow dress with matching ribbon in her brown hair if she could tell Miss Benedict that Captain Lees would like to speak with her. The girl jumped from her chair like a jack-in-the-box, giggled, and ran up the stairs where the bedrooms were usually located. After a few moments, Rachel Benedict came down the stairs and into the library.

Miss Benedict was a short woman in her forties, with black hair, brown eyes that took in all she surveyed with a calm austere gaze. She wore a simple dress of gingham and a white bonnet around her head. In fact, to Lees, she resembled a pioneer woman who might be a better fit riding some Calistoga covered wagon than working as a headmistress for a bunch of escaped prostitutes.

When she spoke, Lees heard a definite Southern drawl. She grabbed onto his hands and pushed them up into the air as if she were refereeing a prize fight, and she was declaring him the victor.

“O Captain, my Captain! What brings you to the Land of Milk and Honey? Haven’t you always wondered how the Bible would use such feminine images for Paradise? Milk from the mammalian breast and honey from the female bee. My work, you see, is to get these little bees busy so they can return to society. Correct, ladies?” She withdrew her hands and spread them wide.

“Correct, Miss Benedict!” The girls shouted. “Bzzzzzzz!”

“Indeed. Now, Miss Benedict, if you will. I would like to ask you a few questions about the girl who was under your roof, one Miss Mary McCarthy.” Lees raised his voice to bring down the frivolity.

The room immediately became silent, and Rachel Benedict frowned. “Mary was one of my best pupils. She worked harder at improving her body and spirit than any student I have had. She had escaped the pit of Hell, you see, and she wanted to be saved from that life. I tried to assist, but just when I thought she was ready to join the community of decent society, she vanished. Right after she got the highest grade on a geography test I had given.”

“Did she say where she was going? What day did she leave your home?" Lees was working toward his primary question.

"No, not a word about her destination. It was on a Sunday. Yes, Pastor Reeves had given the sermon that morning, and I then gave the test. Sunday, the 10. of February." She cupped her right hand around her mouth and whispered, "Is it true what they wrote in the newspapers? Was her young body defiled in such a horrible manner?"

"I'm afraid so. Did anybody bring her to you? Did she have any visitors when she lived with you?"

Miss Benedict looked up to concentrate, and then she raised her right forefinger and smiled. "Why, yes! A young Chinese man brought her to me, and he would visit her from time to time. George, I believe his name was."

Lees' jaws clenched. "George Kwong?"

"How did you know? He was a fine young man. A journalist, I believe. He told me he wanted to save Miss McCarthy from a wretched occupation. He believed she was suited for a much better life."

"His employer, of course, is the same as yours, is it not? When the Methodist Church gives you money to buy girls at the auctions, is George Kwong or his father involved?" This was the point of Lees' questions.

"Why, no. I mean, I wouldn't know about their involvement. I am given money by the church elders with specific instructions to purchase the youngest among the girls, as they are seen as the most salvageable. There are so many Chinese men at these auctions, I wouldn't know if George Kwong or his father were there. Besides, it would be impossible to recognize them, even if they were there."

Lees, who had never attended these auctions, was still hoping he could place the Kwongs at the scene of such illegal business. "Impossible? How is that, miss? Do you not have good vision?"

"I have excellent eyesight, Captain. It's just that the bidders all wear masks. They are quite aware the authorities might be spying on them, so they disguise themselves. Of course, they pay the proper bribes, but every once in awhile, the Chinatown Sheriffs Squad will attend and arrest some of these scoundrels."

"Thank you for this information, Miss Benedict. If I have further questions, will you agree to see me again?" Lees motioned to Vanderheiden to get the door. They both moved toward the exit.

"Of course! I would do anything to help find such a monster. Although, God works in mysterious ways." Miss Benedict's brown eyes glistened.

"Yes? How so?" Lees opened the door. He could smell the foul odors of tobacco and liquors coming from the next-door tavern.

"With a killer like that on the loose, my girls may think twice about the profession they've chosen." Rachel Benedict smiled and closed the door.

"Pretty smart dame, that Benedict," Dutch said, reaching into his vest to pull out a cigar. He lit it with a match he extracted from his watch pocket, cupped it in his big hands, and set the end ablaze by flicking the tip with his thumbnail. He held the flame against the cigar end, blew out the smoke, and grinned. "You think she's on the take at the auctions, boss?"

"Who knows? I'm not after the little fish, Dutch. I am going to press hard about George Kwong and his father, however. They look like the best suspects so far, don't you think?"

"Would seem so. Let's see what the mayor says about the Kwongs. Maybe he wants to clean up the city a bit." Dutch spat a flake of cigar tobacco into the gutter and hitched up his pants.

"Indeed. The excrement does roll downhill." Lees patted his partner's shoulder. "We need to follow the money."

As luck would have it, Lees and Vanderheiden were met by a man running toward them, coming from the direction of city hall. They recognized him as being from the mayor's office. Breathless, he stopped. He wore a dark suit and red tie with red suspenders, and Lees thought at first there might be another murder.

"Captain Lees?" The man was still panting. Lees nodded. "There's been a change in venue. The mayor wants you to meet him in Chinatown. He's dining at the Pagoda Inn on Jackson Street."

"Very well. Thank you, son. We'll head back there."

The office assistant turned on his heels and ran back up the avenue. Lees and Vanderheiden retreated back to Chinatown.

Inside the Pagoda Inn, the delicious odors made Captain Lees' mouth water. He almost could taste the variety of dishes whose smells bathed him in their luxurious energies. Scallion pancakes, shrimp dumpling soup, Peking duck, shredded pork in hot garlic sauce, and chicken chilli. Lees and Vanderheiden often came to Chinatown to eat, as it was their favorite food. Also, many of their street informers were Chinese, so they never had to pay.

"Over here, gentlemen!" Mayor Washington Bartlett was waving from a booth in the back of the restaurant. Lees and Vanderheiden hurried over to greet him.

"*Buenos dias seňores. Como estan ustedes*?" Among other things, including being one of the most prominent officials in San Francisco, who wanted all Chinese immigration stopped, Bartlett was also fluent in Spanish. He was a tall man, a former naval officer under President Andrew Jackson, a life-long Democrat, whose relative signed the Declaration of Independence. His hair and full beard were now all white, and the Six Companies in Chinatown called him "The Great White Whale," not in literary reference to Melville's novel but because he was wide of girth and brash of manner. Captain Lees found it more than ironic that the mayor dined so often in Chinatown, and yet still professed his racism at the table, but mostly in Spanish.

Lees and Vanderheiden squeezed into the booth. Bartlett pointed to the heaping mounds of rice, crackling orange duck, and other delights. "Enjoy!"

"Sorry, Mayor. We're working the McCarthy case right now. I wanted to ask a favor." Lees wanted to get down to business right away.

Bartlett filled his bearded face, with a shoveling action of his chopsticks, from his bowl of rice. "Go on," he mumbled.

"Your man Connolly and his Chinatown Squad have arrested fourteen Tongs. I realize they might be suspect, but to get to the heart of this murder case, I need these men free and out in their community. Violence is bound to break-out if you keep them under lock for much longer, and then my case will become shrouded in anger. I won't be able to get an honest answer from anyone in Chinatown. You can understand my dilemma as a detective, can't you?" Captain Lees pleaded, aware that the motto hanging over Bartlett's desk read, "Honesty in Government."

Bartlett finished chewing, set down his chopsticks, and picked up the tiny teacup filled with oolong. He sipped and smacked his lips. "Of course! I will have them released right away. By the way, how is your case going?"

Lees was taken aback. He had not expected this, and now he was wary. Lees and Vanderheiden had always expected Bartlett to be in on most of the crime going on in Chinatown and that his racism was a way to cover it up from the public.

"Thank you. I'm just gathering testimony from witnesses. There are a few suspects, but releasing the Tongs will improve things substantially. I don't think this murder is connected to any gang rivalries or retributions. I have reason to believe, however, it may be related to something familial. Perhaps a father-son jealousy or something to do with a love affair gone wrong." This was the first time Lees had voiced his suspicions out loud. They sounded coherent enough.

"I know! As an old newspaperman, myself, I understand your concern. Would your suspects happen to be Andrew and George Kwong of *The Oriental* newspaper?"

Once again, Lees was astounded at the mayor's words. How would he know about Kwong? How had word gotten to him so quickly? "Why, yes, I just interviewed them both today. How did you know?"

"I have been in secret communications with them for six months now. I know none of you in the police force could know of this, but Mary McCarthy is not the first murder victim in Chinatown."

"What?" Lees looked over at Vanderheiden, whose eyes were now as large and round as the tea saucer under Bartlett's cup.

"Correct. There have been seven prostitutes killed—all of them Chinese—over the previous six months. When Kwong told me, I immediately knew this information could never reach the community in Chinatown. If so, there would be wholesale panic, and my administration, and even the Sheriff's Department and Chinatown Squad, could become suspect in their eyes. So, I have kept it under wraps. Until McCarthy's murder." Bartlett took another sip of his tea and licked his lips. "You might be interested to know that each of the killings had the same earmarks. The body was flayed and disgorged of innards, leaving the basic skeleton intact."

Lees swallowed hard. "This makes my case a completely different affair! I need a complete run-down on these successive killings. There is not one minute to waste!" Lees pounded his fist on the table, and the dishes and silverware rattled.

Bartlett's white eyebrows furrowed, and his grimace was

vicious. "Listen to me, Lees. If my precious City of San Francisco became aware of these murders, can you imagine what would happen?"

"You might lose your job?" Vanderheiden said, and Lees punched him under the table.

"Not just that. The Committee for Vigilance still exists. If you think the Chinese riots were terrible, word of these murders would have people torching all of Chinatown! We must keep these murders out of the press until we solve this case. Is that understood?"

Sadly, it did make some sense to Lees, even though he was now mentally including Mayor Bartlett on his list of suspects. "So, are you going to get me the list of victims and all the evidence you have on these murders?"

"Of course, O Captain, my Captain! In fact, Andrew Kwong has been keeping all of this information for us."

Lees also thought about where he had heard that expression before. "O Captain, my Captain." Of course! The pioneer woman of the Home for Wayward Women, Rachel Benedict. Did the mayor know her? Were they having an affair?

"Kwong plans to write a detailed story for his readers as soon as we can find the murderer," the mayor continued. "Won't that be special? Let's just hope the murderer turns out to be Chinese. Otherwise, it may not be only my job at stake but yours as well."

Lees again slammed his fist on the table. "I follow clues and discover the truth! I don't give a hang who this killer turns out to be!" He glared at the man. "What you've done, Mayor, is a complete miscarriage of justice. Good day, Mayor."

"Oh, gentlemen," Bartlett called after the retreating officers' figures. They turned back around, and he said, "keep this out of the newspapers, or you will be arrested as well. And you better both pray you find this killer soon."

"Oh, and why is that?" Lees asked. "If the next victim is a person who lives outside of Chinatown, then you can imagine how the anger will escalate."

"Indeed," Lees mumbled. "Hopefully, right up your mammoth posterior."

Isaiah Lees left the mayor, marching down Jackson with his partner, his mind chewing on the rising level of complication. This case wasn't at all what he thought, and if the mayor was right, there was an even more dangerous predator than he'd thought on the loose in his town.

CHAPTER FOUR: THE NEW INVESTIGATION

Tin How Temple, Waverly Place, Chinatown, San Francisco, February 15, 1884.

When Clara met Captain Lees the next morning, inside the Tin How Temple basement, she was expecting a rather mundane police procedural. After stopping at the mansion on Nob Hill to retrieve her friend and translator, Ah Toy, they arrived at their destination at around half-past nine.

Once inside, Clara was surprised by a boisterous scene. There were a dozen policemen present, including Captain Isaiah Lees and his partner, Eduard Vanderheiden, and they had transformed the meeting room into an investigative headquarters. There were eight gruesome photographs affixed to the wall above the Six Companies clan table. They were lurid replicas of women who had been stripped of their skins and intestines, and their bodies were draped over chairs, on beds, and inside closets. These pictures also had arrows drawn, from one to the other, and beneath each photo was a physical description of the woman, including her name, the time of her murder, and the location.

"What happened, Captain?" Clara touched Lees on his gray cape, and he turned to face her. He was obviously preoccupied.

"I'm afraid this murder case has grown way out of proportion, Mrs. Foltz. I was informed yesterday that your clients have been hiding information about seven previous killings of prostitutes—all Chinese—which took place on different dates and locations during the last six months. This was a private affair between the mayor and the Kwongs."

Clara noticed that Ah Toy was standing on the other side of the room, under an ornate lantern, talking with Andrew Kwong. His son, George, was standing next to him.

"I can see that they all have the same operative details." Clara pointed to each photograph. "Do you suspect that the same assailant committed all of these murders?"

"Until I discover evidence to the contrary, I must assume so. The recent murder of Mary McCarthy seems to be a movement in a different direction, obviously. Also, the interval of time between each murder seems to be less." Lees pointed to the dates under each photo. "See? The first one was on August 17, the next September 12, then October 15. But then, from November 17 until February 12, three days ago, there were five murders committed, each one closer to the next by a week. At this rate, we might expect another one at any time. Oh, and here is the affidavit of the journalist who saw George Kwong on Sacramento the night of the McCarthy girl's murder." Lees handed the paper to Clara who tucked it inside her handbag.

Standing with a group of three men, including Jesse Cook, the Chinatown Squad leader, was Sheriff Patrick Connolly, a clean-shaven, red-faced Irishman, with curly-black hair, who was sporting a black frock coat with matching trousers, a vest, and white shirt and tie.

"So, you're the new lass Andrew was telling me about," Connolly said. "Don't pay attention to old Isaiah. His mind was fogged up in London, don't you know?" Connolly was in his thirties, and his accent was very Irish.

"Thank you for the advice, Sheriff, but I can think for myself. Captain Lees was going to show me the intricacies of his investigative technique, but now there seem to be many more cooks stirring the homicidal kettle, if you will." Clara was used to bantering with men, as she was the only female barrister in San Francisco.

"Somebody invoke my name?" Jesse Brown Cook called from across the room.

"Not that kind of cook, me lad," the sheriff said.

Captain Lees knew that it was dangerous having Cook and Connolly in on this investigation, as there was probably a lot of money to be made for a leaked story. However, when Mayor Bartlett gave the order to release the Tongs, he had also decided to inform Connolly and his holy roller pal, kid Cook. Lees had decided to keep all of his findings a secret until he could uncover a suspect, but he would pretend to fully cooperate with Connolly and Bartlett to keep the peace in the ranks. The fly in his ointment was Clara Foltz. He needed her and her translator's help more than ever, and he was going to use it very carefully. He was going to work with her because he trusted the attorney more than he did the sheriff and the mayor. In fact, Mayor Bartlett and Sheriff Connolly were now prime suspects in these murders.

"Sheriff, you and your men are going to question the Tongs about what they know concerning the seven murdered Chinese women. We need to know who they were dating and when, and then we'll need to compare notes to see if there are similar patterns at work." Lees took his Bowie knife from his vest and held it up. "For example, I immediately suspected the killer might have used a blade of some kind to do the flaying of his victim. I even had one of my men question butchers in the city. None of them was suspect, as they all had alibis as to their whereabouts at the time of McCarthy's murder."

"A blade is a blade, me boy-o. It's the sharpness and skill that matters," Connolly said.

Lees nodded. "Correct, Sheriff. But butchers also know how to dispose of the blood and intestines with the least amount of splatter and chaos. Each of these murders has an almost pristine crime scene, so where does that leave us with butchers?"

"Excuse me, gentlemen, but what about a coroner who must perform an autopsy? He or she would also have such grisly expertise. And, what about all of those who work in the burial services? They must also do such work." Clara was using her attorney's logic, and the men were paying notice. "Don't you think you should widen your net to include these types as well?"

Captain Lees was secretly irate. He hadn't expected this woman to divulge what he hoped to keep from Connolly and Cook. He was going to send them out to interview more butchers because there were now more victims. Now he would have to allow them to question coroners and funeral directors.

"Yes, well then, Patrick. Your men can make a list and begin questioning these types. Thank you, Mrs. Foltz." Lees nodded to the attorney. "I need to go now, and I would still like your assistance, Clara. May I call you Clara?"

Clara's face turned red. The captain should have waited until they were away from all these men before becoming so emboldened. "I suppose so. Ah Toy! We must leave with the captain now."

Stepping outside, Lees turned toward Clara. She was surprised at herself for being attracted to the much older man. Perhaps it was his calm, polite manner and English accent. Yes, but she supposed it was his sharp intellect that seemed to coincide with a deeper level in her own personality. When he spoke to her, his attention was riveted upon her eyes, something that other men rarely did. Other men didn't believe women were their equal, but this man did.

"Clara, you can follow me to see how I conduct my investigation. As the defense attorney, you'll be getting all this information eventually, anyway, and I'll be candid. I don't trust the mayor and the sheriff's department. They will not remain objective, and that's what I need right now: objectivity. Now that I have my own list of suspects, I will be proceeding to go back over them and ask more questions to narrow my search. However, there is one other person I want to question who is not on my list. He is the religious leader of this Joss House, the Tin How Temple. He speaks only Cantonese, so I will need Ah Toy's help as a translator. I would also like your legal expertise to help me assess any clues I might come up with later."

"Guan Shi Yin. He has been the minister of this temple for six years, I believe." Ah Toy looked up at the colorful frontage of the temple and sighed. "My people are very superstitious when they are away from home. Mazu, Goddess of the Sea, has become a spiritual presence to pray to, and this man uses that need the way I used the female body in my business. In fact, here in the United States, she is called Goddess of the Heavens, a much loftier title."

"How can you compare a religious man with the business of prostitution? What he does is not illegal. In fact, religious practice is protected under our laws." Captain Lees frowned.

"That's right. Nobody gets hurt praying to a goddess, but I seen a lot of girls beat up by their pimps and Johnny boys." Dutch also had a scowl on his face. "And what about these here murders?"

"To some extent, I agree with you. The way the Hip See Tong conduct business does degrade the women and put them in danger. They treat them like animals, put them in cages, and let the men do just about anything they want to their bodies. When I ran my business, my girls mostly acted for the men."

"Acted? I don't get your reasoning." Clara thought Lees looked intrigued.

"She means she used feminine allure to make money, Captain," Clara put in. "We women have been doing this legally, in marriage, for thousands of years." She smiled over at her friend.

"Yes, nobody could touch one of my women. They could please themselves, mind you, and we provided accoutrements to assist them in this endeavor. I began by doing this alone, and I saw that it worked. I made more money dancing and showing them a gradual unveiling of my female form than I would have if I had to perform intercourse with each of them. Chinese men enjoyed my acting, as it coincided with our Taoist and Buddhist ways. All of life, you see, is a drama produced by the inner God in all people, animals, and in all things."

"But you must have been approached by some men to do more than dance," Lees said, shaking his head in disbelief.

"Of course! But this was the genius of my approach, and it angered the Tongs. I was in control of whom I would allow to do this to my girls. I could carefully screen the applicant, if you will, so the danger to my employee was minimized. My girls received proper medical treatment, and they enjoyed their work. If they chose to marry one of these men, I would allow that also. The Tongs hated me for it, of course, and I eventually had to leave the business. My humane practice was too expensive to their way of thinking." Ah Toy raised the sleeve of her red silk dress to expose a long, jagged scar that extended the length of her left forearm. "One of them did this to me out of anger."

"My God! You never showed me that" Clara touched Ah Toy's arm and winced.

"Come, let's talk with the mystical man. Enough about me." Ah Toy climbed the steps leading to the temple's main entrance. The temple itself was on the third floor of the building. The second floor was where the clan associations met, including the Tongs. Lees could smell the odor of burning incense and perfume as he stepped into the room behind Clara and Ah Toy. Sergeant Vanderheiden held his nose and raised his eyebrows.

Inside the temple, the statue of Mazu sat on the central shrine with her assistants by her side. She was adorned in an Empress dress, all gold, and the ornate detail and jewels inserted in her belt were quite dazzling. Ah Toy pointed to the ceiling above the goddess's head. "Above the shrine are rows of red lanterns donated by devotees. You can see the names of donors that are written on slips of red paper and attached to the lanterns. In front is a table full of offerings. The ritual items such as the joss stick holders were donated by devotees more than a hundred years ago back in China. For a donation, the worshipper may choose from this display of silver-colored seahorse combs, jeweled tie clasps, and small buddhas."

Dutch started to pick up one of the slips of paper to read it, but Ah Toy gently tapped his hand. "You must not touch. In fact, you are not supposed to be here. I suppose you were able to get permission because of the crimes, correct Captain?"

Lees nodded. "It wasn't easy. So, don't get us thrown out of here, Dutch."

"Okay, boss," the sergeant muttered.

"I see there are gifts for women on display. How many females come here to pray?" Clara asked.

"The prostitutes who are superstitious often come here to seek redemption from the gods or to ask for divine intercession," Ah Toy explained.

"I see," said Clara, and she wrote something down on her pad, which she had extracted from her purse.

Ah Toy continued with the tour. "The side shrines are dedicated to many other deities including Guan Gong, Justice Bao, God of Wealth, Wah To, Wah Kwong, Lady Golden Flower and eighteen Guardian Deities, Ji Gong, Lu Dong Bin and God of House Guard."

"You certainly know your gods, Miss Ah Toy," a deep voice came from in back of the shrine's red curtains. The draperies soon parted to reveal the temple minister, Guan Shi Yin, which meant, "hearer of all sufferings."

After Ah Toy translated the man's Cantonese, Lees assessed him carefully. His walk was austere and boldly confident, as this was his domain. As a lowly minister, however, his clothing was humble compared to his spiritual protégé. He wore a simple robe of gold that tied at the waist with a golden sash. He was tall, over six feet, and his face was dark and handsome. He had a cleft in his chin and an attractive mole on his right cheek. His straight, raven hair was pomaded so that it was perfectly symmetrical and parted on the left side with his queue hanging down his back.

Captain Lees knew Guan Shi Yin was thirty-seven years old and that before entering the clergy he had been in the funeral business. In fact, as he still had connections outside Chinatown, he made extra money from doing services for Chinese patrons who had the money to pay for burials. This was the main reason Lees wanted to question him, as there might be some connection between the burial business and a possible murder suspect who might work therein.

"Welcome. How may I assist you in your investigation, Captain?" Ah Toy's translation created a gap in time, and Lees spent it observing the minister's face. He looked sincere enough.

"Where were you on the night of February 12, between the hours of six and eight?" Lees figured he would establish his whereabouts first.

He spoke without hesitation in that sing-song chatter, and Ah Toy said, "He was performing a service in the temple."

"Good. Do you know if any of your—do you call them parishioners? Do you know if any of them have said anything about the murders of prostitutes or behaved in any suspicious way in your presence?" Ah Toy thought for a moment, and then she spoke to him.

Again, he answered quickly, and Ah Toy translated. "No, nothing was said about those murders. When I speak or perform a sacrifice, there is no talking allowed."

"I see. What about your services at funerals? Do you know anybody in your congregation who works preparing the bodies for burial or uses a knife of any kind in his job?"

Before translating Lees' words, Ah Toy explained, "Captain, we do not touch the body when it still has skin. The belief is that the flesh has evil spirits, so we employ white men to do the work of stripping off the flesh. The body is then ready for burial, but we most always send it back to China to be buried with the relatives."

"Thank you, Ah Toy, for that information. I would still like to know if he knows anybody who does this stripping work, whether they are Chinese or white men." Lees knew the sheriff's men would be asking these people also, but if Guan Shi Yin knew anybody, it would save time.

The minister paused for the first time before responding. Ah Toy finally translated. "He says he knows many such men, as he used to be in the funeral business. However, because the work they did is seen as disgusting and servile, he never wanted to know them personally."

"I see. I also saw a woman who performed in the street outside as the psychic medium for your goddess. What kinds of questions or requests does she receive from the men?"

After Ah Toy translated, the minister smiled broadly, and his response was quite long. Finally, Ah Toy offered the translation. "They ask many things. For good health, for a good woman and companion, for a safe trip back to China, or perhaps even to get rid of some specific disease or bad habit. Mazu can create the dance of the gods inside a person so that any problem can be solved."

"Wonderful. And I would expect you get paid handsomely for your part," Lees said, but when he saw Ah Toy shake her head in the negative, he rephrased his words. "I mean, thank you for your help. If I should need it again, would you be open to more questions?"

Ah Toy translated Lees' last words, and Guan Shi Yin again smiled that spiritual grin of his and answered, "Yes, anytime, Captain," Ah Toy translated.

When the group was down the stairs and standing in the street again, Lees confided his assessment. "I want to talk about motive right now. Why would a murderer want to commit a series of killings right under the noses of thousands of Chinese? What do we know about these victims? Now that the mayor and the Kwongs have turned over the details of the other seven victims, I know they had one thing in common, besides the fact they were all prostitutes."

"What's that, boss?" Vanderheiden asked.

"They were all independent prostitutes. This means they were a direct affront to the Tongs and their sex traffic business. I was, at first, angry with Connolly and Cook when they arrested the major Tong leaders, but now I'm not so certain. Could one of them be involved in these murders?" Lees buttoned up his cape, as it was beginning to get cooler.

"I don't think so," Ah Toy responded, buttoning the top button on her red silk *cheongsam*.

"Dear, I think we better get you inside. That flimsy garment won't keep you warm," Clara said. She was hoping the Captain might get the hint.

"Come with me. There's a nice Italian restaurant over on Stockton. It's just a few blocks." Lees began to lead the way.

Clara smiled and nodded at Ah Toy. "See? Chivalry is not dead. Even in the police force."

At Mona Lisa's Ristorante, inside a back booth, all four investigators were huddled together, sipping espressos, and chewing on breadsticks, waiting for their dessert orders to come. Lees sat next to Clara, on the right, and Ah Toy and Vanderheiden were next to each other on the left side of the booth.

"Please continue, Miss Ah Toy. Why is it you believe the Tongs would not want to kill these women?" Lees asked, nibbling at the end of his breadstick.

"I know the Tongs and how they do business. They are ruthless, yes, but they are also pragmatic. They see these women as their product, their source of income. Even women like me, who work alone, are not a threat to their business because we attract men with more money from outside Chinatown. The Tongs who deal with prostitution also deal with gambling, alcohol sales, and opium use. As long as the lone prostitute encourages her client to make full use of the sins available, they never get pressured, much less murdered. I was a threat only when I became a Madame. That made me a fellow business entrepreneur, so I was pressured to leave, but they would never have killed me."

"Show them your scar again," Clara said.

Ah Toy pulled up her left sleeve, and the men frowned. "Yes, I got cut as a warning, and I chose to leave. However, if I had decided to play their game, and give them regular tribute and protection money, I could have stayed in business. I was ready to leave, anyway. I made a lot of money in those fifteen years of work in Chinatown. I was given a Chinawoman's chance to succeed."

"Yes, and that was more of a chance than she would have been given outside Chinatown," Clara said, sipping her tiny cup of strong Italian coffee.

"True, and that leads me to another suspect. Again, this person probably wasn't the murderer, directly speaking, but he could have hired such a person to commit these atrocities." Lees lowered his voice. "Mayor Bartlett hates the Chinese. He got elected on a platform of supporting the national Exclusion Act. And now, from what I hear, he wants to run for governor in the next election. Wouldn't his chances improve greatly if there were wholesale murders being committed in Chinatown? Why, Dutch and I were with him today, and he said as much. Didn't he, Eduard?"

Vanderheiden looked up and saw the waiter bringing the tray of desserts. “Wait up, Captain. I want to taste my Cannoli before I say another word.” He selected the dish with the sweet cheese-stuffed funneled treat. He picked up his fork and took a big slice and pushed it between his lips. “Oh, boy, that’s better than a gift from Mazu herself!”

The others were given slices of Tiramisu coffee cake, and they all ate silently for a few moments, enjoying the experience.

“Sure, the mayor could get a lot of good press from all of these murders. He did tell us he hopes the killer is Chinese. And he threatened our jobs if we found out the killer wasn’t a chink—excuse me—a Chinese.” Vanderheiden licked his fork.

“How ghastly! I never realized there was this kind of racist subterfuge going on at high levels of our fair city,” Clara said, but she was purposefully coy. She played the same “innocent female” in the courtroom. It allowed men to open up even more to expose their weaknesses.

“I received another clue from Miss Benedict at the Home for Wayward Women. There were two clues, but the second may be a coincidence. First, Miss Benedict stated that George Kwong was the man who brought Mary McCarthy into the school. He would also visit the girl from time to time. The second was the fact that Benedict used an expression for me when we first met. She called me O Captain, my Captain. Coincidentally, the mayor called me the same name, and he had never done this.” Lees dipped his fork into the cake and held it there. “I wondered if Benedict and Bartlett might be having a personal relationship.”

“That was from Walt Whitman’s poem about the death of President Lincoln, was it not?” Clara asked.

“Yes, it was. Frankly, I was wondering if it might not be a veiled threat. Assassination being the operative word.” Lees picked up the fork and brought the cake to his lips. He held it there.

“You mean, if Bartlett and that woman are working together to get these girls murdered, then they might also be planning to take you out if you get too close to the truth,” Clara said. “Has our corrupt society come to this?”

“But why would they want the bodies of these women disfigured? It makes no logical sense.” Ah Toy wiped her mouth with a cloth napkin and then set it down.

"It makes sense if you realize Bartlett once owned a newspaper. The more sordid and fantastically morbid a murder is, the more readers want to buy it. It's the old saw of when a dog bites a man, it's not news. But when a man bites a dog, it is." Lees took the forkful of cake into his mouth.

"And if these murders get solved under his watch, and the killer is Chinese, then the White Whale gets his votes for governor. The story would certainly become state, if not national news," Clara pointed out.

"Yes, and that's the sum of my thinking. Of course, there are still George and Andrew Kwong and their involvement in this. Could they be the proximate murderers? If Bartlett paid them a lot of money, they could become killers who would profit from the case behind the scenes." Lees was thinking out loud. He trusted Clara Foltz with this information because he believed she also wanted to find the truth. After many years of fighting the mayor and his private sheriffs, he had finally realized he needed to show somebody what was happening in this city that was preventing real justice from prevailing.

"Captain, I realize you know where I must stand on this. These two men are my legal clients. I must represent their best interests. I am, however, thankful that you are sharing this with me." Clara smiled over at Lees, and he returned the grin.

"You two should get a room!" Vanderheiden laughed, and he drained the last of his coffee.

Sergeant Vanderheiden escorted Ah Toy back to her residence on Nob Hill, and Captain Lees did the same for Clara Foltz. This small team had become closer during the day, and Lees wanted to express his gratitude in a more personal way.

"Clara, I know you didn't get any money today by spending your time with me. Do you think you'll be able to pay for your family to come to San Francisco?" Lees stood at the bottom of Clara's apartment building on Montgomery Street looking into her eyes with his usual direct gaze. Gas lights were lit along the street, glowing with a reddish hue in the fog. Lees was not anxious to go home to his lonely flat, and he wanted to know more about this fascinating woman.

"Thank you for your concern, Captain. I am being paid quite handsomely by the Six Companies, and yes, I do believe I'll be able to soon afford to get my parents and my children back into my arms. I do miss them so. The world of the law, as I know you can appreciate, can be quite arid and without humor. My children make my life joyous and exciting, even though the stress can be of a different variety, if you've spent any time with young ones." Clara smiled. She could tell by the concern on the officer's face that he was a gentle man. He reminded her of her father, Elias. He was the one who steered her toward the law, but it was his spiritual quality as a pastor that reminded her most of Captain Lees.

"I'm afraid I have little experience with the wee folks, except when I'm called to a home that has family trouble." Lees took hold of Clara's hands as the fog rolled in.

"I love to cook, sew and do all of the family things we women were raised to do. My mother, bless her, does this now for me. I became a Suffragist when I had to compete with men for a job. I realized we women had the right to work in any trade we were qualified to practice. I saw that if the laws needed to be changed, I could do the petitioning to change them. If nobody did it, then I had to do it. I also discovered many women who would help me compete because they had been deserted by husbands also, either through death or divorce, it did not matter."

"I agree. These prostitutes, for example. If there were more jobs open to women, then this type of work would soon become less appealing." Lees squeezed Clara's hands, and she returned the pressure.

"Yes! And I know you are under pressure for your legal convictions. My father, who was once a pastor before becoming a lawyer, used to preach the heretical doctrine of soul-sleep."

"Soul-sleep? That sounds quite profound. What does it mean?" Lees asked.

"It means he believed when a person dies, his or her soul does not go directly to God. Instead, it does not exist until the day of the Last Judgement, when all souls are called to argue before their Maker."

"That makes some logical sense. How can one even have a Last Judgement unless all souls are there? If God judged each soul or spirit, when the body died, then there would be no need for a Last Judgement at all."

"I knew you had the same kind of insightful intelligence as my father. It does make perfect sense, but all the Protestant and Catholic religious leaders did not see it that way. Probably because they couldn't tell their parishioners they would get into heaven right away, and this caused consternation and perhaps no tithing at all. Therefore, father was excommunicated to the backwater revival tents, where he still likes to preach, from time to time, even as a lawyer."

"Jolly good for him," Lees said, then bent forward and gave Clara a kiss on her left cheek. She could feel the foggy dew from his mustache, and her face reddened.

"Captain! You must come to the station." From out of the fog, Sergeant Vanderheiden came running up to them. Lees and his partner made it a practice to share addresses whenever they had to split up.

"Slow down, Dutch. What happened?" Lees could see by his partner's face that this was important news.

"Sheriff Connolly has made an arrest for the eight murders. He's got him locked up now at Kearney Station." Vanderheiden was still huffing and puffing, bent over and gasping out the words.

"I told him to wait until we could compare notes! Who is it? Who did he arrest?"

"George Kwong. Connolly says he has enough evidence to convict and have him swinging from a rope on Russian Hill."

"I must go with you, Captain. George Kwong is now my client," Clara said.

"Of course! We must all leave right now. I want to see this so-called evidence for myself. I also want to see what kind of pressure the sheriff is getting from the mayor."

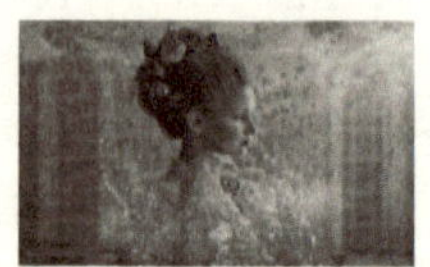

CHAPTER FIVE: THE WHITE WHALE

Jenny Lind City Hall, Police Department, Kearny Street, San Francisco. February 15, 1884

It was twenty past midnight when Clara and Ah Toy arrived at the police station on Kearney. As Clara suspected, Andrew Kwong was there, sitting on the long bench in the squad room. Uniformed sheriff officers and city policemen were busy booking new criminals. Mr. Kwong stood up and waved. "Mrs. Foltz! Over here!"

Clara and Ah Toy walked over and sat down next to him on the bench. The attorney noted that her client's eyes were red from weeping or, perhaps, a head cold. He spoke with his usual enunciated and perfect English, however, and there was no congestion.

"They won't show me anything. My son was arrested in the middle of the night, and now I can't see him, and they won't give me any details about how he could have committed these brutal murders. You have to help me!" Mr. Kwong grabbed hold of Clara's dress sleeve with his right hand and pulled as if he could get a response from her by trying to break her arm.

"Please, Mr. Kwong! Let go of me. I'm here now. I understand your problem, and as your authorized counsel, it's now up to me to find out everything. By law, as George's defense attorney, they must provide me with every piece of hard evidence, and each witness they have that they believe proves your son's guilt. He is not guilty until they can prove, beyond a reasonable doubt, inside a courtroom and in front of a jury, that he killed these women. I will do my best to counter each piece of evidence and rebut every witness."

After Andrew Kwong released her, Clara gently patted his hand. "Please, wait here. I'm going to first meet with the arresting officer, Sheriff Patrick Connolly, and then I will meet with your son. Right now, I don't want you in the room with us, but I will bring you back later when we have to mount our defense strategy."

Ah Toy spoke to Andrew Kwong in Cantonese, and he nodded his head and spoke to her vehemently.

"What did he say?" Clara asked.

"He said it was the White Whale who did this," she told Clara.

Clara wondered who this White Whale could be as she walked over to the desk sergeant. She was asking him about meeting with Sheriff Connolly, when Captain Lees came up to her, grabbed her arm, and spun her around to face him. "I can't talk to you here, but I'll meet you later in the afternoon at your apartment. Is that clear?"

"Yes. I will be expecting you," Clara said, and she watched Lees turn and dash off to the other side of the squad room.

"Go down that hall and turn right at the last door. The sheriff's expecting you," the desk sergeant instructed her by pointing toward a long corridor on the right side of the building. "Walk right in. You don't have to knock."

Inside the sheriff's office, Clara felt as if she had stepped inside a menagerie. There were at least fifteen different animal heads peering down at her from the mahogany walls: bears, mountain lions, deer, and one rhinoceros. Connolly was seated in back of his high desk, leaning back, his hands behind his head, a big cigar in his mouth. He wore the uniform of the Chinatown Squad, so she assumed he had arrested George Kwong, her client.

"We meet again, Mrs. Foltz! Please, take a seat." Connolly pointed toward a small wooden chair near a long bench on the side of the room. Clearly this room was not meant for the comfort of visitors.

"I would prefer to stand right now, Sheriff," she said. "I'm representing the Kwong family in this case, and I need to see George. But first, I want to know what you have on him. I don't need the actual evidence right now, but my legal team will need it eventually. I just want to be aware of what we may be up against here."

Connolly blew a perfect large smoke ring, then blew a smaller one that pushed through the center of the first. "Your pal Captain Lees did a lot of the work to nail this kid. He got the sworn testimony of Boscombe, the journalist who spotted George Kwong at the scene of the McCarthy murder. I was just putting two and two together. I interviewed a coroner across the Bay in Oakland. Name's Goodbody, a fine name for a coroner, and he informed me that Georgie boy worked for him for a whole summer. He told me the lad was especially interested in how to use the U.S. Army post-mortem field kit that Goodbody used. In fact, when we arrested the lad, we found it hidden under his mattress. George Kwong quit his job suddenly, and he took the kit with him. I asked the Oakland doctor whether his little kit could strip a body down like that of Mary McCarthy, and I showed him the photo of her body. He's willing to swear in court that his kit could be used for such purposes."

"All right. I'll eventually need to see that. Of course, that does not prove my client used it on anyone. What motive do you have? What witnesses saw him use it, or what reason would he have to kill those women?" Clara was fishing for clues in Connolly's demeanor. How confident was he concerning all of this tommyrot about George working as a coroner for a summer? Young men need money—especially young Chinese men—and there weren't many jobs that they were allowed to do.

"We talked to Miss Benedict at the Methodist Home for Wayward Women. She says Georgie boy had a big row with his girlfriend, Mary McCarthy, and it was a week before she was killed. Oh, and by the by, we won't be pinning those seven other murders on your boy-o. He may have done them in too, but the mayor wants to hold off." Connolly took another deep drag on his cigar. "One murder conviction will be enough with a white jury, don't you think, Mrs. Foltz?"

Clara was livid. Without the reality of those seven other crimes, she had little with which to fight. She knew no Chinese court testimony was allowed in a courtroom, they weren't considered citizens, and she wanted to use that fact to support her client. Also, what evidence could they provide to prove his hatred for his fellow Chinese women? This single murder of the Irish girl was different.

"This changes things greatly, Sheriff. I want to see my client right now."

"Right. Now don't be getting your bustle in a bunch. I'll take you to his holding cell." Connolly stubbed out what was left of his cigar into an abalone shell ashtray on his desk. He led the way down the hall and out into the squad room. "Smith, I'm taking Mrs. Foltz up to see her client."

Clara followed the two men upstairs where the jail cells were located. She could smell the foul odors of urine and feces, and she could hear the grinding noise of old plumbing. George Kwong's cell was in the back where the Chinese and Negroes were kept.

Smith opened the door with his key, and Clara stepped inside. It was dark and shadowy, lit by a small gas lamp with a protective shield of wire mesh, and it was sitting on a table next to a threadbare cot. George Kwong wore the blue dungarees issued to all prisoners, and his last name was stenciled above his shirt pocket. He stood up when Clara came in, but she motioned for him to sit back down on the cot.

"Your father is outside. I'll soon see to it so he can visit you. How are you feeling?" Clara placed her hand on the young man's shoulder.

"I didn't kill anybody, Mrs. Foltz! I was in love with Mary McCarthy, but she wanted to do things on her own. She didn't think she was lovable. We argued about that, but I never threatened her." Clara could see tears glistening on the young man's cheeks. "I worked for Mr. Goodbody because I wanted to learn a new trade. I don't know how that post-mortem kit got in my room. Somebody must have placed it there."

"All right, George. I'm going to ask you a series of critical questions, and I want you to give me an honest answer. Whatever we share is privileged and protected information. However, if you lie to me, even once, I will refuse to represent you from that moment on. Is that clear?" Clara watched him nod his head.

"Were you and your father working for Mayor Washington Bartlett or anyone else in city government?"

"No, the mayor just wanted us to keep the Chinese prostitute murders a secret. He was an old newspaper publisher, and he told us we could make a lot of money by keeping a record of all the details and photos, but we must not publish anything until he gave the word."

"When did he tell you this?" Clara wanted to pinpoint the actual progression of this most significant negotiation.

"After the first murder. Father was ready to publish the story in *The Oriental*. But then the church officials said to hold off. They said the mayor wanted to see us first. He came down to Chinatown and told us he would put his best men on the case, but he wanted us to keep the murder a secret. When the second murder happened, he again visited us. He said if this story got out into the community, there would be fear and anger generated in the populace, and Chinatown could be invaded by the Vigilante Committee and others. He said his men had to find the killer before we could tell the story, so we agreed."

Clara knew this information agreed with what Isaiah Lees had told them at the Italian restaurant. There wasn't much more she could do until she heard from Lees. She needed to get all the evidence from Connolly before she did her own investigation.

"I'm going to go get your father so he can talk with you. I'll meet with you both tomorrow so we can plan our defense strategy. Right now, I need to go home and get some sleep. Everything will be taken care of, George, so don't panic."

"If I were guilty, I would panic, Mrs. Foltz. Right now, I'm just afraid." George's dark eyes were staring at her with a fixed concern.

"Afraid? What scares you?" Clara took his two hands into her own.

"I'm afraid that when news gets out that I've been arrested for murder, then some person who knows about the other seven killings will try to profit by selling the stories to the press. When that happens, the entire city will be after me."

Clara could see George was in a real panic. He was perspiring profusely, and his voice was trembling.

"It's happened before, and the police could not stop them from executing mob justice on the men involved back in 1856."

Clara could feel the young man's hands shaking. She knew the case about which George was referring. She had to study it for her bar exam. These members of the Vigilance Committee later became the People's Party.

In fact, Clara belonged to the Workingmen's Party, which evolved from the People's Party, because of their support of the Women's Suffrage Movement. She spoke for their candidates, including Denis Kearney, who became its leader.

Clara understood why George and his father would be concerned. They, too, were involved in criminal activities in Chinatown and were newspaper men, just like Charles Cora and William Casey back in 1856, who were holding onto a story that would cause violent repercussions throughout the city.

Finally, the mayor himself was involved, and he was going to soon run for Governor of California. If Bartlett decided to deliver his story to the press about the seven other murders, then Andrew and his son, George, could easily be seen as the Charles Cora and William

Casey of 1884. Their knowledge of the murders would make them guilty, even without a trial.

CHAPTER SIX: A WOMAN ON THE HUNT

Montgomery Street, San Francisco, February 15, 1884,

Inside her apartment on Montgomery, Clara was about to fall asleep when she began to think about her defense strategy to keep George Kwong from the gallows. The power of the press was important. She used it to speak out for women's rights and other issues. What if those other seven murders were leaked—not by Mayor Bartlett's office—but by Andrew Kwong and his church-supported newspaper, *The Oriental*? She wanted to discuss this further with Captain Lees when he came by later. She fell asleep thinking about Lees' dewy kiss late the previous evening, and she smiled.

Captain Lees appeared at Clara's door promptly at nine. She let him in wearing her tennis dress, a striped affair with her corset loose and her bustle small. Unlike her peers, Clara did not feel pressured to constrict her circulation in order to affect the narrow waisted, big bustled look. After giving birth to five children, if a man expected a virgin's hourglass shape then he was delusional. The pleasant smile and fixed look of intelligent interest on the officer's face was enough for Clara to understand he was not impressed by outward feminine appearances.

"Clara, I must talk to you about George. I spent an hour with Connolly, and he wants to get this to trial very soon. We must …"

"Please, Isaiah. May I call you by your given name?" Clara interrupted.

"Yes. Certainly, but …"

"I have had my own discussion with the sheriff. In fact, I wanted to pose a strategy I have in mind to defend George. I know you come from England, where the press is forbidden by law to give out details of a criminal investigation. In this country, however, as you're now certainly aware, since we have a constitutional form of government, we place much more value on the free press being able to get the facts out for its citizenry—even before a case has gone to trial. The First

Amendment was added for that purpose." Clara moved over to her purple couch and sat down. She patted the cushion, and Lees followed her lead and sat down beside her.

Clara watched Lees walk around her apartment gazing at the decorations. She had posters of her speeches at various political rallies and gatherings around California, and the main poster, right above the couch, was one that showed her with Governor Robert Waterman who was congratulating her on the passage of the state law that gave women the right to work at any trade or profession, and this included going to law school and taking the State Bar Examination.

The rest of the display, on hanging shelves, showed photos of her family and her five children. There was also some framed artwork depicting San Francisco and its beautiful landscapes and cityscapes. A long bookcase filled with legal books was decorating the wall next to the small kitchen. She saw that Lees had little interest in the furniture, but he could see her taste was very provincial, except for the purple couch. A stuffed, high-back chair, a footstool, a birdcage with a canary, and a table for tea and coffee service were the practical pieces. No flowers, no frilly doilies or coverlets, no ostentatious European antiques. This was the domicile of a working woman.

"Yes, I know the difference. We at the station call the newspapers the circus because of how they exaggerate the facts. What does your defense have to do with the press?"

"I believe what you said about Mayor Bartlett. He wants to win the governor's race, and he's willing to use the Chinese to do it. The only way he can cause a calamity big enough to attract attention is to arrest George, convict him in a virtual kangaroo courtroom, and then hang him with great hoopla in the press. I want to prevent that from happening."

"As it just so happens, I agree with you. I went over what Connolly has on Kwong, and it's mostly circumstantial. No weapon, no witness who saw George murder the girl, and testimony that reeks of bribery. I still think Bartlett is in cahoots with Miss Benedict the bee lady at the Home for Wayward Women. She could be in on his rise to power." Isaiah Lees took hold of Clara's hand. "Now what's your plan, Clara? Maybe I can help."

"I am going to help Andrew Kwong write an article for

publication. He will not only publish it in his paper, *The Oriental*, but I will take it to all the major papers in San Francisco. This article will explain the facts behind all seven different murders that took place in Chinatown and how Mayor Bartlett was the operational force behind keeping them a secret from the public." Clara squeezed Lees' hand, and he squeezed back.

"I think it's a good plan. The only way you can prevent Bartlett from using these murders to get him elected is to tell your story. Also, this could have an additional advantage."

"Additional advantage? What do you mean?"

"The murderer is still at large. When this story becomes public, the killer will become enraged. I believe these killings may have been used for political purposes, but that doesn't mean the killer is able to be bought. A certain blood lust sets in after several such murders, and the added ingredient of sex lust makes me believe this person will strike again." Lees stood up. From inside his cape, he extracted a small pistol. It was a 45-caliber double-shot model of the small Derringer. "Keep this in your purse. Use it if you need it."

Clara looked down at the pistol in her hand and sighed. As a wife and mother in the wilds of Illinois, she used a weapon to hunt or to ward off predators. This, very personal weapon, was a new experience, and she knew it was meant to kill a human being, the highest order of mammal on Earth. No matter how uneducated or primitive, a human life was sacred. Her parents and her culture raised her to believe this, but now she was being told there were exceptions in the world of police work.

"Thank you, Isaiah. I hope I won't have the opportunity to use it. When I go down this path, I do understand I will be exploring the darkness of mankind, and I respect your experience and your assistance. I now must do it alone."

Standing at the door, Clara stared at Captain Lees. His intense gaze made her believe he was able to see a deeper, intangible beauty within her. She forgot about the little Charles Gunn and his political aspirations at her expense. Lees gave her a dignity that caused her to stand erect, with her back and shoulders set in a firm, immovable position. And yet, she knew, there was a humble and motherly aspect to the slope of her bosom down to her corseted waist, and his eyes followed that path.

Clara allowed this roaming of the eyes from this man, this older, wiser, and battle-tested man. Her first husband had been battle-tested, even wounded, but the experience had weakened him and had made him afraid to be a real man. This male before her, with his concentrated scowl and piercing gaze, had been wounded mentally many times as well, she knew, but he had become stronger and kinder, with a passionate need that she could see was authentic. When he kissed her, she moved into him, and afterward, as her head rested on his shoulder for several minutes, perhaps the length of time it takes to clean a gun, she felt stronger after she withdrew.

***

Later, inside the office of *The Oriental* newspaper in Chinatown, on Waverly Place, Clara Foltz was seated before the desk of Andrew Kwong, the editor. As she spoke, she could see he was distraught, and deservedly so, as his son's neck was virtually encircled by the heavy weight of a legal system that despised his kind.

"Mr. Kwong, I want you to use the information you have collected about the seven murders of Chinese prostitutes in order to show the population of San Francisco that Mayor Washington Bartlett has been using you and your community to advance a political agenda. Indeed, as we have discovered, he wants to run for the office of California Governor, and it has been his intention to do so from the moment he stepped foot in your office after that first murder." Clara could see a glimmer of hope in the man's eyes.

"Of course! That's why he arrested George. He knew George would be at every scene of the crime to take photos, and so when the white girl was murdered, he had what he wanted. And you say we should explain these facts in an editorial?"

Clara stood up and walked over to stand in front of Mr. Kwong. She stared hard into his dusky eyes and her smile was just as dark. "I want not just an editorial about what the mayor is doing to you and your people, I want you to explain what can now happen to all of San Francisco if we don't find the real killer of these women."

Andrew was listening intently to her words. His eyes were riveted upon her face.

"I want you to ask all of the women of the city to write in to explain their fear of being struck down by this predator, and I shall be the first woman to answer your call. I will explain to them why I believe my client, your son, is innocent. I will also tell them I am acting alone as the hunter of this heinous monster, because the mayor doesn't wish to expend the resources to find him. I am alone in my hunt, a woman in the wild, if you will, and I want them to demonstrate against City Hall to show their support for me!"

Andrew Kwong winced. "But, Mrs. Foltz. What if this killer is not captured in time? What if he doesn't kill again? Don't you believe the mayor will go ahead and hang my boy anyway?"

"This murderer doesn't necessarily have to kill again. That is another reason why I am circulating this article of ours beyond Chinatown. I want to enrage the killer so he comes out of hiding. I am going to ask more questions of the suspects we have in mind. I hope to narrow the list to one or two main suspects. Once I know whom to track down, it will be simply a matter of trapping him or her before he or she can kill again."

"How will you do that in so little time? Russian Hill and the Vigilantes are also waiting." Kwong pointed out.

"Don't concern yourself. I believe I now have the bait that will lure this killer out of hiding and into a trap."

"Bait? Another woman? Who would be insane enough to tempt the hand of this monster?"

"You are looking at her," Clara said, and she turned around, walked to the door, and left.

***

The article ran in all the major newspapers in San Francisco, and the national edition of the article ran through the Associate Press and the newer United Press. Eventually, because of the telegraph, all major newspapers had published the story about the woman out West who was confronting the male establishment in order to prove her client, a Chinese man, of all people, innocent.

Because of the danger to attorney Clara Foltz, and the obvious political corruption of the mayor, readers were sympathetic to her plight and were less suspicious of the arrested defendant, George Kwong. Indeed, when they read about how seven murders had been kept secret by the mayor, and George Kwong was a lowly journalist taking photos of the crime scenes, the women became embittered toward the San Francisco legal system.

After they read Clara's letter that explained how she was hired by the Six Companies to protect their business interests in the community, and then she had to protect the son of its most learned and religious owner, Andrew Kwong, they were livid.

Women from all over the United States began to learn that these poor Chinese had no rights in a court of law or in society. They were trapped inside their ghettos of poverty, and Mr. Kwong had converted to Christianity and was trying to save the souls of these poor women being held prisoner in the wicked flesh trade of Chinatown.

Not only were these women's lives being threatened by the acts of Mayor Bartlett, the entire female community was also in danger. Where would this killer strike now? He or she had already broken the racial divide and killed a white girl. Who would be next? It could be any woman in San Francisco! If women could be so easily struck down, what might happen in the communities of any state in the union?

After one week, this single editorial had elicited thousands of letters to the editor, and the demonstrators began to arrive in San Francisco by the trainload. They filled the hotels and rented rooms in the homes of enterprising homeowners, and they met at the churches and in the parks of the city to plan their demonstration against the mayor and City Hall.

***

City Hall, San Francisco, February 22, 1884

Inside the City Hall auditorium, Mayor Washington Bartlett was standing in front of his assembled cadre of uniformed sheriffs, police officers, and newspapers sympathetic to his cause. In addition, Captain Isaiah Lees and his partner, Detective Sergeant Eduard Vanderheiden, waited quietly in the back of the room, subservient yet observant, as the leader of the city droned on.

"I want a full cordon of police presence around this building immediately! I have already responded to that scurrilous editorial, and I want my response circulated on all the press wires around the country. These Chinese and this one woman have usurped the law, and I will not allow a potential murderer out of my jail! The safety of my city must come before any special interests of criminal aliens who care not a whit for our culture or for our system of justice. This is why we keep them out of the country. They have stolen jobs from our good men, and they have brought crime and ungodly practices to our shores."

A few of the sheriff's men shouted their approval. Bartlett grinned back at them.

"I will speak to this crowd of women, and we shall have our day in court! This man, this Kwong, will be hanged if our evidence convinces the jury, and no outsiders will ever sway the method of American justice that has withstood our Revolution against the British, and the many martyrs of our Civil War will have not died in vain."

Bartlett's voice became louder, and his face was red. Sheriff Connolly yelled, "Hang 'em high!"

The mayor continued, "America is for Americans, and we have no room for foreigners who have made their deal with the big business tycoons of New York, behind the people's backs. This foreign treaty has been disavowed once and for all, and these interlopers and pagans will never set foot in this great city, or in any other United States territory or state, ever again!"

Captain Lees and Detective Vanderheiden looked at each other and shrugged their shoulders. Vanderheiden took a cigar out of his jacket pocket, held it under his long nose, and smelled it. "Is Foltz out questioning the suspects?"

"Yes. She told me she has her own ideas about who might have committed these murders, but she wants to narrow down the list." Lees shrugged again. "I gave her the Derringer. What else can I do? She's a hard-headed woman."

"She better not shoot the wrong person, boss." Vanderheiden laughed.

"What do you mean, Dutch?"

"Bartlett ain't going to let her roam around without somebody trailing her, now is he?"

Lees scowled. "All right, you've convinced me. I will make certain she has a clear path to discover what she called the evils of mankind."

Captain Lees knew he was risking his job by allowing this woman to have so much information and trial evidence. However, it was his many years of antagonism that had made him do this. Seeing the vigilante hangings, and then watching the sheriffs become an unfair substitute for this kind of knee-jerk, biased justice had become too much for Lees to stomach. He hated the mayor and his group of private vigilantes called the Chinatown Squad more than he feared losing his job, and he was going to let his natural sense of practical judgement overrule his ego for once in his life.

***

For the entire week, Clara and Ah Toy visited all the main witnesses that Captain Lees considered suspects. Clara, of course, was beginning to have her own idea about who might have committed the murders, but she wasn't certain she wanted to share it as yet. To her way of thinking, proving that the mayor had or had not hired this killer was not relevant at this juncture. Most important was the fact that another woman could die at any moment, and she wanted to prevent that.

She had first questioned Rachel Benedict at the Methodist Mission for Wayward Women in Chinatown. Clara found the woman quite eccentric in her ways, but her answers had been forthright. Had George Kwong ever struck Mary McCarthy in her presence? No. Had he threatened her in any way? No. Had she seen the two youngsters engaged in any affectionate activities? Yes, they often sat and held hands, staring into each other's eyes, and George seemed quite smitten with her. Of course, she could use all of this testimony in the courtroom, if it came to that, and she advised Miss Benedict to be ready for her cross-examination. The teacher agreed, and they left her to her duties.

Clara then traveled to Oakland to question the coroner, Travis Goodbody. She found the gentleman to be quite reticent about talking to her, but when she showed him her credentials as an attorney for George Kwong, the accused, he reluctantly agreed. When she asked him whether the mayor's office had contacted him about George Kwong and his internship, he said yes, He was, however, quite averse about talking further concerning the work the young man did or about the supposed theft of the post-mortem kit. Clara came away believing this man had been perhaps bribed or even threatened into cooperating with Bartlett.

She left the journalist, Stanley Boscombe, and the minister of the Tin How Joss House Temple, Guan Shi Yin, for last. In order to put her plan into effect, she left the same bit of information with each suspect. She told each person that when she went to trial to defend her client, George Kwong, she was going to surprise the jury with the identity of the killer. Clara then looked straight into the suspect's eyes and said, "I know it's you, and you should confess to me right now. Or else, your day of reckoning shall come in court." Of course, not one of the suspects confessed, but she was certain she had awakened the monster within, and that he or she would come after her.

As a matter of fact, Clara had no such incontrovertible evidence. She had suspicions, but she knew the only way to bring the killer out of hiding was to tell every suspect he or she was the murderer. Then, Clara was going to wait for this killer to come to her. The only person Clara had told about this spider-and-fly subterfuge was her good friend, Ah Toy. She believed if she told Captain Lees he would not allow her to do it, and nobody would catch this heinous killer. Ah Toy, on the other hand, was quite excited to hear about setting this trap. She was going to help her do it, and she suggested they discuss the details over a nice dinner at the Hopkins mansion on Nob Hill.

***

One Nob Hill, San Francisco, February 22, 1884

Later, inside the macabre Victorian mansion, Clara was dining with Ah Toy and Mrs. Hopkins. Ah Toy explained before dinner that the old woman was just about prepared to purchase some of Ah Toy's art. "She really wants my landscapes of Chinatown, and the ones I did of the Tin How Temple were especially pleasing to her. I'm afraid the old lady is going daft, however, and you must excuse her at dinner. Don't worry what you say because she will forget it in five minutes."

Clara realized this was true about Mrs. Mary Sherwood Hopkins when she told Ah Toy about her experience interviewing Stanley Boscombe and Guan Shi Yin. "When I told each one he was the killer and that he should confess to me right now, I got some rather interesting responses. The other suspects simply stated their innocence and some wanted to see my evidence. Mr. Boscombe, in a real panic, began to stutter profusely, and he eventually broke down in tears. The minister, on the other hand, began to pray in Cantonese. At least, that's what Ah Toy told me he was doing. His were the angriest prayers I have ever had the displeasure of hearing."

When both Clara and Ah Toy began to laugh at this, Mrs. Hopkins frowned. “You mustn’t provoke God, my dear lady. Even the Chinese gods become belligerent.” This made the levity even more boisterous, and soon Ah Toy and Clara were crying and laughing at the same time.

After they gained their composure, Clara explained how she was going to prepare herself for the probable attack by the killer. “After Captain Lees gave me the Derringer, I knew I had the responsibility to save the lives of women who might become targets of this killer’s wrath. In addition, since the story of the killings has now circulated around the United States, I believe it will not infuriate this murderer, as the captain suggested. Instead, I think this killer will enjoy the notoriety such publicity will bring. Doesn’t it stand to reason? Somebody who kills like this must be an extremely arrogant sort. This person must believe that he or she is doing society a favor by getting rid of these women.”

“Yes, I saw a few of these types in my business as a Madame. They tend to be violent, and I had to restrict their access to my girls because it put them in danger of physical harm.” Ah Toy nodded at the butler Hannigan who was bringing in a tray filled with the dinner’s first course of mixed green salads.

“The mental state of the killer is a key to my discovery of this person’s identity. I believe that when I confronted him or her, I immediately caused fear to take hold. I suddenly became the person who must be killed next.” Clara smiled up at Hannigan, who was placing the salad before her on the laced tablecloth. The butler did not return the smile, as he looked concerned about what she had just said.

“Don’t you believe you might be in immediate danger? Perhaps you should seek protection.” Ah Toy picked up her fork and held it aloft. “I know some Tongs who would do the job. Just give me your permission.”

“No. That would scare off this perpetrator. In fact, it is my guess that I won’t be approached until the trial. I told each suspect I was going to reveal the killer’s identity during the trial, as a surprise. It would be reasonable to assume this megalomaniac, who may be testifying for the prosecution, will also bask in the limelight of such recognition, even though it is the light of truth.” Clara picked up the canter of olive oil and spread it over her salad.

"The truth shall set you free!" exclaimed Mary Hopkins, between bites of her salad.

"I completely disagree! If this killer has any sanity left, he will attempt to kill you as soon as possible. The sooner you are out of the way, the sooner he can kill again." Ah Toy pointed her fork at Clara.

"No, this killer already knows he or she is a suspect. When I divulge the secret identity during the trial, it simply means I believe he or she is the real murderer. The authorities don't believe this, so the killer will simply declare his or her innocence in public, and then I shall truly be in danger of attack." Clara bit off a large piece of lettuce. "It is at that moment I may seek protection from your Tongs or from the police, if they'll give it to me."

"Hannigan! Get this poor woman some tongs. She can't pick up her salad!" Mrs. Hopkins cried.

***

As Clara walked to the streetcar after dinner, she began to feel the danger all around her. Why had she been so bold in her effort to bring this monstrous woman-killer out of hiding? She had five children and a family who depended on her. She wasn't a bachelor like Isaiah Lees. Perhaps her assessment of the murderer being arrogant was misplaced. It was she who was most arrogant. She believed her life was more important than those prostitutes and that the killer would treat her with respect. Why should the killer wait until the trial? Women were nothing to this person.

Clara saw that the slowly encroaching fog was making its way across the streets below Nob Hill. Clara clutched at her wrap, and pulled it down, so that it covered her top half. She had worn a thick cotton brown dress, with a large bustle, so her position while riding in the streetcar was uncomfortable. Her thoughts were even more discomforting, however. The man seated in the row across the aisle was staring at her. He was burly and red bearded, and he had a rather imposing dent in his forehead, as if someone had struck him with a hammer or other such tool. She wondered if her killer might not subcontract another murderer to get rid of her. That would be intelligent.

The fog was thick, as he followed her down Montgomery Street toward her apartment building. Clara heard the man's heavy steps. She smelled the foul odor from the man's cigar. As she increased her gait, he increased his, and her heart began to pound so forcefully that she felt its pulsing in her throat. She opened the top two buttons on her dress. When she looked back, she saw nothing. The fog was too dense. She took a deep breath and began to run. She felt the bustle behind her swaying back and forth like a hot air balloon in the wind. Up ahead, as the fog began to clear, she saw the red awning in front of her building. She looked back, and the hammer head was still following her. She watched, as he began to run to catch up to her.

Was this going to be the moment of her demise? Could he be that mysterious dark figure she saw on the night of the McCarthy murder? Standing in the shadows with the flashing blade? No, she insisted upon living for her children. She extracted the Derringer from her purse and pointed it at the intruder. She felt the trigger on her finger, and her aim was steady. “Stop right there!”

The man raised his hands. “Whoa, Mrs. Foltz. I don’t mean you no harm. Name’s Sergeant O’Brien. Perry O’Brien. I work with Captain Lees. He wanted me to follow you.” O’Brien held open his coat and showed her his SFPD badge.

Clara lowered the pistol to her side. “I am sorry, Detective. The captain didn’t tell me he was ordering anybody to protect me. How long have you been following me?”

“All week. I guess when I was on the streetcar you were spooked by something. I’ve been tailing you so’s you could question all your suspects without harm. And I’ll be watching your apartment while you stay there. Officer Cameron will also wear plain clothes to switch with me so I can get some sleep.” O’Brien took off his derby and held it in front of his portly stomach. Clara saw he was a redhead. “We’ll be with you all next week during the trial. You can rest assured nobody will harm you as long as we’re on the job, Mrs. Old Sherlock’d have me head in a basket if you got harmed! Ever since the mayor fired him and his partner, Dutch Vanderheiden, he’s vowed to help you defeat them in court.”

Clara was astounded. “What did you say? Captain Lees lost his job because of me?”

“I don’t think it was just you, Mrs. Clara. That old Englishman’s been fighting Bartlett and his cronies in the Sheriff’s Department for twenty years now. He says he’s now going to do everything in his power to assist you."

Clara now knew that Isaiah Lees was truly a fine man. Unlike her ex-husband, who ran from any sign of conflict, and chased women like a barnyard rooster, this man Isaiah Lees was showing her his true mettle thorough his actions. She was probably more attracted to him now than she had ever before been lured by any man in her life.

"I must go in now, Mr. O'Brien. Please tell Captain Lees and his partner that I am indebted to them, and I'll certainly be making them members of my defense team."

"Yes, mum. I will certainly do that."

Clara climbed the front steps. When she turned around to see where he was, the detective tipped his derby toward her and grinned. "May those who love us, love us; and those who don't love us, may God turn their hearts; and if He don't turn their hearts, may he turn their ankles so we'll know them by their limping."

Clara turned the knob of the front door, and she felt truly safe for the first time that week.

CHAPTER SEVEN: THE TRIAL

San Francisco City Hall Courthouse, San Francisco, February 23-27, 1884.

On the first day of the trial of George Kwong, there were thousands of demonstrators, mostly women, assembled outside the courthouse on Market and Van Ness Streets. Clara noticed that her friend from the Women's Suffrage Movement, Ellen Clark Sargent, was outside speaking to the assembled and handing out membership flyers. Clara often attended meetings of the Century Club at Ellen's home on Folsom Street.

The City Hall itself was a metaphor for public corruption. Its construction began in 1871, originally planned in the French-style, on the triangular space of the former Yerba Buena Park, which had previously been a cemetery. So many different contractors made a profit from the years of construction that they were fired, and others, even more corrupt, took their place.

The cheap, Greek-style structures that resulted had walls filled with sand, and the city hall buildings had two entrances, one of which faced North toward Van Ness and Nob Hill, where the wealthy could drive-up to the carriage entrance to do their business. The South-facing entrance to the city hall structures was where Clara and the demonstrators were. This was the Market Street side, which included the infamous "Sand Lots," where the labor unrest and Chinatown riots had begun.

As Clara passed by the suffragette group, on her way up the steps to the courthouse, Ellen Sargent waved. "You are our standard bearer, Clara Foltz! Portia of the Pacific, representing the rights of the underclasses, including women, is on her way to victory over the patriarchal powers. Just last year, this male-dominated system terminated the jobs of all the women inside San Francisco's City Hall and replaced them with men. Why? Not because the men were more competent at the jobs. No, they were replaced because men could vote. That's why we need to get that voting rights power, once and for all time!"

Inside the courtroom, the atmosphere and populace that made-up the ingredients of this so-called fair trial were diametrically opposed to the women outside demonstrating. As Clara had deduced earlier, Mayor Bartlett had hastily ordered a kangaroo court against her client, George Kwong.

She had only one week to prepare her case, and during that week she had to assess the tangible evidence, appear at the all-male Voir Dire jury rejection (she had to reject those jurists who were blatant racists), and bring George to the pre-trial hearing, where she argued for most of two hours, with Judge Randolph Hoffman, a man she had never before seen, to allow testimony from Chinese witnesses. She believed it was a pyrrhic victory when Hoffman permitted the testimony, because he warned her that her Asian witnesses could not be used as expert witnesses or eyewitnesses to a crime.

Now, as the trial docket was set, and she moved to her defense table on the left side of the courtroom, she noticed with satisfaction that Captain Lees and Detective Vanderheiden were seated directly behind her and not on the prosecution's side of the room. Since they were no longer members of the police department, the two men would be testifying for her during the trial.

Ah Toy had been permitted to act as the court's translator and her personal legal assistant. Clara could smell the cigar and cigarette smoke coming from the visitors' gallery, and she smiled to herself when she realized that most of the visitors were male as well. The patriarchal hordes. Just the way she liked it.

Clara also had a secret plan she had executed before the witnesses were called to testify. She handed each one a private note that told them a clandestine truth about why they were in the courtroom that day, and Clara believed it would change everything. Even if this were a kangaroo trial, she would be able to flush out the real murderer from hiding. Ah Toy was the only other person who knew about her secret plan.

District Attorney Matthew C. Welles, Jr., was her adversary. He had a contingent of two other lawyers on his team of prosecutors, and they all dressed like pall bearers at a funeral. Black suits and ties, white shirts, and the collective demeanor of funeral directors. She assumed it was George Kwong's funeral they were going to prosecute.

"All rise!" the bailiff announced, standing next to the American flag. "The Honorable Randolph Charles Hoffman presiding in the case of the State of California versus George Bai Kwong, Docket number 53-C, Criminal Court, the State of California."

Clara felt a lump in her throat, as she always did whenever she had to try a case. She had never graduated law school, and there was a voice inside that made her remember that fact. Even though she had made many male graduates look ridiculous, when she took the oral Bar Examination, as her photographic memory could recite most of the California Codes and Criminal Procedures verbatim.

Welles gave his opening statement to the 12 members of the jury. Unlike Clara, he was not a pacer. He spoke from his position of authority behind the prosecution's rostrum, but his voice was a deep baritone, and it was loud, so he need not visit each jurist the way Clara did when she addressed the panel.

"Gentlemen, I represent the people of the State of California. They have appointed me today to show you how the accused, George Kwong, was jilted by the victim, Miss Mary McCarthy, and in response, Kwong did knowingly and willfully attack her in the residence at 814 Sacramento Street at approximately seven in the evening of February 12, 1884."

Clara saw that Welles watched the faces of the jurymen very carefully. To her, they were the key to a successful argument.

"The State has a witness you will hear who will testify that George Kwong had a fight with the victim on the day before her murder, and another witness will explain how Kwong had learned to autopsy corpses while working as a coroner's assistant for a summer in Oakland. The victim, Miss McCarthy, who was trying to become an honest woman, was pulled back into prostitution by Kwong and his father, Andrew, who are well known to profit from such illegal enterprises in Chinatown."

The prosecutor's voice got noticeably louder. Clara knew this was what men did when they wanted to get the upper hand with a woman in any argument.

"We will show that McCarthy was keeping money from such prostitution for herself, and that this enraged Kwong so much that he murdered her and stripped her corpse down to a mere skeleton, using the post-mortem kit he obtained from his job in Oakland. Kwong wanted to make Miss McCarthy an example to other women who would attempt such independence in the future."

There were several gasps and groans from jury members during his speech and a few shouts from the audience.

"We shall also show that this planning against independent prostitutes was well known by the police, especially the Chinatown Squad, and that the Kwongs kept a strict business practice and detested any such absconding of money by women like Miss McCarthy. In fact, their Tong enforcers, the San Ho Jui, or Triad Society, made certain these women were kept in line and paid the Kwongs regularly for their work in the flesh trade."

Again, there were audible gasps from the gallery. Clara noticed that several of the jury members were getting red in the face and fidgeting in their seats. Not a good sign.

"We know this murder can be the tip of an iceberg of corruption in Chinatown, and these criminals, left unchecked, will continue to import and kidnap innocent women to continue their business. Miss McCarthy's murder is perhaps the beginning of a widespread conspiracy to plant terror in the minds of women who would think about going against the dictates of the criminal element in Chinatown. Mr. George Kwong, who is guilty of enforcing the will of his elders, must pay for his criminal act, and we are here to prove his murderous guilt beyond any reasonable man's doubt."

Several men in the gallery applauded, and one even whistled, until the judge finally struck his gavel to restore order.

Judge Hoffman turned to Clara. "Thank you, Counselor. Mrs. Foltz? Would you like to give your opening statement?"

Clara rose from her chair, spread out the front of her conservative, dark-blue dress with the medium-sized bustle in the rear, and walked over to stand in front of the jury. She hoped the intelligent logic of her words could overcome her obvious lack of audible force.

"Shall we get the rather obvious facts out of the way first, gentlemen? I am a female representing another minority, a Chinese man by the name of George Kwong. I have no obligation by law to prove that Mr. Kwong did not commit this heinous murder. No, the only requirement to defend him, since he is not guilty in the eyes of the law up until that moment when Mr. Welles proves his accusations to you, is to show you the number of ways my client may have not reasonably committed the act in question. This horrible act was done to a woman, Miss Mary McBride, who was in love with my client, and he was in love with her."

A few men in the audience laughed. Clara began to pace, moving from one juror to the next and looking each in the eye.

"In fact, the defense will show through testimony and evidence that George was attempting to get her out of her sinful profession and not into it, as the prosecution alleges. I will not argue that Andrew Kwong is innocent of taking money from the Tongs, who run the prostitution and other illicit enterprises inside Chinatown. Instead, I will show how these illicit businesses have come about because of many years of racism and restriction of basic human rights."

When several in the audience booed, Clara felt the obvious prejudice for the first time in that courtroom. She did not look their way, however. Instead, she increased the volume of her voice to its maximum.

"The Chinese in San Francisco came to our city with the hope of eventually becoming citizens. However, their overlords in southern China, the Manchu, and their overlords in this country, the owners of the railroads, conspired together to prevent these innocent workers from gaining any civil rights in these United States. Instead, they were attacked and some were murdered by mobs. They were not allowed outside of their ghettos to mingle with their fellow workers and citizens, and they needed protection just to exist."

Again, there were shouts and cat-calls. Judge Hoffman finally struck his gavel several times to quiet the rowdy crowd.

"The Tongs became that protection, and they were often independent from the Six Companies because they threatened decent men like the Kwongs with violence if they did not submit. Did the authorities help them gain respect and citizenship? No, instead, they appointed a special Chinatown Squad to harass and to subject them to demeaning searches and, in some cases, even killing babies with deadly fumigants and sprays."

Several of the jury members said "No!" Others frowned and coughed.

"Counselor Foltz. Please stay on the topic of murder in the first degree." Judge Hoffman admonished her by striking his gavel.

"It's all related, your honor. The Kwongs were two men who worked the most to show they were part of our community. Andrew learned to speak fluent English, and he even converted from his natural-born faith to become a Methodist. His son, George, worked with him on the only permitted newspaper, *The Oriental*, so they could spread the good, Christian news of redemption and hope to his fellow Chinese. These were not men who detested our culture. These were men who loved our city and our citizens."

Two Chinese men in the back row cheered. They were Clara's permitted witnesses, and the judge immediately said, "Silence! Or I shall have you both thrown out of my court!"

Clara, unbowed, continued, "Why would my client want to jeopardize his future by killing a white woman? We women have so few rights as it is. Why would a good, upstanding Chinese man want to kill the woman he loved and to whom he had devoted his time in order to save her from the world's oldest profession? This is a profession, gentlemen, which women have been forced to enter, when their rights were violated, when men have raped them, and then they have gone unpunished."

Clara noticed, as she began moving from one juror to the next, that her words were having an effect. Their faces softened, and several of them were actually nodding their heads in agreement.

"George Kwong wanted to save his lover, Mary McCarthy, not kill her. Love does not kill. Love preserves. It preserves our human dignity, and it returns our basic human rights to us if we earn them, just as the Kwongs have earned them. Thank you, kind gentlemen of the jury."

"Mr. Welles, you may call your first witness," Judge Hoffman pointed to the bailiff to swear in the summoned person by the witness stand.

"Your honor, I call Stanley Boscombe to the stand."

The young journalist from the *San Francisco Examiner* walked over to stand before the uniformed bailiff. "Please raise your right hand, and place your left hand on the Bible," the bailiff instructed. Boscombe, as well as all the other witnesses that day, did so. "Do you solemnly swear, to tell the truth, the whole truth and nothing but the truth, so help you God?"

"I do," Boscombe said.

"You may be seated," the bailiff said.

Stanley Boscombe sat down in the witness chair next to the judge's raised platform. Clara cross-examined three witnesses that day. Boscombe, whom the prosecution attempted to use as a witness to George Kwong's being present before the murder took place, was rebutted by asking him questions about the purpose of journalism.

"Isn't it the job of a journalist to be on the scene of a crime in order to transcribe what occurred? Could my client have been there to take a photograph of the crime scene? Did George Kwong have a weapon on him?"

These interrogatives were all answered in the affirmative, except the last, which was a "no." Clara knew it was her purpose to put a reasonable doubt in the minds of the jurors, nothing else, and this was what she did.

The second witness for the prosecution was Rachel Benedict, the teacher at the Methodist Home for Wayward Women in Chinatown. She was on Clara's list of prime suspects, even though Clara doubted that she had performed the actual murders. Captain Lees explained that the strength required to flay a woman the way those victims had been dissected, most definitely required the force of a man. Of course, Benedict could still be guilty as an accessory.

Welles's line of questioning attempted to prove that the personal relations between George Kwong and Mary McCarthy had been toxic and that when George left the mission that day before the murder, he was especially angry at McCarthy.

Clara cross-examined Benedict by asking pointed yes-or-no questions. Did the defendant bring Mary McCarthy to you for help? Did the defendant help you by giving money to the home? Did you see George Kwong and Mary McCarthy enjoying themselves? Did the argument you witnessed escalate into anything physical? All of these answers, except the last one, were answered affirmatively, and Clara believed she had planted her seeds of doubt in the minds of the jurors.

The final witness for the prosecution that day was the coroner from Oakland, Travis Goodbody. As predicted, Goodbody was asked to identify George Kwong as the man he employed for the summer internship. The second attorney on the prosecution's team, William Varson, did the questioning of this key witness. Varson had a habit of looking back at the judge after every question, as if he were pleading to God. Clara, on the other hand, always gave her reiterations of witness responses directly to the jury. The jury, after all, decided the guilt or innocence of her client.

Varson continued with his examination of the coroner by bringing forth the Civil War post-mortem kit, the alleged tools used to strip the flesh and hone the body of the victim. Varson asked several highly technical questions about how this process could be accomplished on a female body, and Goodbody swore that these tools could do the job. Clara objected when Varson tried to ask whether George Kwong asked Goodbody any questions relating to using any of the tools to kill someone, and the judge, thankfully, sustained her demurrer, and struck the question from the record.

Clara had her own rebuttal witness, whom she would be presenting after the prosecution was finished with its witnesses, and she smiled over at him after she asked Goodbody her only cross-examination question.

"Do you keep your tools under lock and key?" she asked.

"No," Goodbody said. Clara turned around and grinned at Lees, and he smiled back.

***

Later that evening, Ah Toy told Clara she believed the first day had gone well, especially Clara's brilliant opening statement. The defense team, composed of Clara, Ah Toy, Captain Lees and his partner, Dutch Vandenheiden, were dining together at the Luck Dragon in Chinatown. The large restaurant was filled with many of the visiting female demonstrators from across the United States, and Clara was somewhat of a celebrity to them.

The owner, Stephen Fong of the Hip Kat Company, was personally seeing to it that Clara and her party were given the royal treatment. The table was filled with the most delectable and freshest dishes, and their teapot was refilled regularly during the meal.

"It all seems so choreographed and ritualized. I keep thinking I'm simply talking to walls with animal trophy heads on them. Don't you agree, Isaiah? This is just a kangaroo trial." Clara sipped from her small teacup, and then wiped her lips with a cloth napkin.

"What do you have planned, Clara? You knew this would happen going in because I told you as much. Despite your newspaper victory, and all these demonstrators, the country is still against the Chinese. The economy's been hemorrhaging jobs like blood oozing out of one of this killer's victims, and the Chinese are seen as threats to the few remaining jobs for men." Captain Lees picked up a fried wonton and began to chew it.

Clara looked over at Ah Toy. "Shall I tell them?"

Ah Toy nodded. "I think you need to at this point."

"You never told me you would have one of your men, a Detective O'Brien, I think his name is, following me around day and night. Well, I never told you that I have a plan to bring the real killer out of hiding." Clara stabbed one of her chopsticks into a bowl of fried rice. "I informed every suspect on our list that he or she was the murderer. I also told him or her I was going to prove it as a surprise during the trial."

Lees pounded his fist on the table. "You did what? Are you insane?"

"Now wait a minute, boss. Why would telling them they're guilty do anything to bring them out? Why would they risk killing Clara until they knew what she had on them?" Vanderheiden said, twirling the end of his auburn mustache.

"What do you have on this *real* killer? Who is it?" Lees scowled at her.

Clara looked down at her hands. She felt the same way she had when she lied to her father while she was secretly meeting Jeremiah Foltz. She looked back up and confronted Isaiah's dark eyes. Her fear of real commitment with a man was still plaguing her. "I don't have anything, really. I need to prove a few things first. I just thought since this was a kangaroo court anyway, I would just …"

"Just commit suicide?" Lees roared.

"If the killer tries to get me, then I shall perhaps save some other poor woman. Besides, you gave me the gun." Clara's voice dropped to a whisper.

"I gave you that gun to give you confidence, not real protection. This killer obviously means business. I wouldn't doubt he knows how to wear chest armor or even something like a knight's helmet. We had robbers in England who did this whilst terrorizing a bank. Your Derringer's bullets would be like hitting the killer with two beanbags."

"I agree with Detective Vanderheiden," Ah Toy said. "This

murderer won't risk killing a famous person like Clara. Not unless Clara named that person in court and proved why he or she is guilty." Ah Toy took Clara's hands into her own and engaged her eyes. "Since you won't be showing anything like that during the trial, then there is no danger."

"What do you think is our best way to proceed? I am going to put you on the stand, Isaiah, and the questions I will ask are going to relate to the way this city has its hands in corrupt activities." Clara stared hard at the Captain of Detectives. Even though she had known him just a brief time, she cared about him.

"I can only tell the truth. If my superiors can't handle the truth, then getting my job back isn't worth my time and effort. I've already told you a lot of what you used in your opening statement today. Also, when you wrote that editorial about how the Chinese are being treated, I was completely supportive. I do agree with you about this being the only way to fight this accusation against your client. Without you, Clara, George Kwong would already be hanging from Russian Hill." Lees grasped Clara's hands and scowled.

"All right then. We will attempt to put the mayor and the Chinatown Squad on trial, if that's the only way I can fight. I need to get some sleep now, so I bid you all adieu, my friends. Thank you for your cooperation."

Clara stood up, arranged her hat, and buttoned the top button at her throat. "Once more, into the fray!"

***

The next day in court, the prosecution finished its presentation of evidence and witnesses. Sheriff Connolly, the arresting officer, testified that his men found the post-mortem kit under George Kwong's mattress, and when asked about it, the Defendant had told him he did not know how it got there. Clara was able to get Connolly to admit that anybody with access to the house could have placed the kit under the mattress.

She also pointed out the fact that as the Coroner for the City of Oakland, Travis Goodbody was also affiliated with the police department. She asked Connolly if police did favors for each other in order to get a conviction, and the sheriff admitted that "in order to make the law run smoothly, its officers needed to cooperate to convict a murderer."

Welles and his prosecution team spent the rest of the day presenting detailed charts and statistics that claimed to show how Chinatown profited from its prostitution businesses. When Welles said that it was "common knowledge" that when a woman became independent, she was a direct threat to the profits made by the Six Companies, especially Andrew Kwong and his family, Clara objected.

She explained to the judge that this was hearsay, and without specific contracts or testimony proving that the Kwongs profited directly from Chinatown prostitution, it was inadmissible. Sadly, Judge Hoffman overruled her, and permitted the accusations and statistical information.

Clara spent that night coaching both Captain Lees and her assistant, Ah Toy. They were going to be the first two witnesses she was going to call. She first spent a half hour at the Luck Dragon talking with two journalists from the East Coast who were covering the trial for their newspapers.

One, a gentleman from the *New York Times*, seemed more interested in the fact she was the first woman lawyer in California than he did about the case itself and what it represented. The second, a woman, who was writing for the private newspaper of the Women's Suffrage Movement under Susan B. Anthony, was more sympathetic to the plight of Clara attempting to get a fair trial under such patriarchal hegemony.

After they left, Clara went over what she was going to try to do with her questions the next day in court. "I want to show how the Chinatown Squad was formed, and I want to show how it has treated the Chinese unfairly from its inception. Also, I want to prove that independent prostitution has been permitted in the past, and that women like you, Ah Toy, have actually made a success of it under dire circumstances."

"I think you should talk about the so-called post-mortem kit again," Lees pointed out. "Those tools are too small and flimsy to be used to slice through thick muscle and sinew. When Dutch and I found the body, our first thought was that a Tong member had done the work because they use these large hatchet-like knives that would be ideal for this kind of hideous flaying of a human body."

"Good thinking, Isaiah," Clara said. "I thought those tools looked small. After all, they are meant to be used on the battlefield during the war, as anything larger would have been cumbersome."

"I'll tell you anything you need to relate about the business, Clara, you know that. Besides, if Mrs. Hopkins found out I was in the news she would find it humorous. The first thing she told me when she found out I had been a Madame was that husbands should pay their wives more for that activity. If they did, then maybe the husbands wouldn't have to frequent bordellos so often."

It rained all the next day, and during Clara's questioning, there were flashes of lightning and bursts of thunder. It was as if the gods were taking her to task for the information she was spreading about the corruption of police in San Francisco.

She was objected to five times by the prosecution, but she knew her witnesses had already responded, so the jury was able to hear his testimony nevertheless. It was a trick her lawyer father taught her about being a lawyer. "The horse is already out of the barn," was the way he put it to her.

When she called Captain Isaiah Lees to the stand, there was a hushed stillness inside the courtroom. The newspapers had already informed the city about Lees being fired by Mayor Bartlett, and the story about why the Captain of Detectives had turned against the mayor was also covered. Many people believed Lees was justified for becoming a witness for the defense, but most thought he was a traitor.

Clara, however, knew that the entire hope of freeing her client in that court rested on the captain's testimony. She walked slowly up to him on the witness stand and looked him straight in the eyes.

"How long have you been working for the San Francisco Police Department, Captain Lees?" Clara asked.

"Twenty-three years, six months and fifteen days," Lees replied.

"What reason did the authorities give for your sudden termination on February 22, of this year?"

"I was told I had assisted you, the defense, in this case and that it was against police department regulations to do so." Clara saw Isaiah's forehead begin to sweat, as he was obviously under a lot of pressure.

"Is it true, Captain Lees, that you are required by law to hand over to the defense all evidence and lists of witnesses that will be called by the prosecution before the trial begins?"

"Yes, that's very true. I have often even worked with the defense to make certain they have all of this information or else a mistrial could be ordered by the court."

"I object, your honor! Counsel knows full well that handing over relevant evidence and a list on a piece of paper must first go through the judge's hands. Captain Lees never did this. He is therefore in violation of police department policy." Welles was livid.

"Objection sustained." Judge Hoffman ordered.

Clara decided to get into her main questions.

"Captain, were you working for the San Francisco Police Department when the Chinatown Squad was formed?"

"Yes, I certainly was. The formation of the Chinatown Squad came shortly after the passage of the federal Chinese Exclusion Law by Congress in 1882."

"In your expert opinion, Captain, do you believe this sheriff's department sub-group was acting in the best interests of justice?" Clara rubbed her forehead. "Can you tell the court of any examples of a direct miscarriage of justice caused by this organization?"

"Again, objection! What does this have to do with the first degree murder of Mary McCarthy?"

The judge thought for a moment. Finally, he said, "Objection overruled. This pressure on the Chinese population is relevant to the mental state of the defendant."

"Thank you, your honor. And so, Captain Lees? What happened to cause you to turn against the Chinatown Squad?" Clara looked over at the jury to be certain they were listening. They were.

"I saw a Chinese baby killed from the fumigation by Jesse Brown Cook of the Chinatown Squad."

Several people shouted. There were gasps and jeers.

"The Sheriff blamed every outbreak of disease on the Chinese," Lees continued. "The Chinatown Squad was often more of a hindrance to crime fighting than it was an aide. I also saw men who took money from public officials in order to put more pressure on the Chinese men working in Chinatown."

"Thank you, Captain Lees. And now, what about the so-called murder weapon? The Civil War field autopsy kit that my client, George Kwong, supposedly used on the victims? In your considered opinion, could these tools have been used successfully to accomplish this dastardly and horrendous deed?"

"Objection. Witness is not an authority." Welles shouted.

"The witness was in the army during the Civil War, your honor," Clara said.

"Objection overruled. You may respond, Captain Lees," Hoffman said.

"Let me see that kit. I'll show you why it could never have been used to do the job on the victim," Lees said.

The field kit was carried over to Lees by the bailiff. The captain pulled out the largest scalpel from the kit, which was about six inches long, and held it up for the jury to see. "Mrs. Foltz. Could you assist me for a moment and come over here?"

Clara, who had rehearsed this earlier, dramatically approached the witness stand and held out her arm to Lees. The captain asked her roll up her dress sleeve, which she did. He then held the small, silver blade against the thick part of her forearm.

"This blade could have never been large enough to cut through the sinew of a woman's forearm, much less eviscerate her and slice through the thick muscles of the biceps and the thighs. Even if razor-sharp, it would have taken so much time to accomplish this feat that the murderer would have certainly been discovered." Lees brushed the small blade lightly against Clara's white skin, and again the gallery shouted its displeasure.

"This kit was made for emergencies on the battle field, was it not, Captain? But, what about a Tong hatchet? Could this have accomplished the murderous intent of the killer? Please, Mr. Andrew Kwong. Can you bring over one of your Tong hatchets for the jury to see?" Clara called out to the father, who was seated in the front row on the defense side.

After Andrew Kwong held the large, sixteen-inch blade with an oak handle up, the courtroom again began to shout and whistle.

"Order! I shall have this court cleared if I hear any more commotion!" Judge Hoffman said, slamming his gavel down repeatedly.

"That is all, Captain. I thank you. I wish to call Miss Ah Toy to the stand, your honor." Clara winked at Isaiah, and he smiled back at her as he left the witness stand.

After she was sworn in, Ah Toy took a seat on the stand. She seemed very poised in her red silk *cheongsam*, and she looked over at the men in the jury box. They were all staring at her.

"Miss Ah Toy. At one time, you were working as an independent Madame in Chinatown, were you not?" Clara wanted to establish her witness's professional status.

"Yes, I was. I worked for fifteen years in that capacity."

"Could you show the court why your independent status was superior to the methods of prostitution provided by the Tongs and their sex slavery work conditions?"

"I would be very happy to do that," said Ah Toy, and she stood up. When both of her arms began to undulate in the air, like weaving cobras, the jury panel became transfixed. Clara could see their eyes bulge as they stared at Ah Toy. She then began to wave her bottom in a circular fashion, so the outline of her firm buttocks could be seen clearly under the soft silk.

It took five minutes before Judge Hoffman could become rational. "That's enough! The witness will be seated at once!"

"Your honor, what does this prove?" whined Prosecutor Welles.

"Counselor Foltz?" the judge inquired.

"Miss Ah Toy, were you demonstrating the main method of your female allure that you taught to all of your prostitutes? Were they paid well, were they healthy, and did you even allow some to marry if they so chose?"

"Yes to all of your questions. I made most of my money without having my women engage in any intercourse with their patrons." Ah Toy's voice was clear and confident.

"And, what about the Tong's method?" Clara asked, turning to the jury.

"The Tongs bought and sold their women like sex slaves. They were kept in wire cages, and all of them had to have intercourse or be sent back to China. Profit was the main goal of the Tong method." Ah Toy raised her fist in the air. "Never again should this be allowed!"

The courtroom erupted in a mixture of shouts, cheers, and jeers. Judge Hoffman had to adjourn to prevent a riot.

***

The final day, Clara brought to the stand her Chinese

contingent of witnesses. With Ah Toy acting as translator, she questioned the head of the San Ho Hui, Xi Ming, who testified that he often paid bribes to various police officials so as to keep them from arresting his women. Welles objected that Ming was "no expert witness," and the judge sustained his objection. Clara also interviewed Andrew Kwong at length to explain the good deeds he did for his community and for the Methodist Church and its outreach. He also testified about his son, George, and that he had never had any discipline problems from him at all. Clara interviewed the minister of the Tin How Temple, Guan Shi Yin, who stated that the defendant George Bai Kwong had helped him with religious services and ceremonial duties.

Finally, Clara questioned a Chinese prostitute who knew George. She stated that George was always trying to get women out of the profession and into a "respectable line of work." She also said she knew that was what he was doing with Mary McCarthy.

When instructed by Judge Hoffman to present their final summations, Welles did not speak. He had brought in a special closing argument specialist, one Harold Rossiter, a Sacramento District Attorney. Rossiter, unlike the "pallbearer" Welles, spoke to each of the male jurors individually. His most passionate and affective speech came when he was discussing the threat of violence and disease on womanhood.

"If you allow this man to go free, what are you telling our Christian women in San Francisco? That you care nothing about their lives? For, make no mistake, gentlemen. This killer will strike again. He has already chosen a white woman, and who will be the next victim? It could be your wife, sir, or yours, sir! The bloody handwriting is on the walls of Chinatown's opium dens and inside its brothels. Unless you put a stop to it, it will become an infestation of gruesome murders, and the blood will be on your hands, Gentlemen, unless you vote today for a conviction of murder in the first degree!"

In her closing statement, Clara thought she was not going to do it, but she did. She mentioned the seven Chinese prostitutes who had been killed.

"I know you swore that you never read anything about this case before becoming a jurist. I must say that is how our system works best. Jurors must not be emotionally swayed by members of the press before or during a trial. That is why we have jury sequestration."

Clara moved again in front of each juror as she spoke. There eyes were a bit glassy, so she decided to get into the main thrust of her argument.

"I must tell you that there have been women murdered before Miss McCarthy, gentlemen of the jury. But they were Chinese women, and they were also independent women, trying to be like my witness Ah Toy. They simply wanted to be able to work their way out of this life of sin and brutality in order to see another day of hope. But, they were struck down in their youth, just like the victim in this case."

Clara strutted over to stand before her client, George Kwong. "George Kwong, my client, had no reason to commit this act of brutality. He wanted to save women like her from this life. He could not save the seven others of his own race, and he could not save the life of the one woman with whom he fell in love."

Seeing that the jury members' eyes were again riveted on her, she swayed her bustle a bit to draw their attention even more.

"The weapon was not seen in his hand, the testimony of his anger at Mary McCarthy is mixed, at best, and the fact that he worked one summer as a coroner's apprentice speaks to the fact that my client wanted to learn another trade besides journalism. He was not planning to kill anybody, and he just wanted what his father, Andrew, was attempting to get. Respect as a citizen of San Francisco, who wanted to become a United States citizen one day and sit with you outside the ghetto of Chinatown. You must acquit my client today, gentlemen, for the good of humanity and for the best interests of justice."

Having completed her summary, Clara walked over to her table and sat down. She took George Kwong's hands into her own, and she shed tears. He smiled back at her and whispered, "Thank you."

***

It took only six hours for the jury to deliberate. When they filed back into the courtroom, Clara and Ah Toy had returned from lunch. They stood at their positions at the Defense table. Clara kept staring at the American flag as Judge Hoffman requested the verdict from the jury foreman. The foreman, a short man with a brush mustache, looked tired.

"Has the jury reached a verdict in the case of the State of California versus George Bai Kwong?" Judge Hoffman asked.

"Yes, we have, Your Honor. We find the defendant guilty of first degree murder."

There were shouts and flashes from dozens of cameras inside the courtroom. Outside, there were protesting screams from the demonstrators.

Clara and Ah Toy refused to talk to any journalists. Clara put her arm around George Kwong, who was crying unabashedly. She leaned over and whispered, "It's not over yet. I believe I know who the killer is."

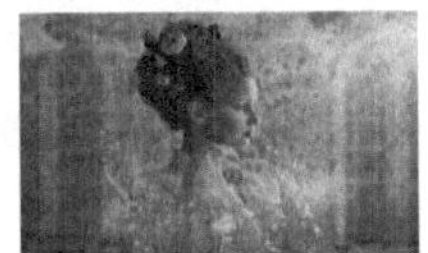

CHAPTER EIGHT: THE KIDNAPPING AND TRAP

One Nob Hill, Hopkins Mansion, San Francisco, February 28, 1884

Clara, Ah Toy, Andrew Kwong, Isaiah Lees, and Eduard Vanderheiden sat around the large, rosewood table inside Ah Toy's bedroom. Since her bedroom in the Hopkins mansion was larger than most living rooms in other houses, the group had more than enough room to discuss the case and plan their next move. Both Clara and Captain Lees foresaw what the result was to be, and thus they knew there must be an alternative to allowing George Kwong to swing from a rope.

After praising Clara and Ah Toy for the job they did at the trial, Lees became his usual, somber self. "I have fought the public hangings in San Francisco from the start. If you have never seen one of these events, then you have not seen the lowest state to which humanity can be reduced. I have seen men foul themselves, cry like babies, trip, curse, hang without dying for over ten minutes, snap the rope, and laugh at it all in a delusional madness. Meanwhile, the authorities, including the conservative merchants of San Francisco, reap great profits from the sinful spectacle. I will not allow it to happen again!"

Andrew Kwong made a karate chop in the air. "I am with you, Captain! What do you suggest we do?"

"I've thought about this long and hard. When your son was first arrested, I knew the White Whale, Washington Bartlett, would never allow George to have a fair trial. Therefore, the only way to save him from Russian Hill is to kidnap him from the jail on Kearny." The scowl of concentration had returned to Lees' face. "And we can bring him here for safekeeping until we can track down the real killer."

"Do you believe me?" Clara took Lees' hand. "I promise you, Isaiah. I know who the murderer is. However, if I give the identity of this monster, I know you will make an arrest. After this trial, I now realize the evidence I have will not be sufficient for the State to convict. The only way I can make the arrest, and perhaps expose any collaborators, will be to lure the murderer to us. And you must promise not to force me to tell you who I suspect until this person is captured."

Captain Lees frowned. "I reluctantly agree. However, if I were still on the force, I would not have agreed. You understand that my first concern is human life?"

"Yes. I understand. However, I must lure this killer out of his or her lair. I can't tell you any more than that."

"Carrie, I knew you had an answer! How will you get the killer here?" Ah Toy used the familiar name for her friend, knowing this was an important moment.

"Carrie? I've never heard you called that," Lees said.

"My parents gave it to me at birth. I changed it later to a more officious title. I believe this killer has an obsession about independent women. Although I don't know what is in this sick person's mind, I do know that if we can escalate the independent threat, then this person will become so enraged that he or she will attempt to come here in order to murder again."

Clara unfastened the top button on her dress and took a deep breath. "Once again, I plan to use the power of the press to arouse the passions of this killer. What if Ah Toy shows women how to use their feminine magnetism to make money from men? We can then advertise a course to teach women these skills. We can say that each course enrollee will have a private meeting with her, beforehand, in this mansion, in order to ascertain the specific needs of the student."

"Yes! That private meeting will tell the killer it will be an excellent way to eliminate me." Ah Toy's face radiated with inner excitement at the prospect of danger.

"I won't be able to guarantee at which appointment the killer will appear, as I would assume he or she would not use his or her real name or true gender. Therefore, I will have to be ready to protect you at every such rendezvous inside the mansion." Clara took Ah Toy's hands in her own. "You are so very brave to be doing this."

"Not only will I be assisting you in trapping this murderer, I will also be preparing the lessons needed to educate a new generation of women who want to gain independence and profit from the male patriarchy." Ah Toy smiled. "I would assume these two powerful men will be helping us in our trap. And, if you need more assistance, I do know some Tong men who would be more than willing to pitch-in."

Dutch Vanderheiden snorted. "Say what? No Tongs allowed. If Mayor Bartlett or any of his henchmen saw even one Chinaman around this place, they'd raid us in a heartbeat. Just keeping Georgie boy inside will be difficult enough."

"Where can we stash the boy so nobody will see him?" Captain Lees liked to get everything prepared before he did anything. "It should preferably be somewhere nobody would wander into by accident."

"There's an observatory in the largest steeple. It's a small room, but it is out of way, and George will be comfortable," Ah Toy said.

"Fine. Show us where it is before we go. I want to be able to enter and go directly up there. The faster we can lock him away, the better." Lees stood up and motioned for his partner. "We need to go now, Dutch. We have to plan our kidnapping adventure before we arrive. It won't be easy, but those oafs in the sheriff's jail can be tricked if we do things correctly."

"Right, boss, we can do it. They don't call you Sherlock around the station for nothing." Dutch followed the shorter man to the door. Ah Toy minced her way over to the door and opened it.

"Lead on, Ah Toy. Clara, you can start drafting your advertisement for the newspapers, and after we return with George Kwong, you can begin your part of this endeavor."

"Good luck, Isaiah and Eduard. I am so grateful to you both. You're putting your careers and possibly your lives at risk," Clara said, smiling at them.

The observatory was a good hiding place. It was up a long, winding stairway, and the room was very dark and sinister, with a skylight that looked out at the stars above San Francisco. A small bed, a lamp, a chair, and a telescope for viewing the sky. Lees and Dutch thanked Ah Toy and left.

***

It was a long walk from Nob Hill to the jail on Kearny, so

Lees and Vanderheiden took the cable car. They discussed how they would break George Kwong out the same way they discussed all their cases together. Lees began by laying out the plan, and Dutch filled in the details.

"Smith knows me, so we can work on him. I've been on hanging details before, so I know the protocol. The prisoner always has to see the doctor before he can be hanged. That always made me scratch my head. Why does the poor bastard have to be healthy to get his neck broken? Because it's the law." Lees took out his Bowie knife from his vest and began to clean under his fingernails. An elderly couple seated in the opposite row gave him a fearful look. Captain Lees just smiled at them.

Lees continued, "We can tell Smith we need to take Kwong to Doc Reed around the corner on Market. I'll tell Smith that Doc Reed gave us permission to escort the prisoner to him. We still have our weapon permits. We need the extra money since we're no longer working."

"But they'll know we were the last officers to be seen with him. What about that?" Dutch stretched his long legs under the seat in front of him.

"We both run like three-toed sloths. We'll just say the kid broke away from us and ran like a deer. We lost him in the crowds of all those women suffragettes. Couldn't shoot because we didn't want to hit a tourist." Lees finished his nails and slid the knife back into its leather sheath under his cape.

"Right. Ha! All those screaming women got us bamboozled." Dutch laughed.

"You take Kwong to the mansion, and I'll go back and tell Smith what happened. I'll say you're still out there hunting for the escaped prisoner, and I just wanted to get word out for a dragnet to begin. You know Connolly will call out the cavalry on this one. The White Whale will swallow him whole if he doesn't." Lees stood up, as they had arrived at their stop.

As they strolled together toward the jail, Dutch began a discussion about Clara Foltz. It had been bothering him from the moment his boss decided to take sides in the trial of George Kwong. Lees had always been somewhat sympathetic to the Chinese immigrants, but it was only based on the fact he was also an immigrant, and his boss's job went more smoothly when Lees treated the Chinese with respect. With Foltz, however, there had been an obvious change in Lees' entire demeanor and purpose.

Dutch took out a cigar from his frock coat pocket, bit off the end, spat out the piece into the gutter, and plugged the cigar between his teeth. He grimaced, took a box of wooden matches from the same pocket, slid the drawer open, took out a single match, and struck it against a lamp post on the sidewalk. He brought the blazing match to the end of the cigar and puffed. Plumes of smoke arose all around him as he walked.

"You really enjoy the company of Mrs. Foltz. I never seen you so attracted to a woman before, boss. Why her?"

"I don't really understand it myself," Lees said, rubbing his goatee. "I suppose she's the first woman I've ever met who has both brains and beauty. Also, she defends her family the way my own mother did. My mother never gave me heartache when I came to this country. She knew it was hard in England for me, and she understood my itch for adventure. That's just the way Clara strikes me. She appreciates an adventurous heart, but she defends the hearth and home."

"I see. I won't be asking again," Dutch said, puffing on his stogie as they came up to the station house on Kearny.

Lees walked up the steps and waved to his partner. "I'll meet you back out here," he said, pushing open the door with his shoulder.

"Okay, boss. Give 'em hell." Dutch turned around and walked to the corner near a lamppost, still puffing on his cigar.

Sergeant Smith greeted Lees. "Sherlock, where's Watson? In the gin mill, as usual?"

"Sergeant, your perception decries the intelligence of your station. I'm here to transport Kwong over to Doctor Reed for his check-up. Dutch is outside. Doc Reed gave us this special detail because we're out of work now. Can you bring him down for me, oh inspirational one?" Lees joked, hoping to keep up his casual appearance.

"Right, Captain. I am sorry about your run-in with Connolly and those sheriff bastards. They've been a thorn in our hide for many years."

Smith turned around and shouted up the stairs, "Goose! Bring down the dead chink. Captain's taking him to Doc Reed."

"The man deserves to be called by his given name, Sergeant.

And, as far as I know, he's still on this Earth." Lees admonished.

"Anything you say, Captain." Smith returned to his desk.

Ten minutes later, Lees greeted the prisoner, who was in shackles around his wrists and his ankles. "Mr. Goose, is it? We won't be needing those chains. Unlock him. I take full responsibility."

"O'Hara, Captain," the officer said, and he looked over at Sergeant Smith. Smith nodded, and O'Hara took a key from his belt and unlocked first the wrist chain, and then bent down and unlocked the ankle chain. "You be a good boy for the Captain, now George," he said.

Outside, on the sidewalk, Dutch was waiting for his boss and Kwong, smoking the rest of his cigar. When they walked up, he flipped the butt into the gutter. "Did Smith question your motives, boss?"

"No, he was his irritable self, but he was cooperative. We need to take Kwong down this alleyway to go to Chinatown. We can't trust the main thoroughfare." Lees took George Kwong's arm and guided him toward the alley entrance. Dutch followed them.

They were almost at Portsmouth Square when Lees stopped. "I will now go back and report to the station about the escape. You take Kwong over to Nob Hill, but go by the side streets and not up California Street."

"Where will I meet you?" Vanderheiden looked around in the shadows of the alley. He heard footsteps, coming fast and hard. Before he could get his gun out of his holster, he was tackled by a large man and held to the ground, with his arms twisted behind his back.

Lees, however, had seen the attack coming much sooner, and his .45 was drawn and pointed at the man holding his partner face-down in the dirty puddles of the alley.

"Captain! Behind you!" George Kwong shouted.

Lees spun around, slipping his Bowie knife from its sheath in the same motion. The Tong gang member screamed something in Chinese as the six-inch hatchet in his hand came up toward the captain's throat, in an attempt to decapitate him.

In a dexterous move for his forty-nine years, Lees dropped down, and he could hear the blade pass over his head. He struck with his own knife, slicing behind the attacker's legs, cutting into his

Achilles tendons in two quick strokes. The gang member fell to his knees, screaming what Lees assumed to be curses, and grabbed at his ankles, which were now bleeding profusely.

Pointing his gun at the other attacker, Lees told George, "Tell him to let Dutch go and to stand up."

Kwong spoke in Cantonese, and the man let go of Dutch and rose slowly, his eyes riveted on Lees' revolver.

"Ask him what they were trying to do," Lees said.

Again, George spoke to the uninjured Tong member, who answered, his head nodding, and his smile beaming back at them.

"He says they saw two white men taking a Chinese somewhere. That's it. They wanted to rescue me," said George.

"Tell them you're already rescued and to get the hell out of here," Lees said, flashing his badge at them from under his cape.

After George spoke to them, the two men in black hobbled off, the uninjured one assisting his partner down the alley.

"You see why we can't have any of those Tongs around the mansion? They're all crazy as hell," Dutch said.

"Again, before we were so rudely interrupted, take George to Nob Hill. I'll meet you there in about an hour, after I report his escape." Lees began to walk down the alley back toward the district station house on Kearny.

***

Inside the mansion, Clara was at the table, drafting the advertisement she was going to include in the daily San Francisco newspapers. Ah Toy was painting beside her, swathing her brush with blue on the canvas depicting a steamship coming into San Francisco Bay. The moon was full outside and was shining into Ah Toy's abode. Each woman, at different moments, looked up to gaze at the moon in reflection.

"Carrie, do you love him?" Ah Toy asked, adding some black to the steamship's deck.

"We don't know each other. Besides, we're both working now. There has been very little time to become really close. He does fascinate me, I must admit. A man of his stature should have been married by now. Do you think it's just because of his dangerous line of work?" Clara stopped, wrote down enough to finish her paragraph, and looked up at the moon.

"You are in just as much danger. I think it may be that very danger that has drawn you both together. Perhaps it will pass when this case is over."

"Listen to what I have written. You'll be teaching it, so you should be aware of how I am selling your skills." Clara smiled. "In 1884, women have few ways to earn a living. Come to our personalized appointment to see if you have the aptitude and the fortitude to benefit from our instruction. Learn from a woman who has become independently wealthy through her own initiative. She can teach you how to manipulate the patriarchal system that rules society. It's the only way women can succeed in today's oppressive business atmosphere." Clara held the paper up and blew on the wet ink. "Well, what do you think?"

Ah Toy set her paintbrush down, minced over to the table and sat down next to Clara. "I like it. However, don't you believe it would be prudent to inform these people that I'm Chinese?"

"Perhaps. After we've trapped the killer. You see, I believe this monster has moved out of the Chinatown hunting grounds. Since we're located in the Hopkins Mansion, the killer might even believe he or she can murder somebody white and wealthy. This would be an important status improvement." Clara took her friend's hands. "Because I am the only one who knows who this murderer is, I will have to be present during all of the interviews."

"All right. I understand that. You mentioned—or somebody mentioned—that the killer may be wearing a disguise. How will you be able to identify this person? Also, don't you think he or she will have to kill us both?" Ah Toy raised her eyebrows and squeezed Clara's hands.

"Of course. That would be mandatory, under the circumstances. But don't worry, Ah Toy, I have a few ways to physically recognize our culprit. This person has a large mole on his right cheek, and a cleft in the chin. I've already informed Captain Lees and his men."

Ah Toy stood up. "We had better leave now. Our men should be returning with Bai Kwong soon. I really enjoyed the excuse you gave to Mrs. Hopkins and the servants as to what will be happening when they bring another Chinese into the mansion."

"I think it stands to reason, don't you? You're an artist, and your subject matter features everything Asian. We have employed a few models for your use. You'll be creating your masterpiece.

Chinese Lawbreaker. George shall be the young miscreant, and Captain Lees and Detective Vanderheiden will pose as the arresting officers. I believe even Shakespeare would approve of this extra bit of ironic art within our larger play." Clara stood up and walked with her friend to the door.

"This will be art imitating life." Ah Toy smiled.

***

The evening fog was rolling in as Dutch escorted George Kwong onto Sacramento Street leading up from Chinatown to Nob Hill. They then crossed over to California Street and arrived at the Hopkins Mansion. It was a steep incline, and they were both winded when the guard at the mansion finally let them through.

The man servant, Hannigan, met them at the front door. Taking a cue from Ah Toy, he shouted up the stairs, "Miss Ah Toy! Your models are here! Shall I escort them up to the Observatory?"

Ah Toy and Clara were standing on the second floor. Ah Toy looked through the spiral staircase leading down to the main entrance and saw Hannigan standing with George Kwong and Detective Vanderheiden. She cupped her mouth and shouted down, "We'll meet you there." Both of their voices echoed back-and-forth through the dark and eerie mansion like wailing ghosts.

***

Back at the Jenny Lind City Hall station, Captain Lees had informed Sheriff Connolly of the escape of his prisoner. Although he fumed, and immediately wired the mayor, Washington Bartlett, Connolly seemed to have accepted the logic behind Kwong's escape. He even understood the ruse about not wanting to fire at the fleeing prisoner because of the many tourists in the streets, although he had his own perspective. "You should have shot anyway, Lees," Connolly barked. "What's a few dead suffragettes? They make more trouble than they're worth."

After the mayor's office was in communication with Connolly, all hell broke loose. The sheriff began running around the bullpen, shouting orders, and slamming his fist on the desks of the officers.

As he burst open the door to the Chinatown Squad Office, he discovered his protégé, Jesse Brown Cook, on his knees with a young uniformed officer. They were praying. "Get up, Cook! That chink Kwong is on the loose! He broke away from Lees and

Vanderheiden on the way to see Doc Reed. Mayor Bartlett wants a dragnet on the whole city. He probably took off for chinkville, so you take your men and comb every building in that infested pig sty. Start with Andrew Kwong's place on Sacramento."

"Don't worry, Sheriff," Cook said, as he strapped his holster around his waist and pulled on his tiger hat. "We'll root out that godless murderer. I know every secret hiding place in Chinatown."

"I'm going to find my partner, Sheriff. If he's recaptured Kwong, or knows where he's headed, I'll be back to inform you." Lees watched Cook as he herded his men near the door. He thought they looked like clowns in P. T. Barnum's Greatest Show on Earth. They were certainly clumsy and ineffective, as they pushed and shoved each other going out into the street. Lees followed them out, chuckling to himself.

***

Inside the Observatory room, Clara and Ah Toy were busy discussing how they were going to carry out their ruse. George Kwong, of course, needed new clothes, although his jail garb was explained by the role he was going to be playing as a model for the *Chinese Lawbreaker* painting. Hannigan had seen much stranger goings on working for the eccentric Mrs. Hopkins, including live peacocks strutting throughout the halls, and a troupe of Chinese acrobats. He was happy to go get the new clothing for George.

"Thank you, Hannigan," Ah Toy said.

When the butler left, Ah Toy turned to Clara. "You have to realize all that you have done, Carrie. You are saving your client's life, but you are also showing other women what can be done if you believe in justice and human rights. So much of the world is dominated by power and influence and not by principles," Ah Toy said, as she set up her easel and color palette under the skylight.

"I understand, Ah Toy, but my mind works the same way Captain Lees thinks. We concentrate on the task at hand and not on the glory to come." Clara turned to Vanderheiden. "Detective Vanderheiden. What happened to you? Your suit is stained with dirt, and you have scratches all over your face."

Dutch looked at Clara as if he were the boy who was caught pilfering the cookie jar. His face reddened, and he tried to sweep the stains off with his hands. "We were in a little scrape in a Chinatown alley. The captain saved my life. We was attacked by a couple of

Tong boys who thought we were kidnapping George here. I guess I wasn't looking and got tackled."

"Captain Lees disarmed that hatchet-wielding thug by using his Bowie knife. He dropped down low, like an Indian, just as the intruder rushed him, and he sliced the Tong's Achilles tendons. His assailant went down like a puppet that just had his strings cut. Wham!" George Kwong spoke with the colorful phrases of his journalist's skill.

"Did I hear my name being used in vain?" Captain Isaiah Lees stood in the doorway, scowling.

In spite of herself, Clara rushed over to Lees and gave him a demonstrative hug. "Thank goodness, you're safe!"

Lees gently pushed Clara away. "What did you ladies concoct about our being here? I was thinking about that on the way over."

"Clara thought of an excellent ruse. I shall be painting your portraits in the Observatory. You and Detective Vanderheiden will be arresting young Bai Kwong, who will be dressed in his jailhouse uniform." Ah Toy explained. "She even thought of a title for my masterpiece."

"*The One that Got Away*?" Lees laughed.

"How dare you insult my creativity!" Clara chuckled. "I entitled it *Chinese Lawbreaker*. It will show the pathos of such a young man being taken in, not having a chance in the world against the powers that be."

"Indeed. You should have seen this powerful one with his face down in the alley mud," Lees said. "As for myself, after all of this is over, I may be the one being arrested in your painting. I'm up to my eyeballs in this illegal subterfuge right now."

"The subterfuge must continue, I'm afraid," Clara said, moving over to the table and picking up her advertisement. "I now have the content that will lure our killer from hiding and into our haunted mansion. The ghost of all these murdered women shall assist me in the capture of such a predator!"

"You will not be alone in this. But it won't be ghosts. You're going to have an armed guard in hiding during every one of your so-called private interviews. We don't even know if this killer will be induced to come into the middle of your spider web. What if he or she attempts the daring deed while you are out and about, or even somewhere else in this house?"

"The captain's right. A smart killer would expect a trap. We need to plan for all the possibilities," Dutch pointed out.

"What? Do you propose we have a police officer in every room of the house and following me everywhere I go? What if this murderer just wants to kill any woman? Ah Toy, me, or even old Mrs. Hopkins might be in danger. Can you protect all of us at the same time?" Clara was using her attorney mind on this conundrum.

"You seem to forget. I was the captain of all detectives in San Francisco. I also have connections with other districts, in other cities. I can have twenty men—all professionals—who can blend in with any setting or crowd. I shall spare no expense when this trap gets triggered. Kwong's life, and our future careers and lives will depend on how well you are protected. In fact, just as you have chosen to protect the identify of this would-be murderer, I am stating that my private detectives shall be unknown to you as well. They will be there, but you won't know it." Lees placed his hands on his cape and puffed out his broad chest. "Agreed?"

Before Clara could answer, a shout came from downstairs. It was Hannigan.

"Miss Ah Toy! You must come down here. There are hundreds of people assembled by the guard's gate outside."

When everybody, with the exception of George Kwong, assembled out in front of the mansion, the sight they took in was at once frightening and comical. There were indeed hundreds of people out beside the guard house on California Street. The guard, in his plumed regalia, was attempting to ward off belligerent members of what was left of the San Francisco Vigilance Committee. The men were pushing and shoving against the gate, causing it to balloon inward like a fishnet on the wharf, bursting with the day's catch.

The spokesman for the group, a tall, elderly gentleman with a walrus mustache and a Confederate uniform from his Civil War days, was shouting at poor Mrs. Hopkins, who had placed herself in harm's way in front of this person's flailing arms.

"You chink-lover! We know you have that killer inside. Bring him out here, or we'll go in and get him!" the old man shouted at the old woman.

The guard, in his protective stance, stood between the two, his rifle pointed at the Confederate impersonator. Having served in the Union, Mrs. Hopkins' old guard was none too patient with such a scallywag. "Step back, you blackguard, or I'll shoot you between your rebel eyes!"

Stepping back, the old man raised his voice above the crowd's yells. "See? She's got a union-buster guarding the plantation. We need to get that murderer ourselves!"

Clara, who noticed there were also many of her fellow suffragettes in the crowd of demonstrators, sprinted out to the guard shack, with Lees and Dutch following close behind. She could hear poor Mrs. Hopkins speaking to them in her nonsensical manner.

"There are no guided tours to my home without prior arrangements. All of you! Leave at once, or I shall have the mayor call out the National Guard!'

Clara took her position beside the old woman. "Listen to me. Everyone, Miss Ah Toy, the artist, is the only Chinese person living here." She pointed to her friend, who was still standing on the front porch of the mansion. "We will be conducting a course to teach women how to become independent and wealthy in these trying times. Why would we risk our reputation by harboring an escaped felon? I was just going to place my advertisement in the daily news. See? Here it is!" Clara held up the handwritten paper.

Lees moved forward to stand beside Clara. He opened his cape to show his sheathed Bowie, and the Colt .45 in his holster. "And my men and I will be here to guarantee that these courses are respectfully and peacefully attended."

Just as Clara expected, the hundreds of women in the crowd began to scream and applaud the news. They had obviously followed the men up California Street when they heard about the rumor of the escaped criminal. "Clara Foltz! Hail, Portia of the Pacific! We want independence for women now!"

"Follow me, independent women!" Clara yelled, stepping past the frustrated Vigilantes. "I'm going now to place my ad, and I want you with me to protect me on my journey!"

The big crowd opened up, like the Red Sea for a female Moses, and Clara began to strut down California Street toward the office of the *San Francisco Examiner*. The women, in their colorful dresses and twirling parasols, swung in behind her, as if they were modern Israelites following their leader to the promised land.

Behind them, the small crowd of men continued to growl

their dissatisfaction at Lees and the guard, but they soon began to disperse, like whipped canines, and began to head back down the street, their invisible tails between their legs, into the waiting fog below.

***

Mayor Washington Bartlett was pacing his office like a caged tiger. The dragnet on his city had commenced, and he was ready to make a speech to the people at the city hall, on the Market Street side. Of course, it was the Van Ness side that concerned him most, but because most of the votes came from the masses, he wanted to assuage them about the danger of their community, while putting the most protection in the Nob Hill and Rincon Hill areas where the rich lived.

The window of his office opened up to a large enclosed platform overlooking Market and the Sand Lots area. There were already thousands gathered to hear the news of what was happening to make the city safe again. Part of them were disappointed that there would be no hanging up on Russian Hill, others were concerned for the safety of their families, and a minority, including former members of the Vigilante Committee, wanted to take matters into their own hands if this mayor proved to be as ineffective as he seemed to be.

Bartlett was ready. He picked up the large megaphone from his desk and held it in his arms as one would hold a baby. It had his last name stenciled on its side in Old English lettering. When he stepped out onto the balcony of his office, the crowd noise was a mixture of cheers and boos. Bartlett brought the voice enhancer up to his full-bearded face and puffy lips, and he began:

"Greetings, fellow citizens of San Francisco. I want you to feel safe this evening because I have ordered a complete search of Chinatown, including the homes of the Six Companies' leaders. I am promising to you, with the authority of my office, we shall have this killer back into custody. He will pay for his conviction of murder in the first degree by hanging by the neck until death up on Russian Hill!"

Cheers were thunderous, but some voices shouted out separate jeering statements, such as "You better get that chink, you crook!" Or, "The Chinese are not the problem, you are!"

"However, I need your assistance to capture this man. If you see or hear anything suspicious, or you see this man," Bartlett held up a large poster with a photo of George Kwong on it, "report it to City Hall or to a local policeman or sheriff's officer. If we work together, we will capture this convicted murderer and keep our city safe, as it should be. Thank you, ladies and gentlemen, and I bid you a good evening!"

Mayor Bartlett turned away from the crowds and walked back into his office. Sheriff Pat Connolly was there to greet him. "Well, what is it? Did you find him?"

"Old Reb Bill and his men tried to scare them with threats. Guess who was staying there with the chink, Ah Toy." Connolly brushed a few bits of cigar tobacco off his Chinatown Squad jacket.

"Clara Foltz?" Bartlett guessed.

"Yes, the chink-lover was there. So were Captain Lees and his Dutch sidekick."

"Oh, really? I want somebody to infiltrate that house and find out what they're up to. I don't care what you do. Tell them there's an epidemic of the plague. Just get inside that mansion and see if they're hiding Kwong!"

"Yes sir!" Connolly saluted and left the room.

"I know he's in there," Bartlett whispered to himself after Connolly left. "If I get him, I can begin to pack my bags for the governor's mansion."

CHAPTER NINE: THE INTERVIEWS

One Nob Hill, Hopkins Mansion, San Francisco, March 2, 1884

Both Clara and Captain Lees perfected their individual jobs before the first interviews were to be conducted that afternoon in the mansion. Clara, realizing she may not have written enough in the advertisement to infuriate the real murderer sufficiently, decided to write an article to emphasize the content of the course to be taught to women. She wrote that the course would be an "empowerment for women, in that it will show females how to establish legitimate businesses based on using women's feminine attraction to make money off men, mostly bachelors. It will not be prostitution (no physical contact), but it will include allure, poetry, dancing and other forms of female sensuality and grace." Clara believed her new article's content, published the day before in the morning papers, would enrage the killer most profoundly because this course will be making "honest women out of former prostitutes in Chinatown and elsewhere." As a result, Ah Toy would become the target for murder rather than some random woman who might show up for an interview.

For his part, Isaiah decided he would import his guardian detective force by giving them staff employment. They would take jobs such as butler, chauffeur, cook, and even maid. The "maid" idea came from Dutch, who believed the killer might let down his guard if he thought it was a woman in his presence. Detective Tom Whitefeather, who looked rather effeminate because he was a beardless young man from the local Muwekma Ohlone Tribe, volunteered for the maid role. Although Tom received some number of good-natured cat-calls and insults, it was soon clear that Tom was so certain of his masculinity that wearing a maid's dress was not threatening to him. The Colt .45 tucked into his girdle would be threatening to any would-be attacker.

There were four women who made reservations to be interviewed that afternoon. Clara was on pins and needles about their possible identities. She had once again gone over the clues she had collected to lead her to the killer. She also knew the two physical traits that she could use to identify this person. Hopefully, this information would be enough to save Ah Toy's life and possibly even her own.

The day before, when she was taking her new article to the newspapers to be published, she also sent a message to her family in San Jose at the telegraph office on Market Street. She did not want to unduly frighten them about what she was about to do, but she did want them to know she was thinking of them at this time of personal crisis. She imagined it was like her husband, Jeremiah Foltz, the Civil War veteran, who told her about how painful it was to go off to battle.

"Carrie, I am not the same man I was because of what I saw. I cannot trust society ever again."

If Jeremiah had become so mentally affected by his war experience, then what was she going to be like after confronting this demonic woman-killer? Would she have to pull the trigger? If she did, and this murderer were dead, then would the evidence she had be enough to convince the mayor and the police? Writing down the message to her family was a brief respite from such thoughts:

> *How are my beloved ones? Are they growing like beanstalks? I so long to have you all in my arms once more! I am working hard to make it so. As soon as I have saved enough, you shall be escorted to me by an entire police force. I am doing important things, as you may have read, Father, and now I will be tested. Do not fear. I will make the most of my trials, I will soon call you to my side for the rest of our lives together! Yours lovingly, daughter and mother.*

Now that Clara was mentally prepared for this ordeal, she went about setting up Ah Toy's room for the first interview. Ah Toy would be seated at the table facing the door. The person being interviewed would enter through the facing door and would sit in the padded green antique chair, which had no armrests. This was to give Clara and the guard easy access to shoot the killer if he or she should pull a gun while seated. Detective Vanderheiden discovered that the late Mr. Hopkins used an ingenious two-way mirror in his study to observe prospective business partners before meeting with them. When the lamp light was shined on the rear side of the mirror, where Clara was, it became transparent, and she could secretly view the suspect. She knew she must be able to identify one or both of the physical traits of the suspect before preparing for the arrest.

The staff and integrated detective force were instructed by Captain Lees to never discuss George Kwong or even the fact that Ah Toy was going to paint a portrait of him in the Observatory steeple. The escapee's presence in the Hopkins mansion must remain a guarded secret until the real killer was captured or terminated. And, most importantly, no guard was to confront or attack a person visiting the house unless Clara gave the word. They all knew about the physical traits of the suspected killer. Lees and Vanderheiden would appear at the mansion during the scheduled interviews in the afternoon.

The four women to be interviewed were Miss Marjorie Potter, Mrs. Elizabeth Baxter-Shaw, Miss Changying Chen, and Mrs. Miriam Levine. Two were single women and former prostitutes who wanted to begin new lives. The others had been married, but Baxter-Shaw was a widow, and Levine was divorced.

Miss Potter arrived promptly at one in the afternoon, and Hannigan brought her upstairs to Ah Toy's office and living quarters. Clara was in the adjoining bedroom, peering through her mirror at the entering applicant. The distance between the suspect and Clara's eye was ten feet. She could see the woman's face, and Clara knew at once this person was not the killer. Even disguised, Clara knew she wasn't the one. Miss Potter was too diminutive. She was an attractive young lady of about twenty-five, with auburn hair rolled into a bun, an hourglass figure, and a professional dress that included a fashionably dark-blue, narrow skirt with a medium bustle. Clara listened to the interesting dialogue between her friend and the young applicant.

"Miss Potter, I want you to forget about your past and especially how you came to your profession. What I need to know is why you want to learn how to work as an independent woman." Ah Toy leaned forward, watching the way the woman conducted herself as she spoke. From her many years supervising young women, Ah Toy had three key questions that she answered by watching and listening: 1. Did she look you straight in the eyes? 2.

Was her grammar and elocution proper? 3. Did she have a sense of humor? If a candidate failed in two of the three questions, then she was rejected, even as a prostitute working for Ah Toy in Chinatown.

Miss Potter gazed steadily at Ah Toy as she spoke, her eyebrows arching somewhat at emotional moments, her tone calmly confident.

"I want to learn to become independent because our society respects those who can make life better by contributing to values we hold dear. As you stated in your advertisement, a woman who knows how to benefit from the finer attributes of life like literature, dance and physical magnetism, can profit without losing her chastity. I have known this to be true, even when I dreamed it during what I now call my fallen days. I watched these women of grace and allure as they paraded in the hotels, and I tried to be like them in both appearance and voice. Sadly, I did not know there were women like you who could save me from the burden of masculine lust and fear that was used to keep us submissive and dependent on our keepers. As I rode the cable car from downtown, I kept feeling inside as if I were climbing up to a woman's Mt. Olympus, where I could finally learn the skills we need to survive the rape of Zeus. Zeus overcame most of his female victims by trickery: he raped Leda in the form of a swan, Danaë in the guise of a golden rain, and Alkmene in the persona of her legitimate husband, and he did not even hesitate to take on so coarse a disguise as that of a randy satyr for the purpose of violating Antiope."

Ah Toy laughed. "My goodness! Where did you learn about Greek Mythology?"

Miss Potter bowed her head in embarrassment, but then she looked up again, and smiled, her blue eyes flashing. "I often acquired my best clients at the library. I had the time, so I read about the foundations of our democracy. The Greek Pantheon was dominated by gods who would fulfill their needs through trickery. I asked myself, if they could do it, then why couldn't we women? Until I read that ad in the newspaper yesterday, I thought it was impossible."

As Clara watched her friend interview the young candidate, she had a deeper awareness of why she loved the United States and its Constitutional experiment. In theory, every person, even a woman such as Marjorie Potter, should have the opportunity to rise above her bad luck and birth right to build a new life. Just as Clara had overcome the infamy of desertion and divorce, so, too, could Marjorie overcome the depression and dangers of harlotry. In America, we must help one another, and we must fight the tyrants who would keep us down for their own manipulative purposes. To do this, our Constitution must be flexible and adapt to new conditions and it must protect our downtrodden and powerless. Laws such as the Chinese Exclusion Act were not in keeping with our Constitutional tenets of "equality and justice for all."

Mrs. Elizabeth Baxter-Shaw also arrived on time at two, but it seemed she was attempting to complain to Ah Toy rather than the established protocol. A recent widow, the applicant wore a scarlet and black satin dress, and a tall, turban-like matching hat that perched on top of her graying black swirl of hair like a buoy in the San Francisco Bay. She also held in her arms, cradled like a baby, a tiny black chihuahua. A tall Negro chauffeur was carrying her black parasol, and he also took the dog from her, as the missus sat down in the chair while keeping up a constant stream of diatribe.

" … and then the cable car conductor began to lecture me about bringing a receptacle for my dog's feces. I pointed to Abraham, my driver, and I told the little man that he was my six feet two inches of receptacle. We drove out to the California Street station in a surrey, only to be insulted by a pipsqueak in a uniform. Our conductors on Rincon Hill are much more decorous to their betters. It must be the steep incline, don't you think? Blood must rush too quickly into their brains. Do you believe in the hidden influence of magnetism?"

Clara briefly surveyed the face of this chatterbox, saw that she was not the killer, and tried to keep from giggling out loud at the woman's audacity. She had known many such women--usually wives of judges or important men in the state legislature--and they often became eccentric after their spouse's passing. However, Mrs. Baxter-Shaw was one of the most humorously flamboyant she had ever met.

"Thank you for coming, Mrs. Baxter-Shaw. I want you to tell me why you want to learn to become an independent woman." Ah Toy covered her mouth with her hand, leaned back, and exhaled, poised in uncomfortable anticipation.

"Now that Reggie's gone, I wanted to find some unique way

to occupy my time. I read your strange advertisement, but since I have already established myself as a femme fatale, by going through four husbands, I thought I might be able to help you train younger women in the fine art of seduction. Why, when I entered the mansion, a man had the nerve to wink at me!"

Clara was watching the Negro. When his employer said "seduction," a faint grin widened the corners of his mouth, and he coughed into his hand. Clara also knew that the winking man was Dutch Vanderheiden.

"I am also an art collector. I know you're an artist, and certainly Mrs. Hopkins knows fine art, so perhaps we can become women who can influence men with our tastes. My second husband, the judge, used to send me all over the world to collect art for him."

Yes, as he probably wanted to get rid of you, Ah Toy thought to herself. She leaned forward, waiting for the opportune moment to interrupt the widow.

" ... I remember, it was a cold day on the hill, and I was gazing out my luxurious bay window at the setting sun. The disappearing sun so reminds one of the sad time when your husband is off on another business ..."

"Thank you, Mrs. Baxter-Shaw. We will get back to you following our assessment." Ah Toy took a deep breath and shouted, "Hannigan!"

Clara was most suspect of the third candidate, as she was late to the interview. She asked Ah Toy to conduct the interview in English, if at all possible, and she agreed. Changying Chen arrived at half-past three. She had, like Ah Toy, bound feet, so her gait was impeded. She was breathless as she minced into the room and sat down in front of her interviewer. The *cheongsam* she wore was blue silk, plain and business-like, and, as Clara surveyed her facial features, she was relieved to see none of the telltale signs of the murderer. The young woman's smiling face was full and healthy, and her clear brown eyes were fixed on those of Ah Toy, waiting, with her small hands folded in her lap, for her interviewer to speak.

Ah Toy first spoke to the young woman in Cantonese. Getting an immediate response in perfectly enunciated English, Ah Toy continued in English.

"I do not want to hear about your past or your negative experiences in the profession from which you wish to escape. Please answer this one question. Why do you want to learn how to become an independent woman?"

Bowing her head of short raven hair, she spoke in a voice that was clearly loud for an Asian woman. "Please, may I be bold, like the crane fishing at low tide on the Yangtze? I am so sorry for being tardy. I was forced to climb California Street because Chinese are not allowed to ride the cable cars. To the kept women in Chinatown, the story of Madame Ah Toy is second only to the Goddess Mazu. Our dreams are filled with your exploits, perhaps somewhat exaggerated over the years, but their import remains the same. If we can remain sane and fix our purpose to your lodestar, we may survive another day. That is what I have done. After six hundred and fifteen of these days of survival, I awoke to read in *The Oriental* that my personal morning star was in San Francisco to share her wisdom. It is my great fortune to be here. So many of my sisters cannot escape the Tong dragon's fire, but perhaps I can be their representative. If I am chosen, I will share my skills to those who also wish to become independent. Madame Ah Toy, I am your obedient servant!"

As Clara watched and listened, there was only one moment when she was struck by what she saw. When the initiate bowed, fixed in the back of her hair was a silver comb in the shape of a seahorse. The attorney knew she must find out where Changying Chen obtained that comb, but she dare not expose herself during this interview. She decided to wait until Ah Toy was finished. When the young woman left the room, it would take her some time to leave the premises because of her bound feet. Clara would therefore be able to instruct her partner about what she needed to know, and Ah Toy could call her back, and Clara could slip back behind the mirror.

After several more minutes of conversation, Ah toy stood up. "I believe you will fit nicely in my class. I will send you the curriculum next week. I'll have Hannigan escort you to the door."

The butler came at once when Ah Toy shouted, and Clara came out of hiding as soon as the door was closed. "Ah Toy, you must call her back and ask where she obtained the silver comb in her hair. Each of the murder victims had this seahorse comb fixed in her hair. She might be the next victim, but I need to know where she got it. I will hide behind the mirror until you find out."

Now it was "Changying" that Ah Toy shouted down the

shadowy stairs of the mansion. After a few moments, Ah Toy could hear the young woman's lumbering steps climbing toward her. After she was back inside, the older woman asked the young prostitute where she was able to procure such an interesting hair clasp. Ah Toy explained that she collected them from all over the world.

"My handler in the San Ho Hui gave it to me as a gift when I left him to become independent. He was one of the rare benevolent Tong members, and I was very fortunate to have had him as my protector. He even told me once that I had the special intelligence to become an independent woman like the great Ah Toy. I consider the comb a talisman of good fortune."

When Clara heard Changying's response, she was immediately relieved. There would be no need to take the drastic action she thought might be necessary.

There was one remaining woman to be interviewed that day. None so far had been the suspect. Clara realized that perhaps her killer might be too fearful to take the bait. Before the last interviewee was to arrive at four p.m., the two women attended to their personal hygiene.

Captain Lees brought Clara and Ah Toy some food. A tray of fruit and bread. He asked them how the interviews had gone.

"Two of the three women have been selected. All is not lost. I thought I might have our next victim, but it turned out to be a false alarm." Clara took a bite of the red apple. "Have you or your men seen anything suspicious around the mansion?" She asked, in-between chews.

"Nothing untoward. Those Vigilante old-timers haven't reappeared. Good riddance. George Kwong is still safe and secure in his ivory tower." Lees jerked a thumb at the mirror. "How has that been functioning for you?"

"I must say, it's an excellent way to spy. I can see persons in the room very clearly, and the sounds are quite acute. I should think you might consider adopting it for your detective needs, Isaiah," Clara said, tossing the apple core into a trash receptacle beside the desk.

"You have one more person to interview today. When you both finish, please come up to the Observatory. I want to discuss the strange goings-on at Connolly's office. My spies have been keeping me informed."

"Very well, Isaiah. We shall meet you there at around half past four." Clara stretched up on her tiptoes and gave the former Captain of Detectives a kiss on the cheek.

Mrs. Miriam Levine wasted no time when she arrived. She burst through the door to Ah Toy's room, pushed up the bustle on her green satin dress, and plopped down in the chair in front of the desk. Her dark eyes immediately fixed upon Ah Toy's, and Clara believed she also looked up and stared directly at her behind the mirror. The woman was in her forties, and her height and facial features immediately eliminated her from the murder suspect list.

"Thank you for coming, Mrs. Levine. I don't want your history. I only need you to tell me why you want to learn how to become an independent woman." Ah Toy leaned forward in rapt attention.

"No, I am afraid you will both listen to me. I am from the Office of Attorney General of these United States. Our men will soon be entering these premises to recapture the fugitive from justice, Mr. George Bai Kwong. You may now come out from behind that mirror, attorney Foltz. We need you to call off your Captain Lees and his undercover detectives or face arrest for aiding and abetting a fugitive." Mrs. Levine opened her handbag and extracted a badge affixed to a leather holder. She set it down on the desk.

Clara decided she must cooperate, so she opened the door of the adjoining bedroom, and stepped out into Ah Toy's living room. Clara picked up the badge and looked at it. It had the name of Benjamin H. Brewster, the Attorney General under President Chester A. Arthur. She tossed it back onto the desk, thinking about how she would proceed. If her client were taken back into custody, then her trap would have to be put on hold, and the murderer would be free to kill again. Clara couldn't hope that the hangman would be postponed because of such a horror, and George Kwong would die.

"Mrs. Levine, if that is your name, I am certain you must be aware that I am the official counsel for the Six Companies and for the Defendant, George Kwong."

"Of course. My name is Miriam Levine. In point of fact, it is your reputation as a brilliant orator for women's rights that caused Mr. Brewster to forgo the warrants for the arrests of both you and your associates in crime. His wife, you see, is a rather vehement supporter of our cause. As a woman, I was sent to explain the Federal Government's purpose in this arrest of your client."

"He is Chinese. You know that's the real reason," Ah Toy said.

"Miss Ah Toy. I have read about you and your story of success. The fact that Mr. Kwong is Chinese has nothing to do with our being here. We are here to protect him from the likes of Mayor Washington Bartlett, about whom we have done undercover detective work of our own. When we discovered that Mrs. Foltz's story about Bartlett keeping the murders of seven Chinatown prostitutes a secret from authorities was true, we immediately began our plan. We also have revisited the homicide trial in which your client was accused of murdering Miss Mary McCarthy. The fact that you were not allowed to appeal because of your client's status as a non-American citizen should not have restricted his access to a fair trial. As a result, we are taking him into our custody to protect him from the local authorities, about whom we suspect of being biased and politically motivated."

Clara sat down in another chair next to Miriam Levine. She grasped the woman's hands into her own and gazed into her dark brown eyes. "Does this mean we can continue with our interviews? Do you believe my client is innocent of these murders?"

Mrs. Levine smiled. "Of course, counselor. You provided an excellent defense for your client in court. We also believe the killer is still out there, and we shall support your effort to trap him or her, but we cannot allow Mr. Kwong to stay here. It is unsafe."

"I understand. But where will you keep him? If you can't trust the local police, then you must have some other place in mind." Clara was toying with the idea of telling this woman about who she believed the killer was, but she didn't really trust her to do the right thing at this point.

"We can't really divulge that information, counselor. You can understand that also. You kidnapped Kwong once, so we can't completely trust you won't do it again. After all, the killer has yet to be apprehended, and the local authorities are not to be trusted, so there you are. It's quite a quandary, don't you think?" Levine brushed a wisp of black hair from her forehead.

"All right, I'll inform Captain Lees, and we'll go get George Kwong. Will you be allowing the undercover detectives to guard us in the mansion? If this killer does appear, we will need the protection."

"You shall have your protection. We just want to keep your client away from harm until this murderer is found." Agent Levine stood up. She reached over and shook hands with Clara, and she then did the same with Ah Toy.

Ah Toy and Clara took Mrs. Levine up to the Observatory to see George Kwong. When they opened the door to the enclosed, circular room, it was empty. Captain Lees must have kidnapped the young man once more, and Clara was dumbfounded.

"I can't believe it! He was here this morning. Captain Lees told us to meet him here after we finished interviewing for the day." Clara ran around the room, looking in the closets, turning back the bedspread, and peering into the small bathroom.

"I'm certain you realize, counselor, if your friend, Captain Lees, knew we were coming, then he is now a kidnapper and subject to federal prosecution." Mrs. Levine took out a pad of paper and picked a pen out of her handbag. She wrote down something quickly. "I must get a wire off to Washington. The Attorney General must be notified. I'm afraid we will be searching for Captain Lees and your client. When we find them, there will be due process of law."

"Does this mean we cannot continue our hunt for the killer?" Clara held her breath, clasped her hands to her breast, and stared hard into Mrs. Levine's eyes.

"I must get permission from Washington. I will tell you tomorrow. Until then, you must not permit any more strangers to visit Hopkins Mansion." Mrs. Levine walked toward the door. "I am sorry this had to happen. I respect what both of you are doing, and I wish you the best of luck."

***

Tin How Temple, Waverly Place, Chinatown, San Francisco, March 2, 1884.

There was one place that the Chinatown Squad had never discovered. This room was inside the Tin How Temple, beneath the giant statue of Mazu. It was behind a secret trap door in the floor, which opened after the statue was moved to the side. This was where Captain Lees and Detective Vanderheiden had taken George

Kwong. When Lees heard about the news that Connolly was spreading about the presence of federal officers in the city, he knew that George Kwong had to be moved again.

Minister Guan Shi Yin had given Lees permission to hide Kwong there, as the young man had contributed greatly in keeping the temple in business. George brought many prostitutes there to pray and to ask the goddess for forgiveness, in an effort to get them back on the straight and narrow.

Inside the room were all the survival accommodations needed to live out a Tong war, or a natural disaster, like an earthquake, or oppression by the city's authorities. Food enough for months was stored inside the lockers in the back of the room, and there was a bed, proper ventilation from a metal shaft that led out to the street, and enough kerosene and lamps to keep the place lit for months. The room had been used by a variety of people, who were being hunted by the police, and Lees and Vanderheiden were the only former policemen ever to be allowed access.

Lees didn't even have to speak Cantonese to Guan Shi Yin, as it was Andrew Kwong, the leader of the Six Companies, who had made all the arrangements for his son to use the secret hideout. As soon as the captain heard about the feds, he simply informed Andrew, and the father of the accused immediately told Lees about the secret room. While Clara and Ah Toy were talking to Agent Levine, Lees and Vanderheiden had taken George Kwong out of the Observatory, through the night streets, and into the Tin How Temple.

"You'll be safe here," Lees told George, as the young man sat on the bed, still wearing his blue jail clothing. "The minister will watch out for you, and we'll be by tomorrow night. I want to tell Clara and Ah Toy about where you are, so they won't be concerned, but I can't chance it until I'm certain there are no feds or local police around the mansion." Captain Lees was standing beside the bed, looking down at his young charge.

"Whatever you think is prudent, Captain. I want to thank you for saving my life once again," George said, his dark eyes glistening under the lamplight.

"Do you think the feds will shut down Clara's trap, boss?" Dutch asked. He was at one of the lockers, rummaging through the foodstuffs, which were mostly Chinese goods.

"I don't really know, partner. However, knowing Clara's skills as a negotiator, I would doubt it. Something tells me the feds came here because of the local corruption and not because of Clara's doings. We really won that trial. You do realize that, correct?" Lees moved over into the light to see the face of Vanderheiden better.

"Win? You do realize that I am a hard-headed Dutchman. I go by what happens and not by what we would like to happen. All I know is that this here kid would be swingin' from a rope if we didn't kidnap him." Venderheiden turned from the locker to face his boss. "Twice," he added, smiling.

"Yes, well, after this second kidnapping, under the noses of the federal authorities, we may be keeping George company on Russian Hill." Lees returned the grin.

"Do you mind not talking about hanging?" George squirmed on the bed and circled his fingers around his neck. "I had almost gotten used to the confinement in the mansion, and now I am back where I began. I feel like a pawn on the hangman's chessboard."

"Good comparison, lad! I'm happy to see you've kept your journalistic repose." Lees chuckled.

"Listen! You all hear that?" Venderheiden pointed up to the trap door above their heads. The muffled sounds of repeated gunshots vibrated the ceiling floorboards, and dust fell on their heads from above.

"What in the hell is happening up there?" Lees sat down on the bed with George Kwong, and all three men stared up at the ceiling, as the continuing cacophony of gunfire and trampling footsteps made the entire temple rumble like a locomotive was passing through.

After about twenty minutes, the noise finally subsided. Lees and Vanderheiden stood up, and brushed off their clothes, which had become quite dusty from all the commotion.

"You think we should go up there now?" Dutch moved toward the portable wooden stairs that served as the method of getting out of the underground room.

"No. Wait. If it's all clear, then the minister will be opening up that trap door," Lees also shuffled over to stand under the exit with his partner.

"Do you think the authorities know we're even in Chinatown?" George Kwong's eyes were large under the lamplight beside his bed.

"Could be," said Lees. "If I know your father, he would do just about anything to save your neck, including starting a Tong war with those authorities."

All three men watched, in rapt attention, as the trap door above them slowly began to open. The sound of the creaking wood seemed like the door to their coffin. Both detectives drew their Colts from their holsters and stood still, pointing the pistols up toward the slowly opening aperture. On the bed, George Kwong held his breath and prayed.

***

One Nob Hill, Hopkins Mansion, San Francisco, March 2, 1884

"Do you have the list of four candidates for tomorrow's interviews?" Clara was having dinner with Ah Toy and Mrs. Hopkins. Their plates contained lamb chops, green beans and mashed potatoes. Hannigan stood to the side, ready to refill glasses of wine and cater to the ladies' wishes.

"Yes, but do you really believe we'll be getting a visit from this killer?" Ah Toy was eating with chopsticks, but she had to first cut her food into small chunks. "You know, back in China, we invented these chopsticks because we were mostly starving. Small bits of food could be picked up easily, and we then had kindling to add to our fire for warmth."

"We'll have no visits from Chinese killers. I don't care if they have chopsticks. Those can be dangerous too!" Mrs. Hopkins shook her gray head, reached over, and snatched the two chopsticks out of Ah Toy's hands. She then stuck them both up into her nostrils. "See?" she grinned. "I could get brain damage from these things."

Clara laughed, but then her face became serious. "I do hope we hear from Isaiah. I'm concerned about where he took our friend George. If he took him back to Chinatown, I don't think Mayor Bartlett will leave a stone unturned until he finds his convicted prisoner."

"We can't be concerned with that right now," Ah Toy pointed out. "We must find this murderer, and that means we have to continue the interviews tomorrow afternoon."

"I am happy we are together in all of this, my old friend." Clara smiled at Ah Toy. "I don't believe I could have done it without your help," she added.

"You once saved my life, Carrie. Remember? If you hadn't defended my business against the San Ho Hui, the little slice on my arm could have easily become a crimson smile on my whore's neck." Ah Toy slid her index finger below her chin, across her neckline. "In our tradition, once your life is saved by somebody, you are responsible to that savior, for life."

"Our Lord and Savior! Halleluiah! Praise the Lord!" Mrs. Hopkins raised her hands in glory.

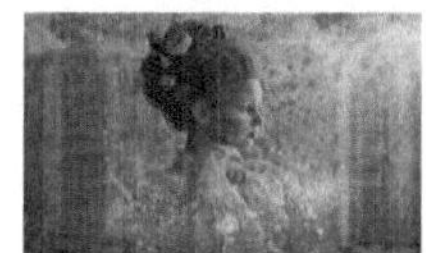

CHAPTER TEN: THE KILLER

One Nob Hill, Hopkins Mansion, San Francisco, March 3, 1884

In order to make herself less of a target, Clara stayed inside the Hopkins Mansion. Ah Toy's room was so large that it had two bedrooms, so it was easy for the attorney to sleep there. When she awoke from a restless dream, in which she experienced herself confronting the killer and being flayed in the manner of the previous eight victims, Clara's mouth was dry, and she probed her body with her fingers, from the neck down, as if it might perhaps be skeletal in form. No, she was still in one piece, so she got up from the bed, dressed in her blue business frock, with a small bustle, and laced up her high black boots. As she arranged her auburn hair into its usual swirl, she heard something being dropped in the other bedroom. She immediately thought about the killer and, for some reason, about the shadowy figure in the Chinatown alley.

Using the shouting habit she had picked-up from Ah Toy, she cupped her hands around her mouth and let loose. "Are you all right in there?"

"It's me, Mrs. Foltz. Hannigan. Miss Ah Toy's not in at present."

Clara picked up her handbag with the pistol inside and walked over to the other bedroom. The door was open, and Hannigan stood there, having retrieved a statue of a Chinese peasant woman that he had knocked over while dusting. "Top of the mornin', missus. Will you be havin' breakfast up here?"

"It depends. Where's Miss Ah Toy?" Clara tucked a stray wisp of hair up into her swirl.

"She's left to do some art shopping. She said I should tell you she would return before the first interview this afternoon." Hannigan dusted the statue before he placed it back on the wall shelf above the bed.

"Really. Do you happen to know where she's doing this shopping?"

"Yes, I do. I brought her the telegram. It was from Mr. Guan Shi Yin at the Joss House in Chinatown. He told her he would like her to see some rare Chinese artifacts he had for sale. It seems the donations have been few these days, and …" Hannigan began.

Clara's mind froze when she heard the name Guan Shi Yin. She heard nothing more. She grabbed Hannigan's arm, and he stopped talking. He stared at Clara's ashen face.

"Are you ill, Mrs. Foltz?"

Many divergent thoughts raced through Clara's mind at once. Ah Toy, her best friend, had, inadvertently, journeyed into the den of the probable murderer. Captain Lees and his partner were gone. The only reason she didn't tell her friends about the murderer was because if she had told them, they would have wanted to confront him. Isaiah might have even taken the law into his own hands and tried to arrest him. At the very least, the fact the minister was Chinese would have been a death sentence. Finally, and most importantly, she never really knew for certain he was the killer. It was true. That's why she wanted the killer to come to her to attempt another murder. However, there was also the other figure she had seen in the shadows on the day Mary McCarthy was murdered. The flashing blade in the darkness. She still remembered that.

Right now, if Clara told the undercover staff about this, they would certainly storm the Tin How Temple, and, no doubt, Ah Toy's throat would be slit before they could break inside. Was Ah Toy even alive right now? Clara's throat constricted and her mouth went dry. There was only one chance, a slim one at that. She had to go to the temple and confront the killer before he murdered Ah Toy.

"I must leave at once, Hannigan. Could you have someone drive me there by rapid means? It's a matter of life and death, I'm afraid." Clara squeezed the butler's arm until his face winced.

"If you don't mind riding a horse, Mum, Detective Tom Whitefeather has the fastest steed. He won a competition the other day between the mansion staff and the detectives on duty. His dappled gray is a swift mare, indeed." Hannigan smiled. "I'm afraid he won't have time to change out of his maid's outfit."

"I don't care about that. I need to get over to the Joss House right now." Clara ran out of the room and into the hall, and Hannigan followed her. "Mr. Whitefeather!" she shouted. "I need you!"

A short person in a long blue and white dress, with an apron and a frilly white cap, came bounding up the stairs from the first floor. As he came running up to Clara, the attorney understood why Dutch Vanderheiden had thought the native would make a realistic woman. His dark lashes were long and flirtatious, and his hairless chin and jawline, and becoming features, were soft and appealing to the eye. When he spoke, however, his deep bass voice assured her this was no woman.

"Mrs. Foltz. I am at your service. What is your need?"

"I need to get to the Joss House, the Tin How Temple, as fast as possible. Mr. Hannigan says your steed is swift afoot."

"She is. I can take you right now. Please follow me." Whitefeather began to run, and Clara tried to keep up, but she was falling behind as he leaped several steps on the stairs on his way down. When he was standing at the front door, he held it for her as she caught up to him. "Come. She is in the mansion's livery next to the guard house."

Clara tucked her small handbag inside her waist sash. She knew she would soon need the Derringer within. When Whitefeather jumped onto the gray, she realized there was no saddle on the back of the horse. However, the young man was very strong, and when he reached over to extend his arms, she noticed his forearms and biceps bulged against the maid's uniform sleeves like those of a strongman she once saw as a child at the county fair. She gripped his hands, and he pulled her up quickly, until her legs were facing sideways behind him. "Mrs. Foltz, encircle your arms around my chest, and hold onto me. Ghost Lady likes to get her lather up when she runs. Until she's into her full gallop, however, you will experience some amount of bouncing up and down."

Detective Whitefeather did not lie. As they took off in a sprint down California Street, at almost a twenty-five-degree angle, it was, to Clara, what she imagined it might be like riding the mythical Greek horse Pegasus. When they galloped past the streetcar, as if it were standing still, she actually believed the gray ghost horse might sprout wings and fly into the air. Thankfully, they stayed on the pavement, and as they raced toward Chinatown, Clara could feel the wind explode in her hair, sending her skirts ballooning outward to embarrassing proportions.

A strange ancillary to this ride was the reaction of all the suffragettes, who were browsing and strolling down the sidewalks of the city. When they saw Clara and Detective Whitefeather galloping by, at breakneck speed in the middle of the boulevard, they hastily assumed the riders were both female. As a result, they began to cheer and wave, lining up along the street to get a better view.

Clara soon realized these hundreds of women believed this to be a creation of female bravado for their benefit. Never to be lacking for showmanship, Clara dared to grab onto her bonnet with her left hand, and wave it in the air at these boisterous women, and when they saw it was their heroine, Attorney Clara Shortridge Foltz, they began screaming louder, "Portia of the Pacific rides again!" and, "Clara Foltz and women's rights!"

When they arrived in front of the Tin How Temple, there was a large group of Tong gang members standing outside. Standing in their midst was Andrew Kwong, father of Clara's client, George. "Mrs. Foltz! There's been a horrible event. My son is trapped inside the temple. And he is with Ah Toy and your two detectives. Guan Shi Yin has taken them all hostage. My men tried to overpower him, but he had weapons down in the hideout beneath Mazu's statue."

Clara slipped down off the Ghost Lady and stood before the leader of the Six Companies. She took his two hands into her own. "How did Captain Lees and Dutch get overpowered?"

Andrew's eyes were wild, and his voice was cracking. "When someone heard Ah Toy's screams, the Tongs tried to break into his temple, and the minister fought back with guns he had secretly stored inside the temple. Miss Ah Toy was there with him looking at artwork he had for sale. He had, at first, with my permission of course, allowed Lees and Vanderheiden to keep my son inside the secret room. I never … he's the killer, isn't he, Mrs. Foltz?"

Clara frowned. She was already trying to think of how to save her best friends. "Yes, I've known he was the murderer for some time. I didn't want to identify him until I could trap him into revealing his evil intentions. Of course, I never thought it would come to this."

"He's inside the shrine with them right now. He says he's going to kill them all unless his demands are met." Andrew squeezed Clara's hands. "You must save my son. He is our only child."

"What demands? This man is mentally deranged, and we must be quite certain he has not killed them already." Clara looked at all of the men surrounding them. “You have to get everyone out of here. I want you to translate for me. Let me talk to this man. I must get to the cause of his hatred.”

Just as she said this, Clara saw that hundreds of suffragettes were approaching Chinatown from the outer city streets. This wouldn’t do. “Get your men to cordon off the perimeter of this street. I can’t have anyone making a commotion while I try to negotiate. If the police or federal officials arrive, tell them it’s an emergency. I need to talk with Guan Shi Yin alone. I believe I can convince him to let your son and my friends go.”

Andrew Kwong moved about the square outside the temple like a man possessed. He gave orders in Cantonese to all the Tongs and other men. The men began to get rope from inside one of the buildings on Waverly Place and string it all around in front of the temple. A guard was posted at every ten feet around the cordon of rope, with a revealing hatchet in his grip.

Nobody was allowed inside Waverly Place. Andrew Kwong escorted Clara up the steps, leading to the temple on the third floor of the building. As she followed the old man up the winding stairs, Clara could smell the pungent odor of burning incense, and cooking stir fry, coming from the clan rooms on the second floor. She felt inside her handbag. The Derringer pistol that Captain Lees had given her for protection was still there, and she fondled its cold metal. She hoped she wouldn’t need it, but this man’s mental state could now be beyond reason.

“It’s right up here.” Andrew turned to look at her as they came to the final plateau in the darkened staircase. The only lighting came from holes, in the shapes of different Chinese gods, in the walls of each landing going up. Kwong was now whispering. “I hope I can translate your words so the minister understands them correctly.”

“I am certain you’ll do well. I have collected some information about your religious practices, but when somebody goes insane, the boundaries of reality and mysticism become disfigured. I’m not quite ready to approach such a task. Any mistake could mean the murder of my friends and your son.” Clara climbed the last few steps and stood with Kwong at the door leading into the temple. She could see bullet holes in it from the earlier conflict with the Tongs.

“Shall I?” Andrew asked, as he held his trembling hand on

the door's dragon-shaped golden lever.

"By all means." Clara thrust her right four fingers in a forward motion, and she held her breath to calm her racing heart.

When Andrew Kwong opened the door to the temple shrine of Mazu, Clara at once saw the glowing light. It was coming up from the open trap door on the floor of the shrine. The giant statue of the Empress goddess was pushed to the side, and in its place, was the figure of the minister, Guan Shi Yin. He was wearing his golden robes, but it was what he was hovering over that riveted Clara's utmost attention.

His hands were gripping the T-shaped handle of a long metal tube that went down into a square box of some kind. The glowing lanterns from the walls of the devotional chamber were casting an eerie glow on his face, which was smiled at her as he was poised to strike, like some kind of possessed demon.

Clara attempted to keep her voice calm, but the sound still came out with a slight trembling vibration. "Hello, Minister. What are you trying to do? Can we be of any assistance?" Clara could hear Andrew Kwong speaking the translated Cantonese behind her. She then listened, as Guan Shi Yin spoke in a rambling, sing-song response.

Mr. Kwong spoke in a low whisper, "He says Mazu is very angry right now. She has given him the gift of millions of years of oceanic wisdom. The dynamite has been cradled in her gift of Diatomaceous earth, so that it will not needlessly explode until he pushes down on the blasting mechanism in his hands right now. Guan Shi Yin says he worked for seven years as the digger of the graves in Oakland. It was then he learned from railroad workers that there was a much easier method of creating the burial sites in the cemetery. Before the invention of the protected dynamite by Alfred Nobel, it seems Mr. Leland Stanford had forced his Chinese workers to use the black powder explosives. Stanford did not care that many of his coolies were blown to bits, as they carried the charges of Chinese-made explosives out to the mountains where caverns needed to be blown apart to create railway tunnels."

Mr. Kwong wiped sweat from his brow and continued, "But then Mazu created the granulated sea earth which now protects these dynamite charges. At first, the minister says, his friend was killing the women by stabbing them with Guan Shi Yin's sacrificial knife—

the same one he used in his tributes to Mazu inside the temple. But then, the brilliant idea came to him. He could terminate the entire prostitution business in Chinatown with one blast and reap a greater reward. This is where we are now, Mrs. Foltz. Guan Shi Yin has connected fifty explosive charges—one for each of our houses of prostitution—and he is going to blow them all if his demands are not met."

Clara's heart began to race again, her brow became wet with beads of perspiration, and her palms were also sweating. "W … what demands?" she managed to blurt out. Also, she wondered, who was "the friend" he was talking about?

"He wants all the houses of ill repute shut down in the United States forever." Kwong raised his eyebrows. "I know, his demands are insane. What can we do?"

"Ask him if I can speak with Captain Lees and Ah Toy." Clara was thinking of a way to work around this quandary. She would need the cooperation of her friends.

Andrew spoke briefly to the minister, who then replied. "He says you can, but you must answer his demands now."

Now? Clara didn't know what to say. If she promised, would this deranged man even believe her? "Tell him I will contact the authorities I know in the government in Washington. If he lets my friends go, then we can see what develops. We will keep him safe until we can get the decision at higher levels."

Kwong translated Clara's words. The killer looked confused for a moment, but then he smiled, nodded, and spoke to Andrew.

"He says you can speak to your friends now," Andrew told her.

Clara moved closer to the trap door's opening. It was still glowing light from within. She could now see the face of the Asian minister more closely. There were the two physical traits she knew. The dark mole on his right cheek, and the cleft in his chin.

"Isaiah? Ah Toy? Can you both hear me?" Clara shouted. She could feel spittle inside her throat, and she coughed. "Did you hear our conversation up here?"

"Yes." It was Captain Lees.

"Clara, I heard everything," called Ah Toy.

"What happened, Isaiah?" Clara asked.

"He had the dynamite ready when Ah Toy came into the

shrine. After the Tongs tried to break into the temple, she was forced down into our room. Ah Toy opened the door, so Dutch and I couldn't get a shot off at him. He has her outfitted as well."

Clara was comforted by the strong voice of her friend. However, she was also confused. "Outfitted? Do you mean he dressed her up in some kind of outfit?"

"No. Not clothing. She is wearing dynamite, which is also fused with his explosive device topside."

Ah Toy had spent many years trying to make her employment of prostitutes safer and less confining. Now, on the verge of teaching women about how to employ their natural charms in a business setting, her best friend and her prospective lover and his partner, were about to be blown apart by this monstrous religious fanatic.

"That's not good, now is it?" Clara became suddenly very calm within. Her voice no longer trembled, her demeanor was slow and perceptive. She believed she was now channeling the millions of years of female survival inside her being. "I'm going to talk with him now. Stay right there, won't you?"

"Don't worry, Carrie," Ah Toy said. "We're not going anywhere."

"Andrew, please translate the following to our minister of the Goddess Mazu." Clara's voice was clear and confident.

"I will do my best, Mrs. Foltz," Kwong said, and he also moved closer to the trap door and the killer.

"Minister Guan Shi Yin, I know your name means hearer of all sufferings. I am going to explain how you will now suffer if you don't release my friends." Clara waited until Andrew Kwong translated. She watched the murderer's face. It became taut, and his jaws clenched. That was a good sign. "I believed you were the murderer of those women shortly after the trial of my client, George Kwong, ended. As a result, I wrote a long dissertation explaining what you had done, complete with evidence that I have gathered, and this written article is about to be sent to all the major newspapers in the world."

Andrew translated, and the murdering minister was now staring at her, his mouth agape in disbelief.

"Oh, yes. If you kill them right now, I have ordered this article to be transmitted by teletype. However, as I do realize you have the upper hands, so to speak, I am willing to make a last negotiation. I know you are a very religious man. I also know I would be the greatest sacrifice for your Goddess Mazu. Why? Because I am the one who has collected all the evidence proving your guilt in these heinous murders. Therefore, if you agree to let me replace my friend, Ah Toy, down in your pit of perdition, I will allow her to destroy my newspaper article. You see, she is the only other person who knows right now where it is. Once she destroys it, she will notify you, and you can release all of us. Is that clear?"

Andrew Kwong took several minutes translating what Clara had said. When the minister spoke, his tone sounded calmer and more deliberate. He punctuated his speech with frequent nods of his head, as he pointed at them with a free hand.

When he was finished, Mr. Kwong turned to speak to Clara, but his face was ashen, and he began wringing his hands.

"He says he never committed any of those murders. It was somebody else who did them. He met this man when he worked in the burial business in Oakland. He says he must have been British, and he knew how to speak Cantonese. A very learned man. He told Guan Shi Yin he would pay him handsomely if he would allow him to stay in the temple's secret hiding place while he practiced his trade in the streets."

"Trade? How can he allow a murderer to practice by taking the lives of young and innocent young women?" Clara's voice was hoarse with emotion.

Again, Andrew Kwong talked to the minister. The translation was finished in several minutes. "He says the man became very efficient, and he allowed Guan Shi Yin to accompany him to each of the killings. The minister helped him get rid of the intestines and other carnage, and the he also planted the seahorses as a distraction. Then, the killer told Guan Shi Yin he would pay him ten thousand dollars to blow-up all the brothels in Chinatown. They both believed these women were a blight and a competition with Mazu and the work of Heaven. No woman should be allowed to live in sin and decadence and pollute the holy marriage union with their filth."

"What can I do to convince him to allow Ah Toy to exchange places with me?" Clara pleaded.

The two men discussed this, and finally Andrew Kwong had

the minister's answer. "He says the brothels must be blown-up, and he doesn't care about dying. He believes Mazu will reward him by allowing him to enter her virginal and heavenly repose. He will allow Ah Toy to go free so as to report exactly what Guan Shi Yin was able to do today to purify Chinatown of these sinful women. You must, however, place the dynamite belt from Ah Toy around your own waist."

Of course, Clara knew, this insane minister wouldn't be stupid enough to attempt to place the dynamite around Clara himself. "Tell him we agree. Get Ah Toy up here so you can take the dynamite off her and place it around me."

Kwong translated Clara's instructions to Guan Shi Yin. The minister yelled instructions in Cantonese down into the trap door to Ah Toy. After several moments, Clara could hear her friend climbing the rickety wooden stairs up to the floor of the shrine. Clara whispered, under her breath, "Be careful, my sister. Don't trip and fall, for God's sake."

The few minutes it took Ah Toy to climb those steps seemed like an eternity. When she finally appeared at the top step, facing them, her mincing little steps made the tension even more excruciating. She took tiny steps toward them, her silk slippers scraping along the floor of the shrine like sandpaper. Seeing her friend safe and alive was exhilarating.

Ah Toy's face was calm, under the circumstances, and Clara realized her friend had also girded herself against any danger that might assail her. Clara remembered her friend's stories about how female infants in China were often drowned because they were seen to be of no worth to the farmers there. Only the wealthy Chinese daughters had access to dowries. Ah Toy had escaped such punishment by learning to work in the fields at age five.

Clara realized all of these young Chinese women were now expendable, not to mention her own life and those lives of her male companions. As Ah Toy crept forward, in the final few steps, with her mincing gait, the attorney understood just how brave her best friend really was.

At last, Ah Toy was standing next to the minister and his insane explosive device. The shrine of the Goddess Mazu was nearby, in all her golden finery, looking down at this small Chinese peasant woman who had progressed so far in her new home country.

Clara believed if Mazu could, she would have patted Ah Toy on the head.

Clara listened, as the minister instructed Andrew in Cantonese on how to take off the suicide belt from around Ah Toy's waist. Finally, her client moved over to stand next to the Chinese woman. His two hands reached out, ever so gently, and unfastened the leather strip that was tied in the small of Ah Toy's narrow back. The three sticks of red dynamite were in a series, and as Andrew brought the strap of leather around with his right hand, these three explosives, which could obliterate the entire Tin How Temple, were dangling in mid-air for several seconds. Clara believed she could hear the three of them as they inhaled slowly and held their collective breaths.

As Andrew was transferring the explosive belt to his right hand, the better to manipulate it so he could bring it around Clara's waist, he dropped it! Clara instantly brought her hands up to her ears, waiting for the crushing blast. Nothing. The minister chuckled and spoke.

Ah Toy translated this time. "He says, Mazu's protective Diatomaceous earth has saved us again. However, it failed to save his son when he was handling black powder for the railroad."

Clara was momentarily struck with empathy. This poor man had harbored a grudge against the powers who took his son's life. This event was the wellspring from whence his insane delusions had come forth. Still, she knew, he was not an innocent. She knew more about his motives than she let on. They were not all delusional.

As Andrew gingerly picked up the dynamite belt, and brought it up to Clara's waist, she inhaled again, as if making her waist thinner could prevent any kind of disturbance.

"Carrie, don't do that. It will be more dangerous when you exhale," Ah Toy explained to her.

Clara let out the air. Andrew, once again, brought the belt around her back and held the two strips of leather between the index fingers and thumbs of both hands. Finally, it was around her, and when Andrew tied it off, Clara began to plan her next move.

Cantonese came pouring from the minister standing at his detonator.

"He wants you to move slowly toward the trap door. Don't make any sudden moves, or he'll plunge down on his handle immediately. Once you get on the top rung of the wooden steps, tell Captain Lees to assist you. He won't plunge down on the detonator until you're below. It will be your final grave to die together."

Ah Toy was now her personal translator, as Andrew Kwong was still perspiring and breathing heavily from his earlier dangerous exercise.

"Tell him I'll do the best I can. I don't go strolling about the town wearing dynamite every day, you know." Clara smiled, as Ah Toy translated. She was proud of herself that she could keep some humor, in spite of the predicament.

Clara believed it was rather ironic. As she moved toward the trap door in the floor of the Mazu shrine, she was taking the same mincing steps that Ah Toy had to take because of her bound feet. Women in North America were not physically bound, but they were, indeed, legally bound. No voting rights, no rights to own property, the list was quite binding and probably as cruel as having one's feet crumpled up like a cow's horn. As she walked, she slowly moved her right hand to her sash in front of her body. Inside the sash, she felt for the small blue handbag, and she opened it.

She had finally arrived at her destination. The dizziness she felt was momentary, as she looked down into the pit of the hideout room below. In its depths, she could clearly see the face of her new beau. He was looking up at her, an inquisitive expression, perhaps one of respect and care. She had always thought his veneration was what she needed most at this time in her life.

Her five children and her parents in San Jose had always admired her intelligence and her fortitude to overcome obstacles that most women withstood because they believed they were powerless. Clara Shortridge Foltz, however, had never, for one moment, believed she was completely powerless.

"Hello! Mrs. Foltz? Can you hear me?" A voice from outside the temple was shouting at them. It sounded like Mayor Bartlett's voice.

"Yes, we're inside—I'm here as well. Please, don't come in!" Clara yelled, trying not to cause a deadly vibration on her explosive belt.

"But your family is here, Mrs. Foltz. They've come all the way from San Jose to be with you. What's happening in there that you cannot come out?" The mayor's voice was its usual demanding tone.

Clara didn't know what to say. If she yelled again, the explosives might go off. If she told Bartlett about the dynamite, her plan would be ruined, as the mayor would certainly order the police to storm inside. Then, all hell would come to them as Guan Shi Yin plunged down on his weapon for the last time.

"This is Lees, Mayor. Get everybody five blocks away from this temple—right now, damnit! I mean it. If you don't, then their lives will be on your head!"

The sound of running feet outside could be heard, and, as the minutes passed slowly, Clara realized it was once more time for her to act.

Clara exhaled with relief that her family was safe, even though her own life and those of her friends were still at stake. She winked down at Captain Lees, who was standing at the bottom step of the hideout. She saw he was smoking one of Dutch's cigars, and the tip of the rolled tobacco blazed cherry-red in the darkness. It was the first time she had seen him smoke. "Can you assist me, Captain? I can't seem to get the hang of these steps."

Clara heard the voice of the killer asking Ah Toy to translate. As her friend did so, Clara knew her final moments were upon her. Even so, she wanted to ask the minister one more question. "Ah Toy! Ask him if he knows the name of the man he helped murder those women."

As she listened to her friend talking with Guan Shi Yin, the hearer of all suffering, Clara curved her index finger gently around the trigger of the Derringer, still in her right hand, and she turned around, took a deep breath, and she pointed the pistol at the man who had caused so much suffering in the world.

Had he helped a crazed killer torture and maim eight innocent women, in the prime of their lives, before they even had the chance to mend their ways or had become enlightened as to the ways of this cruel world? Even if he were telling the truth about not being the actual killer, he had definitely chosen to extinguish life instead of protect it, and for that, Clara thought, in the seconds it took for her to aim at his head, he was guilty.

Her talking target was still looking over at the lovely Ah Toy, who was telling him what this white woman was saying. Between that moment, and the moment it took for Ah Toy to speak to the hearer of all suffering, Clara Foltz, attorney-at-law, pulled the trigger, twice—once for her family, and once for all women. The sound that erupted shook her, as if the explosives fastened around her not-too-thin waist had detonated after all.

When his body fell away from the deadly plunger, harmlessly to the floor of the basement, Clara finally let her breath out in a deep, shuddering wave. Her family was safe, and in her immediate joy, she almost didn't hear Ah Toy's response to her earlier question.

"He said his name was Jack. Jack from London."

CHAPTER ELEVEN: FAMILY REUNION

One Nob Hill, Hopkins Mansion, San Francisco, March 6, 1884

One after the other, in the order of their age, all five of Clara's children greeted her in his or her own way. Everyone in her family was there, including her parents, Telitha and Elias Shortridge. They were learning about the recent case and about the new home they would soon be moving into, thanks to the kind benevolence of Mrs. Mark Hopkins. "My big, gloomy mansion," she said, "would otherwise be inhabited by ghosts."

Eighteen-year-old Trella Evelyn came first, and she greeted her mother by giving her a gentle hug and a brief peck on the cheek She wore a new red dress, with decorative designs on the pockets and a big bonnet. No bustle yet, as grandma forbade it. "It's so grand here, Mother. Will I have my own room?"

"Of course, my love. You're a young woman now, and you deserve your privacy," Clara told her, surprised by how tall she had grown in just a year.

Sixteen-year-old Samuel Cortland came next. He wore a frock coat and short pants, and he chose to shake his mother's hand and smile a crooked grin. "Mother, did you plug that rat in the forehead or the temple?"

Clara frowned. "Sammy, never refer to a human being as an animal of any kind. I had to shoot this man because he could have blown-up most of Chinatown and us with it. It was a matter of life and death, and I really felt a bit sorry for him afterward. Insanity, I now believe, should be determined by a court of law. I was playing judge and executioner."

"Don't you be so hard on yourself, daughter," Elias told her from his seated position on the huge antique living room divan. "You saved a lot of lives that day." Her father's long legs were crossed, and he was smoking a big cigar that Hannigan had given him. Elias wore his best attorney's dark blue suit, with a pink carnation in the lapel of his frock coat. His face was ruddy, his head balding, and his thick mustache was waxy and broad when he smiled.

Mrs. Hopkins, seated to his right, was staring at Elias, reverently, as if he were her deceased husband, Mark. Telitha, Clara's mother, was sitting next to the elderly woman, and she was quite amused by her. She wore a green satin gown that she had worn once to the opera with her husband.

Out on the Persian rug, it was fourteen-year-old Bertha May's turn to greet Clara. She wore a yellow woolen dress with fur at her collars, and her face was streaming tears as she hugged Clara tightly. "Oh, Mama! It's been so horrible without you. Samuel tortures me every day, and I can't find any new friends. My face looks like the craters of the moon."

"My Bertha. This too shall pass. Go sit beside Ah Toy. She will keep you company." Clara pointed to her friend, who was seated on a smaller couch near the fireplace, which was blazing with flames erupting from large winter logs.

Thirteen-year-old David Milton chose to race at his mother from a standing start. At the very last moment, however, he skidded to a stop, and grinned up at her. "What did you get me?" he asked, holding out his arms. His Lord Fauntleroy short pants and jacket, with matching sailor hat gave him a dynamic aplomb.

"I got you a ride on a gray horse called Ghost Lady!" Clara said.

"Yippee!" David screeched, and he ran off to sit beside Bertha and whisper something in her ear.

Finally, little eight-year-old Virginia Knox skipped over to see her mother. Her blue dress with seven petticoats was quite lovely, and her little round hat had a small blue peacock feather. Virginia stood in front of her mother and stared up at her for several moments, as if she couldn't quite believe it was she. "Are you afraid of wolves?" she finally asked, her hazel eyes big and round.

"I would suppose so! They can hunt in packs," Clara said.

"Will you shoot them for me?" Virginia asked.

"Naturally! And if I don't get them, then my friend Captain Lees will," she added, as she observed that Isaiah had just walked into the room along with his partner, Detective Eduard Vanderheiden. They were both wearing their usual suits, and Lees' trademark gray cape was covering his frock coat.

"I think your mother here is a much better shot, however," Captain Lees pointed out. "By the way, Mrs. Foltz, I was meaning to ask. How did you determine that the Minister of the Tin How Temple was the killer of those eight women?"

"I never thought you would ask, Sherlock," Clara walked over and gave Isaiah a close hug and a kiss on the lips. She wanted to show her family just how fond she was of this new man in her life. "When you were showing me how to question suspects, I was taking notes, like a good sleuth. I happened to see that in the photos of all the victims, each woman had the same decoration in her hair."

"Decoration?" Lees pulled a red comb from the back of Clara's tresses and held it out for all to see. "You mean, like this?"

"Do I need to decorate this room again?" Mrs. Hopkins pointed to the lamp beside the divan. "I just purchased that lamp from Tiffany!"

Everyone laughed.

Clara continued, "Yes, except these were the same decorations left in all of the victims' coiffures. As a matter of fact, I also spotted those same decorations inside Goddess Mazu's shrine. They were in the trays, which were given as gifts to worshippers who lit prayer lanterns to the goddess. After I had that information, I deduced that Minister Guan Shi Yin must have placed them there after the victims were flayed. It was a sort of gruesome calling card, if you will."

"The silver seahorse combs!" Dutch Vanderheiden remembered. "Sure, boss, why didn't we see those?"

"After Cook arrested our boy George Kwong, I suppose we got distracted. Thank goodness Clara was alert to that which we had passed over." Captain Lees took the red comb from Clara and placed it gently back into her auburn swirl.

"And how did you determine that the minister was working alone? We thought all along that the mayor might be in cahoots with the bee lady at the Home for Wayward Women. Also, what about this fellow named Jack? Do you believe Guan Shi Yin's story about him killing those girls? Or, was it possibly a dark and imaginary doppelganger scapegoat for his sick psyche?" Lees was bringing out all of the questions he had.

"Elementary, dear Holmes. Although Mayor Bartlett had a lot to gain from using the arrest of George Kwong to win the governorship, he had too much at risk and no motive to be part of the murder plot. He dined at the Chinese restaurant, and he worshipped at the altar of Leland Stanford, who was ambiguous about the value of Chinese labor, at the very least. When I learned that the hearer of all suffering once worked in Oakland as a burial specialist, I decided he had the skills necessary to be able to do the expert flaying of our victims. All of the Chinese deceased also had to be flayed before they were shipped back to China for family burials. As for his meeting up with this Jack, I think he was probably thinking about you, Isaiah and your wonderful British accent. You must have impressed him a lot."

Clara saw Andrew and his son, George, come into the room, and she waved at them. "I also knew George Kwong could have never killed any of those women because he was truly in love with Mary McCarthy."

"Now how could you be certain of something as ephemeral as love?" Clara's mother, Telitha, asked.

"He quit his newspaper job after she broke it off with him while she was in the Home for Wayward Women. He did the summer work in Oakland for that lying coroner," Clara explained. "Of course, he did take all the photos of the victims. I think he was emotionally numb by then, and his journalistic work made him immune to their deaths. When his Mary was murdered, I believe he was truly traumatized beyond emotion. Therefore, he became a prime suspect in Sheriff Connolly's eyes."

"Well done!" Lees clapped. "I knew you were a good student, even though you never graduated from Hastings."

"We women have to make a living these days. Especially if we have to watch out for you men," Ah Toy said, grinning. "Ancient Chinese custom. Get feet twisted to walk daintily for your man. Then he can track you down more easily!"

"I don't want to track anybody down for quite some time," Clara said, opening her arms wide. "Come to me, my glorious family! I want to hold you all in my arms at once, to infuse my soul with your strength. You have done so much to give me inspiration, even though you were far away from me."

All of the Shortridge clan got up and moved to the center of the room to become enveloped in the arms of their mother and daughter. Andrew Kwong, in response, hugged his son, George, and

Mrs. Hopkins took Ah Toy into her arms.

Captain Lees and Detective Vanderheiden each wrapped an arm around the other's shoulder and grinned broadly.

David Milton was the first to break away from the group. He ran to the door and stood there, his eyes glowing, and his body shaking with excitement. "I want to ride the Ghost Lady!" he said, bringing his two hands together in front of his chest, and moving them in a rolling motion, as if he were taking off into the sky.

***

Ah Toy's best friend, Carrie Foltz, was able to love again, and her fight against the fear she had of commitment had disappeared with the further enjoyment of Captain Lees' romantic companionship. She told Ah Toy as much, on many occasions, although the Chinawoman knew her friend would probably never be able to commit to the final obligation of marriage. Clara was too much like Ah Toy. She loved her independence more, and they both understood the fight for female equal rights would take a great deal of time and effort to accomplish.

Ah Toy also watched Isaiah Lees, the crusading law man, win against all odds and return to his job on the police force. It reminded her of her days fighting the Six Companies' bureaucracy, and the Tongs had behaved with Ah Toy much like the Chinatown Squad Lees had to go up against to do his job in the city.

Of course, Captain Lees' dear friend and partner, Dutch Vanderheiden, was also reinstated. Ah Toy had always seen them both as an American version of Robin Hood and Friar Tuck, fighting corrupt law and order and giving back to the downtrodden of all races.

Both Sheriff Connolly and his henchman, Jesse Cook, however, were terminated, as all know that excrement flows downhill. Even though the mayor ordered the kangaroo court trial of George Kwong, Connolly and Cook were blamed.

As for the Mayor of San Francisco, Washington Bartlett, the Great White Whale, he, of course, ordered the termination of Connolly and Cook, so he was therefore able to salvage his reputation. Mayor Bartlett, in an irony not lost on the Chinese community, thus went on to win the governorship of the State of California the next year, but he died from Bright's Disease six months into his new administration to fulfill the prophesy of yin and yang.

During Washington's inaugural speech, which Ah Toy read out loud over morning tea and eclairs with Carrie, the former mayor and new Governor of California spoke about the Chinese in this manner:

"While everyone within the jurisdiction of the State is entitled to and should receive the protection of the laws, still the policy of admitting in such large numbers a race who are distasteful to our people, detrimental to our prosperity, and calculated to breed trouble, cannot be upheld, and it is to be hoped that the National Government may heed the remonstrances that have been made and afford the necessary relief."

On the other hand, Ah Toy observed with satisfaction that Six Companies' leader, Andrew Kwong and his son, George, went on to fight the racism and take their case to court, eventually winning their citizenship and the accolades of their fellows, who would soon follow in their legal footsteps. Immigration became a hot issue, and Clara Foltz and Ah Toy followed it closely.

Finally, the man named "Jack," from London, who had been mentioned in that dark temple basement by a crazed Chinese minister, also headed back to his own country to ply his perfected trade on the Victorian streets of Whitechapel in London's East End. Ah Toy discovered his writings inside the basement hideaway under Mazu's statue, following the near-disaster, and she passed these important writings on to the authorities. In the killer's journal, he described, in gruesome details, how he had committed the murders and that he envisioned this "practice" would make him "a proficient and jolly good craftsman after his return to England."

Ah Toy enjoyed seeing Captain Lees' and Carrie's reaction when she handed them the written journal of this madman. This last twist in the intricate Chinese puzzle was the only flaw in an otherwise brilliant first trial and investigative premier conducted by a new and imposing young female lawyer, best friend, mother, and detective. In honor of her own criminology effort, Ah Toy continued to teach women how to benefit from an independent spirit, and Carrie was often asked to guest lecture.

Ah Toy was still living with Mrs. Mary Hopkins and her best friend in the gray whale of a mansion on Nob Hill, and she enjoyed painting almost as much as she did buying and collecting other artists' work and, of course, playing with Carrie's young ones. Perhaps life did, indeed, imitate art. At least, the Chinese believed it did.

Ah Toy watched the fantastic display in this conflicting world and out in Nature, as she gazed out one of the bay windows of the mansion or strolled in her mincing step down the roiling streets of San Francisco. This beautiful Chinawoman loved to show it all, as dramatically as she could, in her art.

The Spiritualist Murders

Chapter One: The Voice

The Supreme Grand Lodge of the Rosicrucians, 212 Clay Street, San Francisco, May 2, 1886.

"We grow daily beyond our yesterdays and are ever reaching forth for the morrow. The world has had a long night, as it has had bright days; and now another morn is breaking, and we stand in the Door of the Dawn."—Dr. Paschal Beverly Randolph, *Magia Sexualis*

The young woman sat on the bench in the front row. The spiritualist gathering place was inside an old Victorian house owned by one of the members, a Mrs. Virginia Partridge. The girl was crying in the fading San Francisco window light that was illuminating her. Her body was folded over, her head in her hands, as she sobbed, her pale-blue bonnet hanging around her white neck by its frail ribbon.

Clara Shortridge Foltz, Esq., who had been part of the earlier meeting of spiritualists and suffragists, wanted to see if there was something she could do to aid the young woman in her discomfort. With her reddish-brown hair, the girl reminded Clara of her oldest daughter, Trella Evelyn, who was now twenty. Her swirled bun and curly hair were bobbing up and down as Clara walked over and placed a hand on her shoulder. The young woman wore a modest blue dress with bustle, and a satin sash encircled her thin waist.

"My dear, what's wrong?" Clara whispered, not wanting to startle her.

The girl was far from startled. She slowly raised her head, and stared into space, her rouged cheeks slick with tears. Her face was pretty, yet Clara noticed she wore dark eyeshadow, and her eyebrows were red smudges above her glistening gray eyes. Clara had seen this type of shaved eyebrows in photographs of Japanese women, who wanted to affect a kind of mystical quality to their demeanor. The girl finally turned toward Clara, folded her porcelain-like hands into her lap, and cleared her throat.

"I don't know how it happened. I heard the other witnesses, but I still don't believe what they said." Clara noticed the young woman's pupils were constricted, and her words were slurred. The confusing words were perhaps due to a drug-induced condition.

"Witnesses? I don't understand. I am an attorney. Perhaps I can help you." Clara reached down to take the girl's hand, but she pulled back and squealed.

"There were attorneys in that courtroom. All they did was argue about the different witnesses and what they saw. *He* never got called to the stand! He's still out there!" The girl stood up and began humming and shaking her head back-and-forth, as if she were being seduced by a strange, inner demon.

"I can understand why you would want to come to our meeting. We support women's rights under the guise of spiritual communication. What happened to you? Are you drugged? Were you raped? What's your name?"

The young woman's humming began to transform into a chanting of words. Clara thought this might be a method of protecting her body. When she spoke, she clutched her arms across her breasts and looked up into the air at some invisible entity, perhaps a protecting angel or a demigod of some kind.

"Perhaps you can come with me. I don't live too far from here, and I have a friend who knows about the problems of young women such as yourself." Clara took a few steps toward the door, hoping the girl would follow. When she failed to do so, the attorney went back and grasped her arm at the elbow. She guided the young woman toward the door. The girl walked as if she were in another world, looking all about, squinting at the descending sun outside, and continuing to mumble her prayer, if that's what it was.

They took the cable car up California Street to the mansion. The girl seemed in a trance, staring out at the passing pedestrians, horses and merchant carts as if they were phantasms in her personal dream world. Clara realized this when she observed the young woman reach out and attempt to touch one of the passing horses, even though it was at least ten yards from her open window inside the trolley.

After getting clearance from the guard at the gate, Hannigan, the butler, answered the tall gray door of the Hopkins Victorian mansion at One Nob Hill. Clara heard her younger teenage children roughhousing on the stairs. The Irish butler raised his auburn eyebrows and smiled. “Been that way since you left, mum. Banshees, they are, to be sure!”

“Could you please tell Ah Toy I want to see her? We’ll be in the living room.”

“It’s nice to get instructions all civilized like. Miss Ah Toy and her shouts. It’s my opinion, mum, she gets the wee ones all riled up.” Hannigan looked over the girl briefly before he turned to leave, the tails of his black coat bobbing against his backside as he climbed the stairway to the second floor.

Clara, now thirty-seven, had been living at the Hopkins residence since she solved the mystery of the eight murdered prostitutes two years before. Her best friend, Ah Toy, the former Chinatown Madame and now an independently wealthy artist and art dealer, was invited by Mrs. Hopkins to stay with her, and now it was the entire Shortridge family who lived with the widow. These were hard times, as the strikes were on at the railroads, and high unemployment was the result. The big investors and owners of the machines of progress were not being very kind to the working folks.

Mrs. Hopkins, at sixty-eight, was becoming senile, and as such, she was probably more receptive to having all these new, live-in guests to watch out for her. Her confusion was humorous to all of the Shortridge family, and Ah Toy, a shrewd businesswoman in her own right, was making an effort to see that the old woman was not being tricked by sly businessmen or local politicians. The late Mark Hopkins, her husband, was one of the four owners of the railroads in the United States, so he had left his wife with a vast fortune.

Clara was thankful to be able to have this gigantic mansion for her family to live in. One of the main reasons she had taken the murder case in Chinatown was because they paid her enough so that she could finally bring her family from San Jose to live with her. Now that she was back to plying her daily trade of divorce cases and family law, the money was not as forthcoming as the one hundred dollars per hour she received from the Chinatown Six Companies during the murder case. One more reason she was grateful to have this abode.

"Carrie, who have you brought home to us?" Ah Toy was mincing her way over the thick Persian carpeting toward them. As a child back in China, Ah Toy's feet had been bound, which now caused her to walk in tiny steps. Clara was still standing with her charge, whose name, she then realized, she did not know.

The young woman was staring, fixated would be a better word, at one of the oil paintings hanging on the redwood wall in the living room. Its subject was a female medium in front of the Tin How Temple. The woman in the painting had a crazed, inward stare, and her mouth was open. The Chinese men standing all around her were listening intently to what she was saying. The medium's words, according to the belief, were channeling responses from the Goddess Mazu, who was being carried behind the medium on a colorfully decorated cart.

"She seems to be hypnotized by your art, Ah Toy. I found her in this state of somnambulism at my meeting. I think she's been abused by some trauma, and I want your help."

Ah Toy, at age fifty-eight, was still a beautiful woman. She wore a long black silk dress called a *cheongsam* that extended down to cover her bound feet, and her hair was still mostly black, although waves of gray were present, and her temples were completely white. She minced over to stand beside the young woman.

The living room in this Victorian mansion resembled an art gallery rather than a place to entertain guests. Long mahogany benches faced the walls, which were filled with hundreds of oils, watercolors and sculpted designs on wooden platforms. Mrs. Hopkins was one of the biggest art collectors in the United States.

"Why are you fascinated by this piece, my dear?" Ah Toy whispered to the girl. The older woman knew immediately not to burst out in her usually flamboyant voice. The former Chinatown Madame had worked with thousands of fragile young women, and she knew how to handle a damaged psyche. She had been successful in the sex trade because she was gentle, and she had used a woman's beauty and her more mysterious qualities to please men rather than overt and animalistic sexual intercourse.

"I can do this," the girl said, matter-of-factly.

"Do what? What's your name? I am Ah Toy."

Clara listened intently to the conversation. Her detective abilities were on alert, as she sensed there would be an interesting exchange.

"Adeline Quantrill. I can speak in the voices from beyond." Adeline touched her red lips with the tips of the fingers of her right hand. Her face was pretty, oval and Asian-looking, although her eyes were not slanted. It was her jet-black hair and dark eyes beneath the brushes of eyebrows that made her appear Oriental. Her breathing was now regular, and she seemed to be responding well to Ah Toy's questions.

"Beyond. Do you mean voices from our departed souls? Our relatives and friends who've passed on?"

"No. I mean voices from those who are not willing to share what they're thinking to others. Some are dead, but others are alive. They exist in prisons made by men and in prisons created by the mind."

"I see. That's quite a magnificent gift you have! I want to learn more." Ah Toy encircled the girl's shoulders with her arm.

"I found her crying. She told me she was at some kind of trial. The attorneys would not listen to her. She said they kept arguing about what the witnesses had testified. Also, she said that somebody was still out there—a man." Clara stepped over to stand next to her friend.

Adeline pulled away, and her snub nose wrinkled, her mouth turned down, her head began to slowly shake, from side-to-side, and she began to flash her teeth like a caged wildcat. The voice that came out of her was not that of a teenage young woman, however, it was the deep baritone of a tortured male.

"They come to me like lost sheep. I attract them with my recipes for sexual fulfillment, you see. The energies of the body can be harvested for a power much greater than the power men have over them! I can teach them the joys of producing passion as it's linked to the dead. Intercourse with their husbands only leads to death. But intercourse with me leads to the release of the soul into a new realm of power on Earth!"

Ah Toy spoke gently to the possessed woman. "Who are you? Why do you have such power?"

Adeline did not look at Ah Toy. She continued to stare, flaring her nostrils and flashing her teeth. "I am a follower of Dr. Paschal Beverly Randolph. He taught me the gift of animal magnetism before he killed himself in Ohio. Now I have perfected his teachings, and women can at last learn the only way to free themselves from the slavery over their minds and bodies."

Clara was intrigued. Most of her abolitionist and suffragist work had been "allowed" because the Spiritualist Movement, of which Dr. Randolph was a member, gave women a voice that they would not have had otherwise. The male patriarchy forbade most women from speaking in public, and women themselves were fighting the equal rights suffragists because they believed gaining more political power would lead to the same corruption that men had created.

However, Clara and her sisters still spoke out for the rights of women because they knew it was the only truly political path toward ultimate equality under the law. If they had to speak as if they were "possessed" by some otherworldly spirit, so be it. They would speak wherever they could to get their message out to others. But this young woman seemed to be speaking about something more sinister afoot. Dr. Randolph had been a controversial practitioner, and some said his combination of sex and power led to lascivious cravings and ungodly rituals inside the bedroom. Could Adeline be a victim of such practices?

"But how can these women free themselves?" Clara asked the inevitable question.

For the first time, the girl turned toward the voice and stared at Clara. Her masculine voice became a harsh whisper, and what she then said chilled Clara's mind as if this man were in the room and had addressed her personally. She knew after it was said that it was leading her into a morass of dark sexual practices, and the visitation of urges that she thought were only present in men who were engaging in bloody and horrendous warfare.

"They release the souls of their husbands, of course!" The voice said.

CHAPTER TWO: THE CLAIRVOYANT

The Hopkins Mansion, One Nob Hill, San Francisco, May 2, 1886.

When the girl came out of her trance, Clara knew she had to act. If Adeline were ill, then she needed medical attention. If she were somehow telling them the truth, then another course of action must be taken. As an attorney, Clara Foltz understood the importance of memory. In her trial experience as a defense lawyer, she knew how to ask the questions that would demonstrate flaws in memory. This young woman needed to be questioned to determine her ability to tell the truth about her experiences.

"Adeline, are you aware of the voice that just came forth from your body?" Clara took the girl's hands into her own and gazed into her eyes. Her pupils were no longer pinpoints. They looked normal. Perhaps hysteria had caused the effect seen in the meeting house on Clay Street.

"Voice? What voice, madam?" The girl cocked her head to the side and smiled. "If I speak, it is with my own voice. If some other sound came from me, I would remember. You see, mum, I remember every moment of my life since I was eight years of age."

Ah Toy sat down on the other side of the girl on the long bench. "Carrie, we must test her. I have seen this before in one of my girls. When she got off the steamship, I was able to procure her before the Tongs sold her off to the sex slave trade. Yes, her name comes to me. Liu Chunhua."

"What could she do?" Clara asked.

"She could recall every day she had lived beginning back at her village in Guangdong province. She would tell me what was occurring at the exact date and hour—not just her personal experience, but also about those people and events around her. She told me she had two moving pictures in her mind. One was her sight and experience of the present, and the other was the immense pictorial history of her past. She had the ability to order her imagistic memories as one would organize one's closet of clothes and shoes.

Come to think of it, she was very orderly in her personal habits as well."

"We have something more important to contend with here. This girl has been privy to murder. She told me about being at a trial where the lawyers ignored her testimony. Isn't that correct, Adeline?" Clara touched the girl's arm.

"I know every word that was said that day. I can tell you what each witness was saying. Would it help if I gave you their stories about the murder?" For the first time, the girl's face seemed to become animated with something close to joy. It was as if her ability to recite what she remembered was a channel to a personal type of pleasure.

"I certainly want to hear more about this case. What about you, Ah Toy? Do you think Adeline's ability can serve to explore this rather macabre event further? Perhaps we can even discover why Adeline believes she knows who the murderer is."

Ah Toy nodded. "Of course, we have no direct method of verifying the authenticity of her memories. I could do so with Chunhua because she kept diaries of her daily activities in China."

"I keep a diary too! I began keeping it after my parents were killed by renegade Chiricahua Apaches two miles outside Tombstone, Arizona, on April 16, 1876, at ten fifty-two AM, when I was eight years and three months old. After they died, I knew I was going to be alone the rest of my life."

"How did it happen?" Ah Toy asked.

"We were coming out West from New York City, to seek our fortunes, and our train was attacked. Mother and Father were killed with a hatchet by one of the intruders. A Pinkerton guard shot all five of them before they could kill more passengers. I was placed in the Methodist orphanage when we arrived in San Francisco, and that's when I began keeping my diary. I wanted to remember everything from before, and I wanted to remember everything in my new life alone. It's been the only way I can cope with the daily memories and organize them to fit my personal puzzle."

"Good God! Do you have any relatives in San Francisco or perhaps in New York?" Clara was concerned for the young woman's safety and mental health.

"Just a maiden aunt in New York. She has twelve cats and no children, so I am on my own, for the most part. I have been cared for by the Rosicrucians, however, after I turned eighteen."

"This was where you got involved with the alleged murder?"

When Clara said the word "murder," the girl winced and drew back.

"Yes, but the others were very kind to me. It was when *he* came to the meeting that I became involved. There is one problem about all of this, however."

"And what is that?" Clara leaned forward.

"Although I can remember what he said and what he promised us, I cannot, for the life of me, remember what he looks like or what his name is. Isn't that odd?"

Ah Toy stared at Clara. "I would expect perhaps some kind of mesmerizing influence. I have seen it done. One of my ladies wanted to forget a trauma she experienced with a client, and a doctor was able to hypnotize her so that she forgot it completely."

"No court of law would accept such evidence," Clara said. "It's quite difficult to prove this is scientifically possible under strictly controlled conditions. For example, this possession of Adeline's. She may have had a traumatic experience whereby she can now mimic the voice she heard, but I doubt it was caused by spirit possession or hypnotic means."

"Let's start the test to see if she has this autobiographical memory," Ah Toy said. "I propose we use a *Farmer's Almanac*. I believe Mrs. Hopkins has one in the study. It has all the weather conditions recorded for the past years. Chunhua was able to tell me the correct forecast, using the exact dates and times when the weather changed."

"I shall retrieve it. Your bound feet are quite a hindrance when speed is a necessity." Clara got up from the bench and hurried off to the next room, turning right at the front door.

When she returned, she held a mammoth, quite dusty tome in both of her hands. She set it down with a grunt on the bench and began turning pages.

"All right. Meteorology. Which date should I choose?"

"Choose a date that may have a strange occurrence," Ah Toy suggested.

"Here's a good date. April 20 and 21, 1880. What was the weather like in Napa Valley and in San Francisco?"

Adeline moved her forefinger in the air, as if she were turning invisible pages. "It was the greatest rainfall in recorded history. I mean, since 1850, when these weather conditions began to be recorded."

"No need for egotistical levity, young lady," Clara smiled. "What were these grand totals?"

"San Francisco had three and two-tenths inches in twenty-four hours. Oh, and Napa Valley had a quite remarkable fourteen and seven-tenths inches. We had to place burlap bags filled with sand all around the doors of the orphanage on Sutter Street. We could go nowhere for the entire week it was so stormy."

Clara raised her eyebrows. "She's quite correct. Exactly what it says here, to the decimal!"

Both women questioned the girl for an hour about a variety of events and phenomenon occurring in the past, and Adeline was able to answer them all with complete accuracy. She even added personal comments about what she was doing that day, such as what she ate and with whom she socialized.

Clara knew it was time to get Adeline's story about the trial. Even if her testimony today could not be used in a court of law, as the attorney believed, it may lead to clues which might assist them in their hunt for this phantom doctor and possible murderer. When Adeline spoke in this doctor's voice, what was said made Clara's flesh crawl. There was something about the logic and tone of the words which were innately dangerous.

Clara knew she also needed to read more about this doctor's mentor, Dr. Paschal Beverly Randolph. All she knew was that one of the books he wrote, *Magia Sexualis*, was banned from distribution by the United States Postal Service. Therefore, this student of his must have obtained a copy of it secretly from the master himself.

"Carrie! Pay attention! Adeline just slumped over. Her face is pale. I think she may have fainted." Ah Toy raised the girl's upper torso and slapped her cheeks gently. "Adeline, wake up! Are you ill?"

"She must be starving. It's time for dinner anyway," Clara said, looking at the grandfather clock standing next to a statue of Mark

Hopkins, Mary's late husband. "I'll call the children, and you get Mrs. Hopkins. We'll continue this after we eat."

"Yes, I believe you're right. When you mentioned food, she woke up. I'll go tell Hannigan to prepare another setting, and then I'll get the old woman." Ah Toy stood up and began mincing her way out of the huge living room on the ground floor of the mansion. Clara guided Adeline toward the dining room, which was connected to the living room on the east end.

***

The dining room table seats were filled with all five of Clara's children and her two parents, Elias and Telitha Shortridge. For the first time in over a year, the attorney and detective had her family together. The kind owner of the Hopkins Victorian mansion, Mary Hopkins, sat at the head of the table. She was beaming at all these guests of hers, as if she were the queen of a fantasy realm. Her dementia, in fact, was creating within her mind a splendid assortment of dubious realities that Clara and her family enjoyed immensely.

When Ah Toy escorted Adeline Quantrill into the room, everybody became silent and stared at her. In her usual, polite manner, the former Chinatown Madame introduced the newcomer to the gathered family.

"My friends, this is Adeline Quantrill. She has quite a unique ability I am certain you will all find interesting and entertaining. At the moment, however, she is also famished."

The eighteen-year-old guest plopped down into a high-back mahogany chair, as she could no longer stand.

Ah Toy pointed to each of the family members around the table. "Mister Elias Willets Shortridge is the elder of our group. He is Clara's father, and he is also a lawyer and pastor. He presently assists his daughter with her legal practice and saves souls on the weekends."

Elias was wearing his usual blue suit and vest with a gold pocket watch dangling from his vest pocket. He was a balding man with a thick gray mustache, and he nodded at the girl and pushed forward a cane that was balanced against his chair. "Infirmity of age keeps me from keeping up with my daughter, and, most especially, these wild animals called my grandchildren. I shall endeavor soon to cage them and sell them to the passing circus if they don't soon become tamed. I am very pleased to make your acquaintance, young lady."

Adeline gazed at the elder Shortridge, and then smiled. "I see you're a Campbellite Christian, dear sir. Have you baptized your adult children unto their remission of sins?"

The sixty-one-year-old man was taken aback by this girl's knowledge of his religion. "Why, of course I have! There can be no salvation unless the adult is submerged by an authentic Campbellite minister. The Millennium of Christ's return is being ushered in by our reformation baptisms."

"How did you know my father was a Campbellite? I never told you anything about my family." Clara frowned at the young girl. "Who are you? How did you find out about him?"

Adeline whipped her head back and forth until her auburn curls broke from their bun and slashed against her shoulders. "No, good sir! Jesus never baptized even one of his apostles. How can you claim such power over your flock?" She laughed, and then the voice of the phantom minister returned to her, and she bellowed, "Let me have these lovelies! I will teach them how to restore the power they had before Eve. They can become Lilith, controlling the sex act, and reaping what was stolen from them by your false Yahweh!" The girl's gray eyes flashed as she moved her head to stare, in turn, at each of the adult women at the table, including Mrs. Shortridge. She pointed her right forefinger at each one and mumbled what sounded like the same gibberish Clara and Ah Toy had heard earlier.

The sound was so frightening that Virginia Knox, ten, and David Milton, fifteen, got up from their seats and rushed over to stand beside their grandfather to protect him from this possessed young woman. "Grand, you must not allow her to stay here!" David said, frowning.

"I must tell you all. When Adeline becomes agitated and speaks in this deep voice, she has no memory of it afterward." Clara tried to think of a way she could explain it to the younger children. "She is making believe she is somebody else, but she cannot remember it when she's finished pretending. We're going to try to help her with this."

"Do you truly not know what you just said?" Samuel Cortland, eighteen, who was seated next to Adeline at the table, was sharing his mother's intellectual curiosity. He straightened his red silk bow tie. "What is it you feel inside?"

Adeline was watching two of the female servants pouring out soup into the bowls with a large ladle. "May I have some of that?" She licked her lips and pointed.

"Of course, my dear! Sophie, pour some soup for Adeline," Mrs. Hopkins instructed the servant. "Do you do any other impressions? Your Grover Cleveland was quite good! Of course, you're not as rotund."

"I can't understand why Ah Toy believes Mrs. Hopkins is losing her memory. She obviously knows who the president is." Trella Evelyn, twenty, was always defending the eldest owner of their new home. Trella was wearing a Suffragette dress, a long purple affair with a matching necktie draped down the center of her white blouse, and a medium bustle in the back.

"I am sorry, but you didn't answer my question, Adeline," Samuel said.

"Yes, why don't you respond? Perhaps she's the daft one at this table," sixteen-year-old Bertha May said, tucking a cloth napkin inside her high collar to protect her frilly blouse before picking up her spoon.

"She is quite daft! She has bats in her belfry!" Little Virginia squealed.

"Calm down, right now! Let the girl respond," said the sixty-two-year-old grandmother, Talitha Shortridge, from the other side of the table.

The noise was bothering the young woman, and she stopped eating the soup to cover her ears with her hands. She began the humming that Clara had heard her do before at the meeting house and on the cable car.

"Silence! We must all show some respect for this young medium." Ah Toy said, raising her right hand. "Some persons are gifted with the ability to channel the voices from the spirit world. Adeline has this skill, and we must learn from her."

Samuel, who was still staring fixedly at the girl, gradually became her center of attention. Adeline lowered her hands from her ears, turned her head to the left where he sat, and she smiled at him.

"Feel inside? I feel humbled at being allowed at your fine table. What a glorious family you have!" Adeline picked up her spoon again and dipped it into her bowl. "And this tomato soup is like drinking the warm blood from Zeus's lips!" Adeline's white teeth were covered in the red liquid.

"How ghastly!" Virginia's face wrinkled into a prune.

"She's using a metaphor, Clara Virginia," her mother said, using her private name for her youngest. "Children, what is a metaphor of speech?"

All the children's eyes rolled with displeasure in their thinking heads, but only Trella answered. "A metaphor is an image that takes the place of another, more common image, to show a startling comparison. We are obviously not really slurping the blood of the Greek god Zeus, but the image seems to compare our tomato soup with the nectar of the gods."

As if on cue, Samuel, Bertha, Virginia and David began to loudly slurp their soup.

"Enough!" Talitha shouted. "We shall finish our dinner, and then discuss what we can do to help your mother with this young woman."

***

Ah Toy decided that the library was the best room to work with Adeline. Therefore, after dinner, all members of the family over the age of eighteen adjourned to watch her question the young woman. Ah Toy sat at the large table for reading the newspapers and magazines, and the young medium sat next to her. Ah Toy instructed everyone else to stay at least ten feet from where she was, so the rest of the family settled into soft reading chairs from Europe and antique divans from Asia.

This was a library created for one of the wealthiest women in America. It contained over 15,000 volumes, all classified and categorized under the Dewey Decimal System. Ah Toy and the children were able to improve their language skills and locate information for their school work. The Chinese artist and teacher thought it was a fitting location to balance yin and yang and to delve into the mind of a young spiritualist medium. It was a place where the mind and the spirit could meet.

"Adeline, you said you can go back to that trial and repeat exactly what was said by each witness. How many witnesses were there? Also, you stated that your testimony was ignored by the court. Why was that?" Ah Toy kept the tone of her voice calm and reflective. She knew that any aggressiveness or perceived threat on her part could prevent the girl's responses from coming forth.

"There were three witnesses, not including myself. My testimony was ignored because the judge believed me to be mentally deranged. He said I was not capable of sound recollection." Adeline looked down at her hands and then raised her head and stared into Ah Toy's dark eyes. "I was the only one who saw an actual murder take place, but I was not allowed to speak."

"Were they aware of your special talents of recollection?" Clara asked. She was sitting in a chair at the table next to Ah Toy.

"The judge said because I was sixteen, and because I had suffered from so much trauma, he didn't deem it proper for me to speak about matters of evidence."

"But, you were an eyewitness to a murder. Certainly somebody, especially the prosecution, would have listened to you." Clara sounded impatient.

Ah Toy raised her right forefinger to her lips. "Did you speak in one of your voices to any of these court attorneys or to the judge?" Ah Toy wanted to get deeper into the young woman's psyche.

"Yes! It was May 2, 1885, in the court of Judge Holland Wentworth. I was called to the witness stand by the Prosecutor, District Attorney Matthew C. Welles, Jr. at exactly ten minutes after three in the afternoon. I was told before the trial by Mr. Welles that he was going to ask me about what I had seen Dr. McCauley do to the accused, Mrs. Rachel Wilson-Rafferty, at the Rosicrucian Hall. He never asked me about the murder. He just wanted me to tell the court about how Dr. Adam McCauley hypnotized his subjects, as he called them."

"What went wrong?" Ah Toy raised her eyebrows. "Is that why you channeled the voice? Were you angry because they would not listen to you?"

"I never remember what I say after I do it. However, the judge informed me that I was speaking in a male's voice on the witness stand. Even though the other three women screamed when they recognized it, nobody in the court believed I could become a voice from the past." Adeline smiled. "But you believe me, don't you?"

Ah Toy returned the smile. "Yes, my dear. Tell me. What did Dr. McCauley do when he heard you imitate his voice?"

"He smiled. And then he whispered something to Rachel's attorney, Miss Laura de Force Gordon. Dr. McCauley was testifying for her at the trial."

"Laura Gordon? She was defending Rachel Rafferty? She's one of my dearest friends and fellow attorneys. We argued a murder case against each other, and we also worked to get the law passed in California which allowed women to become attorneys and attend law school. It seems that this McCauley could be a possible suspect. I want to talk with Laura about this," Clara said.

"I believe it's a good time to have you channel the testimony of these three witnesses. We shall begin with the first woman. Please, before you go into your trance, tell us the name of this woman and how she knew Dr. McCauley." Ah Toy's eyebrows furrowed in concentration. "Carrie, do you have anything to add?"

"I would also like to know what Adeline observed about these three witnesses. I would assume they were testifying about what was done by Dr. McCauley to Rachel Rafferty, was it not?" Clara leaned her chin forward into the cradle made by her hands. "Was Miss Gordon trying to show that her client Rachel could have been mesmerized by McCauley?"

"Yes, they had all observed the hypnosis which Dr. McCauley used upon the defendant, Mrs. Rachel Wilson-Rafferty. Each one had a different perception about what had occurred. This was what caused the attorneys to get angry. Of course, nobody cared about what I saw. Most importantly, nobody cared that I witnessed the result of Dr. McCauley's hypnosis. I saw …" Again, Adeline began sobbing into her hands.

"Did you see the murder of Mr. Rafferty?" Clara asked.

Adeline stared at the attorney and paused, as if she were remembering something. "Yes. I was working for the victim, Mr. Brian Rafferty, at his home in Pacific Heights. I was the upstairs maid, and on the night of April 3, 1884, I witnessed his wife, Rachel, kill him during their sexual union."

"My goodness! You could have sent that woman to the gallows." Elias said from his seat on the divan.

Ah Toy instinctively knew it was not that simple. "Did anybody in that courtroom believe Rachel was hypnotized by Dr. McCauley to kill her husband?"

"No, of course not! The good doctor was testifying for the defense. He was saying that he knew Mrs. Rafferty was too mentally imbalanced to know if what she was doing was right or wrong. The jury believed it. Women were not capable of the hatred required to commit such murders. Especially of their husbands, who were their sole providers and masters of the house." Adeline wiped tears from her cheeks. "However, I saw her do it, and I could also hear what she was thinking."

"Do you mean to say you are also a telepathist?" Clara asked. "Can you read people's minds as well as recall what they said?"

The young woman laughed. "Of course. It's my curse." She turned to gaze over at Samuel, who was fidgeting while seated upon an old red chair with fringes on the sides and a lace doily on the headrest. "For example, Samuel is now thinking he wants to leave and go play billiards with his friends."

"That's not difficult to discern," Samuel shook his head. "She saw I was uncomfortable, and most young men enjoy billiards. What are my two friends' names then? If you are truly clairvoyant, then you should know that as well."

"One is named Roger. Roger Dowdy. The other's name is Ezra Levine."

There was a dead silence for several minutes. Telitha Shortridge finally stood up and walked solemnly over to the girl. She placed her wrinkled hand on Adeline's shoulder. The girl looked up and gazed into the older woman's face. Telitha told her, "You shall never mention this ability of yours to any living soul outside this family. Do you hear me, young lady?"

"I shall not, Mrs. Shortridge. I have read about what happens to people like me."

"You have? You mean, like what happened in Nathaniel Hawthorne's tale? 'Young Goodman Brown'?" Trella Evelyn asked.

"No, we are now too civilized to kill people for being witches. I once asked Mrs. Young, who was our house mistress at the orphanage, why she was thinking about how attractive the priest, Father O'Shaughnessy was, as he could not return her affection. She became quite enraged, and she shouted at me that they put people like me in the insane asylum. She then picked-up a screwdriver and held the flathead against my temple. She said the doctor would drive a hole into my brain until I could no longer think evil thoughts. She said I was cursed by the Devil."

"Are your prognostications correct one hundred percent of the time?" Clara asked.

"No, it seems I can only read the minds of certain people. I don't know why that is, but there are those who seem to send their thoughts to me." Adeline shook her head. I can never predict when it will happen. It just does."

Ah Toy was getting impatient. "All right. Let us hear your channeling of the first witness. It is now obvious that we can get more than what was given at the court. Perhaps we can learn how this Dr. McCauley was able to mesmerize these women so they became his sex slaves."

"Slaves? Aren't you being a bit overly dramatic, Ah Toy? We don't know this doctor was responsible for the murder." Clara frowned at her.

Ah Toy turned to her friend and smiled. "Remember that we Asians believe in many more realities than just science and logic. Each of us has been gifted with uniqueness that has nothing to do with our social lives. It is our connection with the spirit world. Adeline can lead us into this dark realm, but we can never be the masters over such supernatural powers. We can only follow these powers and discover their effect."

"All I want to discover is whether this mesmerist, Dr. McCauley, has the power to train wives to kill their husbands. If so, then it is he who should go on trial and perhaps be placed into a mental hospital. But we need incontrovertible evidence, beyond any reasonable doubt. At the present, I have many such doubts." Clara cleared her throat. "Please, Adeline, you may now take us back to that day in the courtroom. It would seem we have a lot to learn."

Ah Toy had few arguments with her best friend, but this was an occasion when she had to insist her expertise was to be recognized. She stood up at her seat and addressed the family in a formal voice.

"When I worked in Chinatown as a Madame, there was a Tong leader of the Hop Sing named Fung Jing Toy. Everyone called him Little Pete. Little Pete was my uncle. He had the power over the prostitutes that were brought over from southern China to work. Like this Dr. McCauley, my uncle mesmerized women. After he established his power over them, they willingly had sex with strange men."

"What did he tell them? Was it so they could obtain power from having sex with your uncle?" Clara asked.

"No, it wasn't exactly like it was with Mrs. Rafferty. My uncle told each girl that for every man she had sex with she was gaining dream powers over all men. He would, in fact, get them addicted to opium, and then he would take them to private orgies in the Palace Hotel. He charged the white men a lot of money to participate in these bacchanals. The girls were under his complete control, and my uncle soon became known in the masculine circles as the 'King of Chinatown.' As far as I know, he is still plying his illegal trade, and he even has a white body guard. Mr. C. H. Hunter. My uncle reasoned that no rival Tong would risk killing a white man." Ah Toy sat back down and folded her hands into the lap of her silk *cheongsam.*

"You never told me this," Clara said. "However, I believe your Uncle Pete may be able to assist us when we attempt to confront this Dr. McCauley. Thank you, Ah Toy, for your candid honesty."

"I am always here to extend the patterns of connections between dark and light. Just as your lover, Captain Lees, uses the Tongs as informers to catch other criminals, I also believe the dark side can aide the powers of light." Ah Toy raised her hand. "Shall we begin? Adeline, please favor us with your powers of spiritualism."

Chapter 3: The First Witness

The Hopkins Mansion, One Nob Hill, San Francisco, May 2, 1886.

Clara was now skeptical about what this young woman would present. Adeline was perhaps attempting to gain monetary advantage, knowing now how affluent the family's circumstances were at present. However, the circumstantial evidence was there. She was able to recall the weather, and perhaps when they had access to her diaries, even more proof could be obtained that she was a clairvoyant. She was also extremely traumatized and emotionally distraught. Ultimately, it was Ah Toy's interest in this girl that intrigued Clara the most and made the attorney want to pursue this case to its logical end.

The voice again came from the girl's diaphragm, but this time it was an older woman's voice. It had the melodious tones of a personage who had education and refinement. Someone of the upper classes. This was somebody with status and who came from money. Clara watched the faces of her family members. As the girl spoke, they were riveted at attention, eyes wide and reflective, leaning forward in their seats, hanging upon every syllable of every word. Clara believed they were either watching and hearing a voice from another human in the past, or else Adeline Quantrill was one of the best-trained actresses Clara had ever witnessed.

"My name is Margaret Bennington-Stanton. I reside at 623 California Street, Nob Hill. Yes, I know the accused. She attended the same spiritualist meeting as I. The location? It was on Clay Street. I don't remember the number. My chauffeur drove me."

Clara realized that Adeline was reciting only the witness's side of the questions and answers. Right now, it was easy to determine what was being asked, but the one-sided presentation might get complicated, so Clara walked over to another table and picked-up a notepad and pencil. She brought them back to her seat and settled in, copying those phrases or points about which she might want to clarify with others later.

"I knew Rachel Rafferty from college. She and I attended Berkeley college together. Yes, we were both active in the Suffragist cause on campus. Our husbands were on the university's board of regents together. No, they were not sympathetic to our cause. In point of fact, we both decided to join the Rosicrucian order, so we could discuss politics. It was our only way to openly share these types of political arguments. Yes, of course. We also discussed our personal lives."

Clara made a note to consult with Virginia Partridge about which meeting place these two women might have attended. The Rosicrucian groups were new, but they were sprouting up like mushrooms all around the bay area, especially in the more populous and affluent neighborhoods.

"Rachel was very unhappy with her situation. I was also, but I believe my husband's allowance was more generous than my friend's. Yes, she did. She told me he was physically abusing her. All right. I don't like telling this in public, but yes, she said he was forcing her to perform her wifely duties."

It was interesting to see that her son, Samuel, had decided to remain. When he heard the words "wifely duties" he leaned forward in his doily-covered chair, until Clara thought he resembled a red-headed vulture above a carcass. Were all men alike when it came to physical passion?

"I don't know. She never said she wanted to harm him. She simply became more agitated, and I believe that's when she started taking the laudanum. I told her she shouldn't harm her body with a child on the way, but she got quite angry with me. She told me it was fine with me and my free love ways. Yes, I do have birth control. No, it should not make any difference when my best friend's life was in danger!"

Clara remembered that Adeline told her that each of these three witnesses had very different testimonies. Margaret Stanton seemed to be testifying for the defense. Perhaps all three witnesses were for the defense, and each one was a different perspective. This would have certainly made the case difficult for her friend, Laura Gordon. Of course, because Adeline could never remember what she had said after these channeling exhibitions, she would not be able to explain the context either. This was becoming quite complex, and Clara knew she would ultimately have to track down these witnesses for herself to get the real truth.

"Yes, Rachel told me she didn't know what to do about her husband's abuse. Her drug addiction was obviously just a symptom of this underlying cause. I told her as much. I understand. You have stated a common theme in the suffrage movement. We women, even if we come from the wealthiest families, do not have the legal recourse to confront our husbands about such matters. We become their playthings, their egotistical toys, if you will. When she told me she was afraid for her life, that's when I suggested she begin to gather evidence against him."

Clara realized this was her friend, Laura Gordon, asking the questions. Nobody else would pursue such pointed questions about women's rights. The attorney knew for certain she must question Gordon about this case.

"No, I don't believe Rachel could have planned her husband's death. She was in no mental or physical condition to do so. She was too broken by him and his constant abusive ways." Miss Quantrill's face reddened, and her neck flushed. The voice became a whisper. "I can't tell her about how Rachel said she held a knife over her husband's body as he slept. He had kept her in the basement for two days tied to the furnace. She told me she would have killed him, but the face of her departed mother, Rose, came to her, and she pleaded with Rachel, telling her that her soul would be damned forever if she did such an act. I can never tell them this, or my friend may be convicted!"

Adeline slumped forward, and her eyes lost their radiance from the channeling. When she raised her head, she looked all around.

Ah Toy touched the girl's arm. "Are you all right, my dear? May I get you something to drink or perhaps you should walk around a bit?"

"Oh. I am fine. I simply lost touch with where I was for a moment." The young woman yawned. "I should really get back to the orphanage. They will be expecting me."

"Does she remember what she has just said?" Elias Shortridge was standing now beside his chair.

"No, Father, she told us she never has memories of when she channels these personages. Adeline, I'll have Samuel escort you back to your residence. You have been most helpful. I believe we will be inquiring further into these matters. Can you do this again tomorrow? We can get the testimonies of the two other witnesses." Clara also stood and motioned for her son to escort the young woman back home.

"Thank you all for your gracious hospitality. I shall report back to you, Mrs. Foltz. It's an honor to have you trust me and see in me the possibility of assistance. I just want to save these women from harm." Adeline walked to the front door and waited. Samuel retrieved his frock coat from Hannigan, and the butler opened the door for the young people.

"Don't be taking the lassie over to the park now, Master Samuel," Hannigan said, and he winked. Samuel returned the gesture, but he did so by squeezing up the right side of his face into a grimacing wink parody.

***

Samuel Cortland Foltz did, indeed, escort the young lady in an around-about manner, but instead of the Golden Gate Park, he escorted her to the Chinatown Billiard Parlor near Portsmouth Square on Jackson Street. This was where he knew his friends, Roger and Ezra, would be.

"I know these adults really don't believe you can remember your entire life, but I do. I have thought about this process of recollection quite thoroughly, as a matter of fact." Samuel wanted to impress Adeline with his knowledge, as he found her quite attractive. He especially enjoyed the fact she wore dark mascara and eyeshadow, and that her eyebrows were shaved to resemble what he thought were two red flames affixed upon her forehead.

Adeline, who was walking beside him and looking straight ahead, turned her head sharply toward him, and her gray eyes pierced his soul. "Please, Master Samuel. Would you be gracing me with your bonnie reflection about memory?" she said, trying to imitate the voice of Hannigan.

Samuel did not laugh, as he wanted her to know what he thought. "The way I see it, it's like what the Transcendentalists, like Emerson and Thoreau, talked about. The Over Soul. All our minds are together inside this one big mind. And, some of us can envision a big part of that collective memory, and some of us just have small apertures. For example, enlightened people, such as Jesus and the Buddha, must be able to plug into it all. Most of us, I believe, only get these visions in our sleep. However, you, my young woman, can do it while putting yourself into a meditative trance. You said you see these memories as pictures, is that not the way it is?"

"Yes, there are two frames. In one, I see what everybody else sees in the present. In the other, I see what appears to me rather like Joseph Plateau's Phenakistoscope. Have you seen one? It spins to give the illusion of different moving images on circular display. My images, however, are all different, and they represent my entire life experience going back to my earliest memories. It is like a moving calendar in which I can organize and sort each frame to keep my mind occupied." Adeline kicked a small rock into the gutter, turned toward him, and smiled. "I do like your comparison to dreams, however, Samuel. The images I see of other people's minds do seem like I am dreaming while awake."

As they came upon the billiard house made of wood on Jackson, Samuel could see that his two friends were indeed playing at a table behind the green, frosted glass windows. He opened the tall door for Adeline, and she gazed up at the sign above the portal which said, "I obtained a new billiards table for my wife. Best trade I ever made."

The owner, Chang Bingwen, kept his hall clean and unrestricted to females, so he never sold alcoholic beverages. In fact, most of his clientele came from the wealthy young people who lived on Nob Hill and Pacific Heights, although as they were teenage, he also permitted the Chinese and Negro youth who lived around Market Street and in Chinatown. The children of the wealthy were not as racist as most of their parents. Few of the girls played at the tables. Instead, they would sit on the green felt stools that encircled the sixteen tables, which were laid out diametrically across the room's wide expanse of nine hundred square feet of polished redwood floor and wall space.

The hall had few players at this later hour, and Samuel walked to the back table near the tall desk where Mr. Chang collected the money and distributed the balls for play. He waved at the elderly Chinese man, who wore a frock coat and tie, but Bingwen also had on a red silk skullcap. Chang waved back. His rheumy, humor-filled eyes and wispy-gray, Fu Manchu mustache gave Mr. Chang the appearance of a wise grandfather who enjoyed fraternizing with the young. His English was halting but understandable.

"You bring new customer, Sam? That very good! May Mazu bless you with many children."

Samuel could see Adeline's neck redden, so he quickly turned to his friends, who were smoking long cigarillos and exchanging strokes at the multi-colored balls on the table, banking them against the sides in a noisy cacophony of physics on display. "I see you still enjoy taking Ezra's money. When are you going to play somebody of your own caliber, Ezzy? Or, are you attempting to become the Marquis de Sade of Chinatown?"

Ezra, who was seventeen, was an Orthodox Jew, and he had the long *peyot*, or side locks, under his Yarmulke skullcap. He was always dressed in a suit and tie. His parents were wealthy diamond merchants who came from New York to establish stores in San Francisco and Oakland. They sold precious gems and created magnificent pieces from the plentiful gold. Ezra was also thin as a rail, and his flashing dark eyes quickly surveyed Adeline, and he smirked.

"Wise grandfather, are you certain you are not Jewish? You say this young couple should be fruitful and multiply, in my people's glorious tradition!" Ezra stood, with his stick in his hand, his legs crossed, and the smirk still on his face. "May I be so bold as to ask who this lovely goddess is? She must have lost her way, following after the likes of you."

Roger Dowdy, eighteen, was the handsome, clean-shaven son of a mining engineer and a school teacher, and he was a towhead of over six feet. His almost white hair filled his brown derby and hung down in long strands over his broad shoulders. He never wore a suit or tie, and he dressed like his idol, Mr. John Muir, the famous naturalist. Roger wore Levi's and a vest, with a poet's white shirt beneath. He was soft-spoken and the frequent victim of Ezra's humor. Samuel enjoyed the company of both of his best friends.

"Ez. Are you going to play?" Roger frowned. Samuel saw that Adeline was staring fixedly at the tall youth with the bulging musculature. Ezra turned to look at the table. He bent over, stretched his cue stick out to aim at the white ball, and thrust his right arm forward, striking the cue ball, which, in turn, struck the collection of three billiard balls at the other end of the table.

"This, gentlemen, is Miss Adeline Quantrill. She is a gifted clairvoyant. Mother brought her home from one of her meetings.

Adeline will be helping us find a spiritualist who may have mesmerised a woman to kill her own husband. She was able to tell me what both of your names were, never having met you. She can receive thoughts like a teletype receives messages." Samuel sat down on one of the stools and pulled his feet up on the metal hoop encircling the three wooden legs.

"Mr. Dowdy is now planning to score three potted balls in a row, forcing Mr. Levine to make a foul stroke, thus ending the game." Adeline smiled at the tall Irish lad, and Samuel laughed when Roger's lower jaw hung open as he stared, incredulously, at this obvious witch.

"I would also wager that Adeline has never played the game of pocket billiards. Is this true, madam?" Samuel crossed his arms across his chest.

"No, I have never set foot in such an establishment. I detest smoke, as a matter of fact," she added, wrinkling up her snubbed nose.

Ezra stubbed out his cigarillo into a nearby abalone shell ashtray. Roger, however, took a deep puff, and blew the smoke in her direction. "Science has an explanation for everything. I doubt the young lady has any unusual powers of precognition. Coincidence can happen at any time."

"My mother, as you know, is not one to believe in magic. Yet she believes Adeline can assist her in this important case. In point of fact, I heard Adeline give word for word testimony that she remembered from a trial of which she was part. Adeline says she actually saw this woman kill her husband in the bedroom!" Samuel knew this information would get his friends' undivided attention, and it did. They both dropped their cue sticks down on the green felt table and hurried over to stand around her.

"How did she kill him?" Ezra asked. "If I may be so bold," he added.

Adeline stepped backward and looked down at her shoes. When she raised her head, she looked directly at Samuel. "I never told this to Mrs. Foltz. Shall I tell them, Samuel?" The orphan girl's gray eyes penetrated his being like the lighthouse at Point Bonita.

Samuel lowered his voice. "Go ahead. They won't say anything."

"I saw Mrs. Rachel Wilson-Rafferty kill her husband Brian by performing fellatio upon him." Samuel felt his heart begin to throb in his chest, as he watched Adeline's pouty lips mouth these words. "She stopped twice during the activity to chant something. He immediately fell into a stupor, as I watched from outside the bedroom. I don't know what actually caused his death."

"*Baruch atah adonai*!" Ezra chanted in Hebrew.

"Good god!" Samuel gasped, tugging at his necktie.

"He could have succumbed any number of ways without there being a murder. What did the coroner discover? Did he have a heart condition or aneurism?" Roger was ever the scientist.

"No, the coroner found nothing. No known poisonous substances in his bloodstream. No symptoms of stressors other than sexual. I did hear her thoughts as he died, however."

"Her thoughts? First, it's a bewitching curse, and now you can read minds? Balderdash!" Roger exclaimed.

"Go ahead, Adeline," Samuel coaxed, "what was she thinking?"

"She kept repeating the same two words, over and over. *Magia Sexualis.* It was the book I saw him use at the meetings. *Magia Sexualis: Sexual Practices for Magical Power*, by Dr. Paschal Beverly Randolph. He would teach the women from this book about how to obtain a magical power through the act of sexual intercourse." Adeline again turned away in embarrassment. "I am sorry. I can't discuss this further with you."

"Mother says she will find out about this book and who this mysterious spiritualist you mention really is. Gentlemen, Adeline can remember this man, as she has an autobiographical memory, but she cannot recall what he looks like nor what his name is. I have even listened to her as she has repeated his living voice with a deep, masculine resonance."

"I know one thing that may be possible," Roger said, his upper lip curling. "Adeline may have also come under this magician's spell. Her brain seems quite deranged."

***

"What do you have planned for tomorrow, Clara?" Ah Toy was thrusting into the fireplace wood with a steel poker. The sparks from the logs flew around like fireflies in the evening's glow inside the gigantic mansion. Clara enjoyed these moments together with her friend. They shared a glass of good wine before retiring to their rooms. All of the children, except Samuel, were already in bed. Clara and Ah Toy were still inside the library.

"I want to take Adeline with us to visit Laura Gordon. She knows exactly what happened during that case. I also want Laura to listen to our young clairvoyant channel the other two witnesses. Something tells me she never believed in the girl's abilities. Believe it or not, there are those who are even more skeptical of the supernatural than I. Laura de Force Gordon is one of these people." Clara sipped from her wine glass. The claret went down smoothly and warmed her stomach. After the day's events, Clara needed the anesthetic feeling that alcohol provided.

"I understand, Carrie. The supernatural must be experienced in person. Even then, if the mind is closed to the possibility, the event will never penetrate the intellectual barriers. We Chinese believe the West dichotomizes reality to protect its world of technological progress. What if there are both good and evil and even something more? That is what we believe. That something more is the world of the supernatural." Ah Toy gazed at the flames. Her face still had few wrinkles, and her optimism and acceptance about all possibilities made Clara feel good about life.

"As you now know, the legal profession requires steady logic and a sober outlook. I trust we will be entering a new dimension wherein there will be many more challenges to my training and experience as an attorney and now as a private detective. When you told me about your uncle, were you prepared to discuss with him about how he manipulates women? I mean, in the graphic and anatomical sense?" Clara sat down on the purple divan that was near the warmth of the roaring fireplace. She held her wine glass as a child holds a favorite doll or other toy, cradling it next to her bosom and often gazing down into its contents as one gazes into a reflective pond.

"Yes, I am. I have never done so because I was ashamed of him. In my own way, I believed my methods were the more humane and sympathetic to my female employees. However, I now realize, without my uncle's umbrella of money and power, I would have been ostracized from Chinatown much sooner than I was." Ah Toy turned from the fire and minced over to the divan. She sat, in her gentle way, next to Clara, and the attorney took her warm hands into her own and searched her face.

"This will require much courage from you, and I am so happy you have decided to be with me in this unique quest. I believe we both know how cruel lust can be. My husband, after having sired five magnificent children with me out on the plains of Iowa and Indiana, chose to desert us for a young woman half his age. You never married, and your uncle still uses young women to become rich and powerful. We must have been brought together by some supernatural force, don't you think?" Clara smiled at Ah Toy, and she felt closer to her then than ever before.

"You protected me with your status and legal expertise, and I am forever grateful to you for that. I am now returning the favor. When I explore the dark side of my own family, I am, indeed becoming closer to you. We Chinese have no better ability to withstand the trials that life gives us. We simply attempt to adjust, the way everybody else does. If humans don't learn that one lesson, they break." Ah Toy's dark eyes glistened as she gazed into the wavering flames of the fire. "I almost broke when my husband died on the steamship coming to this new world. However, because he had always told me how beautiful and attractive I was, I knew I could survive. I have used that natural gift these many years, and now I must return to the roots of this power we have over men. Perhaps its darker aspects will teach us both a lesson."

"Yes, when I found that young orphan inside the Rosicrucian home, I instinctively knew she would lead me somewhere that needed to be explored for the benefit of all women. Is this what you mean by supernatural?" Clara squeezed Ah Toy's hands.

"The supernatural is now, and it is all around us. It merely requires an open mind to accept its power." Ah Toy drained her wine glass and stood up. "Now my mind needs to shut down for the evening. Although, as we know, it often opens to the other reality in dreams. May your dreams be sweet, Carrie. And, those of your children."

The front door was opened by Hannigan, the butler, who was still on duty. Clara knew he liked to play Backgammon late with the old chauffeur, Giles Weston, inside the small room near the front entrance to the mansion.

"Who is it?" Ah Toy yelled in her usual way. Even though Mrs. Hopkins had the latest pneumatic telephonic devices installed throughout the house, Ah Toy preferred to shout. Clara said living inside this redwood monstrosity was like being in a canyon of echoing ghosts.

"It's Master Samuel," Hannigan said. "He has no lipstick on his coat, so I suppose we can let him in again. Cupid hasn't shot him yet." Clara wondered if Hannigan was having a glass of port as well.

Clara watched her oldest male child as he strode into the library. He had the black hair and darkly handsome complexion of his father, Jeremiah, the Civil War veteran, but his reflective hazel eyes within deep-set sockets were hers.

"Mother, may I go with you tomorrow to visit your attorney friend? I have some information I believe might concern you and your case." Samuel sat down next to Clara on the divan.

She put her arm around his shoulders and pulled him toward her. "Of course, you may. But what, might I ask, has created this new interest in my investigations? Could it be a certain young clairvoyant, perhaps?" Clara winked.

"Mother, listen to me. Adeline told us tonight what she saw inside that bedroom on the night of the murder of Mr. Rafferty."

Samuel's stern scowl made Clara pay attention. "Yes, go ahead. That information could be beneficial. If it's in detail. Remember. Evidence always requires specificity."

"I know. I've heard you enough times around the dinner table. She said Rachel Rafferty was performing fellatio on her husband, and he then passed out, never to breathe again. The coroner didn't discover any poisons in his bloodstream or was there any aneurism or other natural causes of his death." Samuel looked over at Ah Toy. "However, there was something more supernatural about what she heard," he added.

"What did she hear?" Ah Toy asked.

"She told us she could hear the wife's thoughts. She was thinking just two words, over and over. *Magia Sexualis.* It's Latin for sexual …"

"I know. Sexual magic. Dr. Paschal Beverly Randolph wrote the book. I am going to get a copy of it tomorrow at the library. Mrs. Hopkins has no such tome, as she is a devout Christian and would never have such an abominable text in her library." Clara stood up and put her arm around Ah Toy. "We have in our company perhaps one of the most magical interpreters of such discourse. What do you say, Ah Toy? Will this book unlock the passionate modus operandi of our spiritualist predator?"

Samuel also stood up. "Mother, do you always have to be so dramatic? It is not becoming for a sober barrister."

Ah Toy smiled. "You must keep your passions in reserve. Your mother and I will be exploring the gloomiest depths of male lust. Are you prepared for such an exploration, young man?"

Samuel winced. Clara believed he was hurt. "I believe in Adeline and her powers. It has nothing to do with physical passion! She needs someone who will be on her side. Even though you two older women believe you have her best interests in mind, I don't see her getting through this without support from her age group. She has never been accepted by young people, and she sought out adults only to survive."

"Oh my! That is quite a profound insight coming from one just out of knee britches." Clara tousled her son's dark hair with her extended hand.

"Stop! I am deadly serious, Mother! Adeline's power could turn against us at any moment, and I want to protect you when it happens." Samuel marched off into the hallway and stood near the stairs leading up to the bedrooms. He was glaring back at her.

Clara deepened her voice into a masculine baritone. "Watch what you dream, young master! The Succubus may come to you, and steal your manhood, like a raven who swipes a glittering bauble from around the neck of a sleeping prince."

Samuel let out a burst of exasperated air from his lungs, and lurched, in a stampeding run, up the stairs and out of sight.

Chapter 4: The Second Witness

City Hall, San Francisco, May 3, 1886.

Laura de Force Gordon, Esq. was trying a case. As the only female attorneys working in San Francisco, Clara and she were not only good friends, they were also competitors. The most publicized criminal trial in America took place between the two women in December 1880. They were the first two females ever to try a criminal case in the United States. Clara was able to convict the defendant, Mr. Wheeler, of the murder of his sister-in-law, but the conviction was overturned on appeal because of faulty evidence brought forth by her boss, the San Francisco District Attorney.

Clara knew Laura was now, like she, working on mostly divorce and family law cases, as the public still did not trust women attorneys with the more important jobs of contracts, torts and probate law. They also made supplemental money by speaking at a variety of political venues across the western states. Now that they worked independently as defense attorneys, they shared a lot of pointers and legal information as well as the social discussions they enjoyed as friends.

Clara, along with Ah Toy, Adeline, and her son, Samuel, waited outside the courtroom for Laura to finish. Mrs. Foltz heard the familiar noises and smelled the unique odors of the San Francisco City Hall on Market Street. The clicking of nervous lawyers' and visitors' shoes, which were pacing along the colorful tiles, and the pungent tobacco smoke trailed from the numerous pipes, cigars, and cigarettes stuck in their mouths.

There were also the frantic whispers of family members and newspaper reporters, after a verdict was read, and the variety of colognes, perfumes and body fragrances, coming from the attorneys and the key witnesses, who hoped to make a lasting impression upon a jury. And, if it were a big criminal case, there would be a variety of special interest groups assembled to voice their grievances and to take up the cause of one side or the other. Within the assembled groups would be the smells of popcorn, alcohol, and frankfurters sold by outside vendors to appease the crowds' hunger.

When the double-doors to the courtroom finally whooshed open, Clara stood up to greet her friend. Laura was alone, trailing after the line of gallery visitors, witnesses and opposing attorneys. Clara enjoyed being with Laura because they had much in common, and yet their personalities, dress, and courtroom styles were quite different.

Clara saw her friend was wearing a plain black cotton dress, with a ruffled white blouse showing at the sleeves and at her throat collar. She had puffy shoulders but no bustle. Laura's dark complexion and black hair contrasted with Clara's almost porcelain skin and reddish-blonde hair. Clara's big bustled, red satin "city dress," complete with matching hat and parasol, made the shorter attorney look like a woman of the people, which she indeed saw herself as being.

Clara took Laura's hands into her own and smiled. "By that rather dour expression, I would wager your efforts today for your client were not rewarded."

"It was that old rooster, Judge Ryan. He wouldn't grant me a continuance. He still believes women who practice law are taking jobs from more capable men. To his way of thinking, we should still be at home tending the babies. I divorced because my husband was a philanderer, and, thank goodness, we never had children. However, you and I must lie to the patriarchal establishment and tell them we're widows, or the prejudices we face will extend to our social lives. Must we have to face them at work as well?" Laura nodded at Ah Toy. "Another fighter for women's independence, I gather. How are you, Miss?"

"I am well. My name is Ah Toy, and I am Mrs. Foltz's assistant. We've brought you another freedom fighter you may recognize. Miss Adeline Quantrill." Ah Toy extended her arm toward the young woman, who stood in the back of the group, behind Samuel. When the girl stepped forward, Clara saw Laura's brown eyes widen.

"Oh yes! The Rafferty case. I am sorry you were treated so horribly by those men. We could have kept Rachel out of prison had you been able to testify."

Adeline nodded, but she then retreated to her place behind Samuel.

"Samuel. Have you taken to your mother's profession? Is she giving you the grand tour at last?" Laura extended her arms wide apart. "Did you know that to make more money, the developers of this city hall stuffed sand inside the walls? A carpenter showed me one day. He said it was the oldest trick in the book to make cheap infrastructures appear solid."

"I know. Mother told me. And, no, I am not following in her footsteps. I want to become a professional gambler at billiards." Samuel combed his right hand through his black hair and curled the left side of his upper lip.

"So arrogant! He looks just like his father when he does that," Clara said. "Laura, if it's not too much trouble, could we take you out for lunch? We want to ask you about the Rafferty case. Also, Miss Quantrill can perform a bit of unique testifying for us. Therefore, we'll need a private dining room. Do you know of any nearby restaurant that can provide such accommodations?"

"As a matter of fact, I do. I take my clients over to Pablo's next to the floral shop. It's a Mexican cantina and restaurant with rooms in the back for private meetings. During the Gold Rush, men would negotiate claims in secret inside those rooms. You see, Pablo is deaf. Lost his hearing in a mining accident. All of his waiters and bartenders are also without hearing." Laura smiled and began walking down the hall toward the exit.

"I should have expected as much," Clara remarked, following her friend and motioning for the others to do the same.

***

They all sat in the back room, around a circular table. Pablo, the owner, was pouring lemonade into each glass, nodding his head and smiling as he did so. Clara found him quite agreeable, and he wore loose, white silk trousers and a matching blouse, with a red silk sash tied around his portly middle. His huarache sandals appealed to Samuel, and Clara watched as her son pointed down at them and mouthed, *¿Cuànto questa?* Pablo rushed into another room and returned with several sizes of the same sandal. Samuel matched his size and handed the owner two dollars.

"I do believe had I been married to Pablo, I might have stayed married. He never has to have the last word, the way Harold did, and

I've never seen him eyeing the *señoritas*." Laura laughed, toasting her glass of lemonade. "Here's to a productive meeting!"

Everyone at the table raised his or her glass and then drank from it.

"I've ordered the special. Chiles rellenos and beef enchiladas. I'm certain you'll enjoy them," Laura said, smoothing the cloth napkin on her lap. "Now, what is this unique testimony that Miss Quantrill has to present?" Laura took a fried tortilla chip from a basket on the table and dipped it into a bowl of red salsa. "It's not Mexican hot. It's *gringo* hot," she explained, biting the triangular chip in half.

"First, let me explain the history of our meeting and why we are here," Clara said, her voice taking on its usual lecturing clarity. "I found Adeline at my Rosicrucian meeting. She was quite distressed, so I escorted her to the Hopkins mansion where Ah Toy informed me, after having put the young woman through several supernatural experiments, that Adeline is at the very least a clairvoyant and, quite possibly, even a telepathist."

Laura frowned. "Yes, I'm aware of her so-called supernatural abilities. They were not recognized by the court, as you must now be aware."

"According to Adeline, the judge was a bit prejudiced. This is not important, because what I want you to hear is her channeling of the second witness who appeared on that day in court. And I know what you are thinking. We could simply get the transcript of the trial. However, what is unique about Adeline's ability is that she can also provide us with what the witness was thinking at the time." Clara dipped her chip into the salsa and brought it to her mouth. "She can read some people's minds," she added, thrusting the chip between her lips and crunching down on it.

"Now, Clara. Surely you can't believe …" Laura began.

"My name is Ariel Washington." Adeline was staring into space, and her voice was again different, high-pitched, with a Southern twang. "I worked as Mrs. Rafferty's upstairs maid at the address you stated. I came here from North Carolina in 1885, and I met the Mrs. at the Rosicrucian meeting. Yes, I could attend because the spiritualist in charge was also a Negro. He studied under Dr. Paschal Randolph, the famous mystic who counseled President Lincoln and his wife after their son died."

Laura leaned over and whispered to Clara, "She's repeating the testimony word for word."

Clara squeezed Laura's forearm. "We've heard Margaret Bennington-Stanton's testimony, but I must tell you what Mrs. Stanton was thinking."

Adeline continued, "He told us he must remain anonymous. We were told he was visiting many spiritualist groups around the United States to assist women in their fight for independence. I believe Mrs. Rafferty was so impressed by him that she offered me the job in her home. She believed because he had mesmerized me that I could help her pacify her husband." Adeline looked down at the table in front of her. As Pablo slid a plate with steaming rellenos and enchilada under her face, he stared at her. The owner was cautious, as he saw that everyone at the table had affixed their gazes upon the young woman and were not eating. He almost knocked over her glass of lemonade when Adeline's voice screamed, "No, master! I won't ever tell them about you! Women will never become empowered until you can accomplish your work."

"It's all right, Pablo," Laura said, flicking the fingers on her right hand, motioning for him to leave the room. "We won't need your services anymore."

When Adeline Quantrill came out of her trance, it was if she had never been channeling. She picked the fork up and began to slice into the enchilada as if nothing had happened.

"She never remembers when she channels another person. However, she does recall all of the moments in her personal history." Clara explained the facts as if she were reading from a railroad mechanic's manual, and the young medium was the latest model of steam engine. "When she channeled the testimony of your first witness, Mrs. Stanton, she also told us what the woman was thinking on the stand."

"Is that so. May I ask what those thoughts were?" Laura shook her head. "I was the attorney of record, but she never told me. Although, I can't truly believe I am asking this."

Ah Toy cleared her throat. "As I told Clara, I have witnessed this kind of supernatural ability during my job as a Madame in Chinatown. There are people who can do this."

"Adeline can read minds. I heard her myself." Samuel said, in-between bites. "She knew my friends' names before meeting them, and she knew what Roger Dowdy was thinking when he was playing billiards. She had never played or been inside a billiard parlor before."

Laura tapped the handle of her fork on the glass of lemonade. "Please! Stay on topic. What did my witness, Mrs. Stanton, think?"

Clara smiled. "I see you continue to be the patient attorney. Your lead witness was thinking about what Rachel Rafferty told her concerning her husband's abuse at home. After he tortured her, and kept her locked down in the basement, she held a knife over him as he slept. She told Mrs. Stanton that she wanted to kill him."

Laura frowned. "Torture, imprisonment, and murder threats? My dear Clara, I finally understand what you have uncovered." She pushed her plate away and stood up. "You have revealed the melodramatic fantasies of a teenage orphan!"

Ah Toy also stood up. "No, Mrs. Gordon! This young woman is cursed with her abilities, and I can show you the dark side of such power, if you'll come with us to Chinatown."

"Chinatown? What can you show me there, pray tell?"

"My uncle has this power. He has used his dark powers to control over one thousand young women. They are his sex slaves, and I want you to see how he does it."

"Laura, we believe he might be the key to stopping the murder of husbands like Mr. Rafferty." Clara watched Laura's face. She was still scowling, much the way her lover, and Captain of Detectives, Isaiah Lees, often appeared.

"Murder of husbands? Now we have conspiracy afoot? How so?"

"We believe there is a connection between the book by Dr. Randolph and this mysterious spiritualist that Adeline cannot recall. We think the girl may have also come under his powers, and that's why she has no memory of his identity."

Clara stood up and noticed her friend's scowl had disappeared. Although always a skeptic, Laura de Force Gordon, Clara knew, could never resist proving these spiritualists were fakes. Laura, before she became an attorney, was herself a professional medium.

"Why are you waiting? Take me to the den of this Chinese charlatan!" Laura waved her arm over her head and yelled, "Pablo!"

"Laura, aren't you forgetting something?" Clara smiled.

"What is that?" Her friend asked.

"Don't you remember? Pablo is deaf."

***

Ah Toy was distracted as she escorted her friends to Chinatown. Not only was she going to visit her uncle, Fung Jing Toy, a man denounced by her family back home, but she was also returning to a place where she was, just two years earlier, held captive by a crazed Chinese killer until she was rescued by Clara. She had to survive for fifteen years in a profession that degraded women, and now she was showing these white people just how degenerate her people could be.

As they walked up to the entrance to Chinatown on Dupont Street, Ah Toy could smell the odors and see the sights that had greeted her for those many years. As a ghetto for mostly males, the burning tobacco, frying restaurant food, and pungent incense so intensely mixed with the saloon alcohol and human urine in the alleyways that it made the eyes water.

To Ah Toy, the colorful lanterns strung as decorations between the wooden buildings were symbols of despair. It was as if the entire female population had been stuffed inside many paper lanterns, each one burning like hell on the inside. These trapped Chinese women could only stare from their cages out at the streets beyond, seeing all they were missing, where life in the rest of San Francisco continued in a normal fashion.

Ah Toy believed she somehow had to redeem her people. This was why she had used her influence to allow Clara and her family to stay with her at the Hopkins mansion. And now, she was trying to help her best friend again in a case that might show how her people could help, even if they were criminals.

"Please. Stop right here." Ah Toy turned to address her companions. "You are going to meet a man who represents the dark side of the Chinese population. There are thousands who work in the mines, on the railroads, in the laundries, and in the restaurants, and they never meet such men as my uncle. True, quite often, they must pay money for protection by the Tongs, the gangs which Little Pete represents, but this is often not voluntary. My uncle and his men will tell you they were created because of white oppression and racist attacks. These men, including my uncle, were outcasts in this new land because they came from the poor Han classes back in Canton."

Laura Gordon nodded. "Yes, I've read about that. The Han hated the Manchu leaders because they cooperated with the British after the Opium Wars in the 1840s. The Qing never allowed the Hans to become educated or to hold civil service jobs. Only the Mandarins could compete for work."

"My uncle and his friends formed secret societies to rebel against the Qing Empire of the Manchu and restore the Ming Dynasty, which would return the more populous Han people to control the military and merchants."

"Yes, and most of these class distinctions were based on heredity. Ah Toy's family did not have the money, which was given to these men from the special Manchu families, when they traveled by steamship to San Francisco. These loyal Manchu men were sent to establish order in San Francisco and to force the workers to keep the traditions of loyalty to the Manchu back home," Clara pointed out. Ah Toy had informed her friend about the Toy family, in general, but Clara was not aware of Little Pete's story.

"The secret Tong society became powerful because of greed. In China, gambling is legal, so the Tongs continued that tradition, and the Six Companies also agreed that it was proper. Many San Francisco government officials reaped money from Tong bribes, and when my uncle and others began to expand these services to saloons, opium dens, and, finally, prostitution, none of the men in power said anything because most were getting money from these highly profitable activities." Ah Toy turned around to face the door to the tall, four-story building. It was painted white with blue trim, and a large sign on the second floor said: HIP YEE TONG.

"My uncle heads the Hip Yee group. The Chinese word "tong" means hall in English. Most of his group's money comes from prostitution, gambling and opium." Ah Toy began her laborious mincing walk up the wooden steps of the structure.

"If they're supposed to be illegal, then why do they advertise the name on the front?" Samuel asked.

Ah Toy turned toward Samuel on her right. "I'm sorry to admit, but my uncle and the Tongs belong to secret societies that take pride in their underground methods and unique trickery. In fact, most violence only happens between rival Tongs and not against the public. Because of this, the San Francisco police don't bother them too much, except for the Chinatown Squad."

"As we saw in the murders of those prostitutes, the Chinatown Squad is racist and has a political agenda," Clara said, bringing up the rear.

Ah Toy could hear the commotion inside the hall as they approached the door to her uncle's office on the third floor. She was dreading the meeting, as Fung Jing Toy had always stood for everything she detested about life in Chinatown. She understood the fact that the main population of men had not assimilated into San Francisco society because they did not understand the culture and had always seen themselves as vagabonds from China who would soon return home. They never wanted to make this new society their home because old traditions die hard.

Sadly, because of the rebellion going on against the Qing Empire, many of the men respected Little Pete for his stand against the Manchu back home. Most believed the Manchu sold out to the corrupt politicians in America, the same way they had sold out to the British during the Opium Wars: in order to oppress and control the Chinese Han and now the immigrants.

As Ah Toy opened the door with the golden dragon etched upon the front, she looked back at her friends. Samuel was first, directly behind her, then Laura Gordon, and finally Clara. However, hidden around the corner, in the shadows next to the railing, stood the medium, Adeline Quantrill.

Ah Toy stepped back outside for a moment and gestured toward the girl. "Come, my dear. My uncle is also empowered with your gift. We must, however, praise him to find out what we need to save women."

"Good point," Laura said, and she moved to take Adeline's hand. The girl jerked her hand away, lifted her chin, and followed Ah Toy inside.

Little Pete's office was a vestibule outside the main meeting hall. It was enclosed, about twelve feet square and six feet high, and it contained the group of six men assembled to greet Ah Toy and her friends when they arrived. She recognized her uncle immediately. He was the only man in the room who wore a steel chainmail shirt over his Ming-style black blouse. He also employed a Caucasian bodyguard, a hulk of a man named C. H. Hunter. Little Pete reasoned that no rival gang member would risk killing a white man to get to him. Ah Toy saw that all of the blouses these men wore had the Ming round collar, and in the most rebellious affect, none wore the long queue pigtail demanded by the Manchu leaders in China. They also wore black Western fedora hats folded down over their foreheads.

These Manchu leaders back in southern China, of course, demanded queues, Qing clothing, and subservience from all the San Francisco Chinese, but Little Pete and his men had refused to comply. They told the others they were rebelling out of principle and because they had joined their secret Triad "Hung Mun" or "San Hwo Hui" society, which wanted to return the Ming Emperors back to the throne. Ah Toy knew, however, that her uncle's group was more of a criminal syndicate that used the pseudo-political goals as a front to gain popularity during their take-over. The 1882 Chinese Exclusion Act had restricted new immigration, and these gangsters had filled the vacuum of oppression quickly.

Little Pete walked leisurely over to Ah Toy and bowed deeply. She noticed the same intelligent gleam in his dark eyes that she saw every morning in the mirror, but she did not trust his type of genius. She knew his dark good looks and rakish scar across his brow were meant to impress the white businessmen and officials with whom he contracted his illegal activities, and his excellent English language skills were almost as strong as hers.

"You have not visited me in many years, and my friends have asked about you. Have you been ill? Do you hate your little uncle now?"

Ah Toy's smile was purposely wide and superior. "I do not hate any human. I hate only what humans do. My friends and I have come seeking your specialized assistance. As you are aware, we are working on a legal case that resulted in the death of a husband. We think there may be a supernatural cause. This young woman has the same *wu* powers that you have. She can channel the spirits from the past, but we have yet to hear her channel the dead or any deities. What we need is for you to show us how you train your women to do their work for you. Also, is it possible to train them to kill?" Ah Toy minced her steps, but she never did this to words in a conversation. She knew beforehand that her uncle would be looking for something he could get in return for his "good deed," so she was prepared.

"How impolite you are, niece! You rush into your goal without introducing me to your friends. I am losing face. Not a good thing if you want a favor from me." It was her uncle's turn to smile with indignation.

"My name is Laura de Force Gordon, attorney-at-law. So good to make your acquaintance, sir." Laura bowed, attempting to follow the proper etiquette.

"Clara Shortridge Foltz. I am your niece's best friend and confidant. You are helping us tremendously in this matter. Thanks to you, we may be able to stop the murders of many men."

"Samuel Cortland Foltz. I am her son," Samuel said, pointing his right thumb at his mother.

"Samuel. Yes, my employee, Chang Bingwen, has told me all about you. You are quite good at billiards, and you would like to become a professional gamer one day. A very admirable avocation indeed!" Fung Toy mimed stroking a cue stick across an invisible table.

Ah Toy watched Clara frown at her son, but Samuel smiled back at her. "Do you see? He knows one can make money playing billiards."

"I think I may be able to assist you in your endeavor, my lad," Little Pete noted something on a piece of paper, and then he walked slowly over to stand in front of Adeline. He gazed straight into the girl's gray eyes, as he was the same height, and his face became tranquilized and rigid. He began to moan softly, and soon, she also began to chant her whispering prayers. The room became a cacophony of resonate whispering, humming and deep moaning.

Uncle Pete completed his mesmerizing chant with Adeline by taking his fedora off his head and placing it upon the girl's curly-black hair. "There! Is she not the image of Sarah Bernhardt as the Princess Romanoff in *Fédora*?" Ah Toy knew the reference. Many suffragettes, as a result of the sexy French actress's cross-dressing in the play, had taken to wearing such hats.

"Will you tell us about how you control your women?" Ah Toy asked.

The words were barely out of her mouth when Adeline, in a swift lurch, reached over to Uncle Pete's waist and snatched his foot-long hatchet from under his chain mail. The young woman's eyes flashed and her brows furrowed, as she attacked the huge bodyguard, C. H. Hunter. The razor-sharp flat blade was just about to slice into the tall man's belly when Ah Toy heard her uncle shout, "Desist!" Gasping, and dropping the blade to the floor, Adeline turned toward her spiritual guide. Her gray eyes were wide and pleading for release, or so Ah Toy believed.

"She is indeed a channel for spirits of the dead. I called the spirit of the female assassin, Charlotte Corday, who murdered the Revolutionary French Journalist, Jean-Paul Marat in 1793, during France's Reign of Terror. My faithful guard, Mr. Hunter, became Charlotte's target."

"You mean she would have killed that man had you not called out?" Clara asked.

"My niece asked how I accomplish this control over my ladies. I similarly create a possession of the spirit, but I also need drugs to aid in my mesmerizing task. With this young woman, who is a superb receiver, I needed no such pharmacological inducements. The spirit from the past could be channeled directly into her being, as you have all witnessed." Little Pete, Mr. Chinatown, walked over to the girl, placed his hand on her forehead, and she exhaled. Ah Toy noticed that a look of calm reverie had returned to her face.

"Do you believe the spiritualist who worked with Rachel Rafferty also performed a similar activity?" Laura asked. "I can't believe it. No mind can be controlled to murder."

The gang leader shook his head. "The mind is not controlled, dear lady. It is possessed by a powerful suggestion. The drugs I use, in combination with my innate powers of mesmerism, can channel the correct spirit for the purpose. In most cases, it requires many weeks of isolation and conditioned deprivation before it can work. And, yes, one can eventually create a murderess under the proper circumstances. I have done so myself."

"Uncle, you have gone beyond human decency! I am appalled." Ah Toy had not expected such a confession from her relative. She wondered what Clara thought of her family now.

Ah Toy watched, as Fung Toy, whom she no longer recognized as her uncle, began to pace, like a caged tiger, across the room. "If a rival has taken out a ten-thousand-dollar contract on your life, then you might go to such indecent lengths to stay alive. These women are my property. I paid for them, and I own them. For the most part, when I take them to the exclusive bordellos at the city's Palace

Hotel, to romantically cavort with the high society barons of San Francisco, they live a life better than any existence they could live in China, or in most places in this country. What is one sacrifice to save the life of the person who gives them such opulent joy?"

"Please, friends, we must go. I am so sorry to have brought you here. I never want to see him again!" Ah Toy turned and began mincing toward the exit.

"No, wait. Can you teach Adeline how to stop these murders from happening? If one can cause it to happen, then one can prevent it as well, no?" Clara walked over to stand in front of the short Chinese man. Ah Toy noticed her friend was a head taller than her uncle.

Little Pete looked up into Clara's face and grinned. "Perhaps, but what do I receive for my teacher's fee? I am giving away the secrets of the ancient spiritual guides from my culture."

Laura stepped forward. "First, we have no guarantee this trickery of yours will work or even if it is true. For all we know, you could have set-up this entertainment, with our little orphan here, behind our backs. I am not the indulgent soul that my friend Clara might be. I was also a professional medium, and I know the tricks. I need much more proof than this."

"I see. Then, I must bid you adieu. I have a busy schedule today. Remember, niece, when we first arrived here at the New Gold Mountain? I got my job at the shoe factory and learned to trick the city's restaurants into buying plugs of skate and stingray sold as scallops? And when the Mexicans had those gold coins? We just started shaving them and soon had sacks filled with gold powder. We began making the real money with lotteries, gambling, and the relaxed smoking dens. And you were selling … let's see, what is it you were selling?"

Ah Toy opened the door and stepped out on the stair platform. "This was all a big mistake. We need to leave right now."

"I would like to leave the door open here. If we decide to ask for your help again, may I contact you?" Clara asked.

"Certainly," Little Pete said. "Just remember what I said about payment. Life does not occur without retribution. It is the wheel of karmic justice. You two women are attorneys. I am certain you understand."

“We can see how it applies to your life,” Ah Toy scoffed. As she watched her friends leave, she noticed that her uncle placed a note into Samuel’s palm as he shook hands with the boy. When he was outside with her, Ah Toy asked him, “What did he say in that note?”

Samuel opened the note and read it out loud. “Come to the Chinatown Billiard Parlor tomorrow night at seven. I will introduce you to some money players.”

Clara shook her head. “Oh no. You are not going there to see this man.”

“Mother, you just agreed to keep the door open to allow this gangster to teach Adeline how to become a mesmerist. However, you will not allow me to learn to make money playing pocket billiards?”

“Not alone. I will not allow you to meet with him unless I am with you.”

Samuel began to leap down the stairs, two steps at a time. Adeline followed close behind.

Clara turned to Ah Toy. “He has become more distant the last year. He even said he may want to visit his father in San Jose. What should I do?”

“The more you pressure him, the more he will pull away. You must attempt to bond with him in a way that makes him feel you are allowing him to mature in his own direction.”

“Thank you. I often feel quite alone as a mother. My parents are aging, and both Samuel and Trella have been striking out on their own.”

Ah Toy smiled and placed her hand on Clara’s shoulder. “They all have to search alone, at some point. We can only guide them until they understand that what we have taught them will be inside when they make important choices. Ultimately, it is we who must have faith in them.”

“Faith without works is dead,” Laura interjected. “I heard Clara’s father say that, and I liked how it sounded. I think we still have a lot of work to do on this case.”

Chapter 5: The Third Witness

The Hopkins Mansion, One Nob Hill, San Francisco, May 4, 1886.

Captain of Detectives of the San Francisco Police Department, Isaiah Lees, was waiting for the group when they returned to the mansion. He was playing cribbage with Hannigan in the room near the entrance. At fifty-six, Captain Lees was still robust, and he was wearing the outfit he wore on cases: a brown frock coat and vest with checkered pants and spit-shined Oxfords. He also had his gray cape hanging behind him on the chair, which had become his trademark, along with the Bowie knife he kept in a leather sheath around his waist and under the vest. When Clara kissed him, after he stood up, she enjoyed the tickle of his gray goatee. She remembered his first true kiss at the celebration of solving their first case together that they had in the mansion with all the family present.

"A small bird has told me you have been investigating a murder that was resolved some time ago. Mrs. Rachel Wilson-Rafferty is now in prison for her manslaughter conviction, and you want to prove she was not in her right mind when her husband died." Lees bent over the table and moved his cribbage peg ten spaces and pushed it down into the rectangular board. "Four and four are eight, and two are ten." Clara always enjoyed Isaiah's voice, as it had the British accent she found so romantic. Lees had been born in Lancashire, and he came to San Francisco seeking adventure in 1848.

"Where is Sergeant Vanderheiden? I wanted him to see my new painting of Hunter's Point," Ah Toy said, referring to the Captain's partner on the force.

"Dutch needed to visit his sick aunt in Holland. She was the one who paid his fare to San Francisco when he was eighteen. He and I never got the gold fever, but we certainly got tangled up with you, my golden girls." Lees smiled. "Tell me what you have so far in this case. I have some news that may put some spring in your bonnets. I think you might also need more help."

Clara knew Isaiah had some important news because he never came to the mansion unless it was important. He hated the railroad tycoons, and Mrs. Hopkins had been married to one of the "big four" owners. "Who was this little bird to which you refer? I don't even know if we want help from the police at this stage of our inquiry."

"Trella Evelyn. She was worried that her mother was venturing into dangerous territory, and she wanted me to help you. You know how I get when you don't include me in your little adventures. I feel like the cat who gets left outside the rabbit hole when Alice falls down into it."

"All right. First, Mr. Hannigan, would you please fetch my daughter from her meditation spot, if she's at home. We must adjourn to the library to pursue this matter further, and I want her to be in on the discussion." Clara waved her hand over her head like a cattle driver and began the journey into the library. The rest of the group followed her.

Clara noticed that Laura was walking next to Isaiah, and she felt a shiver of jealousy go down her spine. When they entered the room, she quickly escorted Isaiah to his chair at the table and sat down next to him. Laura sat on the other side of Captain Lees, and then Ah Toy, Samuel, and Adeline.

"I believe you have come at the right time to get involved. We were just about to hear from our young medium concerning the third and final witness's testimony during the trial of Rachel Rafferty." Clara pointed toward Adeline.

Laura touched Isaiah's sleeve, and Clara felt another shiver of jealousy. "I am not a believer in this kind of supernaturalism. You see, before I became an attorney, I made money as a spiritualist medium. I know all the tricks of the trade. This young woman, however, seems to be one of the best impersonators I have ever met."

"Here is Miss Trella, mum," Hannigan said, standing at the entrance to the library. Clara pointed to a chair next to Adeline, and her daughter obediently took a seat. The twenty-year-old cast a furtive glance toward Captain Lees and raised her eyebrows.

"Please, Adeline. Can you commence with your channeling?" Clara nodded at the girl. She began to moan, the way she had done in Chinatown, and soon a strange female voice was taking over the room, as if one of the authors of a book on the stacks along the walls had decided to lecture to those gathered there.

"I worked for Dr. Adam McCauley. Yes, he was the one who mesmerized the defendant, Rachel Wilson-Rafferty. My full name? Elizabeth Harter-Bloomfield. I live on California Street, next to the Hopkins mansion on Nob Hill. I do know Mrs. Hopkins. I visited her quite frequently after her husband passed, as we both belonged to the same church, and we saw each other at various philanthropic clubs. My husband, Jonas, owns the largest mining equipment manufacturing company in California. No, Mrs. Hopkins is not a suffragette. Yes, I am sympathetic to the cause of women's rights. Many of my husband's employees had wives who came to our Rosicrucian meeting." The voice Adeline was channeling had the erudite tones of a wealthy matron.

Ah Toy whispered to Clara, "I've sold two paintings to her. She is a very intelligent and kind woman."

"I did see Dr. McCauley perform his specialty on Rachel Rafferty. However, you must understand that this doctor is not a person who does anything to control a woman. His activities are right out in the open, and everybody in attendance can watch him do what he is trying to do. What is he trying to do? He wants to make the abused women feel more comfortable about themselves and about the traumas they have experienced. After he completes his thought suggestions and relaxation exercises, the women—including Mrs. Rafferty—will always feel much better, and they always thank him."

Clara sighed. "I don't believe this witness will get us any further into this case than we are right now."

However, when Adeline began to whisper, her voice sounded like a frightened woman, and Clara leaned forward to listen. "Rachel said she would kill me if I told them the truth. She learned about a better way to stop her husband from torturing her. Dr. Paschal Beverly Randolph's wife, Kate Corson-Randolph, is still alive in Toledo, Ohio. After reading *Magia Sexualis*, Rachel took the train out to visit Mrs. Randolph to find out if Dr. Randolph has any trusted disciples she can call upon. Most of the men who become sex therapists use women as a way to make men more powerful. Some even advocate the use of prostitutes for the men. Rachel needed somebody who could help her stop Brian from killing her. Murder must be on her mind or she would not have threatened me. But I cannot afford the scandal it will cause my husband and my family, so I must remain silent."

Laura reached over across Isaiah and tapped Clara on her arm. "Is this what you call reading minds?"

Adeline had returned to her normal state of consciousness. Her somnambulant trance was gone, and she looked around at the others, her gray eyes wide and inquisitive.

"Yes, what you heard whispered was the mental projections of Mrs. Bloomfield," said Clara, who had been taking notes on her pad as the young woman spoke. "These thoughts from the witnesses are what make our young clairvoyant so valuable. However, we now must plan our investigation. We have collected enough information to assimilate it into our strategy. This information, especially the thoughts of these witnesses, must be verified. But first I want to hear the news Isaiah has for us." Clara nodded toward the captain and smiled.

Lees brought out a piece of paper from his frock coat pocket, unfolded it, and began to read. "There have been reports made over the telegraph from New York City. Jay Gould, on Wall Street, reported to all police connected by Western Union that three of his close friends were murdered in their beds last week. Two were killed by their wives, and one was done in by a clandestine mistress. This is the important part. Each of these women was a suffragette and a frequent attendant at the Manhattan spiritualist meetings."

"My god! This could be related to our case." Clara scribbled down the information on her pad.

"I am afraid it is. In each instance, the woman had been consulting with an unknown mesmerist, who was supposedly giving therapy to her concerning her intimate affairs with her husband. In the case of the mistress, of course, it was an affair out of marriage." Isaiah cleared his throat, and Clara could see he was embarrassed, as his neck was flushed. "You know how I feel about these railroad rogues, Clara. Gould is one of the worst robber barons in the country. But he wouldn't lie about something like this. When I checked with the New York Police Commissioner's Office, I found out it was true."

"What is happening as a result? I can't imagine Gould allowing this to happen without some kind of retribution against the Suffrage Movement," Laura said.

Lees frowned. "You are spot on, Mrs. Gordon. All of the spiritualist meeting groups in New York have been ordered shut down until this mesmerist is caught, and Gould has contacted his lackeys in Congress to draft a hasty bill to close the rest of the meeting places in the entire United States."

"They can't do that!" Clara was shouting, something she rarely did. "The only places we can speak with each other candidly about our politics are inside those rooms. Laura, we must put up a fight to keep our groups open!"

"Mother, how can you do that when you have already become committed to finding this mysterious somnambulist?" Trella Evelyn pointed out.

"Your daughter is correct. We have enough of our people who live in New York and in Washington D. C. to take up the cause for us. I shall send them telegrams tonight," Laura said.

"I understand. I have had to do so much on my own that I often forget how many friends I have. We must track down this mesmerist and stop these murders." Clara looked down at her notes. "From what we now know, I believe the best course of action is to discover who became a disciple of Dr. Paschal Randolph. I am going to leave for Toledo, Ohio tomorrow. I shall visit Mrs. Katherine Corson Randolph. She should be able to tell me who her late husband was tutoring or to whom he may have bequeathed his mesmerizing and animal magnetism abilities."

"Mesmerizing and magnetism chicanery, you mean," Laura said. "As for me, I will make certain no such federal law gets passed to close our meeting places."

Clara turned toward her attorney friend. "No, delegate that job. I want you to go with Trella and question those witnesses again. I know you are not a believer, but if we can get the truth out of them, we may discover some more clues as to this mesmerist's identity." Clara turned around from Laura and faced Adeline. "Will the orphanage allow you to travel with me to Ohio? I want Mrs. Randolph to meet you. If she sees we are sympathetic to her late husband's spiritualism, then she will be more amenable to helping us."

"Yes, I am certain they …" Adeline began.

Samuel pounded his fist on the table. "Mother, you can't take her. I wanted her to come with Roger, Ezra and me to visit the scene of the murder, Mrs. Rafferty's mansion. Perhaps she can channel more information about the killer's methods."

"You can't go there, Sam," Lees said. "It's still a closed crime scene. Police are guarding it."

"Why? Rachel was convicted and sentenced for her crime," Laura said.

"There's been another murder in San Francisco, I'm afraid. I tried to tell you earlier, but you all became so emotional about this mesmerist and your suffrage groups, I couldn't get a word in." Captain Lees looked down at his piece of paper. "Mrs. Cordelia Fallows, of Rincon Hill, another of your wealthy suffragette wives, was arrested last night. She murdered her husband, Aloysius, after having had sexual intercourse with him. We are keeping her in the women's detention lock-up in the Second District. Since Mrs. Rafferty and Mrs. Fallows knew each other, we want to make certain there was no collusion."

Clara felt her heart begin to race, as she envisioned the possible calamity. Not only could there be a sequence of murders taking place, but the cause for which she had devoted much of her life, women's independence, could suffer a death blow of its own.

"I will go with Mrs. Gordon to see this woman," Ah Toy stood up. "I believe if she was mesmerized, I can discover it. We also need to find out what her relationship was with her husband and if she remembers anything about the spiritualist she might have seen."

Laura stood up also. "Thank you. I must admit. I am not the person to believe in such supernatural hocus-pocus, as I always used my work as a medium as a ruse to make money. But now, after seeing all you have shown me in Chinatown, and what this young and gifted woman can do, I am not so certain. I would greatly appreciate your help when interviewing the accused."

When Clara rose, she looked around the table at everyone. "Good. We now have a plan. There is still a chance that all of these murders may not be connected. We all know about the pressure women of today are under by their husbands. If we can investigate abuses of women in these relationships, as we know were present in the Rafferty case, then perhaps there was no mesmerist at work.

These killings might have been caused by independent women taking the law into their own hands because they felt powerless."

"That was certainly how I handled my defense of Rachel Rafferty. It never entered my mind that she might have been hypnotized to kill," Laura said.

"Yes, but it's still possible at this point, and we must work at this case with an open mind." Clara closed her writing pad and tucked her pencil into her purse. She adjusted her hat, buttoned the top button on her dress, and left the room to make reservations on the Southern Pacific train going east.

***

The Chinatown Billiards Parlor, evening, May 4, 1886.

When Samuel first arrived at the parlor, he knew he was doing something forbidden. His mother told him not go there alone, and he had originally planned to take Adeline with him to possibly read Fung Jing Toy's mind before he went inside. Now that the girl was going with his mother, he decided to keep the appointment with the Tong leader at seven. Samuel heard from those who played at the parlor that big money could be made by playing in the rooms owned by Hip Yee Tongs deep inside Chinatown.

It was after-hours, and the parlor was dark except for a few lit Oriental lanterns hanging from the ceiling over the playing tables. There were fifteen men—all Chinese except for Little Pete's bodyguard, C. H. Hunter—and Little Pete said he would begin by telling Samuel the history of the ancient society into which he was being initiated.

Samuel was first blindfolded, and he heard a variety of voices in the room. They were all speaking Cantonese, so he was also oblivious to their language. He wished Miss Ah Toy were with him to translate the way she did for his mother.

Little Pete told him this initiation was required. It was the only way he could play billiards for money at the various gambling establishments run by the Tongs. He must become a member of the ancient Hung Mun Triad. According to Little Pete, Samuel was now to be initiated into one of the five Grand Lodges, which was controlled back in China.

Although he was frightened, Samuel believed if he became close to Little Pete and his group that Adeline would get the help she needed when the time came. He saw what the leader was able to do with his own eyes. Fung Jing Toy put the young woman under his spell, and she tried to kill that huge bodyguard. At that moment, Samuel became a true believer in the supernatural.

Little Pete's voice was like a spirit hovering over his head. Samuel felt the story being told enter his brain in the darkness, and his mind became a blank screen whereupon the images were projected upon it like the Magic Lantern Phantasmagoria he saw on Halloween each year at the Palace Hotel.

"In 1647, a community of monks who lived in the Fukien Province of China had become masters in the art of war. When a foreign prince invaded China, the emperor sent 138 of these monks to throw out the invading forces. After three months of bitter fighting, they routed the enemy and returned to their monastery laden with gifts and honors from the grateful emperor."

As Samuel listened, his eighteen-year-old imagination began to elaborate his thoughts. Nobody would have to know about his membership in this group. His cue stick would be his weapon of war against his competitors, and the money he earned would be his reward as a member of the Triad. Samuel had been a monk in school for too long. Now he wanted to become part of an exciting new endeavor.

"While the monks were content to resume their lives of contemplation, some of the emperor's ministers were jealous of the favors he had bestowed upon them and persuaded him that the monks were deceptively planning a rebellion. Fearful of their martial arts skills, the emperor decided to attack the monks without warning and sent a strong force of the Imperial Guard, armed with gunpowder, to destroy the monastery."

Samuel watched, as the Imperial Guards burst through the quiet solemnity of the monks' retreat and began to murder them. Some were slain in their sleep, still others stood up to fight back.

"It was said the flames ignited by the blasts soared up to heaven, where they were seen by the Immortals who, perceiving the injustice being dealt the monks, came down to Earth and pushed aside one of the monastery's huge walls, enabling 18 monks to escape. Most of them were so badly burned that they soon died, and the surviving five escaped from the Imperial troops by miraculous means."

Samuel pictured those flames engulfing his school in San Francisco, where he and his fellow student monks studied. If only his boring life in public school could be interrupted by such a magnificent attack.

"After many ordeals, the five monks came to a city in Fukien Province where they founded a Tong whose aim was to overthrow the emperor who had betrayed their loyalty. That Tong exists today as the Hung Mun Triad Tong, and the five monks who founded it, according to the legend, are known as the Five Ancestors. Although the revolt against the emperor failed, the survivors scattered throughout China and established five secret Provincial Grand Lodges, each led by one of the five monks."

In Samuel's mind, he, Roger, Ezra, and Adeline were four of those five monks. They had to escape the adult world of academic imprisonment to become secret rebels, fighting injustice against the youth of San Francisco. Of course, he would never tell his friends about his secret membership. It would mean his friends' certain death.

He couldn't see, but he could feel his body being lifted in the chair by the others. When they were outside the billiard parlor, Samuel felt the Pacific Ocean breezes hit his face. He inhaled the odors of Chinatown; the pungent whiff of urine in the alleyways, the deep-frying of vegetables and meats, and the burnt tobacco from the many pipes smoked by the men. He heard the barking calls of the vendors outside the markets, and the squealing and crunching of the merchant carts' wooden wheels turning alongside him on the brick-paved streets. Samuel wondered what those who saw him were thinking. Why was this white boy being carried through Chinatown? Was he kidnapped? He imagined that they simply accepted it, or they pointed at him and laughed.

After they dropped his chair to the ground, Samuel heard Little Pete speaking to his bodyguard. "Mr. Hunter, please take off his blindfold." He now smelled the distinct scent of incense, a cinnamon-clove odor coming from somewhere in front of him. He heard the melodious sounds of a Chinese flute, zither and drum. The first thing he saw, when the cloth was removed, was an open black door, and the incense was floating in the air from inside the lodge. He also saw the wavering light from standing candles and from multi-colored lanterns suspended above his head from the lodge's wooden rafters, as he walked through the entrance.

The swords came down in front of him, criss-crossing his lanky body to form a steel and razor-sharp "X". There was only one path through, and it was down under. Samuel kept remembering his father when the Army had a wedding for one of his friends. The armed men, including Jeremiah Foltz, formed a path down the steps of the church, under which the bride and groom had to pass. Those swords were raised high, but these swords were very low.

"How many monks were sent out from the monastery to fight the invaders?"

Samuel thought about Little Pete's earlier story back in the billiard hall. "One hundred and thirty-eight," he answered.

"When the Emperor's ministers sent the soldiers to burn down their monastery, who interceded on their behalf?"

Again, Samuel thought. What if he got the answer wrong? Would it all be over for him? Would they kill him? "The Immortals came down and saved them," he remembered.

"How many monks were saved?" Little Pete was grinning at him under the lantern lights like a fiend.

"Eighteen!" he shouted. He remembered that number because his friend, Ezra, said eighteen was a magical number in his Jewish religion.

"Get down on your hands and knees!" Little Pete now shouted at him from off to the side in the darkness. "The Five Masters will guide you through the gauntlet!"

Samuel dropped first to a crouch, and then he pushed his top half forward until he was on his hands and knees. Obviously, they wanted him to crawl through the small opening at the bottom of the crossed blades. Even though he was thin, he could see it would be a very tight squeeze. He grunted, moved his elbows next to his chest along the wood floor, and tried to keep his legs as close together as possible. He still felt the blades brush his shirt, and at one point, as his shoulders passed through, he felt the distinct slice of a blade cut through the cloth and dig into his skin. No pain, at first, but then he felt the warm liquid cascade down his bicep—blood.

He was able to crawl the rest of the way under, and he stood up, looking down at his right arm. "I have never done …"

"Silence! Initiates only answer questions until the ceremony is over." Little Pete stepped to the front of a table that was decorated with five golden statues. Each was a Chinese male dressed in a monk's robe. They all had wide basket hats and were posed in a fighting stance. All of them held a sword in hand, with a bow crossed over each chest, and arrows inside a quiver draped over each man's back.

The same fifteen men were in the lodge, and one of them, a tall man, who was wearing a red silk coat with a golden dragon stitched on the front, brought a silver tray up to Samuel, containing a small teacup and a chinaware pot. "This is the Incense Master. He will invoke the Five Masters, and you will drink the ritual tea."

The dragon master poured the hot tea into the small cup and set it down. He picked up the cup and handed it to Samuel. He said some words in Cantonese.

Little Pete instructed him. "Drink! He will say the 36 oaths."

The musicians played louder, and Samuel felt the hot tea stinging his throat, but he kept drinking. He felt the drum beats vibrate the floor beneath his feet and go up his legs, and the zither was plucked in a repeated, flashy rhythm, filling the room with warlike melodies. The Incense Master kept chanting the oaths.

Three of the men who had the double-edged straight swords called *Jian*, began waving them around in the air to the beat of the increasingly faster music. Samuel had seen men do this in the Chinese New Year's festivity, through the streets of Chinatown, but these men were not celebrating. Their faces were set in deadly concentration, and they were twisting these sharp blades in faster and faster loops around their heads, until he could hear their whoosh as they came near him. He winced from the cut he now felt on his bicep, and he imagined what those two swords would do if they struck any part of his body.

When they stopped, not three inches from him, the men were holding the two blades out at what his father called "port arms," with the swords held in front of their bodies, diagonally across their chests.

"Bring the rooster in now!" Little Pete shouted.

One of the men stepped into another room and came out with a squawking red rooster with a black mane and red combs. The bird was squirming in the man's arms as he was brought up to the two sword bearers.

"This is what will happen to you if you break any of our 36 oaths!"

How could he know any of these oaths? He didn't speak Chinese!

One of the swordsmen flashed out with the sword and lopped off the head of the rooster, and there was complete silence, as the rooster was dropped to the floor. It flopped around, blood spouting from its neck.

Samuel gasped when the rooster staggered onto his shoes, bathing a crimson stream across the toes. The swordsman picked the dead rooster up and collected the severed head. He dripped some of the rooster's blood into a chalice held by the Incense Master.

More chanting and frantic music filled the room until the Incense Master began to walk with one of the sword bearers. He brought the chalice up to the man's arm, the sword came down, and the blade slid across the skin until the line it made began to bleed. The Master did this to all sixteen of the Hung Mun Triad members, including Little Pete.

When they came up to him, Samuel raised his right hand. "Stop!" he shouted.

"How do you dare interrupt the ceremony?" Little Pete was livid.

Samuel thrust out his right leg, bent over, and raised his pants until his bare calf was exposed. "I must use my arm to play billiards," he whispered. "Cut my leg instead. It's all the same blood."

Fung Jing Toy at first glared at Samuel, but then he began to laugh. The musicians stopped playing, and then all of the other men were laughing. The sword came down and sliced the boy's calf, and the Incense Master stooped down and collected Samuel's dripping blood into the Immortals' ceremonial chalice.

The Incense Master then motioned for another man to bring a tray to him. From the tray, he mixed wine, cinnabar and ashes inside a pewter bowl. Finally, he poured that mixture into the chalice containing the collected blood.

One by one, starting with the Incense Master, each man took a sip from the chalice and smacked his lips. When the chalice finally came to Samuel's lips, he was thinking about his father, and how he had been wounded on the battlefield of Gettysburg, during the Civil War. That wound had stuck inside his soul, and he was never the same. It was like the *Red Badge of Courage* in the novel Samuel read at school, except his father had become a coward during peacetime. One day, his father left his family for a younger woman, and Samuel had cried all night.

Now, as he drank from the collective cistern of comrades, the boy believed he had finally become initiated into manhood, and he would be able to protect his family in a way that his father never could.

Little Pete stepped up to Samuel and made three magical signs with his right hand. The first sign was the index finger and middle finger held straight out and together, with the thumb extended and the two end fingers tucked under.

"Heaven," he said, pointing the sign upward.

The second secret sign was the thumb making a circle with the index finger and the other three fingers straight.

"Earth," he said, bending down and touching his fingers to the floor.

Little Pete then made the final sign. The index finger pointed straight, the thumb extended, and the three other fingers tucked under. He brought this sign up to Samuel's forehead, touching him between the eyes.

"Man," he said.

The crowd of the Hung Mun Triad cheered, and tears of joy streamed down Samuel's cheeks.

Chapter 6: Many Questions

The Bloomfield Mansion, Three Nob Hill, San Francisco, May 5, 1886.

"I want to thank you again for coming with me." Laura was standing on the sidewalk at the bottom of the hill leading up to the front door of the mansion of Elizabeth Harter-Bloomfield. Her dress was the usual conservative brown frock, buttoned up to the neck, with no bustle, parasol or hat.

Her companion, Ah Toy, wore a red silk *cheongsam*, and her dark, gray-streaked hair was woven around the back of her head. It was held in place with one of the seahorse combs that proved to be such an important clue in the mystery she pursued with Clara Foltz.

"I believe I can help you distinguish whether this woman is lying. In my job as a Madame, I had to filter the many hysterical and fraudulent ruses of young women under my guardianship. My uncle, Fung Jing, uses his dominant mystical powers to subdue his women. I, on the other hand, used my ability to sense the physical manifestations of when a person was telling me a falsehood."

"Good. I, too, believe I can spot a fraud, having once been such a practitioner in the false art of spiritualist skullduggery. Why, I once claimed to have brought into human form the recently deceased infant of Mrs. Rose Allworthy, the wealthy wife of James Allworthy, the shipping magnate of San Francisco. This grieving mother was so distraught and eager to see her poor baby that when I showed her a doll that had been soaked in phosphorus oil, she fainted. In the shadowy lamplight, one can cause the knockings, the hauntings, and the supernatural affectations needed to dupe most aggrieved females."

"Why, yes! I heard of another female medium named Florence Cook who would bring about the appearance of her constant spirit companion and guide, Katie King, in the 1850s of London. Did you get the idea from her?"

"No, most of my ideas were inspirations from the person or group for which I was planning to perform. I suppose one could call it a tailor-made ruse, as a good dressmaker would fit a design based on the wearer's personality and appearance." Laura reached out and took hold of the silver door knocker. It was in the shape of a round gold panning plate, and when she let it fall, it gave off the tune of "Oh, California," the popular God Rush tune of 1848, sung to the music of Stephen Foster's "Oh, Susannah".

Laura could hear the steps coming to the door, and then it was opened, revealing a tall, thin and curly-headed dark maid, in a black dress with white apron and frilly cap, who curtsied and then extended her arm inward. "The Mrs. is expecting you," she said.

As they followed the maid into the magnanimous confines of the large house, Laura noticed it was decorated with mining regalia and artwork. Paintings of mining camps, Chinese coolies and Irish miners at work digging into the mountains, and scenes of panning for gold, covered the redwood walls. A huge gold display of a pick axe crossed with a shovel beneath a panning tray, was affixed to the living room wall above the granite hearth mantelpiece. The tables were filled with sluice boxes, dredges, trommels, and many other mining tools that Laura did not recognize.

The only different display was a collection of several photos with natives in a jungle setting. In three of the photos, a Caucasian woman and man were kissing in front of a thatched mud hut. In another, the woman was being tattooed by a dark native woman, herself replete with markings all over her almost naked body. The final photo, Laura noticed, was a group of hunters, all males, and they were roasting something that was on the end of sticks over an open fire.

"Those hunters have to hold those tree frogs over the fire to kill them. They then scrape the backs of these frogs with their darts to poison the tips." When Mrs. Bloomfield stood up from the deep cushions of the brown leather divan and faced them, Laura expected her to be wearing a Forty-Niner's floppy hat and bandana around her neck. Instead, she displayed the same confining black frock with bustle that she had worn during the trial of Rachel Rafferty. Laura remembered that at the trial Elizabeth explained why she wore mourning clothes. It wasn't because her husband or somebody in the family had died. It was because she believed she mourned for the women held captive by their husbands and by society in general. Her husband, Jonas, was one of the few men who supported suffrage, so he did not disdain his wife's clothing statement. Laura thought he most likely got his way about everything else, as the mansion's décor had no hint of feminine or family allure.

"Ladies! It's so very nice to see you. I hope I can be of assistance. Please be seated, and Marjorie will bring us some tea and crescent rolls."

Laura sat down in one of the high-backed, blue satin chairs facing the divan, and Ah Toy sat next to Mrs. Bloomfield on the couch. Elizabeth Harter-Bloomfield had a pale, freckled complexion, as her maiden name was New England British. She was twenty-eight, and quite attractive, with dimples in both cheeks, and curls in her tall weave of brown hair.

Laura remembered that Elizabeth was not religious in the conventional sense, and she even bragged to her friends that she had been tattooed by a native female Shaman during she and her husband's marriage voyage to the Amazon jungles of Columbia. She explained that she chose a Maltese Cross pattern. It was etched from charred candlenut bark, on the backs of her legs and on her buttocks. The eight points of each cross represented the eight beatitudes of Christ's Sermon on the Mount. Elizabeth believed she was actually being Christian and not pagan like the natives. Laura believed the woman might be open to other ritual behaviors, however, including the possible mesmerism by a handsome spiritualist.

"Elizabeth, I need to explain why we need to question you again. There have been other husbands murdered." Laura observed the woman's eyes as they grew large. She began wringing her hands in her lap, and the tremor in her voice was from real emotion.

"Murders? In San Francisco? Who was it? Were they in the movement?"

Laura noticed that Ah Toy was also watching Elizabeth's actions. Why was she interested in the movement being implicated? Should she now ask about the thoughts she may have had on the witness stand? The thoughts that the young medium Adeline had channeled.

"There has been one murder in our town. Three other men were reported slain in New York City. Two were husbands in bed with their wives. One was with his mistress. They were all of the upper class."

"Mistress? Oh, my! You didn't answer me. Were these women suffragettes?" Laura noticed that the tremor was now gone. She was angry.

"I know you are concerned about the Suffrage Movement. Clara Foltz has told me about your work for the cause. You even go to jails where suffragettes have been arrested." Ah Toy's voice was calm. Laura supposed she was trying to reduce the anger in the room.

The maid came in with a silver tray containing a tea set and crescent rolls. She placed it upon the table in front of the divan and poured from the flowered pot into each of three matching cups. None of the women made any motions to partake of the food.

"We want to stop the killings and, of course, find the perpetrator or perpetrators behind them. However, I must ask you about your testimony. You stated that Dr. Adam McCauley had no nefarious purpose when he mesmerized Rachel Rafferty. He just wanted to help traumatized and abused women become calm. Is that correct?" Laura observed that this statement caused Mrs. Bloomfield to perspire. Her upper lip was moist, and trickles of sweat ran down her jawline.

"That's correct. I saw the doctor perform his treatment many times. He made a point of doing it in the public setting at our meetings. Rachel became very soothed, and she thanked him when it was over." Laura noted Elizabeth was still wringing her hands.

"Did the doctor ever hypnotize you?" Ah Toy asked. "Do you have any traumas?"

This last question, Laura noted, caused Elizabeth to start, as if she had seen a ghost in the room. She began to stare at empty space in front of her.

"Elizabeth, you know I do not believe in Spiritualism or contacting the dead through a medium. I told you, when I counseled you as a witness for the defense, I know all about the tricks of such paranormal activities because I was once paid to be a clairvoyant."

"Yes, you did tell me that." Elizabeth's voice was vacant of emotion.

"I'm afraid my recent experience has changed my mind about such mystical skills. I met a young lady, a Miss Quantrill, who told me she heard your thoughts when you were answering my questions on the witness stand." Laura was astonished when Elizabeth's head snapped around to face her. Her forehead was wrinkled into a deep frown, and her lips began to blubber with rage.

"My thoughts are my own! Get out of my house this instant! You are both trespassing on my property." Mrs. Bloomfield stood up and pointed toward the exit. "Marjorie! Escort these ladies out."

Laura was transfixed, as she was watching Ah Toy. They were now standing, and Ah Toy took mincing steps until she stood directly in front of Mrs. Bloomfield. She reached forward with her right hand and grasped Elizabeth by her right wrist and pulled her. Laura noticed that the woman's head turned to the left, and she began to stare vacantly into space.

"You are facing Rachel Rafferty. She is telling you something about her husband that frightens you. What is she telling you?" Ah Toy's voice was commanding yet not loud.

Marjorie came into the room and stood waiting. She was also interested in what was occurring.

Mrs. Bloomfield began to talk, and Laura noted that her voice sounded exactly as it sounded when Adeline Quantrill had channeled her thoughts earlier at the Hopkins' residence.

"*Magia Sexualis* is the key to ending my husband's violence, Rachel told me. I visited the master at his hotel room. He studied under the magnificent Dr. Randolph in Ohio. Just before the first great master killed himself. He is so handsome, Elizabeth. You can never understand until he touches your face. The magnetism flows into me, and I am re-born. I am a woman possessed with the innate sexual power of Cleopatra. I can conquer like Joan of Arc. I can bring down the patriarchy that keeps us forever imprisoned with their phallic weapons and their insatiable greed and lust. Only I can stop the violence against women! Only I can help us begin to live again without the shackles of masculine pride and control."

Laura saw that Ah Toy had not released her grip on Elizabeth's wrist.

"Rachel tells me this, but then she tells me if I say one word about what she has learned from the master, she will kill me. And, if she cannot kill me, there are others in her movement who will!"

Ah Toy released her wrist, and Elizabeth's head turned back to face Ah Toy. Laura saw that Mrs. Bloomfield now seemed calm and reassured. "I am so sorry! I don't know what possessed me. Please forgive me for my outburst. You must bring more of your artwork around for me to see. Let me escort you to the door."

Outside, standing on the sidewalk in front of the Bloomfield mansion on California Street, Laura looked back up the garden walk-up to the front door. She realized her perspective on the inner workings of the mind had changed. She still did not believe in messages from the dead, but this was completely different. Ah Toy and her uncle clearly had a psychic ability that seemed to penetrate the conscious veneer of so-called "normal behavior."

"You were able to mesmerize her. How did you do it?" Laura could hear her own words asking the question, but she really did not want to hear an answer. The response, most likely, would change her belief in forensic science forever.

Ah Toy smiled. "I have observed Mrs. Bloomfield carefully. Did you note how she stared into space? She has already been put into an unconscious state by someone other than I. When I grasped her wrist and pulled her toward me, I immediately accessed her subconscious being. When she turned her head to the left, I knew she was mesmerized. The left is the tunnel into the subconscious. I did not hypnotize her, I simply accessed her already mesmerized subconscious."

"Do you mean she was already hypnotized? If you weren't the somnambulist, then it must have been …"

"I believe she called him master. The student of Dr. Paschal Beverly Randolph in Ohio." Ah Toy continued to smile as they both stared back at the front door of the mansion.

Laura felt a shiver through her body. "Do you think she is one of them? One who can kill?"

"I don't know. Perhaps she was simply put under to keep the secret. I know we must now interview Rachel Rafferty again." Ah Toy grasped Laura's arm. "You certainly must be frightened. These psychic phenomena envelope the mind in subterfuge. You will have nightmares, visions, and you will certainly never be the same again. For that, I am sorry."

"Don't be sorry. I am happy to know Clara and Adeline are on their way to Ohio to meet Dr. Randolph's widow. Perhaps we can tighten the noose on this killer and discover him before more innocent lives are taken. Do you think you can do the same thing to

Rachel?" Laura was telling Ah Toy this, not quite believing it herself.

Ah Toy shook her head. "Innocent? We must not be so bold as to affix the label of innocence or guilt so early. Human beings do not become murderers simply from the powers of suggestion. There must be trauma there already for such paranormal skills ever to be effective. I am afraid I do not mesmerize. I can only access those who have already been placed into a somnambulant state by others. The Chinese men, such as my uncle, used these powers to keep the prostitutes in line. I simply cleared their minds of such suggestions, and it did not always work."

"Why? What happened?" Laura touched Ah Toy's arm.

"Some committed suicide. A few went mad." Ah Toy frowned. "The mind is a fragile instrument for some susceptible people."

"Quite right. As an attorney, I should know this. This is why we must always remain innocent until we are proven guilty. Clara's Christianity has always befuddled me. As a god, the Lord Jesus was our savior, so he must have been able to save himself as well. Why didn't he? He was, like us, a human with flesh and blood and a lust for life."

"Not possible. The Buddha was also beyond pain and suffering when he chose to come back to teach us the Four Noble Truths. These redeemers know our world must suffer forever. Of course, they also have the key to transcend that same suffering existence, and this is what they are trying to teach us. I suppose once we learn this lesson, individually, we no longer need this life."

Laura was struck with an interesting thought. "That does make sense. That tattoo on Elizabeth Bloomfield's body. The one with the Maltese cross pattern symbolizing the eight beatitudes?"

"I believe it's from the *Gospel of Matthew*. Clara and I discuss our religions quite often. Her father is a pastor as well as an attorney. In Taoism, similar instructions as these help to balance our daily lives. Confucian rules play the same role. The difference is that in our way of thinking, one must also respect the dark aspects, or negations of these eight instructions. That is, in effect, true balance."

"I just want to keep all of our puzzle pieces together. If Elizabeth Bloomfield was hypnotized, then when did she get put under the influence, and for what purpose? I know these eight instructions by heart, as I attended Catholic school, and we had to memorize them. Blessed are the poor in spirit, for theirs is the kingdom of heaven. Blessed are they who mourn, for they shall be comforted. Blessed are the meek, for they shall inherit the earth. Blessed are they who hunger and thirst for righteousness, for they shall be satisfied. Blessed are the merciful, for they shall obtain mercy. Blessed are the pure of heart, for they shall see God. Blessed are the peacemakers, for they shall be called children of God. Blessed are they who are persecuted for the sake of righteousness, for theirs is the kingdom of heaven."

"Good. Now, it is easy to see how one who wants to manipulate the psyche could use these instructions to twist logic. Each one hinges upon the idea that there are humans who need to be released from persecution and suffering. It's the same in Buddhist and Taoist thought. The person who wants control over people can use these directions to achieve a specific goal." Ah Toy took out a stiletto blade from under the wide sash of her *cheongsam*. The sunlight glanced off the steel into Laura's eyes, and she squinted.

"There is nobody under more control than someone who believes she is doing the work of God." Ah Toy raised the blade in her hand and ripped downward through the air. "We who thirst for divine righteousness shall obey you!"

***

1742 Vance Street, Toledo, Ohio, May 7, 1886.

Clara held Adeline's hand as they walked up to Mrs. Randolph's front door. The house was a white, single-story, wooden affair with a matching picket fence and brick walls on the sides to separate it from the neighbors' dwellings. Clara thought it reminded her of her own home in Indiana when she first met Jeremiah Foltz at age fourteen. He had come to the door because he had seen her, tutoring children, through the classroom window of the house. He wanted her to tutor him. Clara supposed she tutored him until he left her for another, much younger woman. When she had wanted to be nothing but a mother and a wife, he had wanted a voluptuous mother who could keep silent. He believed his war injury gave him that right.

"Let me talk. I will refer to you when the moment comes. We are attempting to extract important information from Mrs. Randolph, and unless she sees we mean her no harm, there will be no cooperation on her part. I have read about her sad travails. She has one son, Osiris Buddha, and she is forced to keep her deceased husband's publishing business going to support them both. We can gain her good favor by showing that you are a gifted clairvoyant."

"Thank you for allowing me to come. You are the first adult who has not thought of me as mentally ill. I have pretended most of my life until I joined the Rosicrucians. When you took me to your home, I became alive once more." Clara felt the girl squeeze her hand. "I felt lost, trapped inside a deep well, and you pulled me up to the light."

Both Clara and Adeline wore green dresses, complete with feathered hats, medium bustles, and matching parasols. Clara had purchased them after they arrived in Akron on the train. All the girl had brought with her were several drab frocks from the orphanage.

"Now you can help me on this case, so we were meant to meet." Clara took out a kerchief from her green dress pocket and wrapped it around her fist. Although she believed completely in the emancipation of women, she still behaved like a lady. Making a loud noise on the door with her knuckles would not be ladylike. Clara rapped three times on the blue door with her muffled fist.

Of course, there was no maid or butler answering the door. Clara supposed it was the son, twelve-year-old Osiris. He was a quite pleasing young man, with wire-rimmed spectacles, red knee pants, suspenders, and matching shirt, and a smile that beamed at them with an intuitive depth. His skin, because of his father's half-Negro blood, was an olive hue, much like that of an Italian or Mexican, as was his curly black head of full hair. Like the photos Clara had viewed of his father, Paschal, Osiris's piercing, oxblood eyes riveted upon Clara, and then they slowly moved over to capture Adeline's gray eyes.

"My mother is expecting you. You needn't buy new dresses. We are all of a communal mind in our house." Osiris turned abruptly, upon his heels, as a little soldier would, and marched into the parlor. Clara and Adeline followed, nodding at each other about the precognitive ability of the young man.

The woman who greeted them in the parlor was a striking beauty. She was Caucasian, but her hair was black and kinky, possibly Black-Irish, and she stood awaiting her company with a smile of affection already on her face and a bowl of mixed fruits in her hands.

"Welcome! Won't you have some fruit? Osiris Buddha just picked them from our garden out back. We have apples, pears and apricots. Trees to accompany us in the Garden of Eden, one might imagine." Kate Corson-Randolph was a tall and slim woman of thirty-two. She wore a plain gingham frock with a white garden bonnet, similar to Clara's wardrobe when she lived in the farmhouses of Iowa and Indiana as a young wife and mother. In fact, Clara knew, Kate was also born in Indiana.

As the four members of this odd group seated themselves on the variety of plush Persian pillows all around the floor, Clara noticed the many wall decorations. Newspaper clippings and magazine articles were displayed of Dr. Randolph, and the most prominent was of he standing together with Mrs. Mary Todd Lincoln, who was a fervent believer in the supernatural. The parlor furnishings, in fact, were a mixture of cultures from around the world. Egyptian lamps and hookahs, Indian and Persian carpets and Chinese paintings and statuettes, which combined with African tribal smoking pipes, animal skins, and even heads of lions, leopards, and hippopotami.

Clara saw that Adeline kept staring at young Osiris, and he at her. She supposed it wise to get to the heart of her purpose for being there.

"Mrs. Randolph, I am here because we are looking for help in a matter which involves some rather strange and ugly activities. To be precise, we believe there are murders of husbands being committed under the supervision of a Spiritualist guru, who may be using the teachings of your late husband as a source of somnambulant mesmerism." Clara noticed that Mrs. Randolph had winced during her introduction speech.

Kate Randolph turned to address her son. "Osiris? What are you sharing with your new friend, and what is she telling you?"

The boy looked away from his transfixed staring for a moment and addressed his mother. Clara could see his forehead wrinkle in concentration. "Her mother and father were murdered by aborigines on a train going to California. She now lives in an orphanage in San Francisco. Mrs. Foltz is using her to discover clues in their new case." He turned back to his obviously telepathic conversation with Adeline.

"We were never married," Kate said. "Paschal and I met when I was nineteen, in 1873. He had experienced a rather horrible accident and was left in partial paralysis. Two trains were converging toward him, and he was inebriated, walking across a trestle. He jumped into a ravine to save himself, and the plunge down the embankment injured his left side and arm. As a medium and spiritualist, the left side is extremely important. It is the hub of activity for the spirit and soul in a man."

Clara was fascinated by what she was saying. These two were never married, and she had met him when he was at his wits end. It must have been after he left Boston, when a fire had destroyed many of his books and writings.

"I see. I understand you have taken up his work and are publishing his books. Were you both Spiritualists?" Clara bent toward the woman, half expecting to be struck by a beam of magnetism emanating from the center of her forehead.

"Yes, as a matter of fact, I assisted him in many seances and meetings of the Rosicrucian Order he had established. We never married because of his jealousy. He believed I possessed a sexual attraction to other men that was otherworldly. You know, of course, about his elixirs?" Kate raised her dark eyebrows and flicked a single curl away from her right brow with her right hand's index and middle fingers.

"No. Not much. I do know about his book *Magia Sexualis*, as it figures prominently in our current investigation. We have read it carefully, but I wanted to hear about Dr. Randolph's teachings from you."

"He sold these drugs to people who needed to improve their powers in the boudoir. They contained legal substances, such as hashish oils and cocaine, which were the prime motivators for his instructions in these books. I helped him write one of his last books called *The New Mola*. In it, he supposed the conditional doctrine of immortality. In other words, spiritual divinity must be earned through the practices he would teach. This led to his drunkenness, I'm afraid."

"What do you mean? Did he fall away from his faith?" Clara wanted to get into what she was really hoping to reveal. But this would do in the interim.

"When in his cups, he would accuse me of being a harlot and a witch, and he even said our child, Osiris, was not his. I had to stop him from attempting to do harm to the boy. One night, after I was presiding over a séance across town, I walked in, and he was holding a Rosicrucian Egyptian sword over his son's head and swearing drunken oaths in Spanish. When he was drunk, he also felt he was cursed by being part Spaniard."

Clara wondered how Kate could speak about the boy in this manner. He was in the same room.

She seemed to read her mind, also. "Osiris wants to become a medical doctor. No magical sorcery for him. Quite ironic, don't you think? The one in our family who possesses the true gift of precognition, and he wants none of it." Kate laughed. "Good riddance, I say! I have had enough of the drugs and alcohol elixirs as well. The men who came around our house before Paschal died were ominous enough. In fact, Madame Blavatsky and Colonel Olcott called Paschal "the Nigger" at that time, and they said he had crossed over into black magic."

Clara sat up straight. "They were the two who founded the Theosophists, were they not?"

"Yes, they had heard in their small sect that Paschal was teaching men from a small pamphlet he wrote privately called *The Mysteries of Eulis*. It may be these teachings which may assist you in your present case. They certainly led to Paschal's demise."

"Please, go on. We are attempting to track down any person or persons who might be using any powers of a supernatural nature upon women." Clara took out her little pad and pencil from her green purse, and she sat at the ready.

"He preached this to me so often in those final days that I still remember it. He told me that no real magic or magnetic power can or will descend into the soul of either sexual participant, except in the mighty moment—the orgasmal instant of both—not one alone. For then, and then only, do the mystic forces of the soul open to the spaces."

Clara noticed that Osiris had stopped communicating and was now staring fixedly at his mother. So was Adeline.

Kate continued, her voice rising in passionate volume. "The eternal spark within us, and which never flashes except when the loving female brings to her feet the loving man in their mutual infiltration of Soul, in the sexive death of both—that intense moment when woman proves herself the superior of man—mutual demise! It was created by Allah—God himself—billions of ages ago in the foretime, and finds its human body only when Sex-passion opens the mystic door for it to enter the man—through him, the woman, through her the world, through them the Spaces, and through it again Allah, God—not as a drop of infinite ocean of Mind, but as a Being in the Heavenly hierarchies!"

Kate collapsed backward upon her Persian cushion and began to pant rhythmically, her chest heaving.

"Mother! Are you all right?" Osiris called out to her.

She sat up, and Clara could see the blood was again beginning to flow slowly into her face and neck.

"Does this mean he believed the participants were becoming infused with god-like powers?" Clara was afraid of what she was asking.

"The four men—his students—certainly believed it. They tried to seduce me, each in his own way." Kate Randolph said, and Clara knew her inquiry had just begun.

Chapter 7: The Noose Tightens

The Hopkins Mansion, One Nob Hill, San Francisco, May 8, 1886.

Now that the group of investigators had grown to seven members, Laura realized that they needed to be in direct communications in order to facilitate developments in the case. Captain Isaiah Lees was an invaluable source, but he could only serve in an advisement capacity. Laura was the person with the most direct information about the case of Rachel Rafferty, so she saw herself as in command when Clara was out of town. After she and Ah Toy had interviewed Mrs. Bloomfield on Nob Hill, she received a telegram from Clara the next day. As a result of the content, she wanted to share it all with her group.

She called for the meeting in the library at eight in the morning, and Hannigan was kind enough to deliver the invitations. Only Trella Evelyn would be late, as she was taking a test for her college course. Laura had sent the telegrams to her suffrage contacts in Washington D.C. about the movement in New York City to shut down the Spiritualist groups. They responded that a congregation of women would demonstrate before Congress to stop such a bill from passing. Both she and Clara had connections in the California legislature, so there should be no closing of groups in California, unless these murders began to increase.

As she greeted Hannigan at the door, she made a mental note to tell Clara's daughter to come with her to question the three other witnesses in the Rafferty trial. Ah Toy had proved so valuable at Mrs. Bloomfield's mansion that she was going to be invited as well. But first, Laura knew, she needed to inform the group about Clara's findings in Ohio with the questioning of Kate Randolph.

"We won't be long, will we?" Samuel Cortland was seated at the library table next to Ah Toy. "I have a meeting I must attend."

"Does your mother know of these meetings? She has never mentioned that you belong to any official groups." Ah Toy touched Samuel's arm. "I won't tell her if you put me under your confidence."

"It's a group that is establishing better cultural relations with the Chinese, if you must know," Samuel said, looking straight at Ah Toy. "I am also trying to learn Cantonese."

"*Nei ling ngo soeng sing wai jat go gang gaa hou ge jan*. Which means?" Ah Toy asked.

"How should I know? I just joined the group." Samuel frowned.

"You make me want to be a better person," she answered. Laura noticed that Ah Toy had the same look she had when she was doubtful of Mrs. Bloomfield's answers. She must ask her about this later.

Captain Lees and Trella Evelyn entered the library at the same time. They sat at the far end of the table, and Laura nodded at them from her position at the head of the wooden rectangle.

"Thank you for coming," Laura began. "I have a telegram that I want to read before we discuss what has been occurring and what we have planned." Laura cleared her throat, spread out the paper on the table, and began to read:

"We have four possible male suspects who learned under Dr. Randolph. Stop. Staying one more day to question Kate Randolph further. Stop. The boy, Osiris Buddha, can read minds."

Laura tucked the telegram back into her dress pocket. "This narrows our investigation somewhat. Ah Toy and I found out from questioning my witness, Mrs. Elizabeth Harter-Bloomfield, that she was hypnotized by someone. Ah Toy can only access those who are under somnambulant control, but we believe whomever is doing this has the ability to suggest things, including possible murderous intent."

"What about the connection to Dr. Paschal Randolph? Are you and Clara suggesting that one of those four students of Randolph committed the hypnotism on these women?" Captain Lees, Laura knew, was almost as skeptical of these supernatural events as she was.

"Correct, Isaiah. I would suppose Clara's purpose for staying another day in Toledo is to get the identity of these men and possibly where they now live. However, at this stage, I would assume, we have to believe all four are possible perpetrators, don't you agree?" Laura liked working with Lees, as he kept his observations objective, the mark of a fine detective.

"We must first question the woman who is accused of this most recent murder, and then go back and see if your client, Rachel Rafferty, has a similar connection to anything this most recent perpetrator knows."

Lees understood the law. In order to convict, the State must be able to assign malicious intent to the act of murdering the husband. This was usually accomplished by establishing a motive and a *modus operandi*, which would usually be a weapon of some kind wielded at the scene by the accused. Laura knew, however, that the motive in these murders could be established through the cause of a spiritualist, who was able to condition one or all of these women to commit murder.

"If a hypnotist were able to mesmerize these women to commit murder, would we be able to prove it in a court of law?" Laura was becoming more doubtful as soon as she questioned the group.

"You are the attorney, but in my experience, there has never been a person who has been convicted of murder through the hypnosis of a perpetrator," Lees said. "Of course, we can always search the facts at the law library," he rubbed his graying chin whiskers.

"That would mean somebody can force others to kill with mental suggestions, wouldn't it?" asked Trella, her eyes wide. "Or, have they been cursed by the Devil, like the witches of Salem, Massachusetts!"

"I have had the displeasure of getting a few of *your* bewitching ocular daggers," Samuel said, contorting his face into a wrinkled phantasm.

"This is quite different," said Laura, becoming impatient. "We have all seen what Adeline can do, and if Ah Toy's uncle can control his prostitutes the way he says he can, then how can we doubt there might be a person with supernatural skills doing these killings through the mind control of others?"

"Even if there is no established precedent for such murders?" Lees asked.

"As Clara would oblige us, there is another child in Ohio, the son of Dr. Randolph, who has the mental telepathy abilities of our Adeline. I, for one, am becoming quite certain that in our investigation we will tighten the noose around the neck of a possible demon. How this demon can control women, and who he is, is our immediate discovery objective."

"What are you proposing?" Ah Toy asked.

"I first want to question my client, Rachel Rafferty again, and I want you to come with me. If she is still under subconscious control, the way Mrs. Bloomfield was, then you should be able to access her. In addition, Trella should come along as a witness, in case we need to use this information in court."

Laura turned toward Captain Lees. "Isaiah, if you would, arrange a meeting for us with Mrs. Cordelia Fallows, the defendant in the newest murder case."

"I can do that," Lees nodded. "I am also going to get one of the law clerks to research capital cases involving hypnosis or mesmerisation. There may be something we can hang our hat on."

"Good. Thus, today, we shall interview Rachel Rafferty, and tomorrow Mrs. Fallows at the women's detention jail on Kearny. Clara and Adeline should return from Ohio in three days. By then, I would hope, we can have some of these puzzle pieces connecting together to add to her findings."

"What about the other two witnesses in your trial that Adeline channeled? She was able to read their minds, as well, wasn't she?" Samuel asked.

"Yes, that's correct. We shall do that the day after we question the most recent accused murderer. I have a strong feeling that hypnosis will play a big part in our investigation from here on out. If you are all as doubtful of this kind of mind control as I am, then our doubts will invariably hinge upon what information Clara brings us from Ohio." Laura stood up. "Are there any more questions for the time being? Are you all aware of your present duties?"

Laura saw nods from everyone around the table except Ah Toy.

"Yes, Ah Toy. Do you have some doubts?"

The Chinese artist and art collector shook her head. "I don't like the fact that Clara kept the door open to my uncle. His dark powers frighten me. In point of fact, I am not a detective, nor am I a respected attorney, but I believe we are missing my uncle as a suspect in these murders. His abilities were demonstrated for us, and yet we refused to believe. Instead, Clara goes traipsing all the way to Toledo, and you, Mrs. Gordon, become enthralled with the possibilities of sexual power by women."

"I beg your pardon." Laura was shaken.

"Don't you believe an evil Chinese man could commit such heinous crimes? I saw it happen before. The killer who came from our clergy at the Joss House. My uncle does not jest, and he most certainly has evil intentions. Why can't we investigate him?"

Laura was suddenly rather proud of Ah Toy's outburst. The group had indeed sloughed off the possibility of Fung Jing Toy being at the center of these murders. She realized how important it was to have all of these intelligent minds working on this important case.

"Ah Toy and Trella Evelyn, please remain. We can discuss your uncle and plan what we shall ask the defendant, Mrs. Fallows. The rest of you, do your best, and make us proud. Write down everything you discover, and report back tomorrow morning, here, in the library, at eight."

The captain and young Samuel left, and Laura turned to Ah Toy and Trella.

"What was it you were going to tell me about your concerns for Samuel? Is it just you who is suspicious, Ah Toy? Or, do you, Trella, know anything about your brother we should know about?"

Ah Toy frowned. "I watched Samuel when he told me about his culture club meeting. As long as he has lived with us at the Hopkins mansion, each time I have caught him lying, his right eye blinks, much the same way as poor Detective Sergeant Vanderheiden, Captain Lees' partner does. Whereas the detective's blink is a frequent nervous tic, caused by nothing nefarious, Master Foltz's blink is invariably caused by a guilty conscience. I don't know what kind of meeting or group he is attending, but you can be certain it is not what he says it is. I say we check with my uncle."

"Ah Toy is correct. Samuel has been caught lying quite frequently. Mother is aware of it, and it is her opinion that Samuel needs the companionship and discipline of a father. Our father, Jeremiah Foltz, left his five children for a younger woman, and Samuel was most affected by it. Captain Lees is now mother's lover, but they have no marriage plans, and they both work constantly. Samuel has been left in a vacuum of inattention. He may be up to most anything, if you want my opinion." Trella pinched her lips together and nodded her head. "Talk about demons at work!"

"We need to be off. I'll tell Clara about Samuel when she returns. The visiting hours at the women's Ingleside Jail end at four. We must take Mrs. Hopkins' surrey. She is paying our salaries for this case, so we must cooperate whenever we can to save her money." Laura picked her handbag up and walked toward the front exit. She noticed that Ah Toy and Trella looked at each other and raised their eyebrows.

"Old Giles is perhaps faster than the two old nags, Lucy and Frank. We may arrive next Thursday," Trella said.

"One must never look a gift horse or nag in the mouth," Laura said, stepping through the opened door and nodding at the butler, Hannigan.

"Did you know, mum? Giles has dressed Lucy and Frank in every costume except the Trojan horses. Maybe he can add that outfit for you ladies."

"Please tell me your Christian name. I have heard Hannigan shouted on numerous occasions, by every member of this household. At one point, I thought Hannigan might be a lost family pet or a ghost. However, your sharp wit deserves a personal accolade using your given name."

"Why, thank you, mum. It's Joseph. Joseph Allan Hannigan," the butler said, staring at Ah Toy as she went past him. "Perhaps others can shout it without scaring the bejeezus out of the wee ones."

"Good day, Joseph, and thank *you*," Laura said.

***

1742 Vance Street, Toledo, Ohio, May 8, 1886.

Kate Randolph allowed Clara and Adeline to stay overnight. They all awoke to the sounds of a sitar coming from the living room. Osiris could play, and the notes were the first Clara had ever heard from such an instrument. As a working mother, she had never had the chance to travel, and living here, even for this short time, was like stepping onto different continents. The sitar sounded to Clara like the breezes blowing upon wheat in the fields, or a fox crying in agony for its lost mate.

They dined on fresh fruit, goat's milk and cheese. Kate and her son were vegetarians by choice, as it was her understanding that the lust for the meat of fellow animals was caused by seeing that animal as a food source rather than for what it really was: a fellow sentient being.

"Sentient means being able to feel or perceive things. I cannot, in good conscience. devour a fellow life form which has consciousness. Even though plants and fruits also have a form of consciousness, we must eat them or die. The fire within must be fed until it is over." Kate touched the arm of Osiris, who was still playing beside her on the Oriental rug they were sitting upon for breakfast.

Clara noted that Adeline was watching the boy very carefully. It was the same vivid perception she had seen in each of her children growing up. There was no more attentive watching than that of a child seeing life for the first time. Perhaps Kate was right about seeing animals as fellow sentient beings. It certainly made a great deal of logical sense. However, her task at hand was to discover the identity of the spiritualist who was training vulnerable women to kill their husbands.

"I wrote to my friend, a fellow attorney, back in San Francisco. She is questioning the witnesses to the murders of two men by wives who attended Rosicrucian spiritualist meetings founded by Dr. Randolph in 1868. We have reason to believe there may be suspects who learned the secrets of sexual power from Paschal and then twisted those teachings into a method of mesmerising a wife into a passionate state of murderous intent." Clara was trying to be clear with her words, but she was afraid this woman was on a different spiritual level due to her pain and suffering.

"Do you really believe a woman, who has the power to bring life into this world, will become a killer based on mere suggestions? I must be honest, Mrs. Foltz, I worked closely with Paschal for four years, and we knew what we did was based on our clients' fears and superstitions, mostly concerning the dead." Kate took a bite of a peach, and Clara watched as the juices spread over her chin. She did not wipe it cleanly.

"I really don't know. I was truly hoping you could help me answer that question. I do understand that many women presently are being held captive by their husbands, and these husbands can often be harsh wardens and even more heartless commanders. You must understand this, certainly, because of your own experience. The mind can become very vulnerable to loving and passionate attention given to it after having lived with harsh cruelty and even torture for many years." Clara was feeding upon her own memories living with Jeremiah, and it gave Kate's words extra meaning. "Even an abusive husband can quickly want forgiveness and promise to never do such acts again. Women can become stuck in an endless cycle of pain and relief."

"I can accept that. I can also accept the fact that men are often slaves to their private passions. The sannyasins who were living under my roof were certainly no exception. I told you, each one attempted, in his own way, to seduce me. Perhaps they felt I was vulnerable because of my husband's drunkenness. They did not understand that I believed in him, and that I accepted it as his sickness."

"What exactly happened? Were they attempting to use on you some of what they were learning from Dr. Randolph?" Clara was slowly arriving to the point she had planned in her mind.

Kate breathed in deeply. "I am telling you about this as clinically as I can. The first was an exhibitionist. He would appear out of nowhere, when I was doing the wash, or cooking, and his torso would be bare. If we women did such things, we would immediately be labeled harlot. He did a lot of manual labor, so his musculature was appealing. He would move to press against me, and I pushed him off, twice, and then he stopped doing it."

"Yes, do continue. He seems like a normal enough cad," Clara said.

"Indeed. The second man was a small young man who fancied himself a lustful humorist. He would also approach me while I was otherwise disconcerted, and begin telling me the raunchiest, most profane jokes one can imagine. How he believed this could seduce a female is beyond me. When I laughed, I explained to him that it was he whom I found hysterically humorous, not his bawdy tales. This stopped him."

"And the third?" Clara picked up a chunk of cheese and popped it into her mouth.

"This man was expelled by Paschal from the house, as he came the closest to raping me. He walked into my bathing area and spied me in the washtub. As he was undressing himself, most obviously expecting to bathe with me, Osiris came home from school. My son and Paschal had a telepathic affinity, so the message was sent, and

Paschal came bursting forthwith into the house, saw what this young man was doing, grabbed him by his collar and by the bottom of his britches, and tossed him out of the front door and onto the front steps. He never came back for his things." Another bite of the peach, and this time Kate bit into it with relish.

Clara nodded. "And … the last man?" She had an idea this man would be somehow much different. Kate was obviously, like a good storyteller, saving him for last for a specific reason.

Before she spoke, Kate glanced over at her son, who was still playing softly on the sitar. "Rheingold Bingham was the first and only man I have ever had a telepathic affinity with. True, Paschal and I would pretend during our seances and presentations, but nobody had ever spoken to me the way Rheingold's voice did on that day."

"This is quite interesting. Please continue," Clara saw that the sitar playing had stopped, and both young people were staring at Kate.

"The three of us were having cordials after dinner, as the other men were out that evening. Paschal and Rheingold were getting into a heated argument about the Hebrew Scriptures. Specifically, the tale of Abraham and his son, Isaac. As Paschal continued to argue, he also continued to drink more wine. His voice became quite loud, of course, and Rheingold's became less so. It was Paschal's contention that Abraham should have obeyed the word of God and killed his son. He said the angel who intervened was not from God but was from Satan. I remember Paschal's direct quotation, 'There would have been not future need for God to send his son, Jesus, as the supreme sacrifice would have already been made!'"

Clara was fascinated, as her father and she were always arguing the Bible together. "No, that cannot be. This was the Hebrew's story to put a stop to human sacrifice, which was going on quite readily in the other religions of that time and place. To this day, Jews and Muslims believe human sacrifice, even that of Jesus, is not acceptable for humanity."

"One would think so. However, Paschal was becoming darker in his philosophy. Remember when I told you about him holding an Egyptian sword above Osiris?"

"Yes. Was this …?"

"It was. And when he did it, Rheingold's voice came into my head. He told me that I could stop Paschal from killing our son by telling him I loved him unconditionally. I did this. I walked slowly up to him, placed my right hand on his dark bicep with the extended sword. I remember. His eyes, when he looked down at me, were so tortured, so abysmal. When I told him I loved him, it was if a dam had burst inside his head, and he began to weep, uncontrollably. He took Osiris into his arms and begged his forgiveness."

Clara felt a great surge of empathy, as she had also come close to avenging her own family against Jeremiah on many occasions, but she never chose love, and this gave her a melancholy feeling. "And how long did this Rheingold stay with you? How did he try to seduce you?"

"He stayed with us until the end. He, in fact, discovered Paschal's body after he killed himself." Kate again looked over at her son, Osiris.

"And the seduction?"

"The seduction is still going on. Rheingold Bingham is my lover."

Clara instinctively knew, if there were any immediate suspect in this case, it must be this Rheingold Bingham. "How romantic! Do you see each other frequently?" She knew she had to approach the two lovers with kid gloves on.

"Not too frequently. Paschal always said that a seer and true spiritualist must work alone to advance the power of love. Rheingold is now out West. He sends me postcards and letters, and he should return at the Christmas holidays. He loves to spend them with us." Kate brushed some cheese particles from her gingham dress, into the palm of her hand, and then placed them on the tray. Clara thought she watched each particle the way God must watch all of His creatures.

"May I see a piece of correspondence from his latest destination? As I said, he may be able to answer some questions which might help us track down this heinous killer." Clara had switched her tactic, and she hoped Kate did not suspect that it was her lover who was under suspicion.

"Why, yes, I'll let you see them all from this year. If you can get in touch with him, please tell him I love him." Kate got up to fetch the correspondence, and Clara waited, smiling at Osiris and

Adeline. After a few minutes, she heard Kate call out from one of the three bedrooms in the back of the house.

"You do know there will be nothing intimate in these letters, don't you?" She shouted.

"No, I did not. Why is that?" Clara shouted back.

"Because those intimacies are shared only by our most intimate organ. Our minds."

The reality of that fact forced Clara to hold her breath until the sound of Osiris and his sitar brought her back to the conscious world of that moment.

***

Ingleside Jail, Ocean House Road, San Francisco, May 8, 1886.

The drive to the jail, which used to be a correctional school, took an hour. It was located seven miles south from Nob Hill along the crowded Ocean House Road. The trip was made even more difficult due to the fog, which was coming in like a pestilence. The elder driver and two horses already had poor eyesight, and the thick fog made their viewing worse. Laura watched old Giles, as he had to maneuver carefully along, honking his fog horn like a ship lost at sea.

Each of the cells had its own lock and key, so when Laura reported with Trella and Ah Toy at the Superintendent's lush office on the second floor, it took another forty-five minutes to retrieve the proper key and deliver it to the guard who escorted them out to the jail building housing the women's unit of cells.

Laura had never been to the jail, as she had always worked with defendants from one of the district lockups in the city. The Ingleside Jail was for the least dangerous inmates who were also allowed to work during their stay, unlike the San Quentin prison. Since Rachel Rafferty came from the upper classes, and her conviction was for manslaughter and not murder, she was considered a safe prisoner.

Laura watched the two women follow the guard out to the women's jail building. Ah Toy walked directly behind the short and slump-shouldered man, who dangled the key ring from his belt buckle like a Judas goat. Trella, who was fascinated by the school-like grounds, made a comment when they approached the steps leading up into the building. "Ah, there are the bars. On the windows!"

"Here we are, ladies. Cell 168. Rafferty, R., prisoner number I-748." The guard held the key on the ring and stuck it into the lock, turned the key, and the lock opened. He swung the door open, and Laura walked inside. As Rachel must have been a model prisoner, she had the niceties of a dresser, a table, and a wooden bed with mattress, quilt and pillow. She was waiting for them, seated at the table in the center of the twenty-five-foot square cell. The restrooms and bathing facilities were communal.

A Calico cat was lounging on the bed, her stomach displayed, and her paws waving abstractly at nothing any human could see. Laura realized that Rachel had the exclusive enjoyment not available to others. She was the only prisoner in the cell, and her gabardine dress was pressed and clean, and her shoes were shined. Her face was made-up, and she created a meager smile for them.

Laura motioned to Ah Toy and Trella to take a seat around the table. "I see you have a furry companion. I have always thought that felines, as a spirit totem, are superb exemplars of self-esteem. Does she help you, Rachel?"

"Yes, my job is in the sewing factory, and Brigette here keeps my ball of twine spinning. She weaves stories for me about her latest escapades with the cell block mouse." Rachel folded her hands on the table and stared at them. "You haven't come to talk about cat-and-mouse games, now have you?"

"Correct. As a matter of fact, we believe we may be able to get you out of here forever. There have been at least four new murders of wealthy husbands, one of whom died at the hands of your close friend, Cordelia Fallows." Laura closely watched Rachel's face.

"Cordelia! She never knew…" Rachel stopped. "I mean, Cordelia wasn't being treated for trauma."

Laura could sense the slip of the tongue, so she pounced, as she imagined little Brigette would do. "She never knew whom, dear? Dr. McCauley?"

"No. You don't understand. We were all fighting for our lives. These are perilous times we women are experiencing. The more pressures that get foisted upon our husbands, the more they push us to the edge of insanity!" Rachel looked up. "Cordelia was already quite insane, you know."

"No, I didn't know. In fact, I will speak to her for the first time tomorrow. Let me be clear with you. You will never be released unless we can prove that there is another party who controls the means by which these women--including you--are able to assassinate their husbands with such alacrity and fervor." Laura took hold of Rachel's hands and gazed deeply into her eyes. "You were not really angry when you murdered Brian, now were you?"

"We know that the secret spiritualist who conditioned you was using hypnotic as well as other means," Ah Toy spoke for the first time, and Laura watched Rachel turn her head to the sound of her voice.

"But I can't tell you who this person is. Also, it would ruin the entire plan." Tears began to run down Rachel's cheeks.

"What plan? Why can't you tell us the name? We cannot get you out of here unless we can prove someone did this to you and to the other women." Laura squeezed her client's hands.

Rachel began looking around wildly, as if she believed somebody could see and hear her. "All right. I will tell you. But not now. I am the only one who escaped the true powers. I can remember the name and for whom this person works. When I was seduced, the spiritualist was on a lower level of supernatural ecstasy. Now that person is much more powerful. I do want to see my children again! Come back tomorrow. I shall tell you!" She broke down into sobs, and she dropped her head into the cavern made by her arms on the table.

Laura stood up. She saw that Trella was now on the bed petting the cat. Ah Toy stood up.

"Don't do it, Laura! You should not trust this woman." Ah Toy's dark eyes were flashing.

"I must. I cannot force her. I am not a spiritualist. In fact, I was a fraud. I was a Judas disciple to the Jesus Spiritualist." Laura looked down at Rachel and touched her arm, wet from crying. "I'll be back. I promise. Tomorrow morning at ten."

Laura stood in the yard beside the women's jail with Ah Toy and Trella Evelyn. Ah Toy's face was flushed. "How can you believe such a woman? She can tell you anything to free herself." It was beginning to rain, and none of them had a parasol.

"I will telegram Clara before she leaves for home. Rachel will tell me who hypnotized her because she wants to be free. Also, I will test her knowledge with the second woman. Even if she can't identify this person by name, she must surely remember the tactics and the overall plan that convinced her to do this horrible act." Laura pulled up her collar. "Where is that old man and his two nags?"

Out of the foggy mist, right on cue, the surrey appeared. Slowly, slowly. Quickly, quickly, escaped the sands of time toward destiny and destruction.

Chapter 8: Poison and Guns

The Hopkins Mansion, One Nob Hill, San Francisco, May 8, 1886.

Clara was meeting in the library with Adeline and all the others. Even though she was extremely fatigued from her trip back from Ohio, she knew if the group failed to act on the information obtained thus far, then the possibilities of discovering the killer or killers would dwindle fast. She had learned about the spiritualists who studied under Dr. Paschal Randolph, and now Clara was certain Rheingold Bingham was a prime suspect.

After hugging her entire family, and giving her thanks to Mrs. Hopkins, Clara took Adeline's hand and guided her back to the library. During the trip with the girl, Clara had also discovered that she had no sense of direction and was constantly getting lost in the smallest of spaces. The result was that Clara was constantly taking her hand to guide her, as she was doing then.

Laura had wired her about meeting with Rachel Wilson-Rafferty the day before, and this was good news. If they could match what the newly arrested Cordelia Fallows knew with what Clara's suspect, Mr. Bingham, knew then they might be close to an arrest.

Isaiah Lees was there as their policing authority, and Ah Toy was the one who could access those witnesses who had been placed under hypnotic trances. Clara went around the table and hugged Laura, Ah Toy, Trella Evelyn, Samuel, and finally Isaiah, whom she also gave a kiss on the mouth. She finally sat down at the head of table and heaved a sigh.

"We have come a long way since our first foray into this case. I do believe we may have arrived at a juncture whereby we can begin to piece together some of the clues. I want to thank you all for coming, and we will get right down to business." Clara took out the pad and pencil from her purse and set it in front of her.

"I must leave with Ah Toy for the Ingleside Jail in ten minutes. We also have the later appointment over at Kearny Street with Mrs. Fallows. These meetings, as I told you in the telegram, may prove to be a linchpin in our case." Laura pursed her lips. "I must admit, Clara, when I began to assist you in this case, I was completely skeptical about the power of the supernatural. However, after what I have witnessed with my own eyes, I have become a true believer."

"Yes, and I will also be on my way again, I am afraid. I must go to San Jose to track down Mr. Rheingold Bingham about whom I told you. He is doing some private spiritual work for Mrs. Sarah Lockwood Winchester, the heiress to the William Wirt Winchester gun manufacturing fortune. It seems Mrs. Winchester was instructed by a medium from Boston to leave her home in Connecticut and go West to create a strange mansion." Clara saw that Trella had her hand raised. "Yes, my dear?"

"Mother, may I go with you and Adeline this time? This trip of yours sounds very exciting, and I have not been back to San Jose to see my friends there in two years." Trella's eyes, Clara saw, were more alive than she had seen them in months. This case had brought her out of her doldrums.

"I don't see why not. The Boston spiritualist knew about her husband's death by consumption, and her daughter's death by marasmus, which is a child's disease wherein the body wastes away in a most deplorable agony. The medium allegedly channeled the husband's spirit through a seance, and Mr. Winchester spoke to his wife and instructed her to build this mansion, with continuous rooms being built, for all the departed souls who had been killed by his manufactured rifles. It was, interestingly enough, the only way to prevent these souls from bringing more curses upon the poor woman's life in the future." Clara wrote something down on her pad.

"Was this suspect of yours, Mr. Bingham, the medium in Boston?" Laura asked.

"No, but I found out from Mrs. Randolph that her late lover, Paschal, knew the Boston medium before a fire burnt down his offices, and he had to leave for Ohio. Mr. Bingham was one of Dr. Randolph's students. He found his teacher's body after Randolph committed suicide in 1875. Rheingold also found out about Mrs. Winchester after he took up with Kate Randolph in an intimate liaison." Clara saw that it was Samuel who had a hand up. "Yes, Samuel?"

"If Trella Bella can go with you to San Jose, then may I go with Ah Toy and Mrs. Gordon to question these prisoners? I need to discuss something with Ah Toy privately."

Samuel's head was downcast, and Clara knew something was amiss. "Why can't you tell me?"

"I said it is private! Must I reveal everything to you? It has nothing to do with your precious case!" Samuel's voice was adamant and loud, once more reminding Clara of his father.

"All right, you may go along. But please remember that kept secrets in a family can lead to untoward and mischievous results."

"Thank you." Samuel folded his hands on the desk and beamed over at Ah Toy, who returned his smile with a nod.

"While we are away again, Laura will be questioning the other two witnesses in the Rachel Rafferty case. We need to establish all the connections we can with the present murders. I would now like to present two theories I have at the moment based on what we know." Clara took out a sheet of paper she had composed upon during the return trip from Ohio.

"May we elaborate upon your ideas with our own?" Laura asked.

"Most certainly. We are, at present, sifting clues and making sand castles from them. One of my theories is that this spiritualist, Mr. Rheingold Bingham, is conditioning these women, one by one, and that he is somehow making money from his talents at hypnosis. Kate Randolph was also in business with Paschal, and this activity was certainly a money-making enterprise." Clara placed a check mark next to her "theory number 1."

"That sounds possible," Captain Lees said. "In my years of experience, most cases of this sort involve greed as the main motive."

"However, from what we extracted from Mrs. Bloomfield, who had been placed under a trance, this spiritualist had motives that encompassed the entire Suffragist Movement. Also, she did connect this handsome mesmerist with your Dr. Randolph, and she mentioned by name his book, *Magia Sexualis*. That certainly bodes well for your theory about Bingham being the culprit behind these murders." Laura pointed out.

Ah Toy nodded her head in affirmation. "I know Elizabeth Bloomfield was entranced. I also told Mrs. Gordon not to trust

Rachel Rafferty, but she ignored my warning. Finally, why have you all rejected my uncle, Fung Jing Toy? He, too, has establishing a working method of turning women into hypnotized slaves to do his bidding. Why couldn't he have sold his technique to this Bingham? He was in San Francisco to establish the first Rosicrucian Lodge after Randolph, and he could have made a deal with Little Pete."

Clara was impressed. "Good. I will put your uncle down as a suspect. Unless other clues appear, we must investigate his possible involvement with Bingham more closely." Clara read from her sheet once more. "My other theory is that these women may have voluntarily cooperated with Bingham, Little Pete, or whomever. Again, money was to be made from their husbands' investments, and we must investigate that angle. Also, the freedom from physical and mental abuse could have been a great instigator for these wives. I, for one, readily admit thinking about doing harm to my former husband. In fact, would it not be possible that these murdering women were pretending to be put under hypnosis to cover-up their murderous intent?"

"Mother!" Trella admonished. "You would never harm father nor would you pretend!"

"I agree. We can't deny either of these theories of yours at this point in time. I shall follow-up on what these women were possibly acquiring from their husbands' deaths." Captain Lees said.

Hannigan, the butler, came into the room, and he held a note. He walked over to Laura and handed it to her. "Mum, this was delivered by a policeman who said it was from the superintendent out at the Ingleside Jail."

"Thank you, Joseph," Laura said, and Clara was surprised her friend knew the family servant's first name. Clara watched her open the letter, and then she saw Laura's thick eyebrows furrow, and she knew it was bad news. "It's Rachel Rafferty. She has been poisoned. There will be a coroner's inquest as to the exact cause of death, and the superintendent is looking into the possibility of foul play."

Ah Toy spoke first. Clara had not seen her this angry for many months. "I told you not to trust that woman! She knew too much, and now we have let her get away with what she knew."

Laura flashed a heated look at the Asian. "This means we are getting quite close to the heartbeat of this mystery. If whomever murdered Rachel was connected enough in the upper-class hierarchy, then that may mean there is a much more dangerous and influential power in charge. We must get out to Kearny Street before Cordelia Fallows is assassinated as well!"

Clara put a check beside her second theory, folded up the paper, and tucked it back into her handbag. "And I must be off to San Jose. Trella and Adeline? Pack your things." She turned toward Hannigan. "Joseph, please make the arrangements for the first train out of San Francisco."

Clara noticed that the butler was pleased by her use of his Christian given name. "Right away, mum. I'll get the maid to pack up your things."

Mrs. Hopkins appeared at the doorway to the library. She was out of breath, and her chest was heaving. "Hannigan. There are many strange women out in my garden. They are shouting something about spirits of the dead. Get them out of there at once! I will not allow witches to put a curse upon my home!"

As it turned out, the women out in the garden were demonstrators in support of keeping the Spiritualist Meetings open. Laura and Clara's suffragettes were there to support them.

***

Jenny Lind City Hall, Police Department, Kearny Street, San Francisco. May 9, 1886.

Laura Gordon left Ah Toy to see about their appointment with Cordelia Fallows. Ah Toy watched the attorney climb the steps leading into the jail located inside the adjunct city hall. Ah Toy was worried about Clara going off on another wild spiritualist chase. She did not trust Laura's sleuthing abilities, because she had not been trained by an expert like Captain Lees, as Clara had been.

"What is it that can be so important, Samuel?" Ah Toy faced the boy, watching for the telltale twitch in his eye. They were standing on the sidewalk, and passersby glanced at them momentarily, but they continued on their way.

"I have some news about your uncle. You must not tell mother nor anybody else." No nervous tic yet.

"I would suspect you have become a gambler in pocket billiards," Ah Toy said.

Samuel's eyes widened slightly, but he continued. "They forced me to join the Triad Society. I could not play for money unless I belonged to the group. I had to take vows that I never understood, and they cut off a rooster's head, and I drank its blood mixed with wine. If I ever tell anybody about the group, they told me I would be beheaded also."

Ah Toy thought Samuel had simply gambled with his friends in secret. She was astounded that her uncle would make the boy a member of his secret society. There must be something behind this. Perhaps Little Pete needed information about the case they were working on.

"I will never tell anyone. You are correct. They would kill you if they knew you told me. Has Fung Jing asked you about this case?" Ah Toy wanted to keep this response a secret from Laura also. She did not know if she would tell Clara. It could mean her son's life.

"No. He just lets me gamble in his Chinatown billiard parlors. I have won quite a bit of money. I was going to buy gifts for everyone this Christmas. And, I wanted to give a special gift to Adeline." Samuel's cheeks flushed red. "Remember. Don't tell anyone!"

Ah Toy decided she needed to tell Samuel one important fact. "I won't. However, I wish you had informed me sooner about this. Remember how I wanted your mother to include my uncle on the suspect list?"

"Yes."

"If he is indeed a functionary in these murders of husbands, then he would not hesitate to murder any one of us who could connect him to such activities. Just as you probably thought you could report to us about him, or use his skills to help our cause, he most likely would use you to keep us at bay."

"You mean, you think he would kidnap me?" She saw the color drain from Samuel's face.

"If he is part of a murder plan, then yes. My uncle would do anything to prevent us from finding out about his involvement." Ah Toy placed her arm around the boy's shoulders and squeezed. "Come. Let us go into the jail. I believe you are becoming a man now, and I am also thankful you told me about this."

***

"What have you two been doing?" Laura was seated on a bench next to the admitting sergeant's desk. She was anxious to interview Mrs. Fallows, and she needed Ah Toy to determine if the accused had been placed in a trance. However, she also remembered that Rachel Rafferty had told them Cordelia Fallows was insane. Could an insane person be hypnotized?

"Samuel has a bit of a crush on our Adeline. He wanted my advice."

Laura watched Samuel's face. She wondered why his eye was twitching. He was probably embarrassed. "I see. We can go back into the women's cells now. The sergeant has checked us in."

A tall and thin young guard came up to them. He wore a sheriff's uniform of blue, with the new double-breasted coat and what looked similar to a Foreign Legion cap on his head. He twirled his mustache at them. "Please follow me. Mrs. Fallows has been placed in an isolated cell. I am afraid she is on suicide watch."

Laura heard Mrs. Fallows before she saw her. She was mumbling to herself seated on the cell's cot against the wall. It was a small cell, and there was no table, so all three of them had to stand near the cot and stare down at the woman. It was stifling hot, as no fans were allowed in the cell block, but there was a block of ice that was kept in a large bucket next to the bed. Laura dipped her hand into the water and rubbed it along her forehead and around her neck. Both Ah Toy and Samuel did the same.

Mrs. Cordelia Fallows was a striking woman of twenty-eight. She could have been a model or a theater actress. Her auburn hair and sad, intoxicating green eyes, were compliments to her olive, flawless skin and hourglass figure. Even in a prison dress of gabardine, her delicate features stood out prominently. Only when she spoke did Laura become aware of the poor woman's confused state of mind.

"The Virgin Mary has given me the power. She appeared to me, and I was lifted up from my slavery and bondage. We are all being lifted up, don't you know? We were called upon to destroy the wretched fornicators who would use us as their playthings. We are making the world clean for the new beginning in the fourth dimension!" Cordelia glanced all around the room, not focusing upon any other human, as if she were conversing with spirits in her private dimension.

Laura did not know how to proceed. This woman was most obviously beyond normal discourse. "Ah Toy? Could you please evaluate Mrs. Fallows?" She knew the Chinese woman would understand what she meant.

Ah Toy stepped slowly over to the seated woman. She reached out with her right hand. Cordelia looked down at it. She then took Ah Toy's hand into her own. The older woman gently pulled the accused inmate's arm toward her. Cordelia's head moved to the left.

"We must know nothing. She told us that this was the beginning of true intelligence. Men always create the concepts, the thoughts about reality, which they enforce with their written laws. They separate the world into nations and states. Good and evil. Love and hate. A dichotomy of three-dimensional pain and suffering. Now we will destroy that world of vague concepts to establish a world based on living in the present where everything is related. Only we free women can understand the present fourth dimension. We shall each have a key."

Laura noticed a strange gleam in Cordelia's eyes. Why did she say it was a woman who instructed her? All of their evidence pointed to a handsome male spiritualist. However, perhaps the woman's insanity was twisting the reality to suit her own diseased mind. If she were sexually abused by this person, then it may have caused a psychotic break with reality.

"It is we who understand a soft touch, a loving glance across a dinner table, a world that has no violent differences based on abstract ideas. I love you is our mantra! I love you is our creed! We are all connected in perfect harmony forever!"

Ah Toy was staring into Cordelia's eyes when Laura noticed the woman wince. Cordelia looked down at her left arm. Implanted in the bicep, dangling like a fishing lure, was a tiny dart. A trickle of blood ran down her arm like a tiny stream from the River Styx.

"Ah Toy! Look!" Samuel was turned around, pointing at the door to the cell. "Someone was standing over there a second ago." He rushed over to look out the bars along the hallway. "I don't see anybody now. But there was someone here a moment before. I swear it!"

Laura screamed when she saw the woman's eyes close, and she slumped over onto the bed. She was quite motionless.

"Guard! Come in here, quickly! The prisoner needs medical assistance!"

***

525 South Winchester Boulevard, San Jose, California, May 10, 1886.

Clara and her two female charges, Adeline and Trella, were driven out to the Victorian redwood mansion of Mrs. Sarah Lockwood Winchester by an old man by the name of Vincent Nicholas. Mr. Nicholas knew all about the rumors concerning the eccentric widow, and he was more than happy to share them on the ride out to the valley estate outside San Jose.

His gray hair was a wispy comb-over, and he wore a worn blue frock coat, brown derby, and bow tie. He would punctuate his sentences with his whip on the backs of the two black stallions pulling the black coach. His voice was still hale and hearty enough to be heard by Clara inside the coach as he bent over and shouted down toward the open window.

"She's got carpenters working shifts twenty-four hours a day. It's truly amazing, but she makes over one thousand a day from her inheritance. I say, why not? She gives people a job around these parts, even if they are making stairs that end nowhere, windows inside the house, and bullseye windows that turn things upside-down when you look through them."

"What about the ghosts and seances? Does she believe in spiritualism?" Clara shouted up at the old man, leaning her body out the window and covering her hands around her mouth.

"Some say it's so, but you know what?" *Whip crack!* "I think she's smarter than that." *Whip crack!* "I think she's building that house to create a place of private meditation." *Whip crack!* "Sarah Winchester wants folks to understand the mysterious intelligence of women."

"How very interesting. Why do you believe that?" Clara shouted.

"My boss owns several properties near her place. He's a Freemason. He told me she belongs to the local lodge, and that she's also one of them Rosy Cross believers." *Whip crack!*

"Rosicrucian?" Clara asked.

"Yep. If she believes in ghosts, it would be the ghosts of Sir Francis Bacon and William Shakespeare!" *Whip crack!*

There were four men to greet them at the entrance to the Winchester house. They were assigned to take the ladies' luggage and escort them to their rooms, of which there were many from which to choose. Construction on the strange mansion had begun in 1884 and continued, unceasing, to this day. Clara could smell the sawdust, paint and plaster the minute she stepped out of the coach.

"You and Adeline go with these men. I want to visit Mrs. Winchester and Mr. Bingham." Clara and the girls were all wearing mourning dresses, in respect for Mrs. Winchester, who had vowed to remain in mourning for all those lives lost because of the misuse of her husband's rifles and guns.

As she walked around the tall hedges, Clara looked at the spectacle in front of her. Men were hammering and suspended from platforms in very precarious formations all around the Queen Anne designed Victorian house. There were some sections that already had violet tiled roofs in conical shapes and with colorful inlays. The driver had said she began with seven rooms in a lonely farmhouse. Now there were over one-hundred rooms, including forty bedrooms, two ballrooms, forty-seven fireplaces, and over ten thousand various panes of glass. The entire property was one hundred and sixty-two acres.

Clara walked up the path toward the front entrance to the main house. She passed a statue of a peaceful brave nonchalantly holding a bow with no arrows. She thought it was probably there to memorialize the natives killed by guns made by the Winchester manufacturing business. As she opened the front door, one of what looked like a collection of a dozen different maids, came up to her. "Yes, mum? May I assist you?"

"I have an appointment to see Mrs. Winchester," she told her, stepping through the doorway into the foyer.

"May I ask who is calling?" The maid wiped her perspiring brow with the back of her hand. She wore the usual maid attire of black dress, white apron, white blouse, and a frilly lace cap.

"Mrs. Clara Shortridge Foltz, Esquire." Clara began to follow the woman down a narrow passageway toward another wing of the house. "My girls are getting our luggage unpacked in our assigned rooms," she added.

"Just so you know the rules of staying at the Winchester home, there is no liquor allowed before dinner, no weapons of any kind on one's person, and lights must be out at ten." The maid waved at the workmen who were busy building new stairs and walls. "This goes on twenty-four hours each day, I am afraid."

"I understand. Where are you taking me now?" Clara asked. The main purpose for her visiting the estate, of course, was to meet Rheingold Bingham, Kate Randolph's lover.

"Mrs. Winchester is in the Sanctum, which is a room in the very center of our home. She and Mr. Bingham are there. Please follow me."

Clara tried to view all of the different activities going on around them as they walked through the house, but it was impossible to focus. Spider-web designed windows, stairs leading to a blank wall, and a skylight embedded inside the parquet floor.

The maid pointed to a floor grating. "We have forced air steam heat that comes up from the huge coal-burning boiler furnace in the cellar. Quite a cozy arrangement during the colder months, as every room has one of these."

There were unique portals of pneumatic communications to other rooms inside the house. The rooms kept narrowing as they reached the inner Sanctum, and when they entered the room, it seemed to Clara a very sparsely furnished and cloistered habitat, almost like a large prison cell.

Of course, when Clara saw the two people inside the blue paneled walls, she lost all sense of proportion. There was only one entrance into this room, but she noticed there were three exits. The maid told Clara that only Mrs. Winchester had the key to the Sanctum.

Seated upon a large, quite ornately embroidered pillow, with his legs in the lotus posture of a Hindu yogi, was the person of Mr. Rheingold Bingham. To his right, kneeling on what looked to be a wooden pew from a conventional Christian church was Mrs. Winchester. The amazing contrast between the two personages was what confounded Clara.

True to form, Mrs. Winchester wore her mourning clothes of black silk, with midnight lace on her hat and down the front of her gown. Her hair was graying, but neatly coiffed, and her pale hands were outstretched toward the man in front of her. She was a very petite yet attractive woman with an intelligent manner.

This man, rather than looking young, the way Clara imagined he would be as the lover of Kate Randolph, was instead gray-haired, and his dark-complexioned face was wrinkled. He was extremely thin, with jutting, bony elbows and veiny, twig-like wrists and bare ankles. His hair was a monstrous, curly weave of smoky-gray locks that hung down over the front of his chest and criss-crossed past his waist.

His mustache and full beard were white, and the strands of long hair also twisted at the end of his chin and curled around his stomach like a snake. He wore brown, open-toed sandals, golden pantaloons, and a crimson-orange, tight-fitting sweater. Colorful beads of turquoise, yellow and red swirled around his neck, and his forehead had the strangest insignia. There were three, one-half-inch-wide stripes that went from his hairline down to the bridge of his long nose; the middle stripe was red and the two outside stripes were yellow. He was chanting something repetitively, and it sounded like the Hindi or Arabic language, although Clara could not be certain.

Mrs. Winchester finally raised her head from prayer, or whatever it was, and saw her. Clara did not know what to say, so she waited.

The maid finally spoke. “Mum, this is Mrs. Clara Shortridge Foltz, Esquire. She has arrived as per your invitation to Winchester house.” She nodded gravely and took her leave out of the center-most exit door, which opened only outward.

Mrs. Winchester stood, emotionless, and nodded to her male companion. “Mrs. Foltz, this is Sadhu Bingham. He has come to teach me more codes to use in my house of Masonic and Rosicrucian puzzlement. Have you just arrived? Where is that young clairvoyant you told me about?”

“So, it is true.” Clara said.

“What is true, my dear?” The first hint of a quizzical emotion surfaced on Mrs. Winchester’s raised brow.

"You are not a spiritualist, who has seances, and keeps building new rooms. You don't need to appease the ghosts of dead victims of the Winchester repeating armaments."

"Those are the myths of the penny press, who wish to make money from these stories of ghosts and a crazy woman trapped inside a haunted house." She took a few steps toward Clara. "No, if anything, my home is a monument to English science and artistry. Francis Bacon, William Shakespeare, and the ingenious mathematician Charles Dodgson are my spirit guides. Of course, Mr. Bingham can tell you about our real purpose here."

Clara wanted to take her chance to inform them about what she knew concerning Bingham. However, she did not want to give away too much, unless he was the suspected spiritualist in her case.

"Thank you, Mrs. Winchester. I am here to instruct Sarah about the ancient and mystical signs of the Rosy Cross. She wants to establish a monument to female genius. Are you aware of the laws of the Fibonacci Sequence and the Kabbalistic numerals? Sir Francis Bacon, like Mrs. Winchester, was a Freemason."

"No, I am not. I was told in Boston that you had studied under Dr. Paschal Beverly Randolph. I thought he was making new inroads into giving women more power through sexual conjugal magic." Clara needed to probe his defenses.

"You must be mistaken. I broke away from his teaching because he was becoming more radical in that area. His elixirs were nothing more than drug-induced rituals in the bedroom." Rheingold was adamant. "I was called by Mrs. Winchester because I plant the magical codes which make her benevolence work for the betterment of society. She met me when I suggested she give a large donation to establish the hospital and research center for Tubercular patients in Yale Hospital, New Haven."

"Sadhu is my personal advisor in all things that relate to the transference of reality to the fourth dimension. My home will be the central point of entrance to all those who solve the coded, mathematical puzzle within my house." Mrs. Winchester walked toward the central exit and stood there looking back at them both. "Please, we must have dinner. I want to meet your clairvoyant. I am not superstitious about ghosts, but I do believe in paranormal events. The Sadhu can cause the waves of light to refract and make seeing much clearer. We can discuss this at dinner."

Bingham followed Mrs. Winchester out the door. “Yes. All of reality is in the present. Thoughts are created to dull the senses and put one into a trance-like state. That was Paschal and his wife’s beliefs. To manipulate human thoughts and control their bodies through mesmerism and animal magnetism.”

Clara was intrigued. Was Kate Randolph lying? This man did not seem to be a supernatural hypnotist at all. Of course, if he were lying, then the tables would turn around again. She knew she needed to talk to Laura and Ah Toy, to unravel the inconsistencies in these two stories. But first, perhaps Adeline could unearth a hidden thought or two on her own. It was time for a much deserved and possibly productive dinner.

As Clara stepped from the Sanctum into the hall, another maid came up to her with a paper in hand. “Mrs. Foltz? This telegram came for you,” she said, and handed the Western Union envelope to her.

It was from Laura in San Francisco. *Both murder suspects are dead. STOP. They were poisoned by unknown assassin. STOP. Come home soon. STOP. We need you to help us put clues together. STOP.*

Clara knew they were getting close to the real killer, and she also suspected something about this house was also part of the mystery, and she wanted to find out what it was before she left.

Chapter 9: The Assassin's Link

Jenny Lind City Hall, Police Department, Detectives Office, Kearny Street, San Francisco. evening, May 10, 1886.

Laura and Ah Toy were discussing the poison used in the assassinations of the two accused women, Rachel Wilson-Rafferty and Cordelia Fallows. The toxicology reports had revealed the chemistry of those drugs, and Captain Lees wanted to inform Laura to see if the link could be made to a possible killer or killers. Lees had also received the information from his legal research assistants about the legal facts concerning murder by hypnotizing the perpetrator. Laura was anxious to hear these new facts, so she and Ah Toy had left the mansion at ten that night to meet the captain in his office on Kearny.

"First of all, my man in New York says none of the women arrested for killing their husbands has been assassinated. That must mean what you have uncovered thus far in San Francisco is frightening the perpetrators enough to want those two women dead." Lees was sitting at his desk near the teletype machines, where all the districts in San Francisco were connected by wireless. Ah Toy sat to his right, and Laura was to his left.

Laura knew their recent interviews of Rachel and Cordelia must have unearthed some toxic information related to the case. But what could they have said to mark them for death?

"Ah Toy was able to access both of these women and their subconscious state of prior hypnosis. We have what they told us written down, but can we put it together to identify a possible killer? Perhaps this poison that was used can give us a clue. What was it?" Laura leaned forward in expectation. She was tired, but these new developments had awakened her like a jolt of adrenaline. Earlier, she had sent off a wire to Clara in San Jose, telling her about the murders and that she should return at once.

The captain twirled his mustaches and stared down at the report from the police laboratory. "I have some bad news about this poison, I am afraid. Our analysis of the liquid on the end of those two darts could not be isolated to any known chemical. We only know how it killed these women. When the poison entered their skin, it caused numbness. Our lab was able to duplicate the effect by using the poison on a mouse. Upon entering the body, this toxin caused muscle and nerve depolarization, fibrillation, arrhythmias, and, eventual heart failure."

"Samuel swears he saw someone who appeared outside Cordelia's cell the night she was killed. He never got a glimpse of the perpetrator, however." Laura wondered if Samuel were placed under hypnosis would he perhaps remember something.

"Laura! I just remembered what Mrs. Bloomfield told us about her honeymoon to Columbia. Do you recall those photos on her walls?" Ah Toy's eyes were round with excitement.

"Yes. She had been tattooed by the female Shaman. An eight-pointed Maltese cross pattern on her back and buttocks. And she told us the hunters were roasting tree frogs over the fire." Laura opened her handbag and took out the notepad. "They wiped their darts against the backs of those frogs. It was poison!"

"Do you suspect Elizabeth Bloomfield? Could she be our assassin?" Captain Lees looked quite interested. "How were these darts used? Did she tell you this as well?"

"She never explained how the natives used those poisoned darts. However, perhaps they shot them from a gun of some kind." Ah Toy said.

"No gun I know of does that. Even if there were some kind of air gun, the noise would have been enough to arouse the guard inside the jail." Lees twisted the paper in his hands. "We need to question this woman again, and this time I will go with you. Poison is not out of the question, and this unknown variety kills within seconds."

"Oh, how I wish Clara were here." Laura wrinkled her nose. "Guns. Clara is at the home of the woman who owns a company that constructs all manner of weaponry. Perhaps she might know. I shall wire Clara again as soon as I can."

"So many clues are floating around in my head right now. I feel like my head is one of those Mexican piñatas. Somebody must strike me to release all my thoughts!" Ah Toy laughed.

Laura wanted to ground their thinking. She did not enjoy the confusion. "What about the research of your legal assistants, captain?"

Lees took out another sheet of paper from his vest's pocket and opened it. "No, there were no cases involving an accused who killed while under hypnosis. However, we did learn about two French doctors who do research in this area. Their names are Jean-Martin Charcot and Georges Gilles de la Tourette. Much of what they've discovered has been used to keep hypnosis out of the courts."

"What do they say? It sounds quite interesting," Laura said.

"They say the only crimes that could be committed while under hypnosis would be rape and theft. They associate the hypnotic state with people who are easily hysterical or quite neurotic. However, the legal requirement of malice aforethought to commit murder could never happen in the mind of a person who is in a trance."

"I beg to differ," Ah Toy said. "My uncle says he can use suggestion to trick the person into believing she is doing one thing when she is actually doing something else."

"Do you have an example of this type of suggestion?" Lees asked.

"He says if he suggests to a prostitute that her client is a spy or a dangerous criminal, she will then lose her moral bearing and kill the man because she has a higher purpose."

"I see. That makes sense. It is not so much that the mesmerist takes over the mind, as he twists the mind's natural proclivity to take revenge upon a person whom it thinks is evil."

Laura nodded her head. "If Elizabeth Bloomfield killed Rachel and Cordelia, I wonder what she was believing?"

"Perhaps we can discover that tomorrow when we question her." Captain Lees moved from his chair to sit on a stool in front of the teletype. "I can send a message to Clara. What do you wish to tell her? The San Jose police office will transmit it to the local Western Union office."

"We still must question the other two witnesses in the Rachel Rafferty case. You should put guards on them in case they might be killed as well. We can do this tomorrow. I just want Clara to know about Elizabeth Bloomfield and that we suspect her. Also, ask if Mrs. Winchester knows of any type of gun that can shoot poisoned darts." Laura stood up and motioned for Ah Toy to do the same.

***

525 South Winchester Road, San Jose, California, May 10, 1886.

Clara once more heard the rhythmic, swaying bounce of the sitar, this time accompanied by a drum. She was being escorted by one of the maids into the dining room of the house. In fact, since each of them was given a separate bedroom, each of them also had a different maid. She imagined Trella and Adeline were being escorted through the labyrinthine maze in other directions.

Instead of a live musician playing, this music was coming from an electronic speaker connected to one of the newest graphophones. It was turning a black wheel, upon which rode a round disc.

"The inventor, Mr. Charles Tainter, sent me one of his newest models from Massachusetts. It won the gold medal at the Paris Electronics Exhibition in 1881. Isn't the sound marvellously melodious?" Mrs. Winchester was seated at the head of the dining table, sipping a glass of port. Rheingold Bingham, who was a vegetarian, and teetotaler, was munching a carrot stick. He reminded Clara of the Mad Hatter from Alice's tea party.

"Yes, I was listening to that instrument while visiting Kate Randolph in Toledo. Her son, Osiris Buddha, played quite well. It is an entrancing sound." Clara saw they were wearing the same clothing as earlier, so she did not feel out of place in the same black dress.

Both Adeline and her daughter were ushered into the dining room at the same moment. It was the Venetian Dining Room, and it had a low ceiling. The dark redwood contrasted with the turquoise silk table cloth covering the round table for six. There was a formal place setting, and above the table was a brightly lit, golden candelabra of gas lighting with six ornate globes of crystal. The gas lights were lit by electric chargers. When all of them were seated, Clara nodded to the servant to pour her a glass of wine.

Adeline, who was seated next to her, looked as if she did not know what to do. Clara decided to instruct her, but Sarah Winchester had other thoughts.

"Is she the clairvoyant? What is the emphasis of her gifts? I have met only two in my life. A gypsy living in Stamford, and a young man diagnosed as mad who was being kept involuntarily at the Willard Asylum for the Insane in Binghamton, New York. This poor, gifted creature was strapped tightly in a holding chair, with some kind of box apparatus over his head. The doctors told me it made them calm. This was where I met the Sadhu for the first time.

He, too, had been committed there by his family. They were the Philadelphia banking Binghams, after which the city in New York was named. My Sadhu, it seems, was quite an embarrassment to them." Clara noticed that Mr. Bingham was still munching his vegetables and was not perturbed.

"I am sorry, but I don't know the title of Sadhu. What does it represent?" Clara wanted to probe some more into the history of Rheingold.

"It means that I was given the task by a guru of separating from the endless cycle of rebirth and death. In this case, it was a guru in India by the name of Shree Shiva Ronchan. I studied with him after Mrs. Winchester released me from the mental prison in New York. I must renounce all worldly possessions and ties, and I must meditate to cleanse my mind of the three gunas of this suffering life." Mr. Bingham's eyes, Clara suddenly noticed, were slightly crossed.

"The gunas are creativity and goodness, motion and activity, and chaos and darkness." Mrs. Winchester pointed out.

"This young lady is Adeline Quantrill. I suppose I, too, rescued her from a mental prison of sorts. Her parents were murdered on a train bound for San Francisco, and she became an orphan. She has the supernatural abilities to remember her entire life and what was occurring on each day of her existence. She can also recall, word for word, what somebody said. In this instance, she has helped me in my present murder case." Clara did not want to divulge Adeline's ability to read minds. This would certainly put the Sadhu on alert.

Mrs. Winchester took another sip from her wine glass. "How fascinating! This case of yours must be quite involved. What does it concern?"

"Five wealthy husbands of women who were members of the Women's Suffrage Movement, were murdered by their wives. Adeline was in attendance at a trial in San Francisco of one of these women. Her name was Rachel Wilson-Rafferty." Clara wanted them to know about the basic facts of her investigation, but she did not want to give away any other details.

"You say *was*. Did she get convicted and hanged, God forbid? I must confess, I read very little of the contemporary press. They are constantly telling tall tales about me." Mrs. Winchester set her wine glass down. "What happened to the poor women?"

"No, neither was hanged. In fact, my friend and fellow attorney, Laura de Force Gordon, got Rachel's sentence reduced to manslaughter. The second accused woman, Mrs. Cordelia Fallows, never got a trial. They were both assassinated by poison, in their jail cells, by an unknown assailant."

"My goodness, how horrid! And what did you want from us? We will most certainly try to help. What is the thesis of your investigation?" Mrs. Winchester, Clara noticed, saw life from the prism of the cultured literati.

Before Clara could respond, another maid came into the dining room with a telegram. She handed it to Clara and stepped away.

We suspect Mrs. Elizabeth Bloomfield of being the assassin. STOP. Please ask Mrs. Winchester if there is a gun that can shoot poisonous darts. STOP. Come home soon. STOP.

Clara looked up from reading the telegram. "It's from attorney Gordon. She now has a person under suspicion for the murders of those two women. I must return to San Francisco the first thing in the morning."

The dining room servants began to ladle out soup into the bowls at each setting. Adeline began eating at once, but Clara put her hand on the girl's arm.

"That must be good news for you." Mr. Bingham said. Clara hoped Adeline was able to hear what he was actually thinking at that moment.

"Laura wants me to ask you about guns. Do you know if there is an armament that can project a small dart with poison on the tip?" Clara figured even if Bingham were part of the conspiracy to murder husbands, this information would not be enough to put him on the defensive.

Mrs. Winchester frowned. "No, I am afraid I leave all the technology to others. I can ask about this tomorrow, perhaps getting an answer before you leave. Would that be sufficient?"

Sadhu Bingham raised his hand. "You know, in my travels around the world, I have been apprised of tribes--especially those in the rain forests of the Amazon--which hunt with poisonous darts. The Matis of Brazil use bamboo devices, hollowed-out, but they are over 14 inches long. I suppose an abbreviated form of these could suffice in the close proximity of a jail cell."

"Yes, I have been the frequent recipient of such projectiles from my brothers and their peashooters." Trella Evelyn spoke for the first time in-between her soup spoonsful.

"Thank you for that information, Mr. Bingham. I shall wire it to my friends tomorrow morning before we leave." Clara picked her soup spoon up and began to ladle it into the steaming vegetable barley.

Following their completely vegetarian meal, each of the diners was escorted by a separate maid servant to his or her room. Clara realized, however, she needed to talk to Adeline about what she might have received from Mr. Bingham in the way of private thoughts.

"May I speak with Adeline first, before you take her?" The other three had already departed the dining room. There were only two maids, Clara and Adeline left. "First, please get me paper and pencil. I wish to send a telegram to Ohio."

One of the maids left the room and returned with a pad and pencil. She handed them to Clara, who began writing. When she finished, she handed the pad and paper to one of the maids. "Please see that goes out tonight, will you? Also, could you both step outside for a moment? I wish to talk in private."

Both of the maids left the dining room and closed the door. Clara turned to the girl. "Well, did you receive anything?"

"No, I am afraid not. I told you before that I cannot control who I am able to access. I was able to hear Osiris, the boy, quite easily. But neither of these adults could be accessed. I am sorry." Adeline looked down at her feet and then up again. "I have been feeling a discomfort in this house. It is the same way I was feeling before my parents were murdered on the train. I would like to stay in your room, if that's possible."

"Of course, my dear. My bed is quite large enough for two." Clara took the girl's hand and led her to the door. She opened it and stuck her head out. "We are ready to leave now. My friend will be staying with me," Clara added.

***

As she raised her head from the pillow, Clara realized her eyes were seeing double. All around this strange room were two of everything. Two standing armoires, two tables, two chairs, and two rugs on the redwood floor. When she saw the two pairs of young women in the same bed with her, Clara shook her head. The images slowly dissolved into singularity. Clara shook her daughter's shoulder. "Wakeup! What happened?"

Trella turned slightly, and her eyes slowly opened. "Mother? Are you there?"

"Listen. Both of you. I believe we were drugged in the night and taken to this room." Clara swiveled her legs around to the edge of the four-poster bed. She pushed off with her hands, but her arms and legs felt as if they had been filled with lead. When her bare feet hit the floor, she could feel the cold wood and the increasing pulsation of her heartbeat. She staggered over to the only door, grasped awkwardly for the silver doorknob, and tried to turn it. It was locked tightly. She screamed, "Let us out of here!"

After a minute, a voice came into the room from another location inside the huge house. It was a male voice, and it sounded like that of Mr. Rheingold Bingham, but Clara could not be certain.

"The room you are in is soundproofed, Mrs. Foltz. No need to scream. I am afraid you must be our guests for some time. We need to ready the physics of Winchester house for the advent of the Fourth Dimension and its subsequent dwellers."

Clara looked all around, trying to discern from which direction the voice was coming. She noticed that Adeline was now awake, and she was glaring at Clara. "What's wrong, Adeline?"

"The revenge has now begun," the girl said. "I warned you."

***

Stanton Mansion, 623 California Street, Nob Hill, May 11, 1886.

When Laura, Ah Toy, and Captain Lees arrived at the Bloomfield residence next-door to the Hopkins mansion, they found it unoccupied. The staff told them that Mr. and Mrs. Bloomfield had left San Francisco because of an emergency and did not say when they would return. Their location was not given.

Although discouraged, Laura said they should continue on to interview Margaret Bennington-Stanton and the maid, Ariel Washington. Mrs. Stanton also lived on California Street, and Miss Washington had gained employment from Margaret Stanton after Rachel Rafferty was arrested for the murder of her husband, Brian.

As they walked up the path through the Stanton's front garden, Laura was sharing the most recent telegram she had received early that morning from Clara in San Jose. "Clara and the girls won't be coming home right now. She says that her suspect, Mr. Bingham, was not at the Winchester house. Instead, he is in Sacramento. They are going to pursue him there."

"How will we pursue our case without her? I don't understand. She was so certain he was there working for Mrs. Winchester." Ah Toy called from behind the others, mincing her way toward the entrance.

"I know one thing. I'm getting the destination location of the Bloomfields traced at all the rail stations and steamship terminals. She is now a major murder suspect in these assassinations." Lees had already reached the front door and was rapping his fist against it instead of using the door knocker.

Laura knew Mrs. Stanton was also a close friend of the now deceased, Rachel Rafferty. They had attended Berkeley College together and were active in the Suffrage Movement. Thanks to Clara and her young clairvoyant, Adeline, she also knew Rachel had been tortured by her husband. As a result, Rachel became addicted to opiates and had even held a knife above Brian's sleeping body, prior to her murdering him during fellatio on another night. Laura had earlier wired Dr. McCauley's office, and the hypnotherapist was also meeting them at the Stanton home.

Captain Lees was wearing his cape, badge, gun, and holster, so the servant let him right in. Laura waited for Ah Toy to catch-up before she entered the house. She hoped the Chinese woman could once again determine if Mrs. Stanton had been placed under a hypnotic trance so they could gain even more guarded information.

They were all taken back to the greenhouse, where Mrs. Stanton was tending to her prize roses. Once again, Laura felt dressed down in her plain brown dress with no bustle. Mrs. Stanton wore an elaborately decorated pink dress with blue lace fringes on the collar, sleeves and front. Mother of pearl buttons were on her garden hat and dainty jacket, and she also had the suffrage necktie. When she heard the maid introduce them, she turned from clipping a monstrously large American Beauty. She was forty-five, but she looked no more than thirty, and her blonde, straight hair cascaded down on her narrow shoulders and over her breasts. Her eyes were a marine blue, her gaze was calm, and her voice was intelligent.

"Why, Mrs. Gordon, it's so nice to see you once more. When I heard the news about poor Rachel, I knew you might be back. How dreadfully vicious! It was in the *Examiner*. On the front page. Don't we get tarred and feathered enough in those liberal editorials? Now the rabble think we're murdering our own." Mrs. Stanton placed her pruning shears down on a white table and motioned for them to be seated in the four chairs.

"I am sorry, Margaret, but this is not a social call. We'll stand. You may not be reading the out of town newspapers, but there were three other murders similar to San Francisco's two. They occurred in New York City. All of the victims were slain by suffragists, and the three were wealthy and prominent in the business community." Laura wanted Mrs. Stanton to know how far the disaster had spread, and she noticed that the woman had to sit down.

"All in the Movement? I did hear about the push in Washington to close down our spiritualist centers. Do you know who killed Rachel and that other woman?" Laura found it odd she didn't remember the name of Cordelia Fallows, as she was a fellow Rosicrucian.

"Cordelia Fallows? She was in your group, wasn't she?" Laura leaned toward Margaret.

"Oh yes. Now I recall. When she had the mental problems, I suppose I failed to keep up with her disgraceful arrest. It's been all too much for me, to be quite honest." She wiped her brow with a silk handkerchief she extracted from her sleeve.

"I know what you testified on the stand during Rachel's trial. However, did Rachel tell you about being addicted to laudanum? Also, did she inform you about Brian?"

"Brian? What about him? How did you know about the drugs?" Margaret's voice was higher pitched.

Laura knew when to cut the rose off at the bud. "Brian was torturing your best friend, wasn't he? He locked her in the basement, and he beat her. That's when she began taking opiates and made an attempt to knife him in his sleep. Isn't that true?"

When she saw the tears begin to flow, Laura knew she had struck an emotional vein of truth. However, before her witness could respond, a young police officer was led into the greenhouse. He looked all around at the flowers, as if he had stumbled into Eden. When he saw Captain Lees, he came to attention.

"Captain, sir. O'Leary here. I'm from the Rincon Hill District."

Lees walked over to stand beside the young man. "Yes, O'Leary, what is it?"

"The body of Jonas Bloomfield was discovered in the attic by the maid." The young officer looked around at the women as if he were embarrassed for them.

"Was it poison?" Lees asked.

"They think so."

"Where is his wife?" Laura asked.

"Nobody's seen her."

"Thank you, Officer O'Leary. I'll be over there as soon as we finish here." Lees shook the young officer's hand, and the man left.

Without being told, Laura watched Ah Toy, as she minced over to where Mrs. Stanton was seated. "Hello, Mrs. Stanton. I don't believe we were introduced." Ah Toy reached out and took Margaret Stanton's right hand, and she pulled it toward her. Laura saw Stanton turn her head to the left before she began to talk. "It is a world suffrage disaster. Unless we act, women will remain in bondage forever. We have each been given a key to a door. We shall meet together to open every door to the new Eden of the Fourth Dimension."

Out of the corner of her eye, Laura noticed the figure of a servant standing just outside the door to the greenhouse. When she turned to look at her, she ran. It was the final witness to the murder of Brian Rafferty, Ariel Washington. "Stop that woman! We need to question her!" Laura shouted.

After they dragged her back into the greenhouse, Ariel Washington kept staring over at Mrs. Stanton, waiting for her to say something. Laura thought it was quite suspicious, but she wanted to get to the heart of the matter.

"Do you both know Mrs. Elizabeth Harter-Bloomfield? She lives next-door to the widow, Mrs. Mark Hopkins." Laura used her best attorney voice. Now that she heard the hypnotic mention of the fourth dimension, she believed it may also be connected to what was going on.

"Yes, we all belonged to the spiritualist group on Clay Street. Mrs. Virginia Partridge's residence, I believe," Mrs. Stanton said.

Ariel nodded her head in agreement.

"Dr. McCauley? Could you come in here now?" Laura called out, and a tall, portly gentleman in a red frock coat and green necktie came into the greenhouse. He was in his fifties, and he had a wide, gray handlebar mustache, and he wore a monocle in his right eye. "Ladies, I am certain you both know the good doctor, Adam McCauley."

"Good afternoon, Margaret. Ariel. I wish we were meeting under more pleasant circumstances, but duty calls. Captain Lees and Attorney Gordon have asked me to put you both under hypnosis. They believe you may have been entranced by someone other than myself." Dr. McCauley sat down on a chair between the two women, who were seated in two other garden chairs. "I have done this before to you, as I was your therapist. Now, however, we may be able to gain information about who may have mesmerised you to plant suggestions in your subconscious mind. May I proceed?"

"I really don't know what this will prove, but I suppose if it's you, doctor." Mrs. Stanton's eyelids were drooping, Laura noted.

"Of course, Dr. McCauley. Whatever you need." Ariel leaned forward with interest. She had only been briefly put under before, and she was obviously anxious to become hypnotized again. Usually, only the wealthy women were allowed such exotic therapies.

Laura had seen Dr. McCauley perform hypnosis on a patient once before, so she knew he was no charlatan, as she had been. Laura had used a large pocket watch, which she swung back-and-forth in front of the performer's eyes, and he or she would then pretend to become placed in a trance.

McCauley, on the other hand, simply used his calm and soothing baritone. He had explained to Laura that hypnosis was successful on a patient because the power of suggestion overcame their will to resist. If a person were steadfastly against any suggestion, then nobody could hypnotize that person.

"Margaret and Ariel, I want you to imagine a most serene setting. It is a place where you are always most comfortable. It is not your bed, as I do not want you to sleep. I want you to hear everything I say to you. It is very important that you concentrate on the sound of my voice. Is that clear?" Dr. McCauley adjusted the monocle in his eye and frowned. When he saw both of the women had nodded in agreement, he began.

"I shall count from ten backward to zero. With each number, your eyelids will become heavier. When I say zero, you will be in a most relaxed, comfortable frame of mind. You will only concentrate on my voice. No other sounds noises in this room will disturb your concentration. Ten … nine … eight."

Laura saw that the women's eyes were now closed, and their breathing was deep and evenly paced.

"Seven … six … five … you are getting more comfortable now … four … three … two … you are approaching your most relaxed state of mind … one … zero. Can you now hear me? Are you in your most relaxed and agreeable state of mind?"

Laura saw that Margaret and Ariel both had slight smiles on their faces, and they were so relaxed that all they could manage was a brief nod of the head.

Chapter 10: The Revenge Begins

525 South Winchester Road, San Jose, California, May 11, 1886.

I am so sorry, Mrs. Foltz. I was not able to receive the exact danger. Will they be coming for us?" Adeline was sitting beside the fireplace, as the room was quite large, although the redwood ceiling was low, similar to the Venetian Dining Room. It also had only one exit and entrance door. Clara was going over the perimeter of the room, for perhaps the one hundredth time, attempting to find some secret aperture or passageway.

"We can't allow circumstances to prevent us from finding a way out," she whispered, although she assumed they were being monitored by the latest invention Nikola Tesla or Thomas Edison could provide. Her daughter, Trella, was taking a bath in the lavatory room. Clara was cheered by the sound of her singing. Despite their being kidnapped, Trella had been keeping up a strong front.

Because she was quite certain they were being spied upon, Clara was keeping her thoughts about what was happening, and about whom she believed was behind it all, to herself. Since the first communication, there had been exactly five informational broadcasts from the male voice of Mr. Bingham. Along with instructions about where their living supplies were, including foodstuffs, he had also assured them they would be released as soon as the final changes were made to the house. Clara was not so certain this would be the case. Bingham must know by now that he was a suspect in the murders, and even if he did release them, he would still be guilty of kidnapping. In fact, if Mrs. Winchester were also aware of what had been done to the three of them, she could also be arrested.

"Do you think the others will be coming for us soon?" Adeline was pushing logs with the poker, and sparks flew up against the grating and crackled.

"Of course. As soon as Laura and Captain Lees find out we have not returned on schedule, they will be out here immediately." Clara continued feeling every inch of the wall, letting her fingers pull against any loose board or crevice. When the voice came over the speaker system, she jumped and hit her head on the ceiling.

"Ladies, we have decided to make an exceptional accommodation for you. Our group will be opening the Fourth Dimension to our members, so we realize we need the verification from the outside world to make our plan noticed. Because we now have the ability to permanently wipe memory from the human mind, the final stage of our process can begin."

Clara moved over to sit on the divan with Adeline. She saw Trella come in from the bathroom, so she motioned for her to sit as well. Her head had a green towel around her hair, and her body was in a yellow bathrobe. When she was seated, Clara wrapped her arm around her daughter's shoulders.

"We have been aware of your investigation for quite some time. In point of fact, it was your young clairvoyant, oddly enough, who gave us the first impetus to extend our goals to reach international proportions. No longer will men be in charge of the nation-states. We have given them over a thousand years to push their agenda of conquest and murder, and now it must stop. As a Sadhu, I was allowed to meditate and use any method--including mind-altering drugs--in order to find a way to harness the power required to wrest control from the leaders of the world. We now know that these males can be conquered in two steps. The first step was what you and your small team observed. We began terminating these leaders in their bedrooms and boudoirs."

Clara now understood why each of the suffragette women was different as to what she knew. The psychic conditioning utilized each woman's particular vulnerability to make her commit murder. Ah Toy told them her uncle was able to accomplish this type of operant conditioning because he could make his women believe they were committing murder for a higher cause than what they normally believed in. Certainly, all militaries of the world functioned the same way. Soldiers were told they were killing the enemy because the enemy was evil, and they were good. They had to kill for a higher purpose, and this belief system bypassed the individual's moral code against killing another human.

"But now, because we have been doing our own investigating into the powers of the supernatural, we can bypass such exploits as murder by spouse and go right for the jugulars, so to speak. Are you aware of the fourth dimension? Imagine this. The first dimension is a line. Just a line on a piece of paper. The second dimension is a line four times, or a line plus a line, plus a line, plus a line, or what we call a square. Next, the third dimension is a square four times or what we call a cube. We live in the third dimension every day, but we can only see things in two dimensions. A first-dimension organism can move only across length back and forth. A second-dimension organism can move in width and length, and everywhere in-between. A third-dimension organism, like humans, can move in width, length, and height."

Clara was following the logic thus far, but she suspected she would have to question Adeline afterward to be certain. She noticed Adeline was paying strict attention. Trella was her usual distracted self, staring at the fire. The idea that they could erase the human memory was especially concerning.

"We can only see things in two dimensions because we see things get bigger and smaller, and the light makes us believe we see all three sides, but it's a trick on the eye. Now, our new theory encompasses the fourth dimension. We believe this dimension is made of height, length, width and one more line, which is time. An organism in the fourth dimension must change, as we all do, but when it does, it makes a permanent mark in time, similar to a photographic image in a long list of sequential photos. This list begins when you are born and ends when you die."

Clara was amazed at this. It explained how Adeline and people like her were able to see their lives in sequential images. They were, possibly, seeing into the fourth dimension!

"We now can create the process of time travel by using people such as your Adeline Quantrill, and sending them mentally into the fourth dimension, where we can literally accumulate enough gambling information, in the future, to take over all the economies in our known world. Not only that, but we speculate that there could also be an infinite number of universes, and, theoretically, we could travel into those infinite places throughout space and time beyond our ever-expanding universe, where our galaxy and solar system exist. So, ladies. we will be using Miss Quantrill as our first-time traveler to create a memorial to the female conquest of our known world."

The speaker was shut off. Clara turned to the two girls. She realized she was on philosophical egg shells, but she definitely wanted some clarification. “I believe I understood most of what was said. However, this idea of time travel quite befuddled me. There would be no gambling wins unless one could somehow travel into the future, correct? Otherwise, there can be no reality of knowing on which investment or race to bet. Also, how can they erase our memories?”

Although she wanted Adeline to respond, it was her daughter who spoke. “This must be a fraudulent device to trick Mrs. Winchester into investing money. Don’t you see, mother? Sometimes, I believe your legal ways don’t allow you to observe the trickery going on around you.”

“Adeline, what are your thoughts on the matter? I believe you do have the supernatural ability about which this person refers. Is it possible to extend it to the future and to prognostications for a profit?” Clara reached out and took the young girl’s hands, as if she were guiding her mind down a dark passageway wherein she could get lost.

“How can I know about this? Really. I have told you, time and again. I don’t remember at all after I access a mind. It does not matter if my mind is in the present or the future. I simply channel other minds, and these minds are imprisoned in their own sanctuaries of fear. I would love to have my memory erased. Most of the time, it is excruciating torture being who I am! Why did you bring me into all of this? My parents were murdered, and that is why I am the way I am. These people are planning to take revenge upon our society, and you can do nothing about it!” Adeline broke away, got up from the divan, and ran into the bathroom. Clara could hear her sobbing within.

“I didn’t mean to ignore you, sweetheart.” Clara now took Trella’s hands. She needed someone to comfort her in this time of immediate peril. “Of course, this can all be a ruse to siphon money from the wealthy Mrs. Winchester. However, there must be something deeper. Perhaps a psychosis of this Mr. Bingham has become overblown. His appearance certainly lends itself to mental illness. We can be certain he never told Mrs. Winchester about the murders of wealthy husbands on both coasts. Mrs. Winchester herself was a beneficiary of a valuable estate due to the premature death of her husband. She would immediately see through any plan to kill-off husbands for financial reward. But what this voice has said is far beyond the realm of legal fraud and even murder. It has become a fanatical vision of monstrous proportions."

Trella leaned forward and kissed Clara's cheek. When she pulled back, Clara could see the first look of pity on her daughter's face she had ever seen. "Mother. We are all in this together. You no longer have to do things alone. We will get over this as women together. I will speak to Adeline and explain any plans you have to get us out of here. I promise."

Clara hugged Trella closely, and they both stared into the roaring fire. Somehow, within the depths of their minds, Clara believed, like a kernel of female survival, a plan could be hatched out of the infinite changes of the moment.

***

The Chinatown Billiards Parlor, evening, May 11, 1886.

When Samuel Cortland Foltz heard that his mother, sister, and Adeline were not coming back from San Jose, as planned, he was livid. "Why do you believe a telegraph message? Anybody could have sent that. We must go to San Jose at once. Mother was certain it was Winchester house that contained the secret to this mystery." However, Laura Gordon and Captain Lees were concerned about capturing the murderer, whom they believed was Mrs. Elizabeth Bloomfield. They told him this Bloomfield had killed the two jailed women with poison darts, and now she had poisoned her own husband. "We can't go galivanting out to San Jose or Sacramento when we have the real killer right here in San Francisco."

Only Ah Toy was sympathetic, and when he left the Hopkins mansion that evening, she nodded her head gravely at him, as if she knew where he was headed. Samuel knew his best friends, Ezra and Roger, would be playing pocket billiards in Chinatown, and it was them he wanted to see.

As he burst through the green wooden doors and lurched down the path leading to the back table, where they always played, Samuel's insides felt panicked and his palms were sweaty. The elderly owner, Chang Bingwen, was behind his counter, and he smiled at Samuel as he rushed up. "Where you lady friend, Sammy? She tell you she see a ghost and run away?"

Ezra was standing next to the table, with his cue stick, and his long sideburns and black hat making him look like some kind of Quaker. Roger was taking his turn shooting.

"Listen to me, fellows. I have news about the women I care most about in this world. So pay attention." Samuel took a position equidistant between the two of them, so he could take turns staring each of them down. "My mother discovered a plot to bilk money from that rich Mrs. Sarah Winchester in San Jose. Remember when I told you she traveled all the way to Ohio with Adeline?"

"Indeed. But, please slow down, my boy. Or you shall burst a piston in your engine." Ezra was his usually sarcastic self.

"You also know that mother's attorney friend, Laura Gordon, has now got it in her head that she's cornered the murderer. When she received a telegram from San Jose telling Laura that mother, my sister and Adeline had left Winchester's house and headed for Sacramento, she believed it!"

Roger, who rarely spoke, set his cue stick down on the green felt table top and turned to face Samuel. "Why shouldn't she believe it? They can trace those telegrams."

"Mother was certain that Mr. Rheingold Bingham was trying to defraud money from rich Mrs. Winchester. He was also the only one who studied under the great Rosicrucian master, Dr. Paschal Beverly Randolph. They traveled to Toledo and questioned his wife." Samuel turned to face Ezra. "You know me, Ez. I never get frightened about something unless I am certain it is true."

"All right. Let us suppose your ladies are still in San Jose inside the haunted money mansion. That must mean they were kidnapped by force. How can you prove this? Send a telegram asking if they have three women locked up?" Ezra chuckled, but when he saw the look on Samuel's face, he abruptly stopped.

"I want you both to come with me and see what is happening there. If we can't locate them, then I shall be satisfied. But we must try to find them. I know they are there!"

"If I were you, I would look behind me at present," Roger Dowdy said.

Samuel turned around. Goose-stepping his way down the green rug was the leader of the Triad Society, Little Pete, and three of his largest companions. Fung Jing Toy motioned to the biggest, his personal bodyguard and white man, C. H. Hunter. "Grab him," Little Pete ordered.

"What are you doing?" Samuel felt the vise-like grip of the man's big hands encircle his wrists and yank his arms behind his back. "I have to save my mother!"

Little Pete strolled up to stand directly in front of him. Samuel noticed, with pyrrhic satisfaction, that he was actually almost a head taller than Pete. "I believe you know why we have come. It has come to our attention that you were having a discussion with my niece. Is this true?" As the gang leader said the words "attention" and "discussion," he poked Samuel in the stomach with his forefinger.

Samuel knew exactly what they were referencing. His confession to Ah Toy about becoming a professional gambler was said in the strictest confidence. Samuel was being harassed because of this one tragic mistake. He now had to think of a way out of this disastrous situation.

Ezra and Roger did not say a word. Samuel supposed they were just as frightened as he was. He realized the only chance he had of escaping possible maiming or even death was to distract them with something which challenged their business income.

"My mother is being held in San Jose by a man who has started a house of prostitution. She was investigating this when they kidnapped her along with my sister, Trella Evelyn and the clairvoyant, Adeline Quantrill. My friends and I were just making plans to go there to see if we can prove they are being held." Samuel observed Little Pete very carefully. He noticed that the older man's eyes squinted, and he rubbed his chin whiskers.

"Who is this man? Do you know his name?" The gang leader was so attentive that Samuel believed his distraction had worked.

"My mother investigated him in Toledo, Ohio. His name is Rheingold Bingham." When he voiced the name, Little Pete swiveled his head to stare at each of his men.

"Yes. I know him. He was in San Francisco working at the various spiritualist meeting groups. I believe you may have something. However, you can never stop this man with your little friends." Samuel noticed Ezra and Roger flinch when Pete said "little friends."

"What do you mean? We cannot raise any suspicion. If you and your gang go with us, there will certainly be a commotion at the Winchester house." Samuel was only trying to distract Little Pete from punishing him. Now, however, the gang lord was becoming a participant in his plans. Samuel wondered what was behind this sudden change in direction.

"Please understand, young man. If I go with you, it will be because I have a personal business disagreement to resolve. My methods of infiltration are both inscrutable and judicious. As you were made aware, we have hundreds of years fighting the emperor and his forces. Certainly, you can see this is like the dragon toying with the hen." When Little Pete began to laugh, his men began laughing, and soon Samuel, Ezra and Roger were chiming in. They were holding their sides and pushing each other. Even the old owner was chuckling behind his counter.

"What about my punishment?" Samuel thought it was better that he got his fear out in the open. If his distraction was not working, then both he and his three ladies could be in danger.

Little Pete put his left arm around Samuel's shoulder and tousled his dark hair with his right hand. "I believe we frightened you enough. Your hair should have turned white, judging from the look on your face when I came in here."

"What shall we do now? We don't have much time. Can we know your plan, or is it a secret?" Samuel pulled away and attempted to gain his masculine composure. He still felt a queasy rippling inside his stomach.

"I think it is best that you do not know what I have in mind. I am well aware of this Mr. Bingham and his spiritualist aspirations. Quite often, one's aggrandisement can be used against one. I believe we shall discover this to be the case at the Winchester house."

Samuel was reluctantly satisfied. "May my friends come with us to San Jose?""

"Why not? Like all great artists, I do appreciate an audience."

***

Much later, Samuel, Roger and Ezra were waiting at the train station for Little Pete and his entourage to appear. They had tickets for the last train leaving San Francisco for San Jose. The nightly fog was moving in, and it became a ghostly ambience around the station. Ezra was eating some cold chicken that his mother had packed for him. Both boys had informed their families that they were going to do a tourist visit at the wealthy Mrs. Winchester's house. Samuel's mother, who was staying there, had invited them.

Samuel who was now impatient, kept looking around, even though the thick fog impeded his view. Their train was warming up, and the sound of the steam engine combined with the smell of the burning coal to again make his stomach queasy.

When the figures came toward him out of the soupy fog, Samuel was astonished. Instead of ten muscular members of the Triad Society, there were that same number of beautiful young women, strutting in long black overcoats, each with a ticket in hand. Only Little Pete and his bodyguard, C. H. Hunter, were there to represent the Hip Yee Tong.

Samuel noticed that only one of the women was Chinese. Nine of them were young white women who wore thick make-up and crimson lipstick. They all giggled as they walked past the boys and climbed up into the passenger car. Were these some of his prostitutes? If they were, then what purpose were they going to serve at the Winchester house? Was this Mr. Bingham running a clandestine brothel right under the nose of the rich Mrs. Winchester? Were Samuel and his friends being duped so that Little Pete could go into business with the spiritualist? If they were being crossed, then how could he save his three ladies?

As the train began to move, Samuel looked out the window. His view outside was as opaque as what he knew was going to happen inside the car. To make matters worse, possibly the most attractive member of the group of ten young ladies was seated next to him.

"Have you been to San Jose before?" she asked him, and he could smell her perfume as she leaned toward him. She was about his age, and her hazel eyes had the maturity of a much older woman. He was not in the mood to explain the history of his family's residence in that town. It all seemed like it had taken place years, if not centuries, before.

Stanton Mansion, 623 California Street, Nob Hill, May 11, 1886.

Dr. McCauley accepted a list of questions that Laura handed him. She wanted information about these specific items because they related to the capture and imprisonment of whomever was behind these murders.

Margaret Stanton and Ariel Washington were completely under hypnosis. At first glance, Laura could not tell, but upon further observation, she could see that each woman kept a steadfast gaze at some point in the air and never looked directly at anything in the room, including Dr. McCauley. It was if they were lost in a private world of somnolence.

"Who was the person who gave Rachel Rafferty her private therapy? Do you know the person's name?" Dr. McCauley read off the paper.

Mrs. Stanton shuffled her feet, and her right hand went up to tug at her right ear. "Dr. Randolph. He was a very handsome man, part Negro. He said he came from so many different lands that he had no home. He was a mixture of all humanity for all time."

Ariel smiled. "Yes, he was very handsome. He told us he worked with Mrs. Lincoln after her husband and son had died. He was in the President's funeral motorcade coach until they saw he was colored and told him to get off."

Laura turned to Captain Lees and whispered, "That cannot be. Clara told us this Dr. Paschal Randolph died in 1875 of a self-inflicted gunshot."

"Perhaps this spiritualist was impersonating him. There were four students who studied under him." Lees nodded toward Dr. McCauley. "Listen."

"Did Rachel want to do harm to her husband? Why was she afraid of him?"

"He tortured her. Dr. Randolph was simply treating her for hysteria. She was medicating herself with drugs, and he told her he could cure her in a more natural manner. He said he was traveling all over the country assisting abused women." Mrs. Stanton cleared her throat. "I told her she needed to see him. When she confessed to me that she had held a knife above him as he slept. My God! She needed help."

"Do you recall what this doctor looked like? Can you describe him? Or, better yet, can you draw him?" Dr. McCauley handed a pad of paper, and a pencil he extracted from his coat pocket, over to Mrs. Stanton.

Holding the pencil above the paper for a moment, Mrs. Stanton paused. “I said he was part Negro. However, I am no artist. I know Ariel can draw. Please, do us this service.” She handed the pad and pencil over to the Negro maid.

“I don’t know. I guess I can try,” Ariel said, and she began to draw on the pad. She was a rather good artist, and Laura could see Ah Toy look over at her work and nod her head in appreciation.

Laura took out a daguerreotype she had of Dr. Randolph and looked down at it. He was quite a handsome man, with dark, negroid hair, an olive complexion, and a rueful stare that displayed a certain transcendental superiority. He also wore a dark suit, white shirt sleeves, and a cravat. She handed the picture to Captain Lees, who showed it to Ah Toy, and then Laura looked over at what Ariel had drawn.

Despite their words about meeting this spiritualist, and then naming and describing him, the pencil sketch Ariel had drawn was nothing like the image of the authentic Dr. Randolph in their possession. This man appeared much older. His hair was long, gray, and braided in many strands that hung down the front of his chest. He also had a full and quite white beard that was twisted like a French Cruller on the end. Upon his forehead was drawn a quite distinctive mark, which had three sections of the same length, extending from his hairline down to the bridge of his narrow nose. The two outer stripes were white, and the innermost stripe was darkened. He also wore several strands of large beads around his neck.

“Dr. McCauley. How can they orally describe this person in one way and then draw him in quite another?” Laura asked.

Dr. McCauley turned to address her. “If they were given post-hypnotic suggestions, then their oral descriptions could be quite different than what they actually saw in person. The actual image of him can come out only under hypnosis and only by drawing it.”

“You mean this sketch is probably the most accurate description?” Laura reached over and took the pad from Ariel and held it up for all to observe.

“Yes, I would say so. This person was posing as Dr. Randolph, so he put both these women under and described his false personage so they would remember it. However, because I have hypnotized them both, the actual image their minds recorded has come out in a drawing."

Laura tore off the sheet. "Ah Toy, can you make a more permanent ink copy of this sketch for us?"

"Of course. Do you suppose this man is the person we should now go after?" Ah Toy took the drawing from the attorney, folded it in half, and tucked it down into the top of her blue silk *cheongsam*.

"Yes. This man is quite dangerous. We also don't know his identity, as he obviously portrays himself differently to his victims." Laura was now worried about Clara and the two girls.

"What about Mrs. Bloomfield? She is the most proximate suspect who had a weapon to kill her husband and the two imprisoned women. I cannot drop that to go after some somnambulist phantom." Captain Lees stood up. "In fact, I must leave now to meet Officer O'Leary at the scene of the murder. If you will excuse me."

Laura watched him stomp out of the greenhouse. "I suppose it's best he does that. However, now I am certain that we must get this image out into the media. If this person is the one who is making suffragette wives into murderers, then he was probably the one who did it to Mrs. Bloomfield as well. If some woman can recognize him from our drawing, then we may have the true guilty party in our sights."

Chapter 11: A Key to Every Door

525 South Winchester Road, San Jose, California, May 11, 1886.

Little Pete decided to keep his girls at a boarding house in downtown San Jose and make his first foray into the Winchester estate with Samuel, Ezra, Roger and his bodyguard. Samuel was able to learn more about what the leader's plans were on the drive out to the valley.

"I met Mr. Bingham in Chinatown. He was using one of my entertainment facilities. He enjoys using opium, in moderation of course, and when he found out how many other establishments I ran, he wanted to meet me. I had never met this man before, but after what you have told me, I can now understand his true motivations."

"What are his motivations? My mother believes he may be the spiritualist who hypnotizes women to kill their husbands." Samuel took out a news story he had cut from the *San Francisco Examiner*. "See? This was the first such murder by Mrs. Rachel Wilson-Rafferty. She killed her husband, Brian."

"I know. I have also been following these murders. I do this because we Chinese are often accused of such homicides even though there is no substantial evidence to prove we did them. I must say, Rheingold Bingham showed no interest in mesmerizing women. All he wanted to know from me was how to work a good house of prostitution for a profit."

"So, when you heard my story about his being at Winchester house for that reason, you wanted to see for yourself what he was doing?" Samuel was immediately frightened. He had no such knowledge about Bingham. The story he told Little Pete was a complete fabrication in order to distract him. To him, it was either a lie or get punished for breaking the Triad's vows of secrecy.

"That's right. I am not about to permit some white devil to use my system to make more money than I do. I am here to convince him to allow my girls to work this house. If he does not agree, then I may have to enforce my will in the usual way." Little Pete took out the hatchet from the waistband of his suit pants and brought it up to Samuel's throat.

Samuel looked down at the razor-sharp blade and swallowed hard. "What about my mother and the two girls? You will save them, won't you?"

"First things first. Profit before favors. We should be able to find out where he's stashed the ladies once he is on our side. I need to first discover what his scheme is with the old dowager. If it's even bigger than just whores, then I will get a slice of that also."

Roger and Ezra, who were in the back of the coach with C. H. Hunter, were staring out at the passing scenery, pretending not to hear. Samuel knew differently. With every bit of information, they were all slipping deeper into a dangerous conspiracy of quicksand.

"Here she is, gentlemen!" The driver shouted down at them from his post above the three horses. "The Winchester residence. Mrs. Sarah Lockwood Winchester, eccentric owner and generous employer."

The five men were taken inside to meet with Mr. Bingham. When the gang leader saw the spiritualist, he walked right up to him and gave him a big hug. Samuel would have believed they were brothers if he had not heard the story from Little Pete. This gentleman was dressed like some kind of Indian. Not an American variety, but an Asian. Samuel even expected Ezra to make some humorous remark, but he was too frightened to do so.

"Pete, it's wonderful to see you again! Come, let me take you to the old lady's Sanctum. We can talk there." Bingham looked over Samuel and the others briefly. "Can we trust them?"

"Of course. They work for me. You know the loyalty I demand from my men." Little Pete followed directly behind Bingham as the mystic led them through the intricate maze that was Winchester house.

"Here it is. The exact center of this huge estate. Mrs. Winchester has the key, but I was able to make a copy. You know me. I make necessary arrangements." Bingham turned the key in the lock, and it opened into a room with blue paneling and three doors opposite the wall. Samuel noticed that inside the room there was only a yoga mat and what appeared to be a pew from a Christian church.

"It is soundproof, so nothing can be heard from outside of this room. Also, those three doors all open outward and not inward. The only exit is from the door we just entered."

Bingham sat down on the yoga mat and folded his legs into an apparently comfortable lotus position. Samuel was impressed. He and the others sat down on a wall bench at the opposite side.

"Bingham, you probably know why I came here. I showed you how to condition women to get ten times the income from these wealthy bastards. What I need to know is what your game is here. I know you can't be expecting much if you're working alone."

Samuel watched the way Bingham brought his hands together in front of his chest, and then the spiritualist bowed his head. "Namaste. I did learn a lot from you, Fung Jing Toy. I learned that fear and intimidation can create slave labor. However, this plan of mine is a bit larger and more complicated than you could ever begin to grasp." The old man had the audacity to close his eyes.

Little Pete's frown became a fixture as Bingham continued his story. Samuel knew the white man was not only condescending, but he was also directly insulting the intelligence of the Chinatown gang leader.

"I am not working alone on this. In fact, since I moved in, there has been a complete changing of the guard here at Winchester manor. All of the carpenters and household staff are now working for me. Oh yes. Mrs. Winchester believes they work for her, but the fact of the matter is that my current partners have much deeper pockets. This tired old witch could only dream about those men who are now backing me in this enterprise and the wealth they represent." Bingham opened his eyes.

"I don't care if you have the United States Cavalry working for you here, Bingham. I want in on it. If you don't let me in, then the silent and imposing death that I represent will creep inside this nutcracker farm like the Black Plague." Samuel shivered at the tone of deliberate threat in the gang leader's voice. He knew this white man had just crossed an invisible line that was never crossed by anybody who wanted to live much longer on this Earth.

"He's pushing a button!" Ezra spoke up, pointing to Bingham's right arm, which was behind him pressing down on something in the wall.

Little Pete nodded to his big bodyguard, and he went into action. Leaping in three steps from his sitting position, he grabbed Bingham's entire body in a wrestling hold. Both of Bingham's arms were thrust upward from behind, and Hunter pushed his right knee into the small of the skinny man's back.

The door opened, and ten of the big workmen stepped inside. Each had a long, Winchester repeating rifle in his grasp, and they pointed the muzzles at all five of them.

"I suggest you release me, Pete. You will then exit the premises with these men in an orderly fashion. If you appear again, they will have orders to shoot you on sight." Bingham's voice was constricted from the pressure of Hunter's grip, but after Little Pete nodded, and the bodyguard released him, he fell forward.

Samuel looked over at his two friends. They had both lost the color in their faces.

***

Back inside the coach, headed for downtown San Jose, Little Pete was silent. Samuel wondered what the Chinese gang leader was planning to do to gain the upper hand on Bingham. The longer it took, the more danger his mother and the two girls would be in. He was also worried about what she would say if she were rescued by them. She had expressly forbidden his becoming involved with the Triad, but he now believed it was an emergency.

"This pompous imbecile will now see how we have survived so long in this country and back in China. I brought these women with us to work. If he had cooperated, they could have become sex workers making a living and getting higher wages for us than they could get back in Chinatown or even in one of my San Francisco hotel retreats. Now, however, they will use their other skills."

"What skills?" Samuel asked.

"Infiltration skills and martial arts that are hundreds of years old. He is very wrong about me. My methods are not all force and power. I do require loyalty, yes, but learning self-defence is using the enemy's strengths against him. My women are superb at this, and this is why they survive." Little Pete again took out the hatchet from his waist and stared at it.

Samuel waited for him to say something, but the small man kept staring into the blade as if it were a mirror into another world. "Are you all right?" Samuel finally asked.

"My ladies are most attractive, and they can penetrate the mind of a man faster and with more delicacy than if I were to use this blade in a pitch-dark room. By tomorrow night, they will know more about Mr. Bingham's new business than he knows himself."

***

The Bloomfield Mansion, Three Nob Hill, San Francisco, May 12, 1886.

Laura had placed Ah Toy's drawn likeness of the mystery man, who was posing as Dr. Paschal Randolph, in the San Francisco newspaper. The inscription read: "Have you seen this man? He may be using the name of Dr. Paschal Beverly Randolph. Please report his location to the nearest police station. Do not apprehend. Very dangerous."

As she was walking up to the location of the most recent murder, which was right next-door to the Hopkins mansion, Laura was thinking about Clara and her "wild spiritualist" chase to Sacramento. Her parents, younger children, and Mrs. Hopkins were all panicked about where Clara and Trella might be. If this unknown man was the person who hypnotized Mrs. Bloomfield so she would kill her husband, and perhaps the other two women, then Clara, Trella and Adeline would be in grave danger. Of course, the man Clara was after may not be the hypnotist at all. Rheingold Bingham was the name of the man Clara mentioned. He was the young lover of the widow of Dr. Randolph. The sketch of this man was that of a much older gentleman.

A handsome policeman on the ground floor, named Rogers, told Laura and Ah Toy that Captain Lees was upstairs in the attic with the coroner. He escorted them, and after they climbed the spiral staircase to the third floor, Laura saw a portable wooden platform that went up into the hidden room above. The climb into the attic wearing her long dress was quite cumbersome. She stared back down as Officer Rogers had to carry the small body of Ah Toy up the stairs. The incline was so steep that Ah Toy's bound feet prohibited her from access on her own.

Laura saw Isaiah immediately in the lamplight. He was standing above the corpse of Mr. Jonas Bloomfield, late husband and owner of the Bloomfield Mining Equipment fortune. He was now not very fortunate, as his body was splayed upon the redwood like a fallen bear. His suit vest was hiked up to his armpits, his bowler hat to the side, and his bearded face was mashed down flat against the floor, so that Laura could not see it. The coroner, a corpulent gentleman wearing a brown frock coat and suspenders, was writing something down in his pad. The wavering beams from the overhead gaslights in the small chandelier made his bald head's surface appear to undulate.

Lees looked over at Laura. "Come here. I want you both to see something. Caruthers here has found a match for the poison in Mr. Bloomfield."

Laura and Ah Toy, still staring down at the corpse, walked gingerly over the creaking floorboards to where the captain was standing. Laura took the laboratory results from the coroner, whom she now recognized from the Rafferty case. "Here you are, Mrs. Gordon. Nice to see you again."

Laura read the lab report. The poison was the same liquid that had killed the two women. It caused the heart attacks seen previously, and a tiny puncture wound was found on Mr. Bloomfield's neck, where residue from the poison was also found. The perpetrator had removed the delivering projectile, probably the dart. Laura looked up and noticed that Ah Toy was rummaging inside an old steel travel trunk in the corner of the attic.

"Now I must summon all of you." Ah Toy held up two photographs. Laura, Captain Lees, and Mr. Caruthers walked over to see what she was holding. Under the meager light, Laura could see they were photos similar to the ones hanging on the hallway walls downstairs. They displayed the jungles of Columbia, possibly the Amazon. Except, in these two daguerreotypes, Elizabeth Bloomfield was standing next to another white man, who was holding in his hands a long fuselage of hollowed-out bamboo. This man was the exact image of the person Ah Toy drew for the newspapers. The person who had impersonated Dr. Paschal Beverly Randolph.

"Is this tool used to deliver the poisoned dart?" Ah Toy asked.

"Yes, they were also in the other photographs wherein the natives were burning the tree frogs over the fire. The poison darts were being wiped upon their backs, and these bamboo devices were seen lying around upon the ground in their midst." Laura was now certain that Mrs. Bloomfield was the murderer. And now, these pictures connected her with the mystery man they were hunting.

Captain Lees held one of the photos up to the light. "These must have been taken in the 1870s, when the couple went on their marriage voyage together. The spiritualist in these photographs looks much younger, but you can certainly see by his outfit and facial resemblance that he is the same man."

"This was where she learned to use the poison. Do you suppose she was also hypnotized?" Ah Toy asked.

"How sad. This poor man, Mr. Bloomfield, had no idea he was on a pleasure cruise to his own demise." Lees took the photographs. "I need these for possible evidence. We have the poison, and now we have the weapon. What we need is the man."

Ah Toy was rummaging around in the trunk. She pulled out some other photographs. "Look at these. This same spiritualist is in California. It's a gold mining camp, and the victim, Mr. Bloomfield, is showing him one of those things that separate the gold from the surrounding rock."

"You mean, a sluice box?" Captain Lees asked. Laura knew the detective had been an engineer during the Gold Rush years beginning in 1858.

"Yes, that's it. A sluice box." Ah Toy passed the picture to Lees.

"What connection do you suppose Jonas Bloomfield and his mining business has with this murder, if any?" Laura asked.

"I'll get my research people on it. There may also be some correspondence in this house. We'll go over it with a fine-toothed comb." Captain Lees turned to Officer Rogers. "Rogers, get the crime scene investigations unit out here. Also, I want you to get our research fellows finding out about anything dangerous that might have been going on at mining sites. I don't mean explosives. I mean any kind of poisons."

"Yes sir, captain. May I help you ladies down the ladder?" The young officer walked over to the attic exit ladder.

"I don't mind," Ah Toy said. "However, please keep your hand off my derrière this time, if you can," she added, smiling.

***

525 South Winchester Road, San Jose, California, May 12, 1886.

Clara was wondering what Laura, Ah Toy, and Isaiah were doing. The voice from beyond had announced that the visitors would be arriving today. Adeline was becoming increasingly panic-stricken, and Trella Evelyn kept badgering Clara about what plan she might have to escape.

"There are many unknown factors in this situation," Clara told them as they dressed. They were given taffeta frocks with silk and lace, but they were black, in keeping with the theme of the Winchester house, Clara supposed.

"We must still have some kind of plan. Perhaps we can signal these visitors, whomever they shall be, that we are in distress." Trella pulled up her bustle. "I am not allowing this to happen without some kind of resistance."

"I still believe Laura and Captain Lees will be coming for us. Others may also be here. Once we were missing for two days, it triggered a search." Clara buttoned the front of her dress and helped Adeline with hers. The girl had not worn such attire, and she was also in quite a daze. Clara believed it might be the stress, and it could also be the fact that she was going to be used in the presentation by Sadhu Bingham.

After they had eaten fruit and eggs provided by their storage bin, Clara and her two charges awaited the visit from the overlords in the house. They sat near the fire, gazing into its primitive allure.

The voice came on. "We are meeting in the ballroom. Please stand by the exit door, and do not be aghast at the men with weapons. We have explained that Adeline Quantrill is a very valuable person. We, subsequently, are making every effort to protect her."

Clara herded Adeline and her daughter over by the door. They waited for the inevitable, until the door lock twisted, and the tall door opened inward.

Two men armed with Winchester rifles stepped inside. The eldest of the two, a grizzled sort with tattoos on his forearms, pointed his rifle's muzzle toward the passageway outside. "Let's go, ladies. Your guests are in the Grand Ballroom."

Clara led the way, and she could feel and smell the tobacco breath of the guard on her neck as she followed the older man down the passageway. Adeline tightly held her hand, as she was quite confused and would have been lost in a second if allowed to wander these passageways alone. Trella walked behind Clara.

"When will they allow us to leave?" Trella asked the younger man, a towhead who was closely watching her.

Clara imagined these men were employees of the Winchester estate, but perhaps Mr. Bingham now had more control than at first suspected.

"It ain't my decision, mum. If it was me, I'd let you go free right now," he grinned.

"Shut your trap, Ainsley!" The older man swiveled his torso to address his partner.

Clara could hear the pipe organ playing as they approached the Grand Ballroom. If she wasn't mistaken it was the Camille Saint-Saëns piece, "Danse Macabre." Inside, the parquet wood floor was covered with the feet of some of the wealthiest men in the world. The American men Clara could recognize from newspapers were J. P. Morgan, the banker and financier, Andrew Carnegie, the steel industrialist, John D. Rockefeller the oil man, and Cornelius Vanderbilt II, whose family had made their money from railroads and shipping.

There were perhaps over forty such distinguished gentlemen inside the small but refined ballroom, and all of their attentions were riveted upon the nude body of a tattooed woman standing upon a raised stage in front of them, her back to them, before the roaring fireplace. Mr. Rheingold Bingham was addressing the gathering, and he was waiting for the music to end.

There were men in turbans, in tribal feathers and loincloths, and in business attire. Clara also noted, with some chagrin, that the only women in the room were the naked young lady on the stage, herself, Trella, and the "guest of honor," Adeline Quantrill. It was most certainly not a gathering of dignitaries who might be sympathetic to the Women's Suffrage Movement.

The silver candelabra chandelier, suspended from the ornately crafted redwood ceiling, cast an eerie light upon the gloomy and serious gathering of men. Clara could see two stained glass windows at the end of the room. They had quotes from one of Shakespeare's plays engraved upon them. One said, "Wide unclasp the tables of their thoughts." The other said, "These same thoughts people this little world."

When the young man finished his playing on the English pipe organ, which was also ornately crafted with the same fine dark wood as the walls and paneling, the men applauded. Sadhu Bingham, wearing his Indian attire, addressed the throng of wealthy dignitaries. He held a pointer stick in his right hand, and he stretched his arm out to touch the back of the naked woman, at her shoulder blades, where the pattern of Maltese Crosses began. They extended down her back and covered her bare buttocks and the backs of her thighs and on down to end at the bottom of her calves.

"Gentlemen, each of these Maltese Crosses has eight points. For our purposes today, I shall read the new beatitudes upon which we will build this monument to man's dynasty over women! Blessed are the wealthy in stocks, for theirs is the kingdom of Earth."

Several guffaws could be heard from these men, and Clara detested the sacrilege she was hearing.

"Blessed are they who speculate, for they shall be rewarded." Bingham was moving the pointer tip to each of the cross's points, but he was moving to different crosses down her voluptuous body. "Blessed are the strong in wills, for they shall inherit the estates."

Again, laughter shook the room.

"Blessed are they who hunger and thirst for good food and wine, for they shall be paunchy and besotted. Blessed are the powerful, for they shall obtain obedience. Blessed are the pure of gold, for they shall see God's wealth. Blessed are the tax dodgers, for they shall be called foxes of men."

Clara was seething inside, but these men were obviously enjoying themselves.

"And, finally, gentlemen, blessed are they who are persecuted by their wives for the sake of their money, for theirs is the kingdom of Hell."

As Bingham swatted the naked woman on her behind with his pointer, the men in the audience laughed and applauded uproariously. They were entertained by their host, and they found it even more amusing to know that Mrs. Winchester, the eccentric shrew who aspired to their own lofty heights, was away at a corporate board meeting at the Palace Hotel in San Francisco.

The Sadhu Bingham picked up an Asian robe and draped it around the naked woman. She climbed off the riser and ran out of the room.

"And now, gentlemen, we will introduce you to what you have all been summoned here to do. I have traveled the world in order to collect women who have abilities which were also thought to be part of mythology. However, the Greeks, in their early empire, spoke about women who could predict the future. The Pythia, or Oracle of Delphi, was consulted by the aristocracy of Athens on the seventh day of each month."

Clara noted that Mr. Carnegie and Mr. Rockefeller both nodded in agreement with what Bingham was saying.

"Her skills at prophesy were never questioned. The Greeks also had Dodona and Trophonius. The Chinese sought to predict the future through numbers in the *I Ching* as did the Hebrews in their *Kabballah*. India has its Akashwani or Asariri, which are voices from the sky that are projected through women or men. In Tibet, the Dali Lama consults the oracle known as the Nechung. I could continue with our own natives in North America and South America and those others around the world."

"Yes, I have seen them on the reservations!" A young man shouted from the back row.

"Suffice it to say, I have collected the women who are representative of these oracles, and you will have access to them in this house of magic numbers and signs, which is predicated upon the precognitive powers of these gifted women."

The organist began playing the "Gypsy Song" by Bizet from the opera *Carmen*. The tattooed woman appeared from another room and entered holding a tray filled with golden keys. She now wore the costume of a Gypsy woman, with a flowing skirt of purple, a red blouse, and a maroon silk scarf tied around her forehead.

Sadhu Bingham took the tray from her and set it down on the dais. "We have a key to a room for each of you gentlemen. You must first solve the puzzle we will give you, which will guide you to your proper room. Inside, there will be one of our oracles, and I have one of them to show you right now. "Adeline, please come up here, if you would."

Clara held her breath, as the young woman she had placed so much trust in walked slowly up to the front of the room, glancing around her at the assembled men, frowning as if she were in the midst of demons. Clara realized that this might truly be an exact assessment.

"This young woman has precognitive abilities, and she is also one of the few spiritualists who can read minds. Please, Adeline, can you tell us what one of these gentlemen is thinking at this very moment?" Bingham waved his hand out toward the audience. Many of the men coughed nervously. Clara suspected they were hoping she was not able to read their minds. Adeline had told her earlier that she was not receiving any person's mental projections. What if she could not perform now? Would they all be wiped clean of their memories and sent on their way?

Adeline's face contorted for a moment, and then she turned to Bingham. "I can tell you what the gentleman in the second row, third from the end has been thinking," she whispered.

Bingham chuckled. "You mean, the great industrialist, Mr. Andrew Carnegie? What, pray tell, was this man thinking? Please speak loudly, my dear, so everyone can hear you."

"He was thinking about whether he should have had the extra glass of wine at dinner. He was also worried about how his stomach looked in his new suit." Adeline spoke out.

"I'll be damned! The girl is quite right. I was thinking those thoughts exactly," Carnegie replied, nervously rubbing his gray chin whiskers. "I shall try not to think of anything from now on," he added, and everyone laughed.

"What will happen now, gentlemen, is that one of these women will be ensconced and relaxing inside a room in this mystical house, awaiting your pleasure. She not only will proceed to give you tips from the stock markets presently existing around the world, but she also has been thoroughly instructed in the art of lovemaking. She can teach you about the animal magnetism present in the wedded bed chamber, whereupon you shall gain extra potency and longer life through the lovemaking you perform with your wife."

One of the men shouted, "What about any woman?"

"Indeed. These *magia sexualis* skills will work with any woman, but the highest apex is reached with your wedded wife, I am afraid." Bingham pointed at Adeline. "But who could resist such instruction from a beautiful damsel like this?"

"What if we don't solve the puzzle?" A man in the back row asked.

"I am afraid you won't get a room. We must have a way to filter out some of you." When Bingham heard a few groans, he added, "Not everyone can become a billionaire overnight!"

There was laughter throughout the ball room. Sadhu Bingham gestured toward the tattooed Gypsy. "Please, Liz, hand out the golden keys. When you are back in your rooms, there will be the puzzle on your desk. Solve the conundrum, and then you may go to your appointed rooms tomorrow evening, after dinner."

Clara knew she had to act quickly. She walked over to stand next to Bingham. "Before you take Adeline to her room, may I speak with her briefly? I want to make certain she is not afraid."

Bingham looked at her and frowned. "All right. But do it quickly. We must proceed with the activities."

Clara took her charge's hand and dragged her over to a corner of the room. "You must not try to escape. I know our friends will be here to rescue us."

Adeline's eyes were wide and fearful. "But, Mrs. Foltz. I have heard from Osiris Buddha, Mrs. Randolph's son. He says that this Mr. Bingham is not the person who was the student of his father. He is an imposter."

Clara nodded her head. "They are both here. Kate must have seen Bingham on the grounds. I sent her a wire because I knew he was too old to be her lover. But now, one must ask, where is the original and authentic Rheingold Bingham? Also, please telepath a message to Osiris that he must get his mother to send a telegram to Laura and Captain Lees. They must know Bingham is an imposter, and they must come to Winchester house at once."

Chapter 12: The Rescue

Jenny Lind City Hall, Police Department, Detectives Office, Kearny Street, San Francisco. May 13, 1886, 8 AM.

Captain Isaiah Lees called the meeting in his office so they could go over the results from the research unit, whose members had worked the day before and all last night going over mining records and the correspondence found inside the Bloomfield residence. Lees already knew that what was uncovered would turn the tide in their murder case.

However, Laura knew information that was even more prescient. When she walked up the stairs to the third floor of the police offices, with Ah Toy lagging behind her, she could hardly contain herself. They had already made reservations for the train to San Jose, and Hannigan had their bags packed and waiting at the station.

"Ladies, good morning. I trust you had a good rest and are ready to attack the battle lines once more." Lees pulled out two chairs near the teletype units.

"Captain, I have news from Clara. Actually, the telegram was not sent from Clara. It was sent from Mrs. Kate Randolph, the woman Clara visited in Ohio. It seems Clara is not in Sacramento, as we had assumed. She and her girls are being held inside the Winchester mansion in San Jose. According to Kate Randolph, 'kidnapped' may be the more operative term to use."

"Kidnapped? How can we be certain this is not another ruse concocted by the killer or killers?" Laura knew Captain Lees was being his usual detective self. At last, she was grateful for it. She now understood how Clara had learned so much from him.

"We cannot. However, perhaps your information can be combined with what we now know to make things a bit clearer." Laura sat down and spread her dress out flat on her legs.

"Adeline is an authentic medium, is she not?" Ah Toy asked. "She may be why they have become trapped inside that house."

Lees sat down and opened his file. "All right. First, here are the facts obtained from the correspondence inside the Bloomfield's house. There were almost forty letters written by a fellow named Bernard Sebold to both Mr. and Mrs. Bloomfield. There was no mention of a person by the name of Rheingold Bingham. What was discussed in these letters is interesting, but my researchers wanted to find out about the name discrepancy."

"Good. This Sebold may have used Bingham's identity for some purpose," Laura said.

"Yes, that may be the case, because when they researched the possible connections, they were led to the admittance records at an insane asylum in up-state New York."

"Insane asylum? What in heaven's name could possibly connect them there?" Ah Toy leaned forward with interest.

"It was the Willard Asylum for the Insane in Binghamton, New York." Lees read from his notes.

"Binghamton? Could he have purloined the name from that? Rheingold Bingham?" Laura reflected.

"Not quite. When patients are admitted, they are given numbers for names, and none of the names is used inside. However, my researchers discovered a strange coincidence in the admissions records. One patient was named Rheingold Bingham, and he was placed in the institution by his parents, the wealthy banking family from Philadelphia. The city of Binghamton was named after them. The other patient admitted was named Bernard Sebold. He was admitted after attempting to commit suicide in an apartment in New York City. He has no family listed."

"I see. So, perhaps this Sebold took on the identity of this Bingham inside the mental hospital." Laura mused.

"Listen to this. Both men were discharged on April 12, 1870. Mr. Bingham left on his own accord after being assessed as mentally stable. Mr. Sebold, however, was released under the custody of somebody whom we all know." Laura hated when Lees played dramatist. She liked facts to be unemotional and quickly assessed.

"Go on, dammit!" She said.

"Sarah Lockwood Winchester." Lees held out the sheet to Laura and Ah Toy so they could read the words.

"That explains it! This Sebold fellow took the name of Bingham and began to impersonate him. He then must have traveled to

California and met up with the Bloomfields." Laura handed the record back to Lees.

"No, the records show he first traveled overseas. This must have been where he learned his spiritualist ways, the same way Dr. Paschal Randolph did. That was why he used Randolph's name as well. He may have even crossed paths with him on his many sojourns. He most certainly must have studied his writings." Lees turned the pages of the record. "Now I have the information about the poisons."

"Wait one moment. This younger Bingham. The *real* Bingham. He became lovers with Mrs. Kate Randolph and was a student of her husband, correct? Meanwhile, out West, this Sebold person was posing as both Bingham and Randolph. Was this the case?" Laura wanted to know because it would certify who was now holding Clara and the two girls captive at Winchester house.

"But where is the real Mr. Bingham now?" Ah Toy asked.

"Wait until I finish reading about this research. There may be further connections to process." Lees picked up the record to read it more closely. "Several of the letters between this imposter Bingham and Mr. Jonas Bloomfield discussed the dangers of quicksilver, which was one of the by-products of cleaning gold deposits inside sluices at the gold mining camps throughout the Sierra Nevada Mountains. Bloomfield told Bingham about how some coolie workers had accidentally inhaled fumes from burning quicksilver, which was left over inside some gold mining pans, which they were using to cook their food over the fire. When this quicksilver liquid heats into vapor it has a very sweet aroma, so nothing was suspected. These men became poisoned, and after a few months, they came down with some quite horrible afflictions."

"Afflictions? What happened?" As a legal prosecutor, who had handled many different ways of murdering someone, Laura was intrigued.

"These men became shy and withdrawn at first. Then, their hands and other appendages began to tremble uncontrollably. Finally, after a few months, they lost all of their memory and slipped into fatal comas." Lees turned the pages. "Now for the *coup de grace*. The changing of the wills of the deceased men in these murder cases."

"After hearing about these poisons, there must be some connection with the deaths of these wealthy husbands." Ah Toy remarked.

"All of the men killed in these cases, even the ones in New York City, had their wills changed to reflect that all estate holdings and business holdings would be going to the surviving wife only. In two instances, this was already the case. But four of the women had their lawyers do this before their husbands were killed."

"What were they expecting? No legal system in the United States would give estate holdings to a woman who had killed her husband." Laura said.

"That's just it. Your case, the Rafferty case, was the only instance whereby the wife was convicted of a crime. All the others were judged as accidental homicides. The tree frog poison was undiscovered, and the result was that the coroners ruled that the husband died from cardiac arrest. This, of course, was how this unique poison acts."

"I see. And thus, my case was unique because there was a witness to the act, and I had proof that Rachel had animosity toward her husband, Brian, who had abused her. Now, what about this new poison? What do you suppose it could be used for, if anything?" Laura was trying to put the pieces together in her mind.

"Perhaps this quicksilver poisoning can be a more fool-proof method. Since it takes months to work on the victim, the cause and effect distance becomes too far to connect it to the poisoning and also to the perpetrator of the act." Ah Toy was using good logic.

Laura decided to put the frosting on their hypothetical cake. "It is also inhaled, which makes it completely untraceable. A murderer's delight."

"We need to catch a train to San Jose. Clara must to be rescued before she, Adeline, and Trella become victims of this madman." Laura stood up and moved toward the door.

When Laura opened the door to exit, a Western Union boy was standing there. "Mrs. Gordon?"

"Yes," Laura responded, and the boy handed her the telegram. Captain Lees gave the boy some change, and he left. Laura read the telegram and stood there in the office for a moment thinking about its contents.

"It's from Samuel. He is with Little Pete in San Jose. They have infiltrated the house with undercover maids. We should meet them at a rooming house in San Jose. They know what scheme is underway inside the Winchester house, and they plan to bust it wide open. Samuel claims they can rescue Clara and the girls without bringing in the police or even firing a shot."

Captain Lees took the telegram from Laura and read it. "I see. Although I tend to doubt Ah Toy's uncle in most matters, I believe we should trust him this time. We can first find out what this scheme entails, and then we can plan our course of action."

"You do so at your own peril," Ah Toy remarked, frowning.

***

525 South Winchester Road, San Jose, California, May 13, 1886.

Clara was now wondering if she were awake or dreaming. Trella was beside her in the bed, but Adeline, poor girl, was now being placed inside a room with only one key. Her destiny was tied to theirs, but was it a supernatural destiny or simply a case of being killed at the end of this nightmare?

That evening would usher the beginning of a macabre ritual created by a man who was bent upon twisting the meaning of female empowerment into a quest for profit and mind control. Clara knew her friends would not forsake them, but would they survive before they could be rescued? Adeline could no longer tell Clara what was happening outside, as she was the only person in communication with Osiris and his mother, Kate Randolph.

The wait inside her own prison would be long and grueling, but it was all she could do. Clara turned in bed to watch her daughter sleep. When she was young, and Clara had the rare chance to be home with her children, she loved watching them sleep. Innocence was personified in the dream world face of the young. Now, in a wretched twist, she was awaiting the possible demise of all that women hoped for. Freedom, emancipation, and equal justice were being ridiculed and preyed upon inside this house of mystery. Powerful and wealthy men would soon be entering rooms that reflected their greed and lust, and where women were being used as pawns to siphon the pockets of these men like so many London guttersnipes.

***

326 Main Street, Mrs. Halverson's Boarding and Care House, San Jose, California, May 13, 1886.

Samuel had listened to Little Pete, and the telegram he sent to Mrs. Gordon and Captain Lees was meant to create a plan which would exact the revenge necessary to return pride to the little gang leader. The women had infiltrated the Winchester house like Ninjas. Ten maids who were previously working there had now been replaced by ten of Little Pete's women. These women had sent a report out to Samuel, Ezra, and Roger, who posed as delivery men. Now they were going to use this report to explain the layout of the house and what these spies had uncovered about Bingham's scheme to hoodwink some of the richest men in the world.

All that Samuel wanted was to rescue his mother, sister, and the young lady he believed he loved, Adeline Quantrill. If Little Pete did not address this during their meeting with Mrs. Gordon, he was going to act on his own. Samuel was in no mood to once more have to live at the snail's pace of adults. He and his two friends would become infiltrators themselves, if need be, and to hell with some grand plan to expose this spiritualist to the world. The world could damned well wait! Samuel wanted his family and love returned to him.

"Hunter, go outside and tell them which rooms we are in." Little Pete was standing in front of the apartment's window facing Main Street below. He was watching the surrey as it approached the rooming house. Inside, were Mrs. Laura Gordon, Captain Isaiah Lees, and Ah Toy.

Minutes later, Samuel could hear the adults stomping up the stairs toward them. Little Pete opened the door and greeted them. Once more, Samuel would play the proverbial fly on the wall and listen to what these people had to say. If they had no consequential plan to find his mother and her charges right away, then he would make his own plan, with his own team of rescuers.

"Come, be seated. I have a lot to cover, and we don't have much time." Little Pete sat around a small table, and the others filled into chairs around him. Samuel listened intently.

"This fellow Bingham has a scheme to steal millions from these industrialists. He is handing out keys, together with a puzzle. If they answer the puzzle correctly they can get the key that unlocks the door to a room in the house."

"He's a complete imposter. His real name is Sebold. Bernard Sebold. He met this Bingham in a mental hospital and stole his identity." Laura Gordon said.

"I don't care. A schemer must have his subterfuge. The point is, my women have discovered that only thirteen of these men are being set-up. They are thirteen of the wealthiest. Their wives have already been entranced and conditioned to reap the rewards of their husbands' slow deaths."

"Do these deaths come by poison?" Captain Lees asked.

"Yes. How did you know? One of my women overhead the plan. Quicksilver is going to be heated in a small container over a gas lamp beside the man's chair. He will inhale the sweet odor, and it will slowly affect his brain. Over the passing days and weeks, he will become a hermit. He will lock himself away, and he will gradually slip into a coma, never to breathe again on this Earth."

"Of course. And then all of the estate and business accounts will become property of the wife. And, I would assume, these wives are suffragists, correct? And, they have been entranced by Sebold, just as he mesmerised his murderess, Elizabeth Bloomfield." Ah Toy pointed out.

"Yes again, niece. We now must enter that house and stop these men from opening the doors to those rooms." Samuel saw Little Pete's scowl return. He meant business. "I want to bring this scoundrel down myself. Is that clear?"

"First, what is your plan? If we can stop this from happening, then we may not have to inform the authorities. He must be arrested at some point, however." Captain Lees said.

"My women will get those keys from the men after they have solved their puzzles. They will collect them, and we will be outside waiting to retrieve them. Once we have them, then we can enter. There are only thirteen armed men. This is a magic number in this house, as you'll see. My ladies will overpower ten of them, and me, Mr. Hunter, and you, Captain Lees, shall relieve the others of either their weapons or their lives."

"Sounds logical. What about Clara and her two girls?" Lees asked.

"The medium, Adeline, will be in one of the locked rooms. We can find Clara and her daughter after we overpower Sebold." Little Pete stood up. "Samuel and his two friends shall wait outside the mansion and serve as look-outs."

Samuel nodded at the gang leader, but he was thinking about something else entirely.

"All right? Let's go!" Little Pete said, and they all headed for the exit.

As they left, Samuel kept whispering to his two friends, Ezra and Roger. His plan was just beginning to take shape.

***

525 South Winchester Road, San Jose, California, May 13, 1886.

As he and his friends had previously penetrated the Winchester house as delivery men, they were again received with nods of the head and smiles. Samuel pointed in the direction he already knew he wanted to go. She was there. The hazel-eyed young woman who had talked to him on the train. When he came up to her she smiled. "Master Foltz. Why aren't you outside? Little Pete will be disappointed."

"Is there a room where guards with weapons have visited? I need to know. It's where my mother and my sister are being held." Samuel understood the logic of the house. The guards were taking care of the most valuable property, so he knew it must have been noticed by Little Pete and his spies.

"Yes, as a matter of fact. I can take you there. I thought you might wait until we overpower these guards, but I can understand your haste. This is your family." The girl headed for the section of the property where the greenhouse was located. She stopped in front of a door guarded by two men with Winchester rifles.

"These men are here to repair the flue in the fireplace," she told the men. She had the key, and she unlocked the door. As she backed away, she dropped down to a squatting posture. When she raised up, her elbows and fists were extended, and she struck the first man with both fists just under his chin. He dropped the gun and fell back, sliding down the wall. As the other man started to raise his rifle to point, she spun around and kicked it out of his hands with her feet. Roger and Samuel picked up the weapons and held them on the men.

"Aurora, go in and get my mother and sister. We must find out which room Adeline is in."

Clara and Trella briefly hugged Samuel, but he was still concerned. "We need to find Adeline," he said.

"She's in the Sanctum. I heard Mr. Bingham instruct another maid to prepare the room for her and her special guest." Aurora took both guns from Samuel and Roger. "Go ahead with your friends. I'll lock these two up for safekeeping and wait for you to get her. We can then meet up with Little Pete and the others."

"May I stay and keep you company?" Ezra asked.

"Don't be silly, Ez. You must come with us. We are storming the Bastille today!" Roger said, and he chuckled.

"Each room has been prepared for entry. I hope Laura and the others are able to stop them in time. Once these men inhale the quicksilver gas, there is nothing to keep them from becoming afflicted." Samuel said, leading the two boys and holding onto Trella's hand.

As they journeyed toward the center of the mystical house, Samuel envisioned himself and his friends as heroes of the hour. His mother and sister were safe, and now his possible true love could be saved. When they came near the narrowing entrance to the inner Sanctum, Samuel and his group were met from all sides by the other invaders. Little Pete, Laura, Ah Toy, and Captain Lees all were there, gathering together with them in the passageway. It was becoming quite crowded.

"What are you three doing here? I told you to remain outside!" Little Pete's scowl unnerved Samuel, but he continued to march into the Sanctum. All around them, music began to play through the pneumatic communications pipes. Once again, it was the organ in the Grand Ballroom playing *Danse Macabre*.

"Did you get the key?" Samuel asked, holding out his hand.

Little Pete handed the gold key to him. "Yes, with no help from you. This is the last room."

After the door was opened, and Samuel entered, he saw it was empty. Where was Adeline and her suitor? Where was Bingham?

Over the speaker in the Sanctum, they could hear the voice of Bingham, the mystical puppet master. This was the only room into which he was transmitting his voice. "My friends! I congratulate you on your resourcefulness. You have stopped my efforts momentarily, but with every apparent conquest comes a moment of truth. Although you seem to have deduced my weapon of quicksilver, you failed to understand that I might have prepared a fail-safe mechanism. Did you not know that my entire plan began with Miss Quantrill?"

Samuel held his breath. What was this monster talking about? Began with his Adeline?

"I met her on my trip out West. Just as I always select women who have been abused, or who have pre-existing mental and hysterical problems, I selected Adeline, and I planted a replacement suggestion in her by which you were all fooled."

Fooled? Was this monster going to slander his love? Samuel clenched his hands into hard fists. Samuel could hear this madman laugh, and he acted. He ran out of the Sanctum, down the passageways, heading for the trap door leading to the cellar. Behind him, and all around him, he heard the doors to the rooms close and lock. His friends were now trapped inside. He dodged the men tied-up along the way, their rifles held by the young Amazons of Little Pete. "Out of my way!" he yelled, pushing past the women and zig-zagging around corners and through narrow doors. All the while the organ played the haunted strains of *Danse Macabre*.

Samuel could now hear the voice all around him through the pneumatic communications. "She did not, in fact, witness her parents murdered by savages on that train. She was their killer. Sad, but true. She murdered her own parents with a knife, in cold blood, and when the authorities arrested her, I followed her to the asylum, where she was taken, and I vouched to care for her for the rest of her life. I explained my own cure back in New York, and the authorities granted my wish. Because of her young age, they were loathed to allow her to rot inside a mental ward, as she seemed to be better, according to the doctors. Her entire story was fabricated just for you, my friends, and now she will assist me in this final *bon voyage*. My dear, do you have the thirteen ounces of quicksilver?"

Samuel could hear Adeline's voice over the speaker. "Yes," she said.

"Please, place it into the boiler furnace. I have set the proper forced air vents so the quicksilver gas will infiltrate every room above the cellar. We will disappear, just as the spirits haunting this house will now be able to take it over forever. And you, my sad, disappointed friends, shall all become gradual comatose victims in a short and brutal life. Unless, of course, you can hold your breaths long enough."

"Watch out behind you!" Up ahead, Aurora was pointing. Samuel turned around, and there, about fifteen feet down the passageway, near the stairs, stood a woman holding something in her mouth. It appeared to be a hallowed-out tube of some kind. Her cheeks were filled with air, but before she could blow, she was tackled from behind by Ezra. They both hit the floor in a heap of tangled legs. Samuel knew he had to continue toward the cellar. He could worry about his friend later.

As he came to the redwood door in the floor near the main entrance to the Winchester house, he stopped. He listened carefully for the whoosh of the forced air. Nothing. Why was it not working? He lifted the door, peered down into the darkness, and, still holding his breath, he began to descend the steps into the cellar.

At the bottom of the stairs, Samuel could see Adeline and a young boy, about the same age as his younger sister, Virginia Knox. He was holding her head on his shoulder as she sobbed. On the floor, in a pool of blood, was Mr. Bingham, better known as Bernard Sebold. Beside his body was a large pail filled with the silvery and quivering mirror-like poison, quicksilver.

"I found my Rheingold," a woman's voice said. She was standing next to a handsome young man who had a pistol in his hand. "Your mother told me about this imposter, and I came right away. Osiris talked with Adeline, and he was able to bring her out of her trance state. She then told us about this room and about Sebold's plan. Rheingold was locked in one of the rooms, and my son found him."

Samuel walked over to stand beside Adeline. She turned toward him, and her eyes were filled with what he perceived to be longing. When he took her into his arms, he could feel the freedom she had just experienced, and his heart pounded in his chest with empathetic joy.

***

The Hopkins Mansion, One Nob Hill, San Francisco, May 15, 1886.

Clara saw that her younger son, David Milton, was standing at attention allowing the adults to enter the dining room. He was telling everyone he was Rheingold Bingham's ghost, and that he could place a curse upon anybody who didn't pay him five cents. Everybody, except ten-year-old Virginia Knox, gave him a nickel, patted his head, and walked through.

Seated at the head of the table, in the place of honor, was the real Rheingold Bingham, the handsome young spiritualist and now husband of the window, Kate Randolph. Mrs. Randolph-Bingham was seated next to him. The rest of the Shortridge family was also assembled, and they included grandparents Talitha and Elias, and Clara's children, Trella Evelyn and Bertha May. Ah Toy and Mrs. Mary Hopkins, who was watching David Milton carefully, as if she indeed believed he was a ghost, were seated at the far end.

Clara could see that the additional company at the long, redwood table included Fung Jing Toy, or Little Pete, Captain Isaiah Lees, Laura de Force Gordon, Osiris Buddha Randolph, Aurora Landis, Ezra Levine and Roger Dowdy. Adeline Quantrill was standing by the fire, holding hands with Samuel Cortland, another hero of the hour.

"I met Mr. Sebold in the mental hospital, as Captain Lees discovered. We became gradual friends, as he was quite curious about my wealthy background and my interest in the occult. We both believed we were condemned because of our supernatural talents. In fact, I still think many authentic mediums and spiritualists are locked inside mental wards around the world." Rheingold held up his wine glass. "To those who are locked in the prison of the mind overlords everywhere!"

"He is right, you know," Kate Randolph said. "The mind of the public would rather condemn the Chinese or the free-thinking women than the politicians who make a career out of keeping outsiders on the outside. Mediums and spiritualists united with suffragists because we needed an open mind to stay free. Freedom is a state of perpetual awareness of our surroundings."

Clara understood. "Without my two close, female friends, Ah Toy and Laura, this case could have never been solved. Through their openness to all things supernatural, they unlocked the inner secrets we needed, such as the fact that Rachel Rafferty, Cordelia Fallows, and, most importantly, Elizabeth Bloomfield, were all entranced by one man, who turned out to be Mr. Bingham's roommate, Bernard Sebold. When I first saw him at the Winchester house, I knew he was not Kate's lover."

"Was it simply female intuition, or are you also a medium of sorts?" Laura asked. "There was no way you could have known Kate and her son could discover in which room the real Mr. Bingham was being held."

"I am not the spiritualist in this dining room. Osiris is. And, most certainly, our Adeline is. By the by, young miss," Clara turned around to face Adeline. "Was that story Sebold told us about you killing your parents true?"

"Of course not! It was a new suggestion he wanted everyone to believe because he believed he could control anyone. Not just women. He wanted to use that money to control society, if he could take it that far. When Osiris began sending to me, I became alive in that house of ghosts. The only spiritual gift that is more powerful than some unscrupulous mesmerist, is the shared communications between empaths." Adeline smiled up at Samuel, who took up her hands and kissed them.

Clara was happy to see her son behaving like a real man. "Little Pete says you can still play billiards, Sam, if you promise not to play poker." Clara said.

"I forbid it. Anyone who is dating a mind-reader cannot gamble in a mind-reading game of chance," Little Pete said, smiling, and rubbing his wispy goatee. "I am happy to extend an invitation to my niece. I have vowed to her that I shall change my tactics. I now see her ways can provide more extended success in the way of family and friends."

"My uncle learns lessons the most difficult way he can find. But I suppose he can make amends like any other mortal soul." Ah Toy said.

Clara decided to raise a glass, as she was very happy at the moment. "I want to say that we all cooperated as if we were destined to solve this mystery together. But we all owe a final debt of thanks to the grand woman of this very house, Mrs. Mary Hopkins, without whom the wheels of justice would have certainly ground to a halt many days ago. Hear, hear!"

They all raised their glasses, and Mrs. Hopkins decided to get the final word in. She turned around to face young David Milton, who was still standing in the doorway, raised her glass, and toasted him, “To the ghost of my husband, Mark. Will you now please sit down to eat with your family?”

The Stockton Insane Asylum Murder

CHAPTER 1: UNDERCOVER

The Women's Section, First Floor, Stockton State Insane Asylum, April 22, 1887.

There she was. Polly Bedford, age twelve, stooped-over in the shadows behind a row of bunk beds. Seated at a scarred wooden school desk, Polly was concentrating on her pencil drawing. She wore the patient's navy-blue frock pull-over with her initials "P.B." stitched on the left arm sleeve. Polly appeared to be drawing her residence inside the Women's Ward at the State Insane Asylum at Stockton. Her tongue tip was protruding from the corner of her mouth, and she kept pushing a strand of black hair back from her forehead, as she looked up from her tablet to view the interior of the ward.

As seventeen-year-old Bertha May Foltz walked up behind her, she could clearly see the bunk beds in the girl's drawing, the wash room, the dining room, and the windows, through which patients could observe their rural surroundings. Except, instead of creating people shapes--patients, doctors, nurses and visitors--Polly had colonised her mental ward with walking and talking medicine capsules. Each capsule, whether it was a patient or not, had stick arms and legs, and every face was drawn onto the top half of its pill torso.

Bertha, after reading the biography of Civil War Superintendent of Union Nurses, Dorothea Dix, became very interested in medicine. She would beg to go with her mother, Attorney and Detective Clara Foltz, every time one of her cases required that she visit the hospital or the coroner's office. When the homicide of ten-year-old Winnifred Cotton took place, just three doors down from where Bertha and her family lived in the mansion at One Nob Hill, Bertha decided she wanted to help her mother with the case. Not only was Polly Bedford a friend of Bertha's, she was also a member of the same choir that sang at Bertha's grandfather, Reverend Elias Shortridge's tent revivals at the sand lots on the Market Street side of San Francisco City Hall.

However, the secret reason Bertha wanted to help her mother was because her older sister, Trella Evelyn, and older brother, Samuel Cortland, had played important parts in the mystery the year before concerning the spiritualist murders. Bertha had watched them both as they pranced around the bedroom, claiming to have discovered this or that clue to contribute in the search for the killer. Samuel eventually broke the case wide open and was able to rescue their mother, Trella, and Samuel's future girlfriend, Adeline Quantrill, at the strange Sarah Winchester House in San Jose.

Bertha May realized that Polly Bedford's art was a probable reflection of the drugs she was being given to alleviate her high anxiety, such as potassium bromide, and to get her moving when she was in the valley of her melancholic despair, Strychnine. Of course, there was some wisdom in the girl's portrayal of drawn characters, as many of the staff could be seen, every night, slipping into the private suites on the top floor to sell cocaine, opioids, and even morphine to the wealthy female patients.

These rich patients never worked in the garden or on the farm. Instead, they stayed on the top floor, playing the piano, babbling incoherently about their paranoid suspicions, and grazing like lowing cattle at the ever-present collection of hors devours placed all around on tables inside their main dining room. They didn't have to sit at the main table downstairs with the poor patients.

In their drugged state, Bertha saw them to be the privileged insane, and every poor patient below, who was required to be shackled when not working outside, gave them envious looks when they spotted these women dancing, like ghosts, back and forth along the carpeted stairwells. They wore fashionable dresses with full bustles and ornate embroidery, and yet they acted like lunatics.

Bertha May was being supervised from San Francisco by her mother. Bertha was there to infiltrate the Stockton asylum, while pretending to be insane, with the sole purpose of questioning Miss Polly Bedford. Bertha was told by Clara that Miss Bedford had been committed by her parents because she had witnessed a murder which had taken place inside their residence, a stately mansion in the Nob Hill section of San Francisco. Clara also told Bertha that the Bedfords did not want Polly involved, and so they were willing to declare their daughter insane to keep her safe and legally out of the way. It was going to be Bertha's important job to discover who or what Polly saw on that night and to report back to Clara.

However, this case was much more complicated than the spiritualist murders. First of all, Bertha knew the murder witness, Polly Bedford. Bertha had played dolls and done homework with Polly, and Bertha had never found the younger girl to be belligerent or mentally strange. Therefore, Bertha was chosen by Clara to find out the identity of the person Miss Bedford allegedly saw commit this murder of Miss Winnifred Cotton, age ten, on January 3, 1887. If she discovered that Polly was not really insane, then she was going to explore how the institution was able to get so many people committed. However, Clara had explained to Bertha, at some length, she was not to steal or commit any crimes during her snooping adventure.

Bertha was going to see if she could determine what made this entire state asylum business run, and even though she knew her mother was looking out for her safety, Bertha was going to take all the risks she needed to accomplish her goal. If her brother, Samuel, could join the Tong Gang and spy on a spiritualist, then Bertha could be just as adventurous—perhaps even more so.

Her mother and the Cottons believed that mental illness was being sold as an easy way to get rid of troublesome wives and children and to secretly formulate a scheme whereby immigrants could be tricked out of their property and wealth by being committed. No money could come from the State of California to the State asylums at Stockton and Napa, unless the patients were ruled indigent.

Therefore, the same panel of doctors and state clerks was employed each year to do this nefarious business of separating the profitable wheat from the insane chaff, resulting in an incredible government statistic that said, "in 1886, alone, one out of every 435 Californians had been declared insane by the State." As this was an important women's and human rights issue, Clara and her team were motivated to uncover any illegal activities that might surface during their murder investigation. Bertha was overjoyed at being part of her mother's team at long last.

All Bertha knew before she was committed by her mother to the asylum was that Mr. Charles Cotton, President and Owner of the Cotton Gin Liquor Imports on Market Street, had deposited five hundred dollars into Bertha's personal bank account. Bertha was going to help her mother do what the City of San Francisco's Police Department was not permitted to do: find the killer of Charles Cotton's daughter.

"I have a new game we can play," Bertha spoke to Polly, sitting beside her chair, down on the lower bed of a nearby bunk ensemble.

Bertha watched the girl place her pencil down on the desk's top. She turned in her school chair and faced her older inquisitor. "Can we play Mental Metamorphosis again?"

It was as if an invisible force had sucked all the air out of the room. After the name of this game was released, the priority was now to breathe and to survive. Nothing else mattered. Bertha also understood what she must do. Using the girl's superior imagination and sensitivities to access her mind was a stroke of genius.

"Of course, we can," said Bertha, reaching out to capture the girl's hands in her own. "Instruction happens so much faster when the message can be implanted directly inside the brain. When you think, you are thinking for the collective good. Unless you control the actors, anything could happen, and that is the path toward chaos."

Polly moved out of her school chair and walked over to where Bertha was seated on the lower bed. Bertha knew this might be the only chance she got to obtain the information she needed. The staff was out supervising the farm and garden work of the others. Only kind old Mrs. Betterman, the baker, was left to mind the asylum, and she was almost deaf. Bertha set the stage immediately.

"What is the kernel of fear? We all have it, do we not?"

Polly stared straight ahead. "Not all. Some have no fear. They get trampled saving children and the elderly. Burnt to a cinder fighting Hell itself. Lost on the battlefields of the wars. I know one person who is the incarnation of Lucifer, the Fallen Star. I saw him murder an innocent. All the murderers are rejoicing. They at last have a hero on Earth to guide them."

Bertha spread out her dress with her palms, smoothing the material against her thin body. She was proud to be thin, and she thought her mother's weighty torso was unbecoming an active Suffragette for international women's rights. Back to her immediate concern, Bertha knew she needed more specific details about this Lucifer. "What did this demon look like? Certainly, he wasn't an apparition. You can't believe in ghosts."

A breathtakingly chilly vacuum devoured the space around them. Polly shivered, the first human reflex exhibited by her.

"You would pray there were ghosts, because no human could stop him. When he turned toward me, I saw his face was a continually changing compendium of different people's faces. I fantasized under stress about the possible reasons for this to occur. I may have eaten something horrid or poisonous. Or, supernaturally, I may have been put under a curse of some kind. Could I be an enemy of the government, who needed to be disposed of?" Polly's face became a bit animated, as she spoke, but her body remained rigid.

"What were you forced to do?" Bertha strained forward to take the girl's hands. "It's time to use your mental metamorphosis. If you become his mind, as he is in the act of killing a girl, tell me what you would be thinking and how you could change the reality of murder into something worthwhile and even redeeming."

The four times previously, when Bertha attempted to access Polly's mind, events kept occurring to interrupt the proceedings. Once it was an earthquake, once a fire alarm, and twice other patients had gone off the deep end and caused a ruckus. This was the moment Bertha had been long awaiting.

The eager smile on the girl's face demonstrated to Bertha that there were conflicting psychological forces at work. Polly, by all academic and social standards, was a genius child, a prodigy, but this turn of events had thrown the social welfare officials and newspaper journalists into an increasingly pessimistic state of conjecture. The idea that a girl's mind, especially a mind that came from such noble breeding, could be declared broken, was inconceivable.

Polly whispered, "I must stop the energy in this poor damsel. If she is allowed to grow older and breed, then the entire society is endangered. One small incision …"

Bertha watched Polly's right hand. It was in the posture of holding a pen or perhaps a cutting utensil. She held it over something, her eyes focused upon the cutting motion being made by her empty but purposeful fingers.

"Polly, dearest. You may now metamorphose your brain and take control of his. What can you do to prevent this immoral act from occurring?"

As a result of public conjecture, Polly's existential reality was the daily emotional fodder for the masses. This or that doctor or nurse (whose efficacy was open to bidding) would secretly tell the press how the girl's parents were to blame and that no child can become insane without a direct influence from the parent figures. Other journalists would speculate that the government was behind a huge cover-up, and so many citizens were being adjudicated insane to keep them quiet. According to conspiracy fanatics, these inmates knew something, and they had to be kept silent.

Bertha could hear the commotion at the asylum's front entrance. The girls had returned from their labors in the garden and on the farm. She took hold of her chain and dragged the ten-pound steel cube across the room to her bunk. Bertha knew that the moment the workers came into the ward they, too, would have these shackles affixed to their legs.

One must always make it profitable for the state-run institution, even if it means a little discomfort during enforcement. A recent statistical survey Bertha read had uncovered the fact that more patient accidents occurred because of there being no restraints, and the screaming dashes made by manic lunatics were not to be allowed. It was Bertha's goal, however, to lift the rock of outside speculation in order to explore the stark reality of the asylum's daily life, which was squirming from the mental disease called fear.

CHAPTER 2: THE HOME FIRES

The Hopkins Mansion, One Nob Hill, San Francisco, April 23, 1887.

When the woman from the Stockton Insane Asylum came to the door, Samuel Cortland Foltz, nineteen, was playing cribbage with the butler, Hannigan. Samuel heard the voice of the woman, and he knew she was the attractive messenger paid for by his mother's suffragist friends. Samuel waved off the butler when he started to answer the door. The written epistle from his sister, Bertha May, would be handed to his mother, Clara Shortridge Foltz, Esq., and then the formal "Walk to the Library" would ensue. As Clara made her journey, inevitably, family members would begin to trail in after her until the chairs around the Library reference table were occupied, waiting for the grand reading by the attorney and leader of the investigative team.

Samuel was without his girlfriend, Adeline Quantrill. The eighteen-year-old psychic orphan, with whom he fell in love during the spiritualist murders case, was interviewing for a research post with Dr. Richard Lobe, the Ichthyologist, who worked directly for railroad millionaire, Leland Stanford. Samuel also knew Adeline was being used by his mother to investigate more closely into what their team was now referring to as the "Mad Money Exposé."

Five of the usual investigative members were there, and they were seated to Clara's right and left. On the right sat Clara's beaux, Captain of Detectives, Isaiah Lees, his usually serious demeanor being attacked by the jubilant woman next to him, Ah Toy, Clara's long-time friend and former Chinatown Madame. On Clara's left were her son, Samuel, her daughter, Trella Evelyn, and, down on the end, the owner and benefactress to them all, Mrs. Mary Hopkins, who seemed to be amusing herself by speaking for an improvised napkin puppet, which the old woman was bouncing against Trella's back. The young woman, used to the magical world of Mary's dementia, was not perturbed.

"Please, may we have some decorum? Or, I may be initiating immediate insanity hearings against Ah Toy and Trella Evelyn for having maniacal and fluctuating changes in their menstrual and uterine habits!"

All the women, except Mrs. Hopkins, began to guffaw loudly and strike the table with their fists or purses. Menstruation and uterine disease were listed reasons for women to be declared insane by California officials, as the group knew.

Clara pounded her fist louder. "Enough! I must now impart the reading." She turned to look down at Captain Lees. He was staring up at her like an Irish Setter at the feet of his mistress. "Go ahead. I know that pleading face. You have more information about our case from the city officials. We usually don't aspire to such lofty heights around here, but, go ahead, Isaiah. Tell us what you know."

Clara sat down and kept her eyes on Lees as he stood to address the gathering. He was wearing the outfit he wore on cases: a brown frock coat and vest with checkered pants and spit-shined Oxfords. Clara wished he paid as much attention to her as he did to his Oxfords, his guns, and the Bowie knife that he kept under his vest.

"Thank you, Madame Investigator. I am certain you are all familiar with our former mayor, and now California's governor, Mr. Washington Bartlett. In the first case Attorney Foltz took on, we had the mayor on our prime murder suspect list up until the last moment. He did, in fact, impede the investigation into the murders of eight women, for which he was never prosecuted." Lees nodded to Clara, who was waving at him.

"I want to get back to our present murder case. How is Governor Bartlett a factor?" Clara said.

Captain Lees was ready for that question. "I understand. Governor Bartlett *is* connected to our present investigation. I just found out from his office, in fact, that the City of San Francisco will not be seeking any criminal grand jury indictment in the homicide of Winnifred Cotton, even though there is reason to believe the victim was pushed down the stairs and did not fall of her own accord."

"Winnie Cotton was a tomboy. She could out-wrestle and out-climb any boy her age. She would never trip." Trella Evelyn pointed out.

Lees continued, "It has also been resolved by the mayor's office that the commitment of Polly Bedford by her parents was legal and proper. Therefore, unless we can discover some evidence that gives us a witness at the scene of the girl's fall, or we get a sane confession from Miss Bedford as to this killer's identity, then Bertha May and Polly will have served their time in the asylum for nought."

Samuel decided to stand and deliver as well. "We began this inquiry when Polly's aunt, Mrs. Jeanne Forester, told mother that she overheard her sister, Louise, and her husband, Ronald Bedford, discussing the commitment of their daughter, Polly. The words Mrs. Forester heard were 'she can't be questioned by the police.' Now we have Bertha inside this asylum risking her life, and Adeline is away to infiltrate the halls of academe, while all we seem to be doing is laughing at suffragette humor."

Clara arose from her chair like an invigorated spirit of human rights. "Enough! We must focus on our present activities." She looked down at the report from her daughter at the Stockton hospital. It was the third such report since Clara had her strategically committed.

Samuel realized that his mother knew that her family and friends looked to her for guidance. They knew that Clara, along with fellow lawyer Laura de Force Gordon, had worked to get the law passed which accepted women into California law schools and gave women the right to enter any profession for which they were qualified. They also knew that Clara and her best friend, Ah Toy, were working to address the injustices of the intolerant culture that surrounded them. This case involved women and children being used as chattel in order to incarcerate them for free into mental asylums. These commitments were being done so the husbands or other relatives could profit, either directly or indirectly, from such confinement.

"Bertha May sends her love, and here is her report for this week. 'I was able to converse with Polly yesterday, but I believe the drugs they give her are dulling her senses and her intellect.' I shall now paraphrase." Clara looked up from the paper at her audience. "Polly describes the murderer of Winnie Cotton as being none other than Satan himself. No horns or other beastly persona for Miss Polly, however. Bertha says that, according to Polly, this devil murderer's face was a constantly moving display of different human faces.

Polly also was certain this visitor was slicing into something just before the murder."

"The Great Liar lives amongst us!" Mrs. Hopkins shouted from the end of the table.

"From what my daughter says about the administration at Stockton, we can at least be assured of getting possible witnesses who will testify that they saw asylum staff selling narcotics to the wealthy female residents in the top floor suites." Clara, always looking for pathways of greed, had been taught well as to the motivation of corrupt persons, especially those who work for the government.

Both her father Elias Shortridge, and her lover, Captain Lees, had in the past been arrested for disobeying arbitrary laws meant to protect the corrupt overseers. And, as the Women's Suffrage Movement also knew, females were seen as the weaker sex for a reason. Without the ability to get out of the home in order to pursue her calling, a woman was also an institutionalized citizen, ripened for the plunder.

Ah Toy raised her hand, and Clara nodded at her. She seemed very poised in her red silk *cheongsam*. Her English was eloquent and well pronounced. "Back in China, the Manchu would have workers join committees that were supposed to root out favoritism and corruption, but the rulers used that information to arrest those who would blame others. In China, if you were committed, it usually meant you would die. In this country, it seems, the institutionalization of humans can mean a profitable enterprise for those who can play the game well."

It was eldest daughter Trella Evelyn's turn to raise a hand. She was wearing the newest female liberation attire, a black gabardine suit, with a crimson tie hanging down belligerently between the breasts, and no preposterous bustle or python girdle to impede the free movement of a woman with a purpose. "I believe Ah Toy has a brilliant idea, even though she has not voiced it. Mother, you have always remarked that ideas are there for anybody to seize, but it is the enlightened person who steals these ideas and puts them into motion."

"Please, Trella dear. Get to the point," Clara said.

"We should form a citizens' committee to investigate the goings-on at Stockton," Trella said, rising slowly to her feet, as her voice gained volume and confidence. “Mrs. Hopkins and her friends certainly have the wealth and political influence to coordinate such a bi-partisan effort. We should keep it away from our suffrage connections, lest the men see through us to our ultimate goal.”

Clara wanted to give her daughter a bit more rope so she could hang herself properly and lady-like. “And what, pray tell, is our ultimate goal?”

“Why, to arrest every member of that corrupt male system in California that makes us the laughingstock of the nation. More Californians are being committed to mental hospitals than in any other state of the union. People are committed for being drunk in public, having hysterical menstrual cramps, and being insane for not speaking English.” Trella’s neck was red with emotion.

Clara was waiting for her daughter’s voice to register near the soprano pitch sung in a Wagnerian opera. There it was. “All right. That’s enough! I appreciate your fervent devotion to justice, Trella, and the idea is good, but the elaboration is not. For us to initiate such a committee, we will need an extremely decorous and judicial approach. Uncontrolled emotions, as you should all be aware, are the Achille’s heel of our movement. Many other women are against the female right to vote because women are important to the home fires. Without a woman’s intelligent touch, so goes the logic, a home can quickly degenerate into chaos and fear.”

Samuel watched his mother gather steam. He had witnessed this often. The unfathomable power of eloquent argument.

“Don’t look at me that way, Ah Toy. You know as well as I that without your sexual allure, you would have never made it out of Chinatown alive. Therefore, we shall form a very prudent, sober, and un-biased committee to investigate Stockton State Insane Asylum. We shall base our inquiry on very specific allegations, and our members will represent a cross-section of the community—both male and female—and our purpose will be to protect the best interests of all California taxpayers and citizens.”

Captain Lees stood up. “You need a member of the legal establishment to sit on this committee. I know a retired judge who would agree to such an appointment.”

Clara turned toward him. “Yes, and father can give us an esteemed reverend from the Christian community. Do we have anybody from academia and labor?”

"I have a professor at Berkeley who can serve. He teaches History and is well respected by his fellow researchers." Trella Evelyn was in college, and Samuel expected she would recommend that professor. She also thought he was dreamy and handsome.

Ah Toy raised her hand and waited until Clara nodded at her. "Chinatown is constantly working to gain advantage in our competitive economy. I believe it would be proper to include a labor official of Chinese descent on our committee. I know of one such respected official, and she is willing, I am certain."

"Thank you, Ah Toy. We now have a framework for our new investigative committee. Obviously, we will need to interview these new appointees, and each of you who spoke will coordinate together to schedule our interview. Be reminded. We are not out to save the world. As of this moment, our task is to prove a little girl has been murdered. Whatever crimes may branch outward from this central search are not of our immediate concern. With God's help, we have members in our international movement who will step in when needed to bridge the gaps."

Samuel knew they would end the meeting with applause. As he joined in, he thought about Adeline. Would she become more motivated by the pull of academic research so that she soon forgot about him? He really had no immediate plans. He still gambled in Chinatown, somewhat successfully. His mother's practice and "The Law" were on his distant horizon perhaps.

Samuel also thought about his sister, Bertha May. He knew that part of Bertha's motivation was to prove she was equal to he and Trella. He and Trella knew the real danger Bertha was in, and the excitement of her adventure exceeded the risk by microcosmic proportions.

He, along with their entire investigative team, knew they would now proceed carefully. The motivation to serve the common good was to always be at the forefront of any investigation they pursued. There was something about that last statement that always made Samuel's chest swell with pride.

***

The Cotton Mansion, Six Nob Hill, San Francisco, California, April 23, 1887.

Clara was in relatively good spirits when she walked through the garden leading up to the Cotton home, five doors down from Mary Hopkins' mansion. She had given direct instructions to her team about how they would collect information in the coming days. Of course, her daughter Bertha was in danger, but unless the murderer were inside the asylum, the risk could be kept to a minimum. Clara believed, of course, in the higher good. Humans needed something to look forward to as well as something to appreciate immediately. Without hope, humanity was doomed.

A tall butler took her shawl and parasol, and Clara adjusted her auburn hair and straightened her new teal hat. The silk teal dress and moderate bustle served as assisting decorations in this important tête-à-tête. The most important task to Clara was how to decorate the questions she was about to ask this special person. She knew just how important it was to have an audience with Mrs. Elizabeth Packard, a woman who, in the 1860s, had been committed to an insane asylum for three years. Like Clara, she was a single mother with six children. Mrs. Packard won her case against the patriarchal authorities, and she turned to the law, in order to enact changes to reform state policies on housing and caring for its mentally ill population. Clara was meeting a woman who had established a national association of experts to address the changes needed at mental asylums in all the states.

As she followed the maid through the mansion, Clara noted how her senses were being distracted away from the usual garish antique furnishings, pungent exotic incense, and even the artwork collections. When one lived inside the beast of capitalism, the opulence quickly became commonplace, especially if one was engaged in legal conundrums that had to do with civil rights for women, the lesser races, foreign cultures, and other lower classes.

Winona Cotton was, of course, still wearing mourning black for her daughter, Winnifred, whose death was the proximate cause of this arranged meeting between Clara and Mrs. Packard. Her eyes were bright, and her hands were warm as she grasped Clara's. "Come. Let me introduce you to her right away. My friends and I, quite naturally, will be leaving the room the moment you give the word. I must tell you. She does have one affectation at age seventy-one. She won't use a hearing apparatus, so she will often not hear you well. You must speak louder than you would normally speak for her to hear you."

Clara nodded and followed her hostess into the study off to the side of the main dining room. Ever the good detective, Clara was making mental notes about the identities of the persons she knew who were inside that study. There was only one personage she did not recognize, a slender man with fashionable mutton-chop sideburns warming his cheeks and framing his blue-eyed gaze. The others were Charles Cotton, Winona's husband, and Clara's close attorney friend, Laura de Force Gordon. Clara assumed Laura was there representing the Cotton family, as she had also represented them during the formal inquest into the cause of Winnifred's death. Laura had been of great assistance in Clara's second case, last year, helping to capture the spiritualist who was responsible for women killing their husbands.

Then, there was the woman Clara really wanted to meet. Mrs. Elizabeth Ware Packard wore a plain, rural dress of dark blue with a white lace apron tied around her middle. The plaid shawl encircled her rather wide shoulders, and the cameo brooch under the white blouse at her neck complemented her calm and inquisitive gray eyes. Her wispy white hair was loose and about her shoulders, and there was something about the way Mrs. Packard leaned forward as Clara approached, and smiled beneath her white bonnet, which caused Clara to say the following to the older woman in a loud voice.

"I trust you are not wearing a corset, Mrs. Packard, lest your father and ex-husband commit you again for purposely cutting off the proper flow of blood to your weak, female brain." Clara took the woman's spotted hands into her own and peered deeply into her intelligent eyes. She at once saw the elder's eyes light up with good humor as she squinted, smiled, and nodded at Clara.

"Ah, Mrs. Foltz. At last, someone who understands the role that simply being of a different sex can mean to one's ability to work and to even breathe comfortably. I keep telling my so-called followers that they need only begin a revolt in the bedroom to get things changed the way they should be. That would most certainly include our women who do their wifely duties in the bordello. Certainly, you'll agree, Aristophanes was onto something when he wrote *Lysistrata*. Women of today simply do not have the gumption to follow the Greek women's plan through. If the corset were on the men's bodies, these gallivanting troubadours of ours would become celibate monks. Just to win a drunken wager at a tavern house, they thought they could escape this mighty garment-python's grip. It is we women who need to gird our loins and, if you'll pardon the expression, herd our collective and closed loins, to put a stop to intolerant male behaviors."

"Oh yes, Mrs. Packard . . ." Clara began, chuckling and sitting down next to her on the davenport. She motioned to her friend Laura to sit down at the end as well, and she did.

"Please, do call me Elizabeth, or even Liz, if you're of the modern set. You must be, as you're so young and flirtatiously attractive." Mrs. Packard adjusted a curl that was sticking down too far on Clara's wide forehead. At thirty-eight, with five children and a robust figure, Clara believed Liz may also need spectacles.

"I'm sorry to be in such a rush. I must be off to another round of questioning in this matter. May we begin? I understand attorney Gordon will be staying to represent the Cotton family's interest in these proceedings. That will be fine, but we need to clear the room of everyone else." Clara glanced around, first at Mr. and Mrs. Cotton and then at the strange gentleman. She made a mental note to later ask Laura who he was. After she watched them exit the study and close the double-doors behind them, Clara turned once again to yell at Mrs. Packard.

"Let me attempt to summarize my predicament at this juncture, Liz," she said, deciding on incorporating the familiar name for this great woman, as it would assuage Clara's own fears of sitting right next to this noble champion of human rights.

"By all means, Attorney Foltz. And, welcome, Mrs. Gordon. I am aware of your courtroom battles to defend the rights of women, some of whom, I might add, were railroaded into mental institutions for the profit of their husbands or other family members." Mrs. Packard folded her hands into her lap. "Certainly, in my own case, back in the 1860s, there were no means of protection to stop the abuses, but now we at least have some protection and even overseers, although law and enforcement are two very different realities, as I'm certain you're both aware."

Clara noted that Laura again wore her plain, dark blue work attire, which reflected her affinity for the masses. No bustle, no frills, and certainly no feminine allure. Whereas Clara used her own grace and feminine stylishness to catch the male opposition off-guard, it had been Laura's strategy all along to come at her opponents with rhetorical guns blasting away, with no regard for a fashionably attractive personal appearance.

Laura Gordon was an efficient and practical San Francisco lawyer, whereas Clara had always tried to look at the big picture, even at a state and federal level, and to plan accordingly. All three of them, Clara knew, had one thing in common. They had all been jilted by husbands who believed women were there to serve them and not there to rebel against their ironclad power.

"Liz, we don't have the membership or far reach that you and your fine organization have. This does not mean our present case warrants your attention out of hand. It does not. Instead, I propose an affiliation based on the understanding that we wish to change the entire mental health care system and not the patients or the people working within. The system must always accommodate the best interests of the individual, whenever possible, with the understanding that organizations must have discipline and order in order to function."

Mrs. Packard was mumbling some words to herself and nodding.

Clara gasped. "Liz?" she said, at a greater volume, remembering about the elder's hearing impairment. "Did you hear anything I just said?"

"I'm sorry, my dear. No, I really did not hear one word. I am fortunate to have you here today. I must remember to tell friends to speak louder when in my company. This is what they called in the asylum a breakthrough, Mrs. Foltz." Mrs. Packard leaned back and sighed. "Sadly, our society often supports isolation and eccentricity, when it comes to research and intelligent scientific and even religious speculation. However, you must always do this under society's auspices, because we all know there is supposedly no such thing as an isolated genius. Without the kiss of approval from society, a genius may as well be a mad person raving, within an asylum, squatting in the corner, excrement in his hands, nude, and with no hope or belief in God or for the future."

"We need your understanding of how things actually function inside these asylums," Clara was almost shouting, and she noticed that Laura was wincing from the sound. In their courtroom debates,

Laura was always the loud one, who could make a jury sit up and listen. Clara, on the other hand, would always come near. Nearer to the judge, to the jury, to the witness. Her speaking method was to fabricate intimate secrets, whereas Laura's technique was to compete directly with the men.

"You have achieved a life about which most women merely dream, Mrs. Foltz. Other women do not realize, of course, that the reality of being given some access to the patriarchal authorities is no guarantee that they will listen. That is when we females use our hidden talents of the supernatural variety, is it not?"

Clara nodded and smiled. She was thinking about the young psychic, Adeline Quantrill, whom she employed to ferret out the identity of a murderer, and who was now being courted by Samuel, Clara's son. The girl was presently applying to assist one of the most prominent and influential families in America, the Stanfords. This bastion of academic exclusivity would be quite surprised to discover that Clara and her investigative team had planted Adeline there to spy on them.

"Some might call madness the isolated genius of a Jesus, a Mohammed, or a Buddha," Mrs. Packard continued. "Or, others might call it the madness of a mind gone off its trolley. I thought I would use that metaphor, as those monstrosities you have going up these Sisyphus hills may as well be circumnavigating between heaven and hell, or mania and melancholy."

"What is your biggest fear about what can happen when society allows the subjugation of human beings for the purposes of isolation away from more respectable members of the community?" Clara hoped her open-ended question would allow Mrs. Packard the freedom to explore her innermost beliefs based on her horrendous personal experience and battle to survive.

"Make no mistake. There are those mental patients who are quite a danger to themselves and to others. They should be the focus of attention at these facilities. Why? They need proper care aimed at preventing physical harm. Whereas, much of the political shenanigans we face have to do with the manipulation of innocent minds for profit, I am quite pleased to be part of your investigation, Mrs. Foltz. My organization and I often become too distracted from the daily realities of our entire society. We become so riveted upon the noble quest to release innocent minds from captivity that we ignore the one true way we can actually cause change. We cannot uncover conspiracies within the organization which point to an evil trend in the very process of caring for the mentally ill. I am proud to serve you in this regard because this is what you will be doing."

A young red-haired woman wearing a nurse's dress rushed into the room, and Clara was at first angry at the interruption, as she had just begun to appreciate Mrs. Packard's acceptance and what it meant to her plans. Luckily, the visiting nurse was talking to Laura Gordon, as she was seated as the closest of the trio to the entrance. After a few moments of intense whispering, back and forth, Laura got up and walked over to Clara.

"She's the messenger from Stockton. She says Polly was confined to isolation. It seems when a fellow patient shared in open discussion about how she knew Miss Bedford to be a secret spy for the government, Polly rushed at the woman and attempted to gouge her eyes from their sockets, or so the written report reads."

Clara felt her heart clutch in her breast. Could someone in that state-employed community have discovered that Polly was connected to Bertha May? And, upon further inside investigation, perhaps they found out that Clara and her group were behind Bertha being committed. It was one of Clara's worst nightmares as a sleuth. That moment when you have discovered that your adversary was one step ahead of you, as you were about to pull the magician's screen back to reveal the real culprits behind the sorcery.

"I have worked to pass thirty-four state bills which directly address these problems. Most often, the guilty party has been discovered by using common sense and an application of human and Christian values. However, in some circumstances, there was a malfeasance committed against a patient that demonstrated evil and even murderous intent. At those moments, I am very happy to turn the authority to investigate over to an honest and caring legal professional, such as yourself." Mrs. Packard nodded at Clara.

Clara smiled over at Laura, who nodded back at her. "We completely agree with you, Mrs. Packard. Even though my own daughter could be in jeopardy, I will not jump to any conclusions before we can hear all of the witnesses to this event. Are you at liberty to travel with us to the Stockton asylum? On the way, I can tell you about the citizens' committee we are in the process of forming in order to thoroughly investigate the entire administration and its staff. We believe this will lead directly to discovering the person or persons responsible for the death of Miss Winnifred Cotton."

"Even during my darkest times inside the Illinois asylum, I was never treated as badly as when I was placed under the roof of my own husband. He locked me up and would not allow me to socialize with anyone. This is what drives one authentically insane. The reality that you are not allowed the privilege of being with fellow humans."

Laura added to the conversation. "Indeed. Isolation recently killed one of my clients. She could not stand her seclusion and committed suicide with purchased drugs she procured on the prison's black market."

Mrs. Packard continued with her memoir, and Clara noted that her complexion became flushed as she spoke more vehemently than before.

"When I was in the asylum, at least I could talk to other women, and we understood how we were being treated, because our every waking moment was monitored by our caretakers. This was not a democracy, but my asylum treatment did not come close to the way the government had bequeathed my husband with the power to imprison me. According to my Christian religion, my Calvinist caretaker should have obeyed the obligation to protect his wife and not to imprison her. We must get that Bedford girl out of isolation!" Mrs. Packard concluded, and she stood up.

CHAPTER 3: THE INTENT OF THE INSANE

Central Pacific Train to Stockton, April 23, 1887.

Clara wanted to use this inquiry into Polly Bedford's alleged assault upon another resident as a way to insinuate their investigation into the life blood of the state asylum's daily activities. Mrs. Packard had already wired the superintendent at the Stockton asylum with instructions to take Polly out of isolation until they arrived.

It was as if this change in circumstance had opened up a new method to eavesdrop, with careful planning, into the heart of murderous intent itself. As an attorney-at-law, Clara understood that most crimes of passion, of which murder was the most heinous, had to be proved in front of a jury, beyond any reasonable doubt, that the Defendant's action was intentional and deliberated upon before he or she made a move.

Along the Central Pacific route toward Stockton, inside their cabin, Clara was able to discuss, albeit at an increased volume, with Elizabeth Packard and Laura Gordon, about why their investigation centered around the murder of Winnifred Cotton. Also, how they needed to prove an intent that went far beyond that of a single murderer's state of mind. Clara was relaxed as she spoke, and she would often turn in her private first-class seat, to gaze out at the passing farm land as they journeyed, the coach swaying, the rails click-clacking like the castanets of a Spanish dancer.

"You see, that's why I wanted my daughter, Bertha May, committed to the asylum. She believes her friend, Polly Bedford, is not insane at all. It's her idea that the administration has been instructed, by whom we know not, to give Polly drugs to keep her in a confused state of mind. I propose we inquire into that area. When an actor is under duress or has been drugged, either voluntarily or involuntarily, his or her actions are not to be considered intentional." When she saw Laura's eyebrow raise, Clara nodded for her to speak.

"Yes, and intent works both ways, my dear. If you believe there is some nefarious conspiracy of a group, then you have the burden of proving intent on their part, as well as showing that each member of that conspiracy took an advanced step toward completing the illegal action, even a murder." Laura shook her dark-brown hair, and Clara remembered that same glint of satisfaction in Laura's eyes that she saw so often during their trials opposing each other in a court of criminal law.

Clara smiled, choosing to circumvent her friend's challenge for the moment. "Naturally, under the present legal circumstances, Miss Bedford has been ruled insane. Thus, her civil rights are completely obliterated. If she is insane, then her intent is nullified, but the same goes for her actions if she were not insane. Why? Because if she is not insane, then the drugs being administered to her for her diagnosed insanity are not warranted. Therefore, the intent of her actions while under the influence of illegally prescribed drugs, is also negated, because she was not lucid."

It was Mrs. Packard's turn to smile, and Clara was so expectant that she reached out and took the older woman's hand.

"What you say is clear," Mrs. Packard said. "It also suggests that you need another expert to add. You need a physician who works daily with committed patients and who can speak with the utmost authority about how drugs affect a patient's mind and body. Most importantly, he must know if their dosage can mitigate intent in the human mind."

"Thank you, Liz. Do you really have a doctor in mind who would do this?" Clara asked.

"I certainly do. He played an important role in my own investigations, when we were attempting to impose pharmaceutical regulations upon several state mental asylums across the country. He traveled with me to seventeen hearings in eight different states. His name is Dr. Andrew McFarland, and he was the superintendent in charge of the Illinois State Asylum for the Insane, in Jacksonville, where I was when I challenged the authorities about my own illegal internment by my husband." Mrs. Packard straightened her collar.

"Is he sympathetic to your cause?" Laura shouted.

"Sympathetic? Well, he quit his employment as the superintendent, due to what we proved was going on under his nose, and he established a private hospital, Oak Lawn Retreat, where he now works as the Superintendent and Assistant Physician. However, I must point out, he will not come to us without the accompaniment of his constant companion, and apple of his eye, his granddaughter, Anne."

"Still another member to join the fray?" Clara raised her eyebrows but smiled. "I suppose having an extra woman will also help us."

"Indeed, it will. I don't know how many times Andrew has informed me he plans to base his entire mental health program for women around his mentally and physically fit granddaughter, as he believes she will make a superb doctor. She will be entering medical school beginning in the new term."

"She is getting quite a special education with her grandfather serving as mentor," Laura shouted.

"Indeed. Anne becomes quite vehement when we discuss the current practice of blaming female mania and nervousness on the patient's menstrual and gynecological disorders. She will instruct you, in the minutest details, about how this policy was instituted in order to reap thousands of dollars from the coffers of every pharmaceutical, gadget, and uterine gimmickry manufacturer known to Man." Mrs. Packard took a deep, resigned breath.

"I can't speak for my entire team, but I believe these two experts will be excellent additions. I want to thank you, Liz, for your assistance. When can they be in California to help us?" Clara's voice was still loud, and she squinted as she spoke.

"Good. Then I shall wire them through Western Union when we arrive in Stockton. They should make it out here in three days, if all goes well. We certainly won't be able to secure a date for our first committee investigation for at least three days, don't you think? That's been my experience in other states. This is the first time I've taken on the system in California. Do you believe it will be difficult?" Mrs. Packard's eyes were glowing with enthusiasm.

Both Clara and Laura were smiling roguishly at that question. Clara spoke first. "California began Stockton's existence in controversy. The first superintendent, a Dr. Reid, was accused in court of using patients as slave labor to add furnishings and a new garden to his personal home. He was also accused of underreporting deaths and using single graves for multiple burials. His trial, begun by the governor, ended in Reid being discharged."

Laura shouted, with her hands circled around her mouth. "Yes, and two doctors—one sympathetic to Reid and the other to the governor—fought a duel over the testimony given against Reid by another doctor who later, coincidentally, became the new superintendent. Luckily, the wounded man, Dr. Langdon, received only a fractured leg when the bullet struck him. As you can see, Mrs. Packard, stories in the penny press about our life in the Wild West are not always exaggerated."

"And, since you speak of aboriginal thinking, what is the overall philosophy at this asylum? Does it accede to the current trend in blaming the body for the condition of the mind? Misogyny, as I have discovered, time and again, often lies at the heart of the way the women are treated inside these state facilities." Mrs. Packard struck her breast with her fist.

"From what we've studied, California mental health authorities subscribe to the theory that social stressors cause mental illness. Allegedly, our Gold Rush and our increasingly complicated industrial society affect our population—many of them from foreign lands—in very negative ways." Clara held her arms out wide. "The cure, so to speak, is for the asylum to be a grand place where the patient can relax, in rural splendor, in order to be treated for mental problems caused mostly by social stress and physical ailments. Thus, we have the water method of keeping a patient's body invigorated by warmth and liquid, thus clearing the mind for more logical thinking."

"Go ahead, Clara, I know you're going to say it," Laura remarked, frowning.

Clara nodded at her friend and smiled. "Yes, and I was especially enthused when you mentioned Miss Anne, the granddaughter of Dr. Andrew McFarland. We have reason to believe these conspirators—perhaps even the murderer him or her self—are profiting from misogynistic practices as well as from the old-fashioned crimes of embezzlement of government funds and outright torture."

Laura snapped back, "The State of California does, in fact, have a very mixed population, and as we know, it is also a very difficult society in which to succeed. Our citizens are under constant threats from labor unrest, we treat our immigrants with disdain, and we move the mentally ill away from these stressors so they can be cured of the mostly attitudinal problems they develop. Attorney Foltz here seems to forget that many upstanding citizens, such as my clients, the Bedfords, need a safe place to commit their obviously insane children. And, the drugs and daily physical regimen are here to assist in medical treatment and not here to aggravate the problem of the patient."

"Oh, it can get quite aggravated when profit becomes a cure, and drugs become the snake oil for the State's coffers," Clara said, and her eyes became livid. She met her fellow attorney's stare with equal resistance.

"As we always say, Counselor, that will be determined in court." Laura adjusted the black comb in her hair. Because Clara was a personal friend, Laura was obviously holding back on her usually antagonistic rhetoric. If they were inside a courtroom, Clara knew, Laura's talons would be showing.

***

This was the third visit for Clara to the Stockton State Insane Asylum. But it was the first involving her daughter, Bertha May, and her companion, Polly Bedford. As they rode out to the institution by rented horse and buggy, Clara reflected upon how different she and Laura Gordon were in one key area of the law. The insanity defense. Clara believed not being able to determine right from wrong was solid proof that the perpetrator did not have the requisite intent. Laura, in opposition, believed only the perpetrator could know about state of mind at the time of the act, so because there was no objective viewpoint from which to judge, there could be no mitigating circumstance of insanity. Judges could not be mind readers and neither could alienists.

Clara enjoyed the sensory panorama riding on the train. The rivers of the California Delta swirled around them. Waves of different odors wafted into the coach: onion, fertilizer, flowers, fruits and many more indescribable and pungent smells. As both Mrs. Packard and Laura were eating fresh peaches, sold from a cart during their trip, Clara reached over and grabbed one from the bag between them.

As she smelled the unique odor of the peach, Clara realized how nonsensical it was to determine the guilt or innocence of a human being upon subjective and often intolerant human reason. According to the patriarchal authorities, one cannot be conscious of one's actions unless one can reason. The animals, even the primates, do not write down their histories and memories. These creatures do not explore the universe nor do they understand the laws of a society created for their own interests.

Ironically, the so-called "insane" person could reason. True, their reasoned world was usually an inner society based completely upon personal and not societal tastes, and on subjective, idiosyncratic status symbols rather than on social whims. Who could truthfully say which reason was superior? If the insane person were kept in the attic, inside an elite mansion, sleeping in satin, prattling to servants, getting featured at Christmas like the other poor oddities in life, then the intent and actions of the insane person were producing a positive result. The insane person's inner society was not part of the outside, and yet it still existed. It was only the social communications network that was missing in this equation.

If the insane person were protected by outside society, then could he or she live another day, without harm, and with a possible hope for the future? For example, in the case of Mrs. Mark Hopkins, Mary, Clara's wealthy benefactress, the old woman's dementia was being protected by Clara's legal knowledge and by Ah Toy's administrative abilities. Without their protection, the old woman could easily be committed to an asylum by unscrupulous types, who had no other concern other than reaping profits from the railroad heiress's formidable estate.

Clara knew that each day was perhaps her last chance to find the connections between that inner, sometimes insane world, and that outer, perhaps eternally insane world. In those moments of breakthrough, when the sick, insane mind sees it is being heard and is being accepted as a legitimate reality, will insanity become open to criticism and possible cure?

Clara also knew this honorable treatment of humans, such as what Mrs. Packard advocated, was at the heart of her own goals as an attorney. Many societal labels were meant to categorize and isolate you from the elite, mostly prosperous, citizens. Status and biased labels, in contrast, were created for both the elite rulers and the poor workers. However, the elite controlled the message propaganda and the enforcement of the rules. The "rub," as Shakespeare would call it, was that the ruling class in 1887 saw most of existence as an extension of themselves: a business.

The name of the gentleman with the lamb-chop side-whiskers, present at the Cotton Mansion inquiry, was Dr. Alfred Rooney, the present Superintendent of the Stockton Insane Asylum. Laura passed that information on, when Clara asked her in the middle of a discussion of the men Laura was seeing romantically. It was a tactic that Clara often used whenever she wanted information from her friend. Laura's mind became so fixated upon making whatever she was explaining correct that she would often answer almost any inquiry with complete honesty.

"My clients want him to be present whenever there is any questioning by any authorities. The Bedfords are on the California State Board of Advisors to the Health and Education Committee. Obviously, they cannot risk any misinterpretation of facts when it concerns the policies at Stockton asylum." Laura's brown eyes were hooded by what Clara called her "focus frown."

"My, that is quite resourceful of you, Mrs. Gordon," Clara said. She knew her good friend did not enjoy being called by her married title. Clara used her own marriage title to protect her and her five children and their social reputations. Clara told society she was a widow when, in fact, she was divorced because of her husband's desertion.

Laura, on the other hand, never had children, and her previous husband was a philanderer. Even though they were both deserted by their husbands, as was Mrs. Packard, it was Laura who came out of the experience angrier. In Clara's opinion, Laura now used men as a soothing balm for her Free Love tendencies, whereas Clara had chosen to remain monogamous and single with the Captain of Detectives, Isaiah Lees, as her lover.

As they neared the steps leading up through the archway into the main admittance room, Clara looked up. The sun was now descending behind the top steeple, shining its weakened rays through the bell tower. Hundreds of fluttering bats were streaming out, like a burst of dark thoughts, and Clara shivered, reaching up to hold onto her hat in the breeze.

There was an ominous foreboding all around her, and even the cooking odors of potatoes and lamb could not assuage the fear the attorney felt deep inside. It was as if a curse had already been placed on this residence, and what they were actually doing was going through a strange ritual meant for all of those who would dare question the human motives behind this portentous cathedral of darkness.

As they walked up to the entrance, on the shadowy grounds of the women's side of the rather eerie Gothic structure, Clara decided to probe a bit more deeply into Laura's legal preparations. Perhaps she knew how the politicians on this advisory board addressed official explorations into conduct that may have led to an assault by one of its residents. Upstairs, a woman screamed, just as Clara and her group entered.

***

The Women's Section, First Floor, Stockton State Insane Asylum, April 23, 1887.

"Thank you, Superintendent," Clara said, sitting directly across from Dr. Rooney inside the asylum's staff conference room. They were adjacent to his personal office on the ground floor's admission area. Alfred Rooney was alone, as his staff was stretched thin, caring for the over five-hundred female residents. "I have with me Mrs. Elizabeth Ware Packard. I would expect you are aware of her special expertise. She has agreed to assist me in this committee investigation of the event concerning Polly Bedford."

The young superintendent shuffled some papers in front of him, cleared his throat, and stared directly at Mrs. Packard. "Of course, I know about this fine citizen. I read the mental health journals, you know, and I have followed her political activities closely. I also know her personal history, and I want to say that she is, most probably, the finest example of what we attempt to create here in our women's facility. As Mrs. Packard advocates, we want our patients to learn to think in terms of improving society and not negating it. The dark land of Hades is not evil, but it does contain only the secrets of dead minds and isolated spirits. Nothing of value can come from retreating deep within oneself, ignoring the society around one, communicating only with the phantoms of illusion and dread."

Clara noticed that Mrs. Packard had brought out her full armaments. She held a rather ornate and collapsible ear trumpet against her right ear as Rooney spoke. It bothered Clara slightly that Liz hadn't used it when she was conversing with them earlier, but this was, obviously, a more important event.

"I am afraid I cannot accept your assessment of what the so-called lunatic community aspires toward, one way or another. I do know your classical analogy is a bit out of context. Hades raped and kidnapped Persephone, his mistress, as she was distracted by a symbol of her selfish, outer beauty, the Narcissus flower. Allow me to explain the myth contextually, just the way I explain it to asylum residents who are confused by their retreat from reality."

"By all means. Please do so," Dr. Rooney said. Clara noted a tone of slight sarcasm.

"Have you, by any chance, Dr. Rooney, ever attempted to go inside a patient's delusion, so to speak? In this method of conversation, you adhere to your patient's mental rules, not to your own nor society's rules. Is that not correct?"

Dr. Rooney was signing an admittance form, probably the same way he approved Bertha May's commitment, and he was distracted. When he finally looked up, he cocked his head to the side like a bulldog. "What was that? I am sorry, but this is the busiest time of year for us."

"That's fine. Your behavior answers my question. The way I approach mental health therapy is to attempt to be on an equal psychic footing with the ill person. You see, although Hades and his underworld can represent a retreat from reality, I prefer to tell my fellow voyager that she has been swept under because she must learn to accept death and the spirit world as a way to learn how to balance her inner world with the outer world. Both worlds are needed for health, but none is more important than the other. Persephone, in fact, is able to convince Hades that a heavenly place was necessary in his dark world, so he created the Elysium paradise for her, which later became the basis for the Bible's Garden of Eden." Mrs. Packard smiled.

"Liz, would you happen to be playing Demeter, Persephone's mother, and the Goddess of Nature, in this story?" Clara asked, also smiling. The attorney believed she knew where Mrs. Packard was going, so she wanted to assist her.

"I play whomever seems to fit with the individual's inner world. Sometimes, I will have a woman who has retreated because she was raped by her father or by some other close family member. This woman will often abuse herself physically, until she realizes it was not her role as a sexual temptress which caused her guardian to molest her. No, it was a social problem that made this woman feel guilty about her own sexual urges. Daughters were taught to love their parents, and when that trust was violated, such as in the case of an incestuous rape, then the violated woman must escape the only way she knows how, inside her own mind."

"I completely understand. However, I must say, we really don't have the time nor staff to explore such deeply disturbing areas. We believe if the body is exercised, cleansed, and kept fit, then the mind will soon follow. There is no need for such a dangerous and peculiar methodology. Sexuality is for the family and the clergy to investigate." Rooney clicked his teeth. "Can we get to the gist of your visit? I have to see to my responsibilities. Dinner is being served, and I must make my rounds."

Clara realized it was time for her to draw the line in the sand. She took out the papers from her purse that officially notified the State of California about their petition to investigate the asylum for reasons of possible improper treatment of patients, unsuitable handling and distribution of drugs, and how residents are wrongly admitted and for what reasons they are admitted. Mrs. Packard had already signed on to be an official on Clara's committee, and Clara was going to explain to the superintendent what they were planning to do in the coming days.

"Mr. Rooney, we are here not only to address the recent handling of Polly Bedford and her confinement, we are also planning to convene a citizens' investigation committee, to evaluate your overall services and health care of all those admitted to these confines." Clara leaned over and handed the copy of the application to Rooney.

She knew the State had its own yearly quality control inspection, but those were usually held on the asylum's schedule, and no process of examination was conducted with any specific purpose in mind. It was strictly a sheet with a check-off list of possible violations. Also, various merchants and wealthy California investors would be paraded past the asylum residents, during what Clara believed to be a pre-arranged dog and pony show, in order to demonstrate to these possible donors just how efficient their system was. However, Clara and her team would be the first truly independent, nationally recognized group to visit these premises.

"I see. And what do you expect to find during your inquest, pray tell? We have been lauded by many different groups for our dynamic and kind treatment of the mentally ill. In fact, we have a medical group from Germany who will soon be studying our research into the hereditary aspects of *dementia praecox* and *mania a potu*." Rooney leaned back in his chair and waved his hand backward toward a row of plaques and awards decorating the redwood walls.

"We want to live here while we work. In addition to Mrs. Packer, we will have five or perhaps six committee members. Do you have accommodations for us?" Clara stood up.

"Yes, we can put you in the first floor guest wing. I'm afraid you will have to live as our residents do. We have a large room with bunkbeds. Will that be sufficient to your needs?" Mr. Rooney also rose.

Mrs. Packard stood up and took the ear trumpet from her ear. "I shall need a larger bed, young man. At seventy-one, I am not as flexible as I used to be. Even my three years in an asylum did not prepare me for old age. If women can escape death during childbirth, they still must face the arthritis, rheumatism, hip dislocations and missing teeth of old age."

Clara and Laura got on either side of Mrs. Packard and escorted her out into the main admissions hall. Superintendent Rooney followed them.

"After dinner, I think I shall roam the wards to meet some of my neighbors," Mrs. Packard said, hitching up her dress. "It is at night when the restless manias come out to play, is not that the case, Doctor Rooney?"

"Why, yes. We have nurses on duty, however, so if anybody gets lost, we can get her safely back into bed. There are also the ghosts, however." Clara looked at the superintendent's face to see if he were smiling. He was not.

"Did you say ghosts?" Laura, the spiritual skeptic, thrust her forefinger into Clara's ribs.

"I did. You may think me an inflexibly scientific sort, but I am actually a great believer in the spirit world. Whenever one of my women dies, if she has not been cured, then I believe her spirit stays around our home until she can be released. Release comes when a new patient is cured. It is the great circle of mental health, is it not?" Dr. Rooney stepped out in front of them to lead them into the dining room.

Clara could smell the lamb and potatoes, and she was suddenly quite famished. Dinner and then bed sounded very comforting. She knew the relief would be short lived, as the curse may still be out there, and now there were these ghosts. At the very least, she would probably have to follow after Mrs. Packard just to keep her out of trouble. Clara might also be accosted by her daughter, Bertha May, but this was to be prevented, at all costs. It may be a long night after all.

CHAPTER 4: ADELINE THE SPY

Leland Stanford Mansion, California and Powell Streets, San Francisco, April 24, 1887.

As Adeline Quantrill walked up to the mansion, which was just a stone's throw from her friends' Queen Anne Victorian abode at One Nob Hill, she was thinking about having been chosen by Mrs. Foltz. It was Adeline's firmest belief that if she were to stand any chance at marrying the attorney's son, Samuel, she would have to show that she could perform well on her first solo mission.

The young psychic was especially concerned, in that her ability to navigate on her own was probably her weakest trait. She had no sense of direction. True. It was her intellectual ability to read minds and telepathically communicate that made her so important to Mrs. Foltz solving the spiritualist murders the year before. In addition, Adeline's autobiographic memory allowed her to access every waking moment of her entire life to remember everything that occurred. This case was giving her all the authority to make her own mistakes, completely alone.

The mansion's structure was more of a Greco-Italian version of an imaginary home somebody so wealthy would build. Whereas the Hopkins' mansion was painted gray, Mr. Stanford chose white. Instead of the Hopkins' tall, cylindrical columns that had the religious appearance of a cathedral, this home had the squat, non-sectarian, and rectangular shape of the Greek Parthenon.

As one of the "Big Four" railroad tycoons, Leland Stanford was not enamored of helping to showcase new artists the way Mary Hopkins was. He was concerned with business and the appearance of grandeur. As Adeline entered through the twenty-foot tall granite and marble Corinthian columns, supporting the front porch entrance, she was not surprised by the type of decorative memorabilia inside. When Adeline, in a low whisper, gave her name to the butler, an older gentleman dressed in formal tails, he nodded, and he escorted her across the redwood floor beneath the house's mammoth circular rotunda.

She asked the butler who had created the statues and paintings, and she was informed it was one man, a Mr. G. G. Garibaldi, who had carte blanche when he furnished the mansion. The ceiling of the grand dome was divided into eight large panels. As she looked up, following the butler's pointed index finger, she was informed that each panel had a picture, four of which were figured with noble allegorical groups of female figures representing the four quarters of the globe. The other four panels were finished with emblematic figures personifying "Fine Arts," "Mechanics," "Agriculture" and "Literature."

As the butler led Adeline into the Library on the ground floor, she recognized the grand figure of Mr. Stanford almost immediately. He was standing in his black suit, vest and cravat tie, and he was looking down at a book opened on the long mahogany table. Hundreds of other volumes looked down upon its sibling from their cases along all four walls. Stanford was leaning on a black cane with an ivory handle, amongst the green and gold chairs, and Adeline noted with interest that Mr. Stanford's legs trembled uncontrollably, beneath his wide girth, as he leaned over to read the text. At sixty-three, his beard hair was almost all white under the gas chandeliers, although he still had streaks of black on top, and in his thick, furrowed eyebrows.

Leland Stanford, Adeline's prospective employer, was speaking to another man, also in a business suit, who was seated. This man, however, was clean shaven, and he wore a bowed tie. The hair around his mostly bald head was gray, and his white, mutton chop sideburns extended below his ears. His upper lip, Adeline noticed, came to a point, giving him a pouty expression. She also noted, with some amount of pleasure, that she could receive his thoughts.

Although she could not read the minds of many people, there were those rare individuals who seemed to have a supernatural affinity for her telepathic reception. One such person was Osiris Buddha Randolph, the twelve-year-old son of the spiritualist, Dr. Paschal Beverly Randolph. The year before, her communication with the boy led to saving Mrs. Foltz and her daughter, Trella Evelyn, from the villain at the Sarah Winchester house in San Jose.

This man was thinking, *I hope he finishes soon. I must make my appointment at Berkeley before noon.* However, when Adeline attempted to transmit her own thoughts to this gentleman, he would not answer. She had experienced this before with others, but not very often. She had known only two people who were only transmitters and not both transmitters and receivers. Either this man was refusing to allow her to know he was also a telepath, or he was afraid to send because Mr. Stanford was in the room.

"After I read your book, I knew you should be the person to formulate my science and psychology departments," Mr. Stanford was saying. "Shortly after we buried my son, I had an apparition of his countenance appear to me during sleep. I was afraid that I would not be able to bequeath anything now that I was bereft of an heir. I was even wondering if I should live anymore. My son spoke to me that night, Mr. Galton, and he said, 'Father, you can give to all of humanity in remembrance of me.' And, that's why you're here, good sir. You can assist me in building the largest university in the world devoted to the betterment of mankind."

If I had known you were a Spiritualist, I would not have come. Adeline heard Mr. Galton's thoughts. When he turned toward her and stared, she believed he might have finally recognized she was listening in to what he was thinking. She then realized that Mr. Galton was actually thinking about Mr. Stanford.

Mr. Galton was moved to reply, "My wife, Louisa, and I were never able to conceive. This is an important part of the over-population problem we face. While the inferior races and the degraded poor are having millions of offspring, we, who have been evolving and producing the superior offspring, are not generating our children fast enough to compensate for the inevitable onrush of the barbarian stock."

"Excuse me, sir. May I intrude? This is Miss Adeline Quantrill. She has come to audition for the laboratory assistant position you need for Mr. Galton."

Both men turned toward Adeline, and she thought she smiled at them. However, when she saw her reflection on the wall mirror behind Mr. Stanford, the disfiguration of lips beneath her nose resembled that of a gorilla or chimpanzee attempting to mimic the grin of her betters.

"Thank you, Frederick. You may go." Leland Stanford chose that moment to swivel his rather portly back side down into one of the library chairs. The expiration of breath, as he fell into a seated position, was then followed by an expiration of stomach gas. The latter sound was so loud as to frighten a lounging Persian cat from the table.

Adeline, at nineteen, could not resist chuckling, as the feline scurried, slipping and sliding, from the library's confines, away from this creature with such great sounds erupting from it. Adeline thought momentarily of following the cat to safety.

Without any embarrassment, Mr. Stanford reached for a file on the table, took out its contents, and began his inquisition into her life.

"Young lady, Miss Quantrill, thank you for coming. This gentleman has come all the way from England, at my request, in order to work on a particular task of monumental importance. It is our immediate aim to take your experience and character into consideration, but please be aware that our questions are not meant to be an imposition upon your value to society. It's simply that we have a private agenda in mind. Is that clear?" Mr. Stanford looked over at her, and she was reminded of the way the judge and social welfare experts had looked at her after her parents were murdered on the train to San Francisco. Adeline wondered how much he already knew about her.

"I am honored to be here," she replied. "Your grand purpose must be important, and I can't help but wonder why you chose me as a candidate. After all, I have just begun my studies at Berkeley, and I have yet to declare my major study discipline." Adeline hoped her answer would be enough to extract the hidden reason behind their request to meet her.

"Very well. Since I am not the person who will be working with you, I am going to give Mr. Galton the opportunity to question you for his needs. Is that permissible, Miss Quantrill?" Mr. Stanford leaned forward and squinted at her.

"Of course. If I shall have the honored gentleman as my supervisor, I am eager to hear what he requires from an assistant." Adeline turned toward the Englishman, and she heard him thinking about her.

She is the only candidate with no parents. Good. That means she will not have any direct familial bonds to distract her from being objective. "Miss Quantrill, are you familiar with the two most important science books in the world, written by my cousin, Charles Darwin? *On the Origin of Species*, published in 1859, and *Descent of Man, and Selection in Relation to Sex,* published in 1871?"

Not only had Adeline read these books, she had also committed them to her prolific memory. Her autobiographic recall was pulling their images up on her inner brain screen as he was speaking the titles. She and Samuel had discussed the most controversial applications of what Mr. Darwin posited in their many arguments concerning the importance of biological inheritance in modern society.

"Yes, sir. I know those books quite well." Adeline replied.

"In point of fact, I was honored by having my own studies cited eleven times in his second book. Do you believe that breeding and natural selection form the building blocks for the evolution phenomenon, including the development of humankind and its resulting civilizations?" *This should open up her thought processes sufficiently for me to evaluate her abilities to reason on a higher level.*

"Although I respect Mr. Darwin's work, and I can completely agree with him as to his ideas concerning the methods of adaptation and survival that our natural world contains, when he extrapolates his theories into our own society, I am afraid I must begin to disagree." Adeline watched the face of the distinguished researcher and explorer. His manner was relaxed, and he smiled back at her. He was even keeping his thoughts private.

"Since you would be a close assistant, I am going to tell you a fact about myself that will allow you to understand how important Darwin's theories are to my own. When I was a bit older than you, and I was about to take my honors exams at Cambridge, the very thought of spending eight days and five and one-half hours of each day, writing about mathematics and statistical analysis, in order to prove my worth to my professors, was too much for my mind to process. As a result, I did not earn my doctorate, I withdrew from college, and so my credentials may not appear on paper to be sufficient." Mr. Galton looked over at Mr. Stanford and smiled.

Mr. Stanford struck the table with his clenched fist, and Adeline winced from the noise. "Balderdash! Give me a man who works with his hands and sets sail to travel the world to prove his theories correct. That is why your cousin chose your work over others."

"Please. I want you to look at a letter I wrote to my dear sister, Adèle." Mr. Galton took a letter from his vest pocket and handed it to Adeline. She read it to herself slowly:

"*My Dear Adèle, I am 4 years old and I can read any English book. I can say all the Latin Substantives and Adjectives and active verbs besides 52 lines of Latin poetry. I can cast up any sum in addition and can multiply by 2, 3, 4, 5, 6, 7, 8, 9, 10, 11. I can also say the pence table. I read French a little and I know the clock.*

FRANCIS GALTON,

Febuary 15, 1827"

Adeline returned the letter. "I am astounded, sir. You were obviously a child prodigy. Excepting the misspelling of the month, your epistle is perfect."

Mr. Galton folded the letter carefully and slid it back into his pocket. *Now I shall ask her the question which will prove her worth.* "My sister was an excellent and patient teacher. However, do you believe it was her skill as a teacher that allowed me to learn so quickly? Or, was my ability innate, a product of my family's excellent ancestry and long line of successful athletes, gun merchants, bankers, and academics?"

Adeline realized she had to respond in the way Mr. Galton required. She decided she would risk it all with her attempt. "My differences are not with your esteemed cousin's research and logic. His scientific examples of natural selection and species adaptation are impeccable. And, I do accept the fact that it was your excellent breeding and family's evolution that gave you your mental ability and strong character."

Her inquisitor nodded. "Yes, but what about your difference? I am curious. I believe your intelligence is superb, and you can show me how well you think from what you tell me now." *You had better not make a mistake at this point, or your chance at becoming my assistant will disappear.*

"My difference was voiced in the argument made by Mrs. Antoinette Blackwell in her book, *The Sexes Throughout Nature*. Mr. Darwin's theory of natural selection by females, in her opinion, was defrauding the advancement of womanhood." Adeline inhaled, believing it was best to quote a source who had credibility, even as a woman, in the dispute. She noted that the faces of these men were not irritated. Their expressions remained attentive and interested.

Therefore, she continued, "Darwin said that merely by choosing tools and weapons of superior quality, man had become superior to woman. I say, however, that choices first must be permitted by a society, and our society does not allow us women to make those same choices and learn those same trades that make men superior."

Mr. Stanford frowned for the first time. "Those choices, my dear lady, are often fraught with danger and possible death. What about inevitable war and conflict? Women are the keepers of the home and hearth, are they not?"

"Saint Joan of Arc, who was burned for heresy for her bravery, helped the French win the battle of Orleans during the Hundred Years War. Most recently, my dear sir, there were, by conservative estimates, over five hundred women who clandestinely took up arms during our Civil War."

Adeline was almost going to read off her photographic memory's list of the exact names of the women she knew who had fought in battles, but she refrained from doing so. Because of the reddened face of Leland Stanford, she believed it was time for her to soften her rhetoric.

She continued, using a technique she saw Mrs. Foltz use when arguing. She smiled, and then she made her voice into a lilting, sing-song refrain. "In effect, are not many women, in the best families, being kept like household pets? We cannot vote; we cannot make contracts; we cannot own property; we are children with adult bodies. We are a species Mr. Darwin ignores. Are we being given the same chances as men to prove our innate qualities? Perhaps, with the same educational and political opportunities for both males and females, our society would evolve twice as quickly as it is doing today."

Mr. Galton stared at her for several minutes, placing his right forefinger to his chin and holding onto his elbow with his other hand. His gaze was pecuniary but not malicious. Adeline did not hear him thinking negative thoughts about her. He finally sighed deeply and walked over to where Mr. Stanford was seated. He bent over and whispered into his ear for another two minutes.

At long last, Mr. Galton turned back toward her, and Adeline held her breath. This could mean her future. She needed to impress Mrs. Foltz, so as to win the heart of Samuel, and perhaps even be accepted into the hallowed world of male influence.

"One last question, Miss Quantrill," Mr. Galton said. "Do you enjoy working with identical twins?"

Adeline was dumbfounded. To what on earth could that question be in reference? "I must admit. I have never had the pleasure of seeing identical twins. However, I would most certainly find it intellectually stimulating and amusing to study or investigate such miracles of birth."

You will most certainly have your time filled with these twins. Mr. Galton puffed out his chest and looked over at Mr. Stanford, who returned Galton's stern gaze and nodded. "When can you begin? I cannot promise to be with you more than one or two hours per day, but I can certainly get you started on your new work."

Adeline coughed into her fist. "I don't want to appear presumptuous, Mr. Galton, but what wage will I be earning for this work? Will it require the nursing care of children or babies? I would expect a bit higher wage if that were the case."

Indeed. You are most certainly an American capitalist. "I am prepared to pay you the sum of fifteen dollars per day, which will include room and board. Also, my twins are actually identical triplets, three each, of both genders, and they are eighteen and twenty years of age. The ladies are eighteen, the lads twenty." Galton's walk to the library entrance doors was, to Adeline, quite resolute. His stride, in fact, was almost a march cadence. He turned the gold handle, opened one of the doors wide, and shouted into the hallway.

"Roberts! I say, can you bring in the twins? We're ready."

What occurred next was to live in Adeline's dreams, in the form of vivid nightmares, for weeks following. There were six adults who entered the library, but it was their physical composition that sent a shiver down Adeline's spine. Two sets of the twins were conjoined. The males at the hip, the females at the chest and thorax. The other two identical siblings were normal. Adeline believed, however, that the term "normal" could hardly be accurate. Even if each three did not live together, the psychological pressures of being identical, combined with the physiological limitations of being fused together, must have been tremendously bothersome to all of them.

Even with their dragging feet, slumped-over torsos, and crab-like ambulation, these future laboratory subjects were quite handsome and alluring, in a uniquely macabre way. The conjoined men and women had exactly the same bodies and clothing as their siblings, and their faces were so exactly identical that Adeline kept scanning from one face to the other to see if there were even the slightest differences. No more exact replicas could have been created, even if they had been brought to life in some kind of successful Dr. Frankenstein laboratory experiment.

"These are the Falcone Triplets and the Johansen Triplets. Roger, Jerimiah and Claiborne were born in Edinburgh, Scotland in 1867, to Sir Robert and Emily Falcone. The Falcones come from a long line of nobility, extending back to the First Scottish War for Independence in the Thirteenth Century. The Falcone males fought with William Wallace in their attempt to seize power from King Edward the first. Each generation, the Falcones improved their status and wealth, with men who worked in Civil Engineering, fought for the King's military, explored scientific research at Cambridge, and managed four tobacco plantations in the New World, until the War for Independence by the United States, after which they sold their interests at a very good profit." Mr. Galton nodded to the lone Falcone, Claiborne, who stepped forward.

"Thank you, Mr. Galton. My name is Claiborne, and I am the eldest, at ten minutes. My brothers, I like to say, were so obnoxious in the birth canal about who should go next that they became fused together at the hip from the heat of their combined invective and fisticuff exchanges. However, we have all graduated from Cambridge with honors, and we hope to begin teaching there following our present work under our esteemed polymath and professor." Both Roger and Jerimiah applauded. Claiborne stepped back to stand beside them.

Claiborne, Adeline noted, unlike his two conjoined brothers, was tall and muscular, about five feet and ten inches of full manhood, with a pomaded black pompadour that glistened under the chandelier lamps. They had no facial hair, which was very appealing to Adeline, as her love, Samuel, also twenty, preferred shaving his face as well. Each young man had a most adorable curl, which snuck down at the upper-left corner of the forehead, like an added comma, as if to connect the grammatically perfect physiology of their hawk-like, amber eyes, with the matching facial accent of one coiling dimple in each triplet's cheek. They all wore light-brown cashmere frock coats, matching trousers, and vests that dangled gold watch fobs with chains.

These young women, on the other hand, were no suffragettes. They had no sense of seriousness or purpose. Flittering about in their city finery, these three beauties knew they were attractive, and they knew how to use that temptation to its fullest extent. The satin frock with the large bustle was made uniquely to fit both bodies of the sisters who were fused together. Blonde, silky-smooth tresses curled over strong shoulders and down between six passionate globes of bounty.

Mr. Galton was not about to do the same introductory courtesy, and so he merely waved at the girls the way a child would wave at the caged tigers in a passing circus parade. "Trust me," he said, his pointy upper lip thrust forward. "these ladies are from the finest families and the noblest stock."

One of the sisters decided she would step forward to introduce them to the officious gathering. "We are honored to be part of this noble experiment for the betterment of civilization. My name is Deandra, and Susanne is one of the Thoracopagus duo, residing happily on the left, and Matilda is the artistic genius on the right. Her paintings are selling internationally. Susanne and I perform in a chamber ensemble in Stockholm. I play the piano; she, the violin. Matilda really pays no attention to us, as she paints while we play."

"All right now, pay attention please. This is Miss Quantrill. She has been awarded the pleasant task of being appointed your ward, tutor, and ombudsman. I expect that you will give her the utmost respect, as she is my direct representative when I am not present." Mr. Galton's voice rose at the end of the sentence in expectation.

"Yes, Mr. Galton!" The six answered in rehearsed union.

Mr. Stanford got up and addressed them. "I am afraid I must leave you all now. Congratulations on your new endeavor and best of fortunes building the roots of our new, progressive society!"

Not until Stanford had gone did Mr. Galton again begin to speak to them.

“We are not going to hide what we are doing from you. The instruction I shall give to Miss Quantrill tomorrow will also be given to you. I am of the belief that a society moves that much faster when it knows the ultimate purpose behind its labors. I must remark at the outset that I am very proud to have you all as important parts of this monumental study. I have been told by our benefactor, the great philanthropist, scholar, and world traveler, Leland Stanford, that we must move to the state asylum in Stockton to do this work. We shall have complete privacy, but I hope it’s not an inconvenience to the newest member of our research group.

Adeline’s pulse quickened. She had some previous experience with mental wards. When you are a girl who tells adults she can hear their thoughts, and then they realize that you do indeed know what they are thinking, the tables, as Jesus would say, begin to turn. They put you into a white room, with padded walls, and with one small hole in the giant door in front of you. Imaginary snakes and vermin also use that hole.

“No, sir. It would be no imposition. I am proud to be a part of your research, and I am very happy to meet all of these fine ladies and gentlemen. I will do my utmost to teach you all that I know about what it takes to advance in this society, and I will follow Mr. Galton’s directions exactly, in the best interests of science.” Adeline turned to face Mr. Galton, who was busy taking the thumb prints of the triplets. He took each one by his or her thumb and pressed it firmly down on individual cards laid out on the table in the center of the room. Adeline knew he had recently written a paper about his study concerning finger print marks. Mr. Galton believed that each print was completely unique and that it could conceivably be used as a means of identification for the police or other proper authorities.

You have the misconception that I cannot hear you. Say something. I will respond.

Adeline heard these words, and her blood turned icy. She reacted rather than pondered the consequences. *Thank you for being honest, Mr. Galton. However, I might never have believed you were a telepath in addition to being a polymath.*

He laughed. His voice was high-pitched and effeminate. Adeline wondered vaguely if he might even be capable of humor. She believed the home of Swift and Pope should have nobles, even noble scientists, who could appreciate a satirical jab or two, or three, or four.

Oh, Miss Quantrill. You shall enjoy your new appointment. I chose you exactly because you are a telepath. I also know you are far more talented than your lowly academic status would bely. Your mind is a literal box of history as it was lived. Yours is the most historically accurate mind of all. To me, your value is inestimable.

Mr. Galton turned to the six youths. "Off to bed with you! We must move tomorrow, and I want you all rested."

All six came to give Mr. Galton and Adeline a personal hug before retiring. When Claiborne came up to her, Adeline became a bit nervous. Again, her pulse quickened, but this time it was because she imagined her brain to be shrinking to the size of a pea, and the resultant pressure was driving her arteries insane.

"Good meeting with you, Miss Quantrill," Claiborne bent forward and whispered in her ear. "We are really Jews. Surname is Feldman. This man is insane. Get out while you can. I am staying here only to protect the others." Claiborne's gray eyes were glistening with emotion, and Adeline felt his chest heave, with a deep inhale, as he turned on his heels and left the room.

CHAPTER 5: THE FIVE

The Women's Section, First Floor, Stockton State Insane Asylum, Morning, April 25, 1887.

Francis Galton had his projects organized as if he were spending his own money. The voyage to San Francisco had given him the time to arrange the stages of his experiments. He was also able to study the backgrounds of the five subjects that were being provided to him by Dr. Alfred Rooney. Francis understood that his reputation as a scientist was at stake, so he was prepared to proceed like a scientist.

Like his benefactors, Francis believed that the problems of minority races and hereditary genetics were growing exponentially in the United States. In order to provide the proof necessary to convince lawmakers that change was needed, Galton was given this chance at the Stockton State Asylum to do so. He knocked on the door of Rooney's office with a firm conviction. The Superintendent was waiting for him, and he answered the door almost immediately.

"Francis Galton! What a pleasure. We've been corresponding all these months, and now I have a chance to meet you in person. Quite an honor. Quite an honor indeed." Francis followed the taller man into his large office. He sat in the leather chair in front of Rooney's wide mahogany desk.

"Thank you, Alfred. I am pleased to finally meet you." Francis took the five files from his briefcase, leaned forward, and placed four of them on the top of the superintendent's desk.

Rooney pointed to the obligatory photo of Washington Bartlett, the current California governor, whose white-bearded face was smiling down at them from the wall behind his desk. "He's a Jew, you know. This is what our so-called democracy allows. The insinuation into our midst of the race that killed Jesus."

Francis nodded and opened the file of the first woman chosen to become one of his research experiments. "I trust you have the five women domiciled in a secure location?"

"Of course. Do you mind if I call you Francis? I feel like I know you already." Rooney smiled.

"I don't mind at all. This appears to be the informal way you California chaps do business." Francis looked down at the record in his hands. "I want to go over these five women and their backgrounds. Then, if possible, I would like you to introduce them to me."

"Of course, Francis. They are interred on the second floor, in a locked suite, with five beds and a separate washroom. They do not mingle with the wealthy patients or with any other member of my staff other than me." Rooney leaned forward in his chair. "Are those the files I sent you?"

"Yes, they are. As you've already broached the topic of race, let's discuss our first subject, Miss Sidney Reyes. I believe her family and friends call her Kitty?" Francis looked down at the photo of the young woman. She was wearing the navy blue uniform of the asylum, with her initial "SR" stitched on her left shoulder. She had the inferior expression of her Filipina-Asian ancestry: slanted eyes, oval face, weak chin, and wide nose. Her black, stringy hair was parted down the middle, and she was seated on her chair with her legs apart, like a man, and her hands on her knees.

"Reyes. Of course. They all receive Spanish surnames since Spain's occupation. She came alone to the United States in 1885, and arrived in San Francisco. Her parents sent her away because they were members of the movement for independence, and they were afraid she would be hunted down. When she found out her parents were executed in Manila, for following the novelist and rebel, José Rizal, she became withdrawn and secluded. She has retained the rebellious streak of her parents and her kind, and yet her mental illness also contains a proclivity for retreating into a private, fantasy world, known only to her."

Francis picked the photo up and looked at the notes beneath it, which he had made about this woman. "And yet, it says you committed her for neurasthenia. It was love sickness that placed her here, and you are aware that this type of perverted amorousness makes her my candidate."

"Yes, Francis. I am well aware. She was in love with another female." Rooney frowned. "Not only was she disobeying the laws of nature, she was also a moral degenerate."

"This type of illness can be traced to her heritage. The Asiatic mind is filled with immoral fantasies, and their genetics make them prime candidates for my experiments. I am anxious to meet her." Francis closed the folder on Miss Reyes and picked up the second folder from the desk.

"I understand. California has become, as in many other states, a refuge for the Asian, especially from China. They were supposed to go back to China when they worked on our railroads, but they decided to stay. That's why we passed the federal law against further immigration of these pagans. They were trying to take the jobs of white Americans, but many of them go insane, so we have to house them." Dr. Rooney coughed into his fist. "Please, continue, Francis."

"This woman has auburn hair, and her name is Angela Thoma. She is married, and her family calls her Angie, or Ang. We have reason to believe her hysterical activities are hereditary by nature, as the entire family has been known to follow her into deserted battle fields, graveyards, and other insane asylums looking for ghosts. The alienist, a Dr. Forbes of San Jose, said she was committed when it was determined she could not have children. That's when she began to go out alone to trespass and to put herself at risk of arrest and even death. She insists she has the ability to speak with the dead, and this is why she hunts for their spirits, even if she must break into such private domiciles to do so."

Dr. Rooney struck his fist on the desk top. "Quite right! We know that these types of hysterics are often faking it in order to gain sympathy and to get out of household work. The hysteria is frequently caused by the reproductive problems they have. Quite often, as you may know, they are brought out of their delusion by bringing them to orgasm and by using techniques such as cold-water showers, interruption of their breathing, shaving their heads, and disgracing them in front of their family members. In this case, the husband is as delusional as the wife. He insists she can communicate with ghosts, as he has seen her do it."

Francis closed the folder. "I want to determine how such a physically attractive woman, in her thirties, can become such a mentally unstable patient. Once I can determine the actual source of her hereditary disease, we can perhaps provide a cure for all such hysterical cases."

Francis picked up the third folder from Dr. Rooney's desk.

"This woman. This Melissa Kay Wilkinson. She is the only criminal lunatic of our five, is she not?" The Englishman held up her photo.

"Correct. She was adjudicated insane by Judge Samuel Crawford of San Francisco in 1885. We moved her to Stockton this year as you requested."

Francis placed the photo down on the desk and picked up the notes on the woman inside the folder. "I believe her type of murderess, quite possibly, can be traced to a genetic cause. She was found inside her mansion on Nob Hill, wandering the luxurious halls, still wearing the same wedding dress, but it was bloodied and in tatters. She was quite hysterical and mute. Although her family is intelligent, with artists and poets among its members, they all have eccentricities that are against the norm. Our young lady, Pepper, as she's called, stabbed her newlywed husband, Jeremy, on their wedding night. When asked why she had done this, she replied that he had refused to allow her to dip her food into the condiments of tomato ketchup and salad dressings."

Dr. Rooney chuckled. "Yes. That's our Pepper, all right. As you can imagine, she is not allowed near any object that can be dangerous to her or to the other patients."

"And yet, her gaze is quite penetrating, and it says she is a social chameleon. She loves to imitate the postures and affectations of whomever she's with. She writes long, anti-patriarchal diatribes with the finger paint supplies you provide to her, and she's quite sociable for being a hysterical mute."

Francis closed the folder. "If we can isolate the cause of her obsessions and get her to speak, I believe we may then trace the hereditary problem to its root cause."

"I admire your ambition on this case, Francis. I assume you have special tools with which you'll be working to do this?" A knock sounded on the office door. "Come in!" Dr. Rooney shouted.

The door opened, and Mrs. Betterman, the baker, tentatively stuck her head inside the doorway. "Dr. Rooney? Sorry to disturb. But that committee group from San Francisco is here again. Mrs. Foltz, the attorney, wants to know where they would be staying."

"Put them in the dining room until I'm finished here." Dr. Rooney brushed her away with his hand. "Such a bother! Can't you see we're busy?"

"Yes sir! I shall do so immediately." Mrs. Betterman, her face flushed, turned around, and closed the door behind her.

"Committee? What is that?" Francis inquired.

Dr. Rooney scowled. "We have a young patient, a Miss Polly Bedford, twelve years of age. She attacked another youngster, and because this Bedford child was committed by her quite wealthy parents, the newspapers follow her goings-on quite regularly. Some say she was witness to the murder of a ten-year-old girl at her parent's mansion. Others say she may have actually committed the act itself and then gone mad. This committee, as a result, is here to investigate our entire facility."

"And, this Foltz woman. Who is she, and who are these committee members?" Francis took up a pen and was ready to jot notes on one of the folders.

"Don't fret. I will not allow them to access any of our research areas. They will be restricted to the patients' quarters, the dining room, and my office. Mrs. Foltz has assembled this group, and I will be learning their full identities after we finish here. I will keep you completely informed, you can be certain."

Francis picked up another folder and opened it. "Indeed. We need to maintain the strictest secrecy in these matters, Alfred. It's a matter of life and death."

"We understand the stakes. My reputation is also on the line. Who do you have in that folder?" Dr. Rooney took out a cigar from his waistcoat pocket and offered it to Francis. When the Englishman refused, Rooney lit it with a flint lighter on his desk and puffed leisurely.

Francis read his notes on the fourth patient. "A most interesting woman. She has a delusional identity, among other problems. Her Christian name is Katherine Sue Yantis, but she believes she is Annie Oakley, the famous sharpshooter. I believe the actual Mrs. Oakley is now touring with the Buffalo Bill Wild West Show at the present moment. Mrs. Yantis claims this other woman is a fraud. They are both from Cincinnati, but Mrs. Yantis came west to seek fortune with her husband during the Gold Rush."

Dr. Rooney blew a smoke ring. “Yes, I knew she would be a good candidate for your experiments. This woman was certified as a modern witch, after she claimed to be able to change cats into women who would do her bidding. Her family also made macabre mementos from the hair and fingernails of known murderers, which she inserted into lockets and watches and sold at their hangings. They also put cremated ashes of pets and loved ones inside antique vases, statuary, and other artistic pieces. Several noted industrialists have done business with her and her family.”

Francis smiled. “She is an obvious genetic freak with delusions of grandeur. I have just the remedy for her type, and if it proves to work, then we shall have evidence that witchcraft can be conquered with modern science.”

Dr. Rooney laughed. “If you can simply rectify the delusions, it would cure over one hundred women presently inside our asylum. We can then work on the Congress of the United States.”

“I agree. Once Eugenics has been recognized for what it causes in our general population, the government will pay attention. This Yantis woman is quite spirited and attractive to the eye. She should make a great story for your newspapers once I’ve cured her.” Francis closed the folder and picked up the final one from Dr. Rooney’s desk.

“This is our youngest patient of the five. Miss Jessica Adkins. At the age of fourteen, she witnessed her best friend, Sarah, being murdered. She became a vicious and beautiful demon, refusing to go to school, to become socialized, or to learn the proper behavior of a young lady. Today, she believes that we are all figments of her personal dream.” Dr. Rooney stubbed out his cigar in an ashtray.

Francis chuckled. “I see. I have had that perception myself, from time to time. I can understand her wanting to believe she is the center of existence. Our entire social realm is an attempt to frustrate that concept. As a lunatic, this young woman has become traumatized by the act of murder. As a result, she is protecting her own mind by believing she is, in fact, projecting all of what she observes, and that we should appreciate her for that act of kindness, if you will.”

“I have never thought of it in just that manner, but yes, I can see what you mean.” Dr. Rooney splayed his hands together, thrusting the intertwined fingers and palms forward, until they made an audible cracking sound. “What are your plans for Miss Adkins?”

“She is most important to my entire experiment in that I believe she will be able to unravel the puzzle that is Miss Polly Bedford, the entitled patient of whom we both understand to be witness to the murder which took place on Nob Hill. That murder, in point of fact, is the linchpin in the rebellion against my philosophy of Eugenics. The wealthy race of Caucasians, upon which most of the world’s civilizations rest, cannot become victims of such atrocities!”

“Yes, Francis, but how can you stop such acts of rebellious murder? Certainly, an insane person is behind this murder.” Dr. Rooney leaned forward, expecting a more focused response.

“The experiments I shall perform on these five women will give us the answer. As it was stated in Shakespeare’s *Hamlet*. When the young prince sees the ghost of his dead father, the King, he says, ‘And therefore as a stranger give it welcome. There are more things in heaven and earth, Horatio, than are dreamt of in your philosophy.’ We must be open to the magic this youngest and strangest of the five brings to us. She may be the key to communicating with lunatics everywhere.”

***

Clara wired her son, Samuel, to tell him to take Dr. Andrew McFarland and his granddaughter, Anne, out to the Stockton asylum. He was to use one of the buggies from Mrs. Hopkins’ stable on Nob Hill, and meet them at the train station in Stockton at three in the afternoon the following day. In the meantime, Clara was going to speak with the committee members who had joined them to meet with Dr. Rooney when he completed his business conference with an unknown visitor. The kindly baker, Mrs. Betterman, had escorted them into the patients’ dining room on the first floor.

The members of the investigation committee had dwindled fast. Three of them, in fact, did not want to journey out to the asylum, giving a variety of excuses as to why they did not want to participate. Captain Lees said his judge was busy with a court trial, Ah Toy’s labor representative mentioned something about “evil spirits,” and her daughter, Trella Evelyn’s favorite professor told her his reputation as a scholar could be held in question if he were to become involved with what he had termed the “insane academy.”

Trella told Clara that her esteem for this professor had consequently lessened because of his rebuff.

There were now six on Clara's committee, including the two arriving the next day. Laura Gordon would also be participating, as an attorney for the Cotton family. As she sat at the head of the physician's dining table at the front of the dining room, Clara nodded to each of her fellow investigators. Ah Toy sat on her left, and she was talking to Mrs. Packard, who was in the chair beside her friend. Captain Lees was to Clara's right, and Laura sat next to him.

"May I have your attention? I want to discuss our method of inspection before Superintendent Rooney appears." When they all turned to look at her, Clara continued. "Governor Bartlett has signed the authorization papers, which now give us authority to inspect the premises, interview staff, and talk to patients. However, and this is a rather great exception, if you ask me. We cannot visit, under any circumstances, the second floor rooms where the wealthy patients reside. Bartlett has always been a protector of the upper classes, as we know from our experiences with him as Mayor of San Francisco. I believe we can use subterfuge to enter these quarters, as I have been informed that Adeline Quantrill, my son's friend, is now working inside the asylum on the second floor."

"Do you know what she's working on?" Ah Toy held her pencil above her pad, ready to jot down notes.

"No. It seems to be a top-secret endeavor. Since we have only three days ourselves to complete our inquiry, we shall have to wait to speak with Adeline following her duties upstairs." Clara cleared her throat. "Did you all sleep well last night in your new accommodations?"

Mrs. Packard, who held her hearing aid, spoke up. "I visited with a few wandering patients last night. They seemed tranquil after I told them of my own experiences in Illinois, and I was able to tuck them into bed. However, I did not see any of the ghosts. Thank goodness. If I had, then I might have considered becoming a resident myself."

They all laughed.

"Our method should be to discover how this asylum conducts its own subterfuge. The theories we've established will mean fewer persons to conduct searches, and yet we still have two important people in our group who can help us. Mrs. Packard, of course, will be able to interview patients, and Dr. McFarland and his granddaughter can investigate the use of tranquilizers and other drugs on the site."

"Don't forget that we still have your daughter Bertha here," Ah Toy pointed out.

"I certainly have not forgotten our implants, and that includes our psychic and mind reader, Adeline Quantrill. Our fishing expedition shall be conducted with a net that can gradually surround all the suspects at once, slowly tightening its grip until the guilty are aroused from their evil grottoes and attempt to escape from our confines." Clara took out a sheet of paper and scanned it with her forefinger. Her brow furrowed. "This is a list of our most possible suspects at this point. If you have other suggestions, please let me know. We can always add or subtract to it."

"Shall we be pursuing only the hunt for the murderer? Or, if warranted, will we be searching for bigger sharks, swimming in deeper waters, who may have ordered such a crime?" Isaiah Lees sat up straight in his chair and twisted his mustache. "My weaponry will always be at the ready to protect any of you who may get into danger."

"Polly Bedford is still a suspect in the murder of Winnie Cotton. She was the only person present in the house. What we learned from Bertha was that Polly was perhaps too drugged by Dr. Rooney to have a clear memory of the killer. That brings us to our second suspect, Dr. Rooney. He wanted to be personally involved in this investigation, to the point of making certain the Cotton family was represented by counsel."

Laura Gordon smiled. "And I am still in that employment," she said.

"Not a problem. We are also investigating with the best interests of the Cottons in mind. However, I am afraid, dear Laura, that your clients are our suspects three and four." Clara frowned. "Unless you can provide them with a proper alibi."

Laura returned the scowl. "There are no charges as yet, my dear. Be assured that if you do provide such warrants, I shall protect them."

"Finally, we cannot rule out Leland Stanford." Clara noticed the silence and the human question marks on their faces. "I told you I believe this entire plot could entail a culprit from the highest levels of society. It cannot be mere coincidence that the murder was committed on one of the most distinguished families in San Francisco. We must always be on the hunt for connections that tie us into the upper classes."

Elizabeth Packard raised her hand, and Clara nodded at her. "We discovered three such connections during our investigations of different asylums. One was indeed related to the murder of a patient, and the two others were drug overdoses prompted by illegal sales to the wealthy clientele, who had become addicted. The murderer was the superintendent, and I applaud your listing of Dr. Rooney. He was on my personal list of suspects also."

Clara looked down at her paper. "That brings me to another five suspects who were not calculated earlier."

"Five suspects? What in blazes?" Captain Lees stood up next to Clara and took hold of her arm. "What do you mean, Clara?"

"While Mrs. Packard was roaming the wards and causing a distraction, I was also roaming to a rendezvous with my future daughter-in-law, Adeline. She has informed me that her employment has been delegated from Leland Stanford to one Francis Galton."

"Galton? Isn't he the British cousin of Charles Darwin?" Trella Evelyn asked. "We've been studying them both in Biology. He has rather strange theories about heredity, does he not?"

"Indeed, his does, daughter. He also has five residents housed in this asylum, who shall be his personal laboratory test subjects. One is a convicted murderess, and the other four are also quite insane in their own right. Not only does this Galton want to prove something here, he also may want to establish links to identical triplets being capable of insane activities."

"Triplets? How so?" Ah Toy asked.

"Actually, they are not patients here. He brought them from his world travels to this place. For some unknown reason, he wants to prove something, and I do not rule out possible mind control for murderous intentions." Clara heard the door at the end of the dining hall open. When Superintendent Alfred Rooney entered, her pulse quickened, and she sat down, pulling Isaiah down with her.

"Ladies, and gentleman! So glad you have arrived. I have some news of my own to share," Dr. Rooney exclaimed, as he strode confidently toward them, his shiny leather dress shoes clicking on the newly polished tiles of the doctors' dining enclave. "After I tell you, I shall have someone escort you to your new room, as I must assist Francis Galton with his research."

CHAPTER 6: SEX, MAYHEM AND SQUALOR

The Women's Section, Second Floor, Stockton State Insane Asylum, Morning, April 26, 1887.

Sidney

None of these other women was her friend. Sidney "Kitty" Reyes was alone and hungry when they picked her off the street in downtown San Francisco. She did not know where she was, and she had lost the love of her life, Maria, a former slave who had come to town to work for Mary Ellen Pleasant, the "voodoo queen." When they discovered from Maria that Sidney was in love with her, in a very physical way, the young Filipina woman was chosen to become one of the lunatic subjects to be studied by a famous scientist from England, Francis Galton.

One of those nurses who frowned at her whenever she had to provide Sidney with new linen, or bathe her, take her for exercise, or administer ordered treatments, unlocked the door and entered. "Reyes. You're to come with me."

Sidney followed the short and stoutly swaggering older woman. It was the first time out of that room, and Sidney's black eyes observed every board in the floor, color on the wall, and other patients, who were wandering the upstairs. The Filipina could smell the noxious odors of French perfume and talcum powder wafting from these well-dressed women, and many were dancing alone, twirling their skirts, swirling in a circle, their diaphragms undulating their bosoms like the bellows keeping the fires lit in a house of ill repute. She could hear the sounds of freedom in the steps of these wealthy women, as they would never be hungry, on the move over rugged terrain, or cast their eyes frantically, wondering if they would be murdered and raped or forced to sell the last commodity known to be a good woman's product: her flesh and intimate talents.

"Here it is, number 75. Dr. Rooney and Mister Galton are in here, and I want you to understand your place. You hear me?"

Sidney nodded obliquely to the nurse, wondering to herself if she should curtsy or spit in their faces. When she passed into the room, she inhaled deeply, and she did what her mother in the Philippines always told her to do, "Prepare for the worst, expect the best, and you won't be disappointed."

"Aha, Miss Reyes! I see you've come at last." The old man with the grizzled gray lambchop sideburns and an old owl's penetrating gaze, rushed at her, arms extended. She darted away from him, twirling her entire torso so her right shoulder grazed his expensive blue waistcoat. She had done this, many times, to get away from drunken bounders in the streets, who poured out of the taverns by the dozens, looking for the restorative power of a receptive woman.

"Write that down, Dr. Rooney. Her physical proclivity is against the aggressive male form. It may be about the father, or the authority figure, and we shall certainly find out! Get her prepared. I want to begin immediately. I shall retrieve the Johansen ladies." The older man left the room.

The superintendent sat her down in a chair beside the window. He pulled up another chair, sat down, took hold of her hands, and stared at her. Sidney recoiled within herself, afraid of this man, but he slapped her face, and his palm caught her left ear. She slowly turned toward him, ear ringing, furrowing her brow, trying to remember the voodoo curse Maria had taught her, so she could inject it between this old man's rheumy eyes.

"You are very fortunate to be here, Sidney. Why, you might even become a woman who is talked about in research journals and at meetings of insane asylum leaders from around the world. We are going to attempt to discover the source of your abominable sickness. Have you always lusted after other females? Even back in the Philippines? I have read that in that island nation your kind are locked away forever inside Spanish prisons. Aren't you happy to be in the United States, where we attempt to cure you?"

Sidney now wanted to spit in Dr. Rooney's face. Instead, because she had learned how to survive in this nation by pretending to be submissive, she curled her lips into a possum-like smile. "I know my thoughts are sinful, Doctor. My mind is my enemy, and I am very happy to be under your care. What will he be doing to me?"

It was Dr. Rooney's turn to smile. She believed his smile was even more pretentious than hers. "Good. I am not aware of what Mr.

Galton is going to try. You may rest assured, however, that it is in your best interest and in the best interest of the future of mankind."

The door opened once more, and into the room, walking sideways like a crab, Sidney watched the two, identically beautiful and blonde young women enter, attached together at their chests and throats. Their fine silk dresses, with scarlet petticoats, violet bustle and trim, belied their tiny, shuffling feet and the absurd connection of bone, sinew and flesh, which forced them into a sisterly union of a most uncommon and macabre sort.

Francis Galton, the man Sidney already feared, entered behind them, gazing upon these freaks of nature like a proud father. "Matilda and Susanne Johansen, from Sweden. Matilda, on the right, is an artist of the finest caliber. Susanne, on the left, has given concerts to King Oscar II of Sweden. Ladies, this is Miss Sidney Reyes of the Spanish kingdom of the Philippines."

Sidney stared at these two women. Their faces were identical, and each head, although the same shape and size, seemed to exist in different worlds. Matilda was gazing into space, her ruby lips pursed, her brow furrowed in concentration. The one he called Susanne, on the other hand, was watching Sidney like a hawk, her eyes wandering, most obtrusively yet fetchingly, up and down her body. It was Susanne who spoke.

"Miss Reyes. We are charmed, I'm sure."

"We shall now leave you ladies to your own devices. We want you to become acquainted. You will not be disturbed, as it is most important that you learn all about each other. The fragile mind of Miss Reyes can be affected very easily, and I want you twins to behave. You are the ones who are world travelers and sophisticates. Remember your *noblesse oblige*. Good morning to you, ladies. I shall return at noon to see how you've gotten on together."

Sidney's breathing quickened when the two men existed and closed the door. It was locked, and she was together with two women whom she did not know, but whose beauty, sophistication and physical abnormality attracted her in a unique way.

"My sister is the one who loves her own kind." Matilda spoke for the first time.

Sidney thought her voice was without sentiment. She was speaking as if she had done this, quite often, before.

Matilda continued, "I have learned to meditate from a Rabbi's son in Budapest. As you two women exchange your familiarity, I shall be focusing within, into my dream world, preparing my next work of art."

With those words, Matilda closed her eyes, began to breathe deeply and regularly, a slight smile hovering upon her lips.

Sidney stood up, walked slowly over the creaking wooden planks, to stand next to the identical twins. The bold stare from Susanne made Sidney's hair follicles prickle and tickle upon her olive skin.

"We can also be one, my lovely young maiden," Susanne said, reaching out with her alabaster right arm, with the delicate, bejeweled ring on her heart finger and the diamond bracelet encircling her thin wrist.

As Sidney pressed her lips to the top of Susanne's soft hand, she felt a joy enter her body that she had never experienced before. Her life of poverty, even the momentary dalliance with Maria, disappeared in a puff of exquisite perfume from between the white globes of this female monument to unique loveliness. Passion rose inside Sidney like the dawning of the rising full moon upon a lake filled with water lilies. She now wanted, more than anything else in the world, to touch her lips upon this beautiful woman's neck, and then, most slowly, and most lovingly, move down to enter the dominion of Sapho, in an expression of undying and forbidden love.

Angela

Angie plunged deep inside herself whenever she talked to the dead. Contact had to take place in the exact center of the white-hot reality that was non-being. Zen meditation was what it was. The way her Uncle Dill said it was. He had studied Zen under a master in Kyoto, Japan. True Zen, he told her, reaches the smooth path between the living and the dead. The spirits of these magical beings came floating above you, and you were able to snatch them out of the air. The catch, however, as Angela Thoma discovered, was that one had to be in a special place, where the dead's spirit essence was still trying to participate with the living.

Pulsations and hunger were the physical manifestations of Angie's manner of necromancy affinity. The pulsing took place in her erogenous zones. The small of her back, just above the spreading meadowlands of her passionate zones below; her lips, spread wide for the darting tongue of any human sexual spirit; her breasts, rising up, like two peaks of firm, silk-adorned dunes, decorated at the tops with pink buttons of dimpled delight. Her mouth would begin to salivate, setting off the oral and nasal battle between her taste buds and her odorous follicles, joining together with the delicate softness on the underside of her wrists, her neck, her belly, and her womb. The voices came to her, only when she was deep inside herself, and it was like standing on the edge of the Grand Canyon and jumping down into its stupefying beauty, without having to die in the flesh.

Instead, you melted into the mountains, the rivers, and the forests, like the natives, and you began to talk with the anxious ancestors.

"Thoma! Get your rump over here. I am taking you to meet somebody." The tall nurse, who, to Angie, resembled a puffy-headed crane, standing on one leg, had her right arm outstretched toward her. Angie shook her long auburn hair, and looked furtively at each of the other four women, as if she needed their permission to leave. She stood up from her bed, wrapped her arms tightly around her shoulders, and walked delicately toward the nurse, who was now standing just outside the doorway.

"Speed it up, Missy. I have things to do. You walk like you're inside a molasses vat." The nurse held the door and drummed her right hand's fingers upon the door-frame. When Angie finally passed her, and stood out in the hallway, the nurse slammed the thick door shut and locked it with a key she had hanging on a shoelace around her neck.

Angela had lost her way since her family decided to admit her to the asylum. They found her locked inside the remains of an old mansion down in the Bowery, on the Barbary Coast. The New Orleans-style building was owned by a French pirate, and it became deserted, after he was arrested and hanged on Russian Hill for shooting a gold miner in a game of poker.

She was called there by this pirate's spirit, she told her husband, Allan, when he found her there, and he drafted the commitment papers that same day. Even though Allan had believed she could communicate with the dead, when she was making money from her efforts as a medium, she was then no longer doing her motherly and household duties, so he believed she needed the repose and treatment. The rest of her family agreed, even though her youngest daughter, Camille, believed her mother could, indeed, talk to ghosts, and the family had to pull her off Angie's skirts when they took her away to the Stockton facility. Dr. Rooney, after seeing what her mental problems were, decided she was perfect for Francis Galton's research project.

"Go inside. She's waiting for you." The crane nurse opened the door with another key from around her neck. As Angie walked inside, with her arms still wrapped over her shoulders, her body's waist became a magnet, and she gasped when her feet felt frozen in place.

After the nurse closed and locked the door, Angela experienced a strange sensation. It was a gravitational pull that centered within her loins. She could not move, no matter how hard she tried. As the pulling became stronger, her entire body was shuffled along on the floor, without Angie taking one step of her own. It was if she were a spirit that no longer needed its body for locomotion.

"Angela, don't be frightened. I understand you." The young woman now holding onto both her shaking hands, was speaking, and yet Angie could not hear her. Her full concentration was upon a voice vibrating within her stomach, traveling up to her lungs, and then circling into her esophagus and into her ear canals. It was an eardrum-splitting shout that filled Angie with a terror she had never felt before, during all her years of searching out abandoned houses, and probing inside haunted buildings.

I died here, and now I am being called to murder another one. You must tell them to remove these strangers from the asylum! Unless I am free to roam, without intrusion from outsiders, there will be hell to pay!

When the sound became too much to bear, as it was so loud and so nauseating to her body, Angie crumpled over into the strange woman's arms and breathed into her ear in a panicked whisper, "You must leave here. You and whomever else are here from outside. Unless you go at once, there will be a murder committed!"

Katherine

Before the door to Katherine Sue Yantis' new reality opened, she was thinking about how to escape this prison of mental defectives in order to return to her family and to her employment with the Buffalo Bill Wild West Show. Her trigger finger was itching, and she smiled at the prospect of blasting her way out, watching all the rich women on the second-floor run, screaming for cover, the frilly petticoats getting soiled as they fell, their thick make-up running like a desert flash flood of tears. Or, she could turn any one of her psychotic roommates into cats, who could then infiltrate this hell hole and get the keys. There were so many possibilities when one was a witch.

Katherine knew, when the door opened, she was going to be taken to a place where she could be understood. The knob was turning, as the key was inserted, and she watched it swing open. The woman standing in the doorway was not a nurse, however. She did not wear the white dress and frilly cap. Instead, her look was cosmopolitan and well mannered. Her full-length dress had a stylish bustle, and it was orange, with black buttons down the front, and a matching hat that was shaped like a stove pipe but with a small bouquet of white flowers in the band. The silver cape she wore looked as if it were from some Eastern European court, with spots on its fur-lined insides and edges, as if the Czarina herself had ordered it.

This woman, as expected, sauntered directly over to Katherine, her gaze only vaguely taking in her compatriots. When she stood before her, Katherine could smell the expensive odor of her perfume. Her cheeks were rouged lightly, and her lips were puffy and scarlet. Her forehead was wide, and her ears were delicate, with passionate lobes and angelic, serenely blue eyes.

"Mrs. Oakley? I am here to invite you to a meeting with his royal majesty, the King of Sweden. He has heard of your skill as a markswoman and the magical prestidigitation you possess. Oscar the Second is going to be here in a fortnight. Can you accept his invitation to rendezvous under these rather squalid conditions?"

"And, who are you?" Katherine asked, sizing this lady up for a possible shape-shift into an orange tabby.

"I am the King's foreign secretary. Madeline Olsen. In Sweden, women are not as subservient to male domination as you are in these

States. I have the authority to arrange such meetings, you can be assured. Here. Look at my passport."

With her right hand, Miss Olsen reached into an orange bag, suspended by a leather strap around her left forearm, and took out a square piece of parchment. She handed it to Katherine and smiled.

It had the royal seal of the King of Sweden, and her name, "Secretary to the King, Madeline Olsen," was stamped in the middle in raised, gold lettering. Katherine handed it back to the woman.

"Will he provide me with a weapon? I cannot demonstrate unless I have a Winchester rifle." Katherine was already plotting her escape. This was a fortuitous occurrence, but it made sense, as her fame must have spread to Europe by now.

"Most certainly. The king has not come all this way by ship not to be entertained. Your superintendent, Dr. Rooney, has guaranteed me that you may participate outside. It must be completely private, however. The king has made it quite clear that he wishes to possibly hire you to train his female recruits in the art of sniper warfare."

Katherine was quite overjoyed. At long last, her talents were being respected, in the manner she believed they deserved.

"Just tell me when and where, and I will be there."

"You shall be notified anon. I am very glad to have met you, Mrs. Yantis. I will forward your response to the king. You are assisting women in their quest to gain the militant skills worthy of the Amazons. May God bless you and keep you."

Miss Olsen turned around and began to walk toward the door. The four other female patients stared at her as if she were a specter out of a dream. Miss Lisa Wilkinson pinched herself. Jessica Adkins crept-up behind her and felt her dress from behind. Kitty Reyes sang a song about lost love, and Angela Thoma, awakening from a bad dream, screamed aloud.

When the door was finally shut and locked, Lisa spoke to Katherine. "If you believe all that, then I have a bridge in Brooklyn, New York, I want to sell you."

Jessica

Whenever possible, Jessica preferred to stay near the light. Inside the private room for the five women chosen by Dr. Rooney as special studies for Francis Galton, the fourteen-year-old brunette was huddled beneath the window ledge, staring out at the others.

Her blue eyes darted from one face to the next, expecting one of them to remonstrate her for being there, just as they had when she fought them to have the bed closest to the window.

It was her belief that her best friend, Sarah, had commanded her to be on constant guard against all outsiders who would take away her gift of dream. Jessica Adkins dreamed everything around her. She knew once her imagination took over, the details of daily life could change. It was this private change that was the only certainty, Sarah had told her, in one of their frequent philosophical discussions. Sarah's boyfriend, Dennis Leary, never acknowledged Sarah's gift of genius, but Jessica had.

"What you dream is what is real," Sarah had informed her, on that lazy summer day. They sat together upon a large branch of a sugar maple tree in the front garden of Sarah's mansion on Rincon Hill.

Her parents, Richard and Elouise Fremont, had come from England to San Francisco in the 1850s to help finance the Gold Rush. A banker and investor, like Jessica's own father, Raymond, Mr. Fremont helped invest in the newly established bank, Wells Fargo, and hired Raymond as its first manager.

The two families, the Fremonts and the Adkins, lived next-door to each other in the wealthy neighborhood. Jessica and Sarah loved doing things only boys were supposed to do, and tree-climbing was the least dangerous activity they enjoyed.

Sarah had once suspended Jessica by her ankles from the back of a cable car going up California Street to Nob Hill. A much stronger and taller girl, Sarah helped Jason, their Irish butler, cut wood, and she knew how to ride a horse when she was five. The day she told Jessica about dreaming, she was being harassed by Dennis, and the girls had climbed the tree to escape him.

Jessica's daily adventures with Sarah were a ritualized performance. To her, Sarah was both a mentor and a spiritual adviser, so when she informed Jessica that she was dreaming her own, and all of the world's, existence, she believed her at once.

"You mean, everything around me is being imagined by my mind?" Jessica asked her friend on that fateful day.

"Oh, yes! The truth is, each of us believes he or she is dreaming a private reality, and it's true. There is no shared existence whatsoever. There are only accidental meetings and coincidental rendezvous, which each dreamer creates inside her own vivid imagination."

Sarah picked a large leaf from the branch and held it in front of Jessica's wide eyes. "See? I am dreaming this leaf, and every event that happens around it. You see it too but only because our dreams have intersected for a brief time. When we separate, only our separate dream-weaving will exist."

Sarah then told sixteen-year-old Dennis that she no longer wanted to dream him, and he became enraged. He was at the base of the tall tree, staring up into the branches at the two girls.

"I will show you who is imaginary!"

Dennis began to climb the tree, and as he did so, Sarah began to climb as well. Jessica watched, in fascination, as her best friend ascended ever higher in the tall maple, stepping on a branch, pulling herself up, and then reaching for the next, higher branch.

Dennis kept up his chase, however, and soon Jessica could see them both above, suspended precariously, in the highest branches. The next words she heard from Sarah would live forever in her dream world. As her friend reached out, Jessica looked up through the branches into the summer sky on Rincon Hill. Dennis reached out to grab onto Sarah, but she would not accept his touch.

"Our dreams have met, and now they shall be over!" Jessica watched, in abject horror, as Sarah fell from the tree. She landed on the hard ground, her neck breaking her fall, and her limp body tumbled down the hill.

As she climbed down from the tree, branch by branch, Jessica began to believe. Everything around her became more vivid and more important to her. She understood that her destiny, and the destiny of the entire world, were inside her imagination. That summer's insight became Jessica's passionate fixation forever.

Jessica dreamed the man with the lamb-chop sideburns and the pointy upper lip. He had come into the room, escorted by her imaginary doctor named Mister Rooney. They were both standing above her, looking down, and she knew she could make them disappear at once, simply by closing her eyes. She decided to listen to them, just to see what she could invent next.

The older man with the strange accent addressed her. "Hello, Jessica. There is another young lady I want you to meet. Her name is Polly Bedford. She can also dream and talk to spirits. I am certain you'll be great friends."

Jessica saw him wink over at Dr. Rooney. *Why did I make him do that? He sounds very interesting. I'll have to ask Sarah the next time I see her.* "I can make you all disappear, you do realize that? However, because I am becoming very bored with these old women in here, I shall go with you to meet her."

"Jolly good!" The old man reached down, took Jessica's hands, and pulled her up. Jessica dreamed what he then said, and she smiled at him when he said it. "You will both be changing what we all dream. I can assure you of that. We shall come for you once we arrange the meeting with Miss Bedford."

Melissa

Melissa was exhausted. She wondered why she had to waste her precious time conversing with idiots. When she finally broke her vow of silence to speak to the older married woman, Katherine, Pepper immediately decided to go back into her perpetual mummery. These reprobates did not deserve her wisdom. Let them succumb to the patriarchal establishment that was controlling their destinies inside this mad house. She was going to become the avenger of women everywhere, and to this end, she might have to endanger them, not to mention putting her own genius in jeopardy.

"Wilkinson! Come out here at once!"

The voice was obviously summoning her from beyond the room's enclosure. Did they really believe she was stupid enough to go out into that snake pit? And yet, something about the masculine baritone of that voice made her body quiver with sexual interest. It sounded like her departed husband, Jeremy's voice.

If she could change anything from the past, she would have not stabbed her poor husband on their wedding night. He was not to blame for the insane logic of the times. He did not create the lust, the greed, and the constant mayhem of living under a system dominated by the male hierarchy. Jeremy's hands were gentle, his touch sublime, and he was the first person to call her "Pepper." She stabbed him out of an ocean of resentment built inside her soul. He was the dead canary within her coal mine of hate for much greater and more powerful evils.

"Pepper! Won't you come out? I have unlocked the door for you."

Melissa watched the other four women. Nobody lunged forward to escape. They all just stared at the door like the lunatics they indeed were.

"All right. I'm coming. If you harm me, then you will forever be haunted by my evil spirit." Melissa believed this curse, as she moved toward the door. Before opening it, she stared out through the wire mesh rectangle. Nobody was out there. Could the door be unlocked?

She reached down and turned the knob. It turned a full turn, and she heard the necessary click, releasing the lock. The heavy door opened, squealing its usual resistance. When she discovered no person out in the hallway, she turned around and peered inside from whence she came.

"Come on, ladies! What are you waiting for? It's our chance." Melissa realized she had broken her vow of silence once more, and that was when a shadow came out of the passageway, and she saw a long arm push the door shut, with a grunt coming from the man who had slammed it.

The tall man, dressed in all-black, grabbed her by her right arm and pulled her—dragged her—along the hallway. When he came to a room, she saw that it had a number, "13." He unlocked it with a key he extracted from his waistcoat pocket. She stared at the back of his head. He had black hair, and his cheeks were shaved.

"Quickly, get inside, Pepper. I need to tell you something."

That voice again. She was mesmerized by it. The inside of the room was grimy and dank. It was one of the few unused rooms in the asylum, with stacks of flour, wheat and other cooking supplies and foodstuffs. It smelled of disinfectant and yeast.

Melissa took a good look at this man. He was clean on his face, and his dark brown eyes penetrated her being the way Jeremy's used to do. It was like being breached sexually, but she had never gotten to that. She had left Jeremy frustrated and staring quizzically at the bloody knife she held in her hand that night after their church wedding.

"I want you to have this," the young man said. He extracted a leather strap with something dangling at the end. He held the large, oval medallion up to her eyes in the dark room. "It belonged to the

Empress Dowager of China." She saw the design on the silver backing. It was the shape of a swirling dragon, with tiny jewels inserted as the eyes and over the body of the snake-like demon.

"Here is the answer to its secret identity." He grasped the bottom of the medallion with his right thumb and forefinger and pulled. To her surprise, a six-inch steel blade came into her view.

Why would this man give her this? Was it a trap? She would surely be placed in solitary confinement should she accept this weapon of death.

As he placed the sheathed medallion around her neck, and tucked it under her asylum smock, he did the unspeakable. He nuzzled his smooth chin against her neck, kissing it warmly, and with passion.

"I am a prisoner, just as you are, Pepper. I know all about you. You want to stop the real killers who oversee this mad house. I have been entrusted by Francis Galton and Dr. Rooney to trick you into murdering someone on these premises. You shall not stab anyone until I give you further instructions. I trust you will not. Why? Because your entire family will then die. We must learn that we are working for a higher cause. When I give you the order to kill, we can then escape, and I will take my brothers with us. When the time comes, do not listen to anyone else."

As his strong arms turned her around, he gazed into her eyes, and then she watched his lips, and they came down to hers, sucked the air from her lungs, and then gently moved up to her eyes, kissing them closed, up to her forehead, delicately placing lip pressure upon her third, also hidden, eye. This man understood the power of persuasion, and she loved him for it. Despite his words, she knew she could find a way to trick him, if need be, as it was always a constant struggle against such passionate desires that made her what she was.

"I will explain to you how I came from a life very similar to yours, and we will soon become closer as a result. For now, I shall return you to your prison, and I shall return to mine."

CHAPTER 7: LOST SOULS

The Women's Section, First Floor, Stockton State Insane Asylum, Morning, April 26, 1887.

The first investigations would now begin, and Clara was inside their private room, seated with her notes, at a small desk in the middle of the room beside a Franklin stove. The men, Dr. Andrew McFarland, and her lover, Captain Isaiah Lees, were sharing one bunk bed in an enclosed area next to the bathroom. Mrs. Packard had her own bed, with a wood plank for her back beneath the mattress. Clara and her best friend, Ah Toy, were sleeping in the bunk bed next to the door. Laura de Force Gordon was sharing the final bunk bed with Dr. McFarland's granddaughter, Anne, next to Clara and Ah Toy. In deference to their group's privacy, Laura had already left the room for breakfast.

Clara realized she would need to better coordinate communications now that her group of investigators had dwindled to six. The other member was her friend and rival attorney, Laura Gordon, but she was playing the role of friendly adversary. Clara wanted to use her friend as a devil's advocate for the group's thinking, since Laura represented the interests of the Cotton family. Since both Adeline and Bertha were working undercover, one of the first items on the agenda was to figure a method of communicating with them inside the asylum. Adeline had already informed them that she was working for Francis Galton and not Leland Stanford.

Finally, the news that Superintendent Dr. Alfred Rooney brought to them the day before made Clara wary. He said Governor Bartlett had approved Stockton asylum as an extension for mental health research at Stanford's new university. That meant it would be more difficult to investigate the activities of Galton and his group. If they were indeed connected to the murder of Winnifred Cotton, then it meant the source of the conspiracy could be right there, under their noses. As they were sniffing downstairs, the real culprits could be upstairs planning more insidious activities.

"May I have your attention?" Clara watched her colleagues, as they were in various stages of dressing. The two men were, of course, unseen behind what Clara was calling the "Wall of Jericho," a long blanket suspended on a clothes line in front of the bunks. When she heard an assortment of grunts and responses from them all, she continued. "Today, I would like Dr. McFarland and Anne to interview the physicians concerning the medications administered in the facility. We would like to see if the drugs being prescribed are appropriately matched to the patients who must take them. Ah Toy, you and I shall question the nursing and household staff." Clara cupped her hands around her mouth and shouted, "Mrs. Packard? I want you to interview all the residents on the first floor. Try to assess their relationships and their mental stability, especially as it pertains to the drugs being given."

All of them were now dressed, and they stood around Clara at her table. The women decided to wear the same clothing as the female patients; the simple, navy-blue frock pull-overs. Captain Lees adjusted his Colt 45 in its holster around his hairy chest, beneath a red shirt tucked into blue denims, which was the uniform worn by the male patients of the asylum. These men were housed in another wing. The Bowie knife Isaiah usually carried was not worn in deference to a patient Dr. Rooney described to Clara as a "murderess who stabbed her husband to death."

Dr. McFarland, despite being a grandfather of sixty-four, stood tall and straight, with gray, curly hair and a ruddy, Irishman's complexion. His granddaughter was an intellectual sort, with spectacles, and her brown hair was in a neat bun.

"I want to thank you, Dr. McFarland, and your granddaughter, Anne, for lending your expertise to our cause. If we can discover who was responsible for the murder of Winnifred Cotton, we believe her death may also be related to this institution and how it is run. The drugs being given to Polly Bedford, in fact, may be the connection we need, so your assessment of her is very important to our case." Clara smiled up at them.

"Thank you, Mrs. Foltz. If there are any shenanigans about, you may rest assured we will uncover them." Dr. McFarland took Anne's hand. "As for the methodology of the asylum, my granddaughter is an expert at finding all the accounting and other tricks such organizations have for hiding their misdeeds."

"I am certain you will, as my esteem for Liz Packard is such that her recommendation of you both is quite sufficient." Clara stood up from the desk and took in a deep breath. "Shall we briefly discuss how to make our contacts with our two spies? Bertha and Adeline need safe havens in which to impart their information."

Mrs. Packard, who now had her collapsible hearing aid, nodded her head. "Yes, I believe I saw a place that may suit your needs, detective Foltz. I was escorting Dorothy, the patient I found wandering the halls the other night. She informed me that the angels came down in the morning during breakfast. When I asked her where these cherubs might be, she showed me a trap door in the ceiling beneath the staircase. It pulls down by a lever, and there are stairs leading up into a portion of the attic used for storage. I believe if you should rendezvous with your daughters up there, it would be safe. You could place someone at the bottom to be a look-out."

Clara chose not to explain to Liz that Adeline was not her daughter, as yet, but the idea struck her as quite good. "Yes, that could work very well, Liz. Thank you. We will use that means and call it by the code name Jacob's Ladder."

"I suggest you make certain you're already up there first," Isaiah pointed out. "Your helper could then open the door for your guest, and stand guard while you're both up there conducting business."

"Bravo! I can see why we have you on our committee, Captain. I have read about your detective exploits in the newspapers." Dr. McFarland slapped Isaiah on the back.

"Isaiah has instructed me in the finer arts of sleuthing, and for that I am forever indebted to him." Clara pulled down at the waist of her patient's frock, as she was self-conscious about her weight. Her daughters, especially Bertha, were often reminding of her extra baggage. "Shall we adjourn to breakfast in the dining hall? Afterward, we can begin our appointed rounds. I wish you all the best of luck, and may God be with us."

"Please remember," Anne McFarland said, bringing her hands together at the mention of prayer. "These are lost souls. They can only be rescued by the grace of a higher power. We are merely conduits to lead them back to our Maker's orderly universe, where they may hopefully join us once more in our daily struggles."

"Amen," Ah Toy said, and Clara smiled at her. She then followed her Taoist friend out the door, followed closely behind by the others.

***

The Women's Section, Second Floor, Stockton State Insane Asylum, Afternoon, April 26, 1887.

Bertha May Foltz was spying on the conversation between Francis Galton and Dr. Rooney. The scientist did not trust Adeline, as she was able to read his thoughts, so Bertha was chosen to be the spy. Elizabeth Packard, who was interviewing patients that day on the first floor, had also informed Bertha of the clandestine hiding place wherein she and Adeline were to meet, individually, in order to communicate directly with Mrs. Foltz about what was happening upstairs.

After infiltrating the second floor by a dumbwaiter used to send food from the kitchen to the second-floor rooms, Bertha was now using that dumbwaiter to listen in on Galton and Rooney. She leaned against the plywood door with her ear pressed against it.

"We have set the wheels in motion for all my experiments, Alfred. Phase two will begin tomorrow." Bertha could tell the voice of Mr. Galton, as it had the British pronunciation of words.

"How did you establish your link to each of my patients? Also, what will happen in phase two? Perhaps, one day, I shall write my own book concerning the experiments we have conducted." That was Rooney's voice. She would know that raspy, Irish baritone anywhere.

Bertha could hear papers being shuffled. "Let me see. Here we are. Subject 1, Miss Sidney Reyes. My conjoined twins have established the necessary lustful attraction, and Susanne tells me she should soon have complete control over this Filipina's mind. In phase two, I want to see if that control can lead to murder."

Murder? Bertha's pulse began to race. *If these men want to create murderers, then perhaps they are behind the murder of Polly's friend, Winnie Cotton.*

"You can't mean you will allow her to kill in my asylum. We just gained approval from Governor Bartlett . . ."

"No, you idiot. She will not kill anyone. I just want to see how far her hereditary rebelliousness goes. This will allow us to establish the necessary causal proof we need to show the Congress of the United States why we need to change the laws immediately to protect the safety of society's elite."

"I see. Now I understand. And, what about the second patient? Mrs. Angela Thoma?"

"I had my psychic assistant, Miss Quantrill, impersonate a voice from the dead to arouse this woman's sick psyche into a state of suspended belief. She can now be easily manipulated by this means, and the same test will be applied to her."

"Attempted murder?"

"Correct."

Bertha's heart was now racing. She knew she had to get this information to her mother as soon as possible. She twisted inside the small compartment, and the box she was in dropped slightly on the pully, making a squealing sound. *Good God in Heaven! They will find me!*

"Did you hear that?" It was Francis Galton's voice.

"No. What was it?"

"It sounded as if it was coming from that wall."

"Oh. Correct. The kitchen staff uses that dumbwaiter to send up food to our wealthy patients and to our room. It's close to lunch, and they're probably sending something."

"Jolly good. I am getting rather famished."

Bertha exhaled and held her stomach, which was beginning to gurgle at the mention of lunch. *This blasted dumbwaiter and my own stomach are turning against me!*

"Please. Finish your explanation. Then we can eat something."

"Patient number three, Katherine Yantis. My Swedish solo triplet, Deandra, shall impersonate King Oscar's personal secretary. At the rendezvous, Mrs. Yantis will be tested to determine if she can kill with a Winchester repeating rifle."

"Oh, good. I shall have my staff prepare for this meeting with the king. Who will get to play Oscar?"

"Why, with a bit of physical alteration, I think you would make an excellent royal personage, don't you?" Bertha pictured Dr. Rooney as a king, and she shuddered at the image. He already had complete power over all the men and women in this asylum. As a king, what would he do, pray tell?

"Thank you, Francis. I will forever be indebted to you!"

"The fourth woman, the girl, Jessica Adkins. She has agreed to meet with Polly Bedford. I have a drug I've been testing, and I shall use it on the Adkins girl. With her present psychosis, we can see how far we can extend her dream world. Hopefully, it will enter into homicidal tendencies."

"What is this drug called? I don't believe I am familiar with such a pharmaceutical. It would seem it could be used in our military, for good purpose, no doubt."

"Hardly. This drug has sparked wars on the Asian continent between my own country and China. Combined with an already hysterical mind, like that of young Adkins, opiates prove to be the most conclusive prescription for homicidal ideations."

"How interesting! Why didn't I think of that? I suppose this is because the drug is used in so many legal medicines, such as laudanum. Our Congress will certainly want to know how murders might be increasing because of its use."

"Yes, well, we have a specific purpose in mind, don't we? We need not tell the authorities that our young lady was given such medication before she tried to kill Polly Bedford."

Kill Polly? These men are plotting bold experiments, indeed!

"I am almost afraid to ask about Mrs. Wilkinson. She has already killed. What purpose do you have in mind for her?"

"Ah, yes. My lone identical triplet, Mr. Claiborne Falcone, has enamored the woman with his masculine charms. He has also given her a weapon and a purpose. What she does not know is that the weapon is harmless. The tin it is made from is constructed to fall apart once it is used. We shall, however, have proof that her hereditary disposition can move her to kill once more, very easily."

"How ingenious! This will give us five demonstrated tests to prove our case to Congress."

When Bertha heard the dumbwaiter door being opened, she fumbled for the pulley with which to descend, but she was not fast enough. The face of Francis Galton, his pointed upper lip quivering, was staring at her. "Put this girl in isolation. Immediately!" She felt his arms encircle her body and yank her forward into his arms. Bertha was most saddened because she would not be able to inform her mother; and her sister and brother, Trella and Samuel, would be ashamed to be related to her.

"Who is this girl?" Francis Galton was watching Dr. Rooney, as he grasped Bertha by her arm.

"Deidra Watkins. She was admitted last week. We found her wandering around Golden Gate Park in a transfixed state. She has no parents or relatives that we could locate." The Superintendent grabbed her by the shoulders. "She could be a malefactor. Miss, why were you in there?"

Bertha thought she might be able to talk her way around this capture by using her wit and guile. "I am friends with Polly Bedford, sirs. She told me she saw who the killer of Winnie Cotton was. I knew the nurses wouldn't let me come up here, so I used the dumbwaiter to reach your room."

"Oh, is that so? Quite interesting. And who would this perpetrator be? Be informed. If your evidence proves to be invented, you will never see the light of day again." Dr. Rooney twisted her arm, and Bertha winced in pain.

"She said it was Samuel Foltz, her neighbor on Nob Hill." Bertha kept her face unemotional and grave, just the way she had seen her mother speak before a jury in a San Francisco court room.

Francis Galton's bushy eyebrows rose on his forehead. "Foltz? Is he a relative of our inquisitor downstairs? Attorney Clara Foltz?"

"Yes, he is. He's her son." Dr. Rooney loosened his grip on Bertha's arm, leaving a red mark on the skin. "I read about him in the *Chronicle*. He assisted Clara Foltz in her case concerning the mesmerist murders of wealthy husbands."

"We may be able to end this committee's investigation and also establish a criminal motive of the utmost importance to state authorities." Galton raised his right hand's thumb and forefinger to his chin. "Of course, we shall have to bring this young Foltz in for questioning at once."

"Wait a moment, sir, if you don't mind. Can't we use this important information in another way?" Dr. Rooney touched Galton's forearm.

"Another way? What does your Yankee ingenuity have in mind?"

"We could turn Samuel into a spy for us. If he did kill Miss Cotton, then we can dispose of him later. If he did not, but he is too afraid that we shall tell his mother, then he will certainly work for us."

"I know a better way, Dr. Rooney. My employee, Adeline Quantrill, is in love with this Samuel Foltz. She told me so. Her job with me is her way to impress Mrs. Foltz and her family so that she can become worthy of their respect."

"That's very interesting. Please, go on."

"We can tell Mr. Samuel Foltz that unless he works for us, his love, Adeline, will receive the worst employment review that has ever been created by a scientist of my stature." Galton smiled. "That should make him work for us with no qualms whatsoever. And, as you say, if he proves to be the murderer of Winnifred Cotton, then we can indeed turn him over to the authorities at the conclusion of our experiments."

Bertha's mind was spinning. Was she still going to be put into isolation? Would she be able to tell the others before Samuel began to work for these scoundrels?

"What about our little intruder? Hasn't she heard too much?" Dr. Rooney again took Bertha's forearm in his vice-like grip.

"Yes, she must be placed in solitary confinement until we can execute our plan. Take her away."

***

The Women's Section, First Floor, Stockton State Insane Asylum, Evening, April 26, 1887.

Clara was happy the day was over. She and Ah Toy interviewed the entire staff of seventeen nurses and other employees, but other than hearsay allegations of alleged cruelty toward some patients, there were no leads about activities which could prove to a court of law that the asylum should be closed down. The others in her group were assembled at the doctors' table inside the dining hall. The patients on the first floor had previously been fed, as well as the staff physicians and nurses. Clara's group was privately dining on roast brisket of beef, mashed potatoes, garden carrots, and salad.

"Liz, how did your day progress? Were you able to inform Bertha concerning Jacob's Ladder?" Clara purposely sat next to Mrs. Packard, so as to be within close range of her eardrums.

"Yes, she is now aware, and she told me she informed Adeline Quantrill upstairs. It seems they have surreptitiously arranged another endeavor on their own during lunch. I am not privy as to its details, purpose, or goal, however." Mrs. Packard cut into her meat, in the European tradition, with her knife held in her right hand, and her fork in her left. She brought the meat to her mouth and nodded. "Quite good. Rare, the way I prefer."

"Dr. McFarland and Anne? What about your questions of the doctors on staff? Any skullduggery afoot?" Clara dabbed her cloth napkin to her lips.

"We went over the patient records and matched them with the script from the doctors. Nothing untoward as yet. Anne and I still want to interview the pharmacist. Sometimes, in these cases, there can be a secret arrangement being made that's quite illegal." Dr. McFarland sipped from his wine glass.

"Isaiah, what about your rounds? Have you discovered any inappropriate activities?"

"No. I was accosted by several women, however. I suppose my male uniform harkened them back to the Christmas Dance that I'm told allows the sexes to mingle for a night of frivolity. As you are quite aware, dear Clara, I do not dance with my two left feet." Captain Lees chuckled. "Women, especially these women, can be quite forward."

The entire group began to laugh, and soon they were teary-eyed with frivolous entertainment, at the expense of the burly police captain. Clara extended her hand across the table to grasp Isaiah's hand in her own. She smiled at him, and pursed her lips into a pucker of affection.

CHAPTER 8: THE VISITOR

The Women's Section, Jacob's Ladder, Stockton State Insane Asylum, Morning, April 27, 1887.

When Clara learned about the incarceration of her daughter, Bertha May, she was inside Jacob's Ladder talking with Adeline. Clara realized her committee needed to increase its pressure on the authorities of the asylum. Dr. Rooney had mentioned that he was going to keep the female, Deidra Watkins, in solitary confinement, so the committee could not interview her anymore. Unless her group discovered a way to overrule Rooney's authority, Bertha would remain in isolation. One less spy for them to use, and perhaps Dr. Rooney might even attempt to torture her daughter for information.

Downstairs, beneath the ladder leading up into the attic storeroom, Captain Lees was holding vigil as their guardian. The light inside the room was a dim reflection coming from a small window on the far side. Clara could barely discern Adeline's face in the shadows, but it was the importance of her information that she was focused upon.

"What has been the motivation of these two men upstairs? Who are these five women, and what do Dr. Rooney and Francis Galton plan to do with them?" Clara was trying to remain calm, as the news about Bertha had increased her tension and fear.

"I am so sorry, Mrs. Foltz. I am not allowed to see these women. Mr. Galton contracted with Dr. Rooney to have them locked in a private room. All I do know is there are going to be experiments done on them."

Clara could tell by the tremors in her young voice that Adeline was quite emotional. "Don't be frightened. However, I am afraid you are now our only link to their endeavors. Until we can come up with some hard evidence to force our way into their research, we will have to rely on what you tell us."

"Only link? What about Bertha May?" Adeline reached out to grasp Clara by her right forearm. "Has she been harmed?"

"Oh, no. Dr. Rooney informed us she was placed in isolation due to some serious infraction of the asylum's rules. Therefore, we have nobody to watch over Polly at the moment. Mrs. Packard is attempting to interview the girl, but there is always a nurse standing by, so her questions are limited." Clara moved next to Adeline and put her arm around her shoulders. "Please continue, dear. We must know whatever you have been able to perceive, including your psychic abilities."

Instead of becoming calmer, Clara could feel Adeline's body begin to shake with emotion. "Francis Galton is also a telepath. He informed me that my psychic talent was one of the major reasons he hired me for this job. He knew I had access to past history. I discovered we could read each other's thoughts when I was being interviewed at Leland Stanford's mansion. I have to be so careful around him, Mrs. Foltz. It is giving me nightmares about being found out. What if they do discover what I am doing? Would they kill me?"

Clara was sorry for the girl's fear, but she knew unless she was completely honest with her, the entire investigation could be placed in jeopardy. "No, not unless they are directly responsible for the murder of Winnie Cotton. We have no reason to believe they are, at this point. Although, we do have suspicions that their overall philosophy toward the mentally ill may be suspect. What can you tell me about that?"

"They don't allow me to be there during their conversations. I am presently a tutor and ward of the identical triplets."

"Identical triplets? Who are they?" Clara was quite surprised by this new revelation.

"Two sets of identical triplets. They came from Europe and Scandinavia with Mr. Galton. Two in each set are conjoined from birth defects. One each is not, but they were all born identical in appearance and mere minutes apart. The three males are named Falcone, and they're from Scotland. And the three females are named Johansen, and they come from Sweden. They are quite nice, actually, and we get along with each other very well."

"How is Galton using them? Are they being questioned, or are there formal scientific experiments? Are they being harmed in any manner?" Clara thought this might be a key to being able to intervene upstairs with their investigating committee.

"I don't know. Mr. Galton calls for each separately, except for the conjoined set, and then they all reappear later in the day inside our room. They tell me nothing about what they're doing, except for one. His name is Claiborne. When I first met him, he told me he and his brothers were Jews, with the given surname of Feldman. Claiborne says he believes Mr. Galton to be a madman and that Mr. Feldman is staying in the asylum only to protect the others."

Clara was intrigued. "What proof does he have that Francis Galton is insane?"

"He has stopped talking about that. Claiborne has gone back into a shell of conformity for some reason. I shall keep trying to get him to tell me. Do you think I should tell him what I am really doing working for Galton?"

"No. Don't do that. We can't know at this point whether or not this young man is simply trying to bring you out at the behest of Galton's private instructions. Just keep watching him." Clara stepped back. "Anything else? I need to return to my group downstairs."

"There's to be a visitor today. Dr. Rooney informed us. A psychiatrist from Munich, Germany, by the name of Dr. Emil Kraepelin. They will be giving him a tour of the asylum and discussing European standards of care."

Clara believed this might be a break in their investigation they had waited for. "I must discuss this with my group, especially with Dr. McFarland and Elizabeth Packard. In the meantime, try to spy on them to overhear what they say. I know, I am putting you at risk, but this may be very important to our case. Can you do that for me?" Clara again grasped Adeline's arm.

"Yes, I can do that. You have done more than that for me. I will report back to you after he is given the grand tour. Please tell Samuel that I miss him."

"I shall, my dear, and thank you for being our spy in the sky. We can rendezvous here at the same time, after breakfast, tomorrow."

"Goodbye," Adeline said, and Clara began to walk back toward the ladder. "Mrs. Foltz?"

"Yes?" Clara turned around.

"I dreamed about you last night. You were visiting me, here, in our private room. You were conjoined with Samuel. Francis Galton was standing behind you both, and he told us you were his most recent experiment."

Clara laughed. "That is indeed a bold experiment! My son Samuel would sooner be hitched to a mother grizzly bear, I am afraid." Clara bent down and rapped three times with her knuckles on the trap door. After a few moments, she could hear Isaiah climbing up the steps.

***

The Women's Section, Second Floor, Stockton State Insane Asylum, Evening, April 27, 1887.

Bertha May could hear the voices coming down the hall toward her room. For hours, it had remained eerily silent. She never heard anybody, not even the wealthy lunatics who prowled the halls at all hours babbling their incantations. Her fear was not for herself. She was more afraid that Polly Bedford would be harmed in some way. If that happened, then her mother would be furious at her.

She needed to collect herself before these people come into her room. Bertha mussed her hair and decided she would play the game she played with Polly: Mental Metamorphosis. She covered her face with her hands and concentrated. *My insanity can be the way to invoke the real truth from these visitors. I must think the way mother does. Trickery is in my genetics.* When she completed her metamorphosis, and sat up straight on her bed, Bertha had become her sleuthing character, Deidra Watkins, the orphan found wandering alone in Golden Gate Park.

The door opened with a squealing groan. Three men entered, and Bertha already knew two of them, but the third man, a short, handsome man, with an all-white suit, white hair, gray goatee, and black eyebrows, walked right up to where she was sitting on the edge of the bed. He stared down at her, and she stared up at him, for about three minutes. She was not going to turn away, or be intimidated, no matter what his importance.

"Do you think about why you are here?"

"No. Do you?" Bertha saw, too late, from the corner of her eye, the flat hand, striking at her from the side. She was hit hard, and her head snapped to the right. The skin of her left cheek stung like needles had stuck her, and she knew it would fill with blood, turn a flushed crimson, and leave a ghastly purple bruise.

Dr. Alfred Rooney, who had struck her, was smiling, rubbing his right palm against the front of his frock coat. “We get these types quite often, I am afraid. Our effort to rehabilitate often meets a dead end when it comes to these girls in their teenage years. They wander on their own, so they become hardened by the streets whereupon we find them.”

“I understand. However, I find in the clinical setting, the wild ones provide the best testing results.” Bertha twisted her head away, when this strange doctor attempted to stroke her cheek with his outstretched hand.

“That is what I am attempting. The five I told you about have been prepared for hereditary experiments.” Francis Galton walked over to stand next to the visiting clinician from Germany. “However, this one has told us she overheard one of our patients identifying who the murderer might be in a case involving a young girl from a wealthy San Francisco family. The murdered Cotton girl was one of the transmissible elite we have vowed to protect.”

“We have a plan to get this murder suspect, Samuel Foltz, into the asylum where we can employ him. His mother, Clara Foltz, is the head of the investigating committee about which we told you.” Dr. Rooney took out two pairs of steel chain shackles from the inside of his waistcoat. “I am taking you down to see Polly, Miss Watkins. Our first experiment is about to commence. We want you to elicit from her the name of Samuel Foltz as the killer of Winnifred Cotton. Since you were caught spying, we must keep you restrained.”

Francis Galton furrowed his brow and turned to address the German. “Do you suggest we allow this girl speak to Polly before we admit our subject, Jessica Adkins, into the room?”

Bertha watched, as Dr. Rooney first put the chains around her wrists, and then, stooping down, encircled her ankles with the second pair.

“One moment. If this Foltz is the murderer of the elite Cotton youth, then why not place him in the room with them both? I find that psychosis can often be broken when the patient experiences the traumatic effect again. Don't you agree?”

"I see what you mean. If Polly Bedford becomes lucid after seeing Samuel Foltz, the killer, again, then she can testify against him in court. Rooney, take those off, and then go pay a visit to young Foltz." Galton walked over to the door. "Emil, please come. We can do the second experiment. She's an actual murderer who stabbed her poor husband on his wedding night. I have followed your advice this time, in that my subject will be given instructions to use a harmless placebo knife on another patient."

"You must keep a full record of what transpires. Our international group will require such proof to move forward."

Bertha watched the three men as they left the room. She knew she had to find a way to escape before Samuel entered the fray. Unless her mother could take action, then she might be representing her own son in criminal court. Why had she put him into this predicament? Did she harbor some kind of sick resentment of her own against Samuel for being their mother's favorite? Perhaps all this time inside the asylum was working to unhinge her mind. Was that it? Bertha walked over to the door and peered through the rectangle of wire mesh. One thing was certain. There was a bigger conspiracy happening than just one murder. This international group must have ideas of its own about why people murder and perhaps become insane enough to attempt murder.

Panic had finally set in. Bertha's plan, before she was caught, was hatched with Adeline Quantrill, inside Jacob's Ladder. They were to go together to spy on Claiborne Falcone, one of the identical triplets being used by Galton in his work. Adeline believed Falcone, whose name actually might be Feldman, could possibly work with them. They needed to get information concerning Dr. Rooney and Francis Galton and what they had planned for these five experiments. Adeline would now have to go it alone until Bertha found a way to escape. Before she could get out of this room, Samuel might have already proved Bertha to be a liar. And then, she thought, they could really have her committed.

***

The Women's Section, Second Floor, Stockton State Insane Asylum, Evening, April 27, 1887.

Melissa Sue Wilkinson was ready. She kept fingering the Chinese medallion around her neck beneath her smock as she sat on her lower bunk near the door. Even though she regretted stabbing her husband, Jeremy, to death, she still had the urge to stab things. The handsome young man who kissed her said she would be able to use the knife soon. She simply had to wait for his instructions. Waiting, however, was not one of Melissa's better character traits.

For example, the other four women in her company were getting on her nerves. They were really much more mentally affected than Melissa could ever become in her wildest dreams. Kitty Reyes, her bunk mate, kept moaning and crooning Philippine love songs in some gibberish language that sounded more like a duck quacking than musical lyrics of lost love. Katherine Yantis was constantly turning on Melissa and pretending to draw guns from an invisible holster around her waist. Kathy even took an apple from lunch and placed it on Kitty's head. One crazy girl singing, and the other one playing Annie Oakley with a rifle. What lunacy!

Oh, and then there were the other two. Melissa almost pulled the blade out of her medallion when Angela Thoma woke her out of a sound sleep one night to tell Melissa there was an evil spirit hovering just above her. Angie then said she was talking to it, and that she could convince the spirit not to kill her, if Melissa would give Angela her portion of potatoes at dinner time. Jessica Adkins was the final straw. She kept telling them all that they were figments of her dream world. The teenager even asked Melissa, while they were bathing, if she would prefer to have larger breasts. If so, Jessica could promptly dream them up for her!

These were the lunatics she had to live with each day, and the experience was enough to send Melissa over the edge. If it was not for the handsome, dark-haired stranger, life would no longer be worth the struggle.

Melissa got up from her lower bunk and walked slowly over to the door. Her thoughts became a muddled mess. She remembered how her Uncle Joseph used to sing to her alone, inside the family's library. Then he began to molest her sexually, and she remembered his hands, everywhere on her twelve-year-old body, and when his actions became bolder, she picked up a letter opener from the library desk, and she stabbed him in the hand.

Inside, something became infused in her psyche that became a way to cope against what she saw as the ever-increasing, daily harassment by the overlords, the dominating males in charge of most everything around her. Her uncle, in his fear of being discovered, never said anything, but Melissa knew there were others, outside the family's domain, that would not stop. They would kill her if she tried to protect herself, so she was ever-vigilant, ever protective of her body, and, most importantly of her mind.

As she gazed out of the rectangular meshed window to the outside hallway, Melissa felt regret that her mind had become so fearful on her wedding night. Jeremy, sweet Jeremy, became just another male intruder. The boiling rage that had built-up over the years had made her snap, she believed, and now she was inside this monstrous place with nowhere to turn, and nobody to talk to who understood.

When those dark eyes appeared at the window, Melissa was thinking about him. *Is it time to act? Are they going to finally accomplish the feat which will ensure their escape from this madhouse forever?*

The lock on the door clicked, and the door swung toward her. Melissa stepped backward, and the dark stranger walked in. He looked around the room at the other women, who stared back at him, as if he were an archangel come to rescue them all from perdition.

His whisper was hoarse, as if he had rehearsed what he was telling her many times. "We must go now. You must do as I say, and you must never hesitate for one second. Our lives depend upon it. My brothers will meet us when we take him hostage."

"Who is him?" Melissa stepped out into the dark hallway, and he shut the door and locked it.

"You shall see. Now. Follow closely behind me."

As she walked behind him, she felt like his shadow. In fact, in her mind, she was sucking in his power, his male animus, and her body become infused with a new energy she had only experienced once before: when she stuck the letter opener in her uncle's hand.

As they came to the corner of a passageway leading into the wealthy patients' dining room, Melissa could see Dr. Rooney standing in the doorway with two other men. They also looked like officials or doctors, and they nodded to her escort.

Dr. Rooney smiled. “Take her inside. Rosemary is waiting. She is one of the elite patients about whom I told you.”

Melissa watched him nod at Dr. Rooney, but then, as they walked slowly into the large dining room, he turned around to whisper in her ear. “Slowly, very slowly, pull out the blade. Once you have it in your grasp, you will begin to walk toward the woman inside. Keep the knife out of sight. The men will follow. Move so you are in front of Dr. Rooney and facing her. At the last moment, I want you to turn around and grab the superintendent and hold the knife at his throat. We will use him to get out of here. Do you understand? This is our only chance at freedom!”

The word “freedom” rang inside her being like the cracked bell she once saw in Philadelphia. She had always pictured that bell as an icon for women’s rights because it, like most women in the United States, was a used and damaged instrument, ringing out its message of liberty every day, but that message was falling upon mostly deaf ears.

The three men followed Melissa and her escort into the room. About five yards away stood her intended victim. A statuesque damsel with auburn hair, a blue bell bonnet with a matching dress, and tiny, red satin slippers. She was smiling at Melissa as the space between them grew smaller. Melissa held the blade in her hand and glanced back to see where Dr. Rooney was standing. He was about five feet from where Melissa now stood.

“I have the hand of God in my grasp, my dear lady. Do you want to touch the hand of God? Come to me. I will allow you to experience a joy that no human, other than myself, has ever experienced!”

Melissa decided to act before being told. “I can’t go through with this! I am ill, and you won’t help me?” She turned around, and she held the knife blade limply against her side as she shuffled across to stand in front of the other gentleman wearing a white suit. She had strategically placed herself so that Dr. Rooney’s back was facing her back.

“Oh, kind sir, won’t you help me?” she cried to the white-haired stranger. Before Dr. Rooney could turn around to see what this strange gentleman was going to tell her, she spun, lifting her knife up so that it was held in her right hand, the sharp side of the blade toward her.

"Achtung!" The man in white yelled, as Melissa grabbed Dr. Rooney around his slim waist and thrust her blade around his neck until it was being held about a half-inch from his jugular vein on the right side.

"Dr. Rooney. You will come with us. We want you to open the main entrance and allow us to leave. If you do this, you will not be harmed." Her dark escort pointed toward the exit from the dining room.

Expecting to push the doctor toward the exit, Melissa tightened her grip on the handle of the blade and spread her legs apart to gain traction in case the other men attempted to lunge at her.

For a few moments, everything went as planned. Melissa shuffled along with Dr. Rooney toward the door and then out into the hallway.

"Stay back!" Her escort ordered the other two men. They did as they were told and stayed behind, as Melissa waltzed with Dr. Rooney and her dark stranger toward the front entrance of the asylum.

From the side, Melissa could see that Dr. Rooney was smiling. Why would he do that? Did he know something they did not know?

"What is going on here?" An old woman walked toward them out of the shadows.

Dr. Rooney regarded her. "Don't worry, Mrs. Packard. This is merely an experiment. The knife is not real."

The knife is not real? How can that be? This was their only chance to escape, and her dark stranger had lied to her? Her mind was again flooded with the insane fury of that night inside the bridal suite, with her newly wed husband, Jeremy. He had also lied to her about being kind and thoughtful. He was forcing her to eat in a "civil manner." She could hear the constant chomping of his own food, and yet he wanted her to eat in a manner he dictated as most proper for a lady. Why was dipping one's food so barbaric? The Swiss had their fondue. The Egyptians ate with their hands. The Chinese had sticks. Proper should be flexible to the person in charge of his or her own mouth; her own body was her own temple, was it not?

"Believe me, Dr. Rooney, that knife *is* real." Her dark benefactor walked over to stand next to her. "Open that door at once!"

Melissa ran her thumb against the sharp edge of the shiny steel blade. It felt real.

"It cannot be real. I gave you the tin blade myself," Dr. Rooney began, and when Melissa felt his body begin to turn around to face her, she took action.

Her left hand grabbed onto the lower face of the superintendent, and she pulled his face to the left, so the right side of his neck was exposed and under tension. With her blade facing forward, she stabbed the neck slightly behind his right ear, jamming the knife in to the hilt. Then, while pulling the knife out, she knew she needed to push forward so she could rip through the arteries and open a hole in the doctor's neck. The blade sliced deeply into the carotid-jugular beneath the skin, and the blood spewed forth, like a visual animation of the red on the flag standing next to the front entrance door.

As Melissa watched Dr. Rooney's body collapse, she saw that her right forearm and shoulder blade were covered in fresh blood. Her eyes were wide as she watched Mrs. Packard walk toward her, smiling, reaching out to her.

"Let me have it, my dear. You must let me have it *now*." The old woman's voice was calm and reassuring. Was she the one who would finally listen? With a questioning, wide-eyed expression, Melissa handed the bloody knife with the dragon handle, once a possession of the Empress Dowager of China, over to the kindly old woman.

The other two men had grabbed onto her dark stranger, and the last thing she heard, as she followed Mrs. Packard out of the main room and into the side room where the other committee members were, was her escort's strained voice.

"I never put that blade in there! This was only an experiment. I am a Jew. They wanted to blame me for this. I know it. They needed another martyr for their insane cause!"

CHAPTER 9: RIGHT FROM WRONG

San Francisco City Hall Courthouse, San Francisco, Afternoon, April 29, 1887.

Captain Isaiah Lees immediately took the patient, Melissa Sue Wilkinson, into custody on April 27. She was transported to the jail in Stockton that same day, and this was where it was discovered that she had never stood trial for the murder of her husband, Jeremy. The Wilkinson family was very wealthy, but their money came from gold, so their status in the community was not from heredity, but their influence was certainly applicable when money was the method of reason in the courts. Although she was not judged legally insane, the courts had accepted the payment of ten thousand dollars to transport Melissa to Stockton State Insane Asylum. This was the pleading agreement issued by the judge and arranged by the family's attorney with the Judge for the State of California in San Francisco.

The San Francisco judge, William H. Cathcart, under direct orders from Governor Bartlett, had ordered a special hearing at the courthouse. This hearing was to determine the sanity of the defendant, Melissa Sue Wilkinson. If proved sane at the time of the homicide, she could then be put on trial for First Degree Murder. However, if she were proved insane, she would again be confined to Stockton State Insane Asylum. This time, however, she would be given the official designation of legal insanity, which would place a permanent mark of shame upon her family.

Clara decided to represent Mrs. Wilkinson in the hearing, and this news spread like wildfire in the press. The irony of the case was that the family, because of the shame that an official insanity decree would inflict upon them, did not want Clara to win. They would, in fact, prefer that their daughter be adjudicated sane, and face a murder trial and possible death sentence. Clara thought this was ludicrous, although she understood the reasoning. Social stature was important in San Francisco, and the Wilkinson family was not from a distinguished line of wealth. They had been one of the many families made rich during the brief Gold Rush, in the 1850s; so their social standing, if Melissa were judged insane, would be such that they would not be accepted into the elite echelon of San Francisco clubs, civic groups, and schools.

The State of California believed it had made the best appointment to argue at this special hearing. Laura de Force Gordon had successfully won against her rival, Clara Foltz, in a previous murder trial, even though it was a victory made after an appeal. Gordon was also quite familiar with the insanity plea, as well as with the evidence and characters involved at the scene of the homicide. Therefore, the San Francisco District Attorney's Office had appointed Mrs. Gordon as the lead attorney and state's prosecutor at this hearing.

Clara was inside a locked counsel room, adjacent to the court, with her team of advisors. Captain Isaiah Lees, who had been the arresting officer, was also sympathetic to Clara and Mrs. Packard's cause, so he was there. Mrs. Elizabeth Ware Packard, of course, was an important advisor to Clara, as was her best friend, Ah Toy. As a resident superintendent and psychiatrist in Illinois, Dr. Andrew McFarland was also being used as an expert witness.

Meanwhile, back at the asylum, Adeline Quantrill was now serving as their only undercover spy. Bertha, as well, was still participating, but she was confined, away from the asylum population. And, in a wicked twist of fate, Clara's son, Samuel Cortland, was working at the asylum for Francis Galton. Clara had no idea as yet why he was doing this, but Ah Toy and Trella told her he was probably trying to be close to Adeline, to protect her.

Clara stood at the head of the conference table, with all the paperwork they had assembled in the two days they had prior to the court-mandated insanity hearing spread before her on the table. The research and interviews they accomplished in forty-eight hours had been phenomenal. Clara, Liz Packard, and Dr. McFarland had interviewed their client, Melissa Wilkinson, extensively. They agreed that putting her in front of the judge, to testify, would not be proper, so Clara was going to explain the case for insanity to the court, and she would also call upon Mrs. Packard and Dr. McFarland as expert witnesses.

The main issue Clara wanted to discuss with her group was what they believed Laura Gordon had up her sleeves. Since this was a hearing, and not a trial, they had no access to evidence, other than the witness testimonies that would be given concerning the homicide of Dr. Rooney. These were in the form of sworn affidavits, which Laura and the D. A.'s office had obtained. The judge would have these, and Clara's team had received copies. There was, of course, no public gallery allowed during this hearing, just members of the press, and the court's goal would be to determine if Mrs. Wilkinson was to be tried as a sane woman for the murder of Superintendent Dr. Alfred Rooney. It was Clara's job, of course, to argue that her client was insane when she committed the stabbing. Clara wanted to explain what she was going to be doing so that her expert witnesses understood her overall legal philosophy.

"Thank you for being here, ladies and gentlemen. I know, I have put on my courtly demeanor, but this is the way I argue. Perhaps I maintain my formal elocution because I have no law degree. I will also be using my feminine character and wardrobe, which will, no doubt, irritate Laura Gordon and all the other suffragists who read about this hearing in the newspapers."

Clara tucked the loose end of her white-frilled blouse's collar into the top of her red dress, which had lion-headed gold buttons running down the front. She also wore a full bustle, and a scarlet, ostrich-feathered hat was on the table in front of her. Finally, she would be wearing long black boots when she entered the courtroom. Isaiah had suggested she also carry a riding whip, and should crack it against the floor, as she strode down the aisle. She did not laugh at his attempted humor.

"The court, as we know, will be using the usual study questions pertaining to an insanity plea. Not only must we prove that our client passes the M'Nagthen Rules test, established in Common Law, but we must also be certain our experts, that's Liz Packard and Dr. McFarland, understand the current prejudices of the courts pertaining to their expertise." Clara picked up a sheet of paper from a folder in front of her. "Have you both read the list I gave you?"

Dr. McFarland nodded. "Yes, in my previous testimonies around the country, I have often spoken to the points made in your list. Having it to study, however, has been quite a boon, and I thank you, Counselor."

Clara was a bit irked that the psychiatrist was attempting to mimic her formal tone. "And you, Liz? Do you understand these points?" Clara saw that Mrs. Packard was using her collapsible hearing trumpet at long last.

"Of course, Clara. When one has had to fight the legal system in order to escape the insane clutches of the asylum, one tends to remember why one was placed there in the first place."

The others chuckled.

Clara cleared her throat and continued. "I intend to remark upon those items which are brought up by our prosecutors, including their expert witnesses, Francis Galton and his visiting doctor from Germany, Emil Kraepelin. This will, of course, be in the form of rebuttals. However, my main argument shall hinge upon proving that our broader society has become such a pernicious and unjust breeding ground for insanity commitments that our client was simply a tiny mote in the public eye, especially when she is compared to the gigantic beam of unfairness blinding the populace from the greed and graft going on, in the background, in the name of mental health care."

Dr. McFarland struck his fist upon the table top. "Hear, hear! I applaud your analogy and your biblical reference, counselor."

"What about number three on your sheet, Clara?" Ah Toy held up the sheet and pointed. "Let me read it. *Careful attention should be paid to ascertaining the nature of the stressors that may have produced the insanity, including any history of an aversion to assume a duty or job to which the individual now must subscribe, especially that of a soldier.* Since Mrs. Wilkinson was never judged insane in her first encounter with the law, and she had no employment, would the prosecution use her quite obviously stressful experience with her husband as a way to prove she was feigning her insanity?"

"Excellent point. I am certain the prosecution, and the judge, for that matter, will not allow that previous altercation to be raised at all. If I attempt to raise it, I know they will object. And, to be truthful, even though we know it's related to Melissa's mental state, it is not relevant to the case at hand and to what we are obligated to show in the M'Nagthen tests." Clara pointed to the list. "Most of these items, as we now know, point to proving that the accused is feigning insanity. We have all gone over these points with Melissa, and she is aware of the methods of the prosecution to prove she is trying to defraud them. Now that she has been examined by the court, we shall see how well our tutoring worked on her."

Clara noticed that Isaiah was squirming in his chair. "Yes, Captain? I see you're uncomfortable."

"This is what irritates me about the court side of justice. It all seems to become an orchestrated Shakespearean drama. We coach our client, they coach their witnesses, and the judge places them inside the ring as if it were a bloody dogfight. Whatever happened to spontaneous truth in the heat of passion?"

Clara frowned down at him. "Must I again explain to you the dynamics of a hearing of this nature? There will be spontaneous truth that will come to light. No matter how much both sides prepare, the moment two adversaries begin to argue, the immediacy of that argument, when the snarls and scratches begin, truth becomes a product of that confrontation. It is the Hegelian dialectic. I admit, in some foreign jurisdictions, as in Europe and Great Britain, the adversarial approach is seen as rather barbaric and crude. Especially our jury trial and our First Amendment interventions. However, since I work within this legal system, I find it most scintillating and appropriate for the times in which we live."

"Well stated, Clara. What do you plan to use to prove the M'Nagthen tests?" Dr. McFarland raised his caterpillar-gray eyebrows, as she knew he was asking because of his own part in this procedure.

"The law states we must prove that, at the time of the committing of the act, Mrs. Wilkinson was laboring under such a defect of reason, from disease of the mind, as not to know the nature and quality of the act she was doing; or, if she did know it, that she did not know she was doing what was wrong. In point of fact, the person who was actually acquitted of murder, Daniel M'Nagthen, in 1843 England, would have been proved guilty under these tests had he been tried under them."

"Do tell. I never knew that." Elizabeth Packard remarked.

Clara's voice was calm and assured. "Yes. I plan to use the argument that our client was not only diseased of the mind so that she knew not what act she was committing, but that she was also so much under the patriarchal pressure of Superintendent Rooney and Francis Galton, that she snapped, in an insane and homicidal rage."

"I understand now. I like the questions you have for me and Mrs. Packard. You have encapsulated the points in this legal test nicely, and our testimonies will now help you prove them."

"I believe we can now adjourn to the courtroom, ladies and gentlemen. Captain Foltz, you may sit in the back, as you are not officially a part of my legal team. Please remember this. I am going to attempt to hitch our legal star onto the dramatic philosophical argument I will extend to the court. Our purpose is to show the court and the world what is happening during California's current mental health crisis—and it is a crisis—and when we are finished, even the powers in Washington shall know what they are really trying to do inside the Stockton State Insane Asylum."

Clara's group applauded, and they all adjourned.

***

Clara Foltz, Esq. strutted down the center aisle of the courtroom, but she was thinking about how she had lost her last two criminal trials due to the prejudice and misogyny that existed in the legal arena. Both she and Laura Gordon understood those problems to be faced by women who wanted to argue cases before an all-male jury, a male judge, and a mostly patriarchal press and audience. Still, they persisted in their jobs because they believed that one day, when society awakened from its mummification created by hundreds of years of keeping women away from powerful appointments in the public and private sectors, the sexes would be seen as equal, under the law.

At the front of the room, on the right, her friend Laura was seated with her witnesses, two of whom she knew, and one of whom she did not. Laura was wearing her usual plebeian court attire, navy blue dress with no ornaments, no hat, no gloves, no fashionable female accoutrements. Laura saw herself as a woman of the people, and even her arguments were made with that kind of firm, masculine resolve and spirited delivery. Clara, on the other hand, kept her tone intellectual and even feminine, in a polite manner, even though she always used her tall attractiveness and fashionable attire as a way to lull her opposition into a state of calm reflection. Clara believed humans were more prone to agree when their passions were not riled up, and Laura believed the opposite.

"Good morning, Mrs. Gordon. Mr. Galton. Dr. Kraepelin." After they acknowledged Clara with a nod, she turned back to her side of the courtroom where Ah Toy, Dr. McFarland, and Elizabeth Packard sat awaiting her. She took off her hat and placed it gently on the table, and then she looked up at the bench at Judge Cathcart, who was perusing documents, his pince-nez reading glasses suspended at the tip of his nose like mirrors leading into Alice's Wonderland. She knew nothing of his politics or his reputation for being strict or liberal. She did not bother with this type of research. In her experience, the court could be quite prejudiced, and no amount of logic was going to change the verdict. Such had been her recent trial experience representing the Chinese journalist, George Kwong. This had been a kangaroo court wherein she had lost her battle even before she presented her case. Since this was just an insanity hearing, Clara believed she stood a better chance at winning.

"Attorneys for the state and defense, please approach the bench." Judge Cathcart announced.

Both Clara and Laura got up from their seats and walked down the center of the aisle to look up at the judge. There were only the two sides inside the courtroom. It was empty of visitors, except for the press, who had assembled in the upstairs gallery and were hanging over the railings, notepads and cameras in hand, staring down at the activities like the hungry vultures that they were. They must have looked so ravenous that the judge recognized this.

"Ladies and gentlemen of the press! I must warn you before we begin. No camera photos until I give you permission, and no ruckus or noises, no matter how emotional you may feel about what is being argued. If I have reason to believe you have reported any untruths about these proceedings, I shall ban you from future coverage in the San Francisco City Hall."

The press mumbled acquiescence in low tones, and then were silent, staring down at them with eager attention.

"Assistant District Attorney Gordon, have you assembled all of your witnesses, and are you prepared to present in this matter of the defendant, Mrs. Melissa Sue Wilkinson?"

"I am, your honor." Laura nodded, and then she turned around to stare directly at the one witness Clara did not know.

"Your honor, may I enquire as to the identity of the third witness, sitting next to our German visitor? Mrs. Gordon failed to inform me of him." Clara wanted this information right away, and she was rather aggravated she had not been informed earlier.

"His name is Claiborne Falcone, your honor. I did not include his name because he was not a factor in this presentation until this morning. He has volunteered to provide eye-witness testimony that figures rather importantly on this insanity hearing." Laura smiled at Clara, and it was the smile of the Cheshire cat variety she knew so well. It meant her friend was attempting to sneak something past her.

"I object, your honor. We have not had time to resolve his identity or to ask questions of him. Can this be fair to my client?" Clara kept her tone diffident and warm.

"I understand, Mrs. Foltz. The court will allow you to ask questions of this witness, and Mrs. Gordon shall provide you with his written testimony, which has just now been given. From what I can tell, he was at the scene of the homicide, and, in fact, he played a significant part in the entire experiment." Judge Cathcart stared down at his paper. "I shall allow his personal testimony based on reflection, as it is crucial to the state's argument."

"Thank you, judge. We are now ready to present our case." Laura turned around and swaggered confidently to the podium in front of the court.

Clara took the paper from Laura and almost ran back to her comrades. She knew that only Mrs. Packard, from her team, had been present during the homicide, and only she would know who this man was and what he was doing on the day in question. Clara handed the paper to Elizabeth, let her read it, and then listened.

"Yes, he was there. From what I know, he is one of Francis Galton's patients. He is from Scotland, and he is one of three identical triplets. Two of them are conjoined, and they are serving to help Galton and the late Dr. Rooney in their experiments." Mrs. Packard sighed. "Doctors attempting to make names for themselves in the field of mental health. I suggest you question them sternly about their purposes, Clara."

Clara was worried about this turn of events. "I shall, but I know my friend. She does not present last minute witnesses unless she believes she has her opponent over a barrel of some sort."

"Your honor, my two expert psychiatrists have examined the defendant, and their conclusions are based on established president concerning whether or not an individual passes the M'Nagthen tests. I am here to argue that not only is the insanity defense a miscarriage of justice, it is also a tactic that was originally established by a court in England. My main witness, Francis Galton, is well aware of how the courts in England work. As his testimony will show, the recent scientific advancements that occurred after the publication of Charles Darwin's research have now been adapted by the mental health community. We shall demonstrate that the defendant, Mrs. Melissa Wilkinson, was quite sane on the day in question. In fact, she was so deliberate in her actions that the other legally insane women in her room were frightened of her. Deliberation of intent, as we in the legal profession understand, is the prime requisite in any criminal case involving the *mens rea* factor. The defendant knew exactly what she was doing when she methodically and viciously stabbed the knife into Dr. Andrew Rooney's throat. It was no fantasy. It was no figment of her crazed imagination in some alternative reality. It was a cold and calculated action based on her hatred and her conviction that the so-called patriarchal powers of society were out to keep her from living her rather obviously antisocial lifestyle. May I please call my first witness, Mr. Francis Galton?"

"Francis Galton, please approach the bench to be sworn in."

The middle-aged appointee of Leland Stanford got up slowly from the State's table and walked over to the bailiff, who was standing near the witness stand, next to the flags of California and the United States.

"Please place your right hand on this Bible." The portly bailiff, in civilian clothes, extended the Bible to him. "Do you, Francis Galton, citizen of the United Kingdom, vow to tell the truth, the whole truth, and nothing but the truth, so help you God?"

"I do."

"Please be seated." The bailiff pointed to the riser where the padded chair was, and Galton climbed the two steps and sat down.

Laura walked over to him and smiled. "Thank you for being here, Mr. Galton. I know you are very active in your work with patients at the Stockton Asylum, and it this work that I want to ask you about."

"Your honor? What does this witness's activity as a researcher have to do with the insanity of my client?" Clara was a bit surprised that Laura would go in this direction. She suspected only a discussion of the events on the day of the alleged murder.

Laura turned and addressed Judge Cathcart. "Your honor, this witness is one of the most renowned scientists in the world. In point of fact, his research was quoted by Charles Darwin in his second text, and he has traveled to do his research almost as extensively as his cousin. Mr. Galton's testimony about his experiments will help prove the sanity of the defendant. Indeed, it will also help to instruct the United States on how to address the increasing epidemic of mental diseases, which now are plaguing this great nation of ours."

"Objection overruled. You may proceed, Mrs. Gordon."

Clara took out her papers concerning Francis Galton and his qualifications. She was ready to rebut his testimony, but she knew she would need to extend her points to meet the wider range of discussion. The points she could not address she would refer to Dr. McFarland or Elizabeth Packard.

"Mr. Galton, why did you arrive at the conclusion that Mrs. Wilkinson was sane when she stabbed Dr. Rooney to death?" Laura was wasting no time. The question burned into the quick of the matter.

"She was part of our experiment. You mentioned my cousin, Charles Darwin. One of the first experiments I did, in 1869, was to prove that his theory that gemmules, from all the cells in the male and female bodies, circulated freely, and then combined to determine the heredity of their offspring, was false. To disprove his hypothesis, I transferred blood from rabbits of different breeds and showed there was no such transfer of characteristics. Instead, I demonstrated, once and for all, that it was the sperm and the egg which determined the hereditary ingredients of children. No psychological events or traumas that occurred during their lives ever changed their basic genetic make-up."

Clara stood up and faced the judge. "Again, how does this information support the contention of sanity in my client?"

"Please, your honor. This man is a genius. He will arrive at his conclusions momentarily. Scientific logic works as an inductive flow, not deductive, or syllogistic, as Mrs. Foltz may wish us to believe." Laura turned toward Clara and smiled.

Judge Cathcart struck his gavel hard three times upon the wood square on his desk. “Please continue, Mr. Galton. And, Mrs. Foltz. Refrain from your objections. This is not a trial. I want to hear what the gentleman has to say.”

“Thank you, Judge. As I was about to say, I have studied the heredity of many famous personages, from around the world, and it is my determination that the only way to save the elite, within our Caucasian race, from being polluted and overrun by such aberrational races as the Negro and the Chinese, is to control the breeding of the female population. As we now know, the careful selection of mates is the only way to ensure the continuation of genius and the best possibilities of both mental and physical superiority. The best bred aristocrats have known and have voluntarily practiced this kind of select breeding for many generations, and they have produced the superior leaders, thinkers, athletes and warriors down through the ages. And, I might add, they also produce the best cattle, horses, sheep, dogs, and chickens.”

The gallery of newspaper journalists laughed.

Clara was about to burst inside. She and her team had fought this bigoted attitude before, only to have the national government pass a bigoted law forbidding the Chinese from immigrating to the United States. As for the Negro, she believed, along with millions of other Americans, that the Civil War had decided in favor of giving full citizenship to them. But today, Negroes were still prevented from being full citizens, especially in the South. And now, this supposed genius scientist was telling everyone that the only way to ensure a perfect civilization was to control the breeding of the women? What about controlling the men?

“Mrs. Wilkinson, as you may see in her test results, is of a superior intelligence quotient. In addition, before I selected her for my experiments, I gave her a special questionnaire to determine her ability to critique possibilities between very controversial topics, such as the reasons why the male of the species has risen to be the head of a family. Granted, she completely rebelled, in some ways, saying that women needed to fight men to gain their individual freedom. However, this fighting against the patriarchy, as she termed it, demonstrated a strong will. Since she also came from the upper classes, I concluded she was quite sane.” Francis Galton folded his hands and looked over at his colleague from Germany. Dr. Kraepelin returned the smile.

The rest of the presentation of the witnesses for the State was a stream of basic reinforcement of what Francis Galton had established. Mrs. Wilkinson was sane because of the I.Q. and other tests given to her by Mr. Galton. He was the expert in racial superiority and class achievement, and there was nothing Clara could say to rebut that fact. She had been silenced by both Judge Cathcart and by the metaphorical Survival of the Fittest experiment going on inside that hearing room.

When Laura called the last witness, Claiborne Falcone, Clara was almost relieved to have it concluded. Her only hope was to turn the tables during her presentation, but the odds were building against her being able to penetrate the wall of intolerant science growing all around her.

"Mr. Falcone. What were your instructions by Mr. Galton on the day Superintendent Rooney was killed?" Laura paced before her witness like a victorious cat.

"He told me that the knife I gave to her was a tin variety, quite harmless. Mr. Galton also said the experiment was to see if Mrs. Wilkinson had the male strength of character to be able to kill upon command. It was to be the final proof that she could withstand the pressures of leadership." Falcone smiled over at Clara. He was quite handsome, and Clara understood why Melissa had been so smitten by him.

"Therefore, as far as you knew, when she stabbed Dr. Rooney, she believed she was performing under your direct order and not under the authority of someone else. Is that true?"

"That's quite true. When the knife was discovered to be a real blade, I was as astonished as everyone else."

"The entire experiment, up to the moment of the homicide, was planned completely by Mr. Galton and his associates?" Laura was moving in for the kill.

"That's true. I was instructed to tell Melissa that she was helping me to escape the asylum with my brothers. We have no reason to believe any one of us could have switched the blades during the experiment." Falcone frowned. "She is quite a beautiful and trusting woman. I do not wish to harm her."

"Did you show affection for the defendant in any physically demonstrative way?" Laura stopped pacing. She stared directly into the young man's dark eyes. "Were you not, in fact, in love with her?"

"Yes, I was. I don't see what this has to do . . ."

"Your honor. This is the most convincing evidence so far that Mrs. Wilkinson was sane when she committed this homicide. She was capable of love, and she was determined to do the bidding of her lover. I would like to call my final witness, Dr. Emil Kraepelin."

Clara was astounded. What was she doing now?

The German was sworn in, and he took the stand. Claiborne Falcone sat down.

"Dr. Kraepelin, what did you see just before Mrs. Wilkinson stabbed the victim, Dr. Rooney, in the throat?" Laura inhaled and then blew out her breath in one stream. "Take your time. If you need a translator, I can provide one."

"That is not necessary, thank you. I saw Mrs. Wilkinson rub her thumb on the blade of the weapon before she used it."

"If the court would allow. The witness has stated that he saw Mrs. Wilkinson run her thumb over the blade, to test it for strength, just before she used it. This purposeful act proves a deliberation in the mind. And, coupled with her obvious amorous affection for Mr. Falcone, she was doing it for both love and to save her lover from his prison."

Clara could hear the gasps from up in the gallery, and she knew her case was all but lost. She looked over at Dr. McFarland and Elizabeth Packard. They were frowning, with downcast stares. The presentation she would give in this hearing, no matter how eloquent or logical, was going to be a race to the bottom.

CHAPTER 10: THE OTHER EXPERIMENTS

The Women's Section, First Floor, Stockton State Insane Asylum, Afternoon, April 30, 1887.

It was almost a relief to Clara when they returned to the asylum to continue their investigation of the murder. Laura Gordon had been an excellent barrister. She understood the reality of the moment, she applied her direct questioning and developed her thesis. And she concluded with intelligent aplomb. However, when she met with Clara and her committee later, it was as if she were the attorney who had lost. She was downcast, hesitant in her speech, and apologetic to everyone involved with the hearing in San Francisco.

They were discussing their plans inside the committee's private room on the first floor. All were back wearing their patient attire, increasingly appearing to be actual members of the insane academy. It was Laura who made the first foray into what they should be doing to foil the plans of Francis Galton and his ambitions to create a bigoted and misogynistic paradise for the elite white class.

"I am so sorry, Clara. I had no idea this man was so filled with rancor for the working and lower classes. You know I am not in favor of any kind of class distinctions based upon racial or class privilege. I was only doing my duty as an advocate. I told the District Attorney that I will refuse to prosecute this woman in any subsequent murder trial."

Laura clasped her hands on top of Clara's as they sat together on the lower bunk. They looked as if they were two patients who had been given shock treatment. Their eyes were tearing up, their nostrils were red from crying, and the others were standing around them, trying to console and cheer them up.

"I am not depressed because I lost the hearing. I am afraid for that poor woman's life. She is now being tried for murder in the first degree, and I know that I can do nothing to protect her unless I can solve the mystery of how she was fooled into using a real blade. She has completely shut down again. She will not tell us, or anyone else, anything about what happened. How does one defend somebody who won't speak? On top of it all, we have a mental hospital that is obviously being used to promote some kind of laboratory for creating homicidal maniacs." Clara stood up and turned toward Captain Lees. "What do you think, Isaiah? I tried to show the court that what Galton was doing was inhumane cruelty. Judge Cathcart just sloughed it off as a unique way to train prospective spies for undercover military duties in the government interest."

"I know, Clara. I have faced this kind of thinking my entire career. There are those in the majority who see an encroaching take-over by the teeming masses in Asia, Africa and anywhere else where the social structure might have different values than what they see as Christian, patriotic and civilized. We have to find the murderer who is responsible for the death of Rooney, and, quite possibly, for the death of little Winnifred Cotton."

"We gave them all the statistics about the faulty diagnoses of mental illness, especially for women. Your judge was simply too impressed by this Galton to see how these insanity commitments could be caused by greed and improper procedures." Mrs. Packard put a warm hand on Clara's shoulder.

"We have to understand that we were simply outgunned inside that court room. Now we have to work harder to find corruption going on here. I agree with you, Clara. It must be part of some strange experimentation to show how poor heredity affects the brain." Dr. McFarland walked toward the door. "I'm going to question the other doctors and nurses again. Perhaps they know what's going on upstairs. Anne, please accompany me." His granddaughter followed him.

"All of you. Please be careful. There is a murderer at large. I believe it is someone inside this asylum, and I will be trying to eliminate the suspects, one by one. I also need to speak with Adeline. Ah Toy, would you please inform her? I shall meet her at noon inside Jacob's Ladder. I also want to get Bertha May out of isolation." Clara walked with Isaiah out the door.

Ah Toy followed closely behind. She tapped Clara on the shoulder. "Clara, I have noticed there have been new patients being admitted. Can't we get the State to stop this until this killer is found? The more who live here, the more sheep for the wolf."

"Very good idea. I shall wire the Governor's Office immediately." Clara was the last to exit the room, so she shut and locked the door.

Later, after Clara was informed by Ah Toy that Adeline would meet her in Jacob's Ladder in one hour, she sat down inside a little nook where she could watch the passing of other patients and nurses doing their daily rounds. Both the mental patients and the nurses were obsessively compulsive. She was as well, she realized, especially when she was working on a case. She opened the folder in her hands while seated on a rickety school chair. Her number one suspect had been Dr. Rooney, until he became the victim.

As for the five hidden patients, she only got to briefly know one of them, Melissa Wilkinson, and the poor woman was now being tried for the murder of Rooney. The others were working for Galton in some kind of dastardly experiment. The Cotton parents were still on her list, and Clara had even thought about Polly being a possible killer, but now that another murder had occurred, under the direction of Francis Galton, she doubted they were involved. The final addition to her list was the lone triplet and supposed lover of Melissa Wilkinson.

Mrs. Packard told her she heard him say something quite interesting after Melissa had stabbed Dr. Rooney, but the court had not believed it related to the defendant's sanity. He said he was a Jew and that he never put the blade inside the knife Melissa used. He said they needed a martyr for their cause. Clara wondered if he could, indeed, be Jewish. Also, who was "they," to which he referred? Was it Galton and the people behind his effort to purify the white race? Somehow, she still believed this killer might be a lone assassin who had a more private motive. Why? Because if the murderer were part of this Eugenics movement, then he or she was killing the very persons this group was trying to protect. The white elite. This case was becoming more complex by the moment.

The *modus operandi*, why this killer was motivated, was the most important factor in Clara's final assessment of a suspect. Isaiah had taught her that motive also applied to criminals who were insane. The mentally ill develop purposes based on imaginary realities, but how was that really any different than what societies invent? Isn't a tribe, a society, or even a government, a type of personal creation invented by someone? This was a fact which frightened the social beings so much and comforted the loners and artists. The artists and the insane intuitively knew that the best power source for creativity came from the white-hot kernel of the lonely person's mind. However, dictators and the elite knew this as well. "Therein," said Shakespeare, "lies the rub."

That brought Clara full circle. She was meeting with the one playing card in their deck who could penetrate the masculine power force now holding the asylum in check. Once they could break that binding evil, the true wisdom of what Mrs. Packard believed to be at the heart of any mind—especially the mind of the completely focused lunatic—could finally make its presence known. The lunatic is cured. The society is healed. The angels gather to help us. We need only do what Alexander Pope prescribed when he said that in order to appreciate great art, one needed to suspend one's disbelief concerning all existence.

In other words, the only Truth was that anything was possible and that change was the only common denominator. Somewhere, the killer was ready to strike again. That event, she knew, was inevitable. The murder of a child and a doctor was lurid. One needed a bold and sophisticated reason to do it. This was no spontaneous act of aggression. Clara hoped her future daughter-in-law, Adeline Quantrill, could help her uncover that solipsistic reason before death reared its ugly head once more.

***

The Women's Section, Stockton State Insane Asylum, Morning, May 1, 1887.

In four different areas of the asylum, the fictional dramas were being created. Each one had been carefully orchestrated by the research team of Francis Galton and the German visitor, Dr. Emil Kraepelin. All the required players were costumed, and the entire asylum seemed to be breathing along with the zealous jealousy and anger being developed, inside each patient, like a purple blossom of Deadly Nightshade.

Within a locked room on the second floor, Sidney Reyes was becoming a passionate damsel who was reacting to scorned love. After days of ardent love trysts with the lovely Filipina, Susanne Johansen had promised her new love a voyage back to Sweden, where they would be allowed to live together without being afraid of being locked up. Sidney believed this would change her life, and she would no longer be afraid of staying inside the cold and tortuous confines of the asylum. She sang to herself, smiled at all who passed her by, or served her needs, and she insisted that the nurses and Francis Galton call her Kitty. She was Susanne's little puss, all ready to curl her lithe young body next to her lover inside the regal family's castle in Stockholm.

Kitty was watching Susanne play the violin, the sweet strains of a Beethoven concerto wafting throughout the cold room. Attached to her identical sister, Matilda sketched them both on her pad, as they watched each other with fervent adoration. Kitty wore her navy blue patient's smock, and the sisters wore matching, green-silk evening gowns. Matilda also took sips from a blue goblet, inlaid with gold, that the new attendant, young Samuel, had brought her. Just as Susanne struck the last notes, she frowned and glanced over at her identical sister, who was, of course, attached to her body at the neck and side.

Susanne stood the varnished instrument up against the red satin Turkish pillow, upon which they had reclined their backs, as the music was being played. Kitty watched her love bring the bow up to her lovely face and point it directly at Kitty's heaving breasts. In her mind's eye, Kitty pictured Susanne as a female matador, ready to drive the short sword into her heart at the conclusion of a bullfight.

All Kitty could see were those ice-blue eyes staring back at her. It had been this way before, on each of the days when they had met. Susanne would always point the bow at her and keep staring, until Kitty's will began to exude out of her body, like a stream of white light, and she was transformed into a mechanical doll in the P. T. Barnum Museum of Oddities. Weaving in place, Kitty was ready to do her love's bidding. Kitty danced nude, she did cartwheels, and she became a bull, rushing full-speed at the red cloth held in front of her face. Kitty Reyes was under Susanne's complete power, and now, today, was the final test.

"Look at me, Kitty. What do you see within my eyes?" The girl could see only the two eyes, and the rest of the room became a foggy blur.

"I see you, my love, for all eternity. You make me come alive once more. I am no longer a girl of the streets. I am just as noble and as artistic as you. I will do anything you ask. Just take me away from here! I cannot stand this prison that keeps us apart." Kitty was panting and flexing her fingers, unconsciously, still swaying from the rhythm of the violin, which had ceased playing. Those eyes were engulfing her entire being, until she felt them encircling her, and her body became an aperture into another dimension. It was a place where she could find solace and peace at long last. Her parents in the Philippines would be so proud of her. She had found her true calling. She was an Angel of True Love, ready to respond to the most wonderful power imaginable.

"I love you so very much, my darling! Just tell me what to do." Kitty writhed on the floor, extending her dark arms toward Susanne's glowing beacons of Aryan hope.

"I am sorry, but my sister has told me she cannot allow you to come back with us."

The words were floating out of her love's pert, crimson lips, but Kitty could not quite fathom their meaning. "She told you what?"

"You cannot be with me, my love. There is only one way. You must strangle her to death. We do not share any vital organs. I can be free of her at last. Don't you see? The doctors will slice away her useless body from me, and I will be yours forever. Please. You must. Get up, and take this scarf from me." Susanne untied the thick, mint-green scarf from around her thin waist and thrust it toward Kitty.

The mesmerized young Filipina stood up, and reached out, taking the scarf into her two hands and wrapping the ends around her fists. As she shuffled toward Matilda, she could hear the woman scream, but the sound gradually faded. It became a weak background noise inside a phantom tune. Kitty could hear only the revolutionary battle hymn of her home country, as she stood behind the screaming blonde beauty, her scarf held taught between her closed fists. The screams melded into the music, until Kitty brought the stretched silk up over Matilda's head and down around her ivory throat. Matilda tried to pull away from her sister, but she was imprisoned as always.

As Kitty twisted the material tighter, she watched Matilda's face gradually flush, and then turn crimson red. Kitty kept glancing, back and forth, between Matilda's wide "O" mouth, her silent scream of asphyxiation, and her lover's dagger-blue eyes.

"Stop! I command you to desist." Susanne was now screaming at Kitty, but the young patient did not cease her strangulation. Only when Matilda's form was slumped over, and the victim's throat was pulling on the skin between their two necks, did Kitty's wide brown eyes begin to relax. But Sidney Reyes continued to hold onto the scarf, as if her freedom were contained inside Matilda's lifeless body, which had previously been compelled by birth to be a millstone anchor. Now Matilda had been miraculously transformed into filial detritus calmly drifting upon an ocean of true love.

***

Angela Thoma was being asked to search for the spirit that was the asylum murderer. Francis Galton had entered the room to tell her what she had to do.

"Angie, I am releasing you into the patient population. Do you remember Mrs. Wilkinson?" The old Englishman pointed to the empty bunk in the middle of the room. She was the only patient in her group of five who was still inside their room on the second floor. The young Filipina had been taken in the early morning. The deranged woman who believed she was sharpshooter Annie Oakley was gone about ten minutes later. Finally, the dreamer named Jessica was escorted out by a young man named Samuel, just before Mr. Galton arrived.

Angela nodded and smiled at her caretaker. The only thing she remembered about Mrs. Wilkinson was that she used to mimic the behaviors of everybody in the room.

"The evil spirit with whom you conversed took over Mrs. Wilkinson's body. She then stabbed Dr. Rooney to death with a knife. She is now in jail facing murder charges. You were correct, Angie. The ghostly presence you heard is now wreaking havoc upon our asylum population. It can enter and possess anybody at any time. This is why I want you to go out into the population and track this entity down."

His eyes were wide with fear, and Angela could sense the foreboding in his voice. If a famous scientist like Mr. Galton believed in her, then she finally must be getting well. Perhaps, if she could find this demon, Mr. Galton might even allow her to return to her family.

"Here. Take this." The Englishman handed Angie a small Derringer pistol. "I am afraid the only way we can stop this demon spirit is to trap it inside a dead body. The released soul of the victim will kill the demon before it is released to heaven. Keep it inside your pocket. Don't show it until you have found the evil spirit, which possesses the poor body of one of our patients."

Angela felt the hard steel of the pistol, and she tucked it inside the pocket of her blue smock. She now believed she was on a mission to rid the asylum of a potential threat. If she was successful, she knew it would mean she would be released to her family.

As she passed by Mr. Galton's body, Angie could feel the heat from it. She knew that her intuitive ability to connect with the spirit world was radiating inside her once more. She felt the same powers she had whenever she searched the cemeteries, the haunted mansions, and the underground crypts with her family. It was if she had become a gigantic magnet that could sense the spirit world's presence.

This was the first time she had been allowed outside the room alone. The crane nurse had taken her to meet the unknown woman who had inspired the mystical awakening inside. She heard that voice of doom. If she could find this voice again, she knew it would be the one Mr. Galton said had possessed Mrs. Wilkinson.

All of her senses were on high alert. She could smell the perfume wafting from one of the wealthy women, who was standing near the stairs that circled from the second floor down to the main level. The woman was tall and gangling in her beautiful red gown, and she was singing an aria from *Aida*.

Angie could feel the pull from downstairs as she stood beside the insane woman. The notes from the woman's full-throated, soprano voice bathed Angie's ears like a lovely waterfall. In her mind, Angie was transforming into the young slave girl from the opera.

It was the fourth act, and she knew she must find the vault wherein the Egyptian court had sentenced her lover, Radamès, to be buried alive. As the woman sang at the top of the stairs, Radamès had refused to renounce her. Angie gently stepped down the stairs, leading her toward the lower depths of the burial vault. She knew that this demon spirit's voice was inside the same tomb where she, Aida, was supposed to die with her true love. Could it be that the same spirit that mourned for Aida and Radamès has also possessed women inside this asylum and made them kill others?

All around her, on the first floor, Angie could see the other slaves, groaning and wailing, the steel shackles on their legs dragging along the wooden, feces-stained floors. The sounds of their agony forced Angie to cover her ears with her hands. She could still search for the demon spirit with her loins, with her breasts, and with her soul.

Angie, in abject fear, lugged her body along the walls, her hands probing for a secret passage. Her ears were on alert for the sound of the demon's voice, and she pressed the right side of her face against the graffiti-adorned surface. The words of the scrawled curse seemed to penetrate into her head. *Let me out of this hell on earth!*

Her eyes were wild, as she shook her auburn tresses in exasperation. No sounds were coming to her yet. She must open her body to the passionate Devil, she must find the vibrations, the odors of extinction and lost love, the monstrous roar, and the touch of death. This voice would finally tell her that she had found the person the demon now possessed. Her freedom could be around this next corner, in another room, down another hallway.

When Angie did find the vault, and the killer's spirit, would she be able to shoot the body that held it? If this demon were possessing a human form, then the only way she could end its power over humanity would be to kill the body of the possessed. The possibility of freedom exalted her being like nothing she had ever felt before. Her fingers encircled the pistol in her pocket, and she took in a deep breath of possible salvation.

***

Earlier . . . the new assistant, who told Katherine Sue Yantis that his name was Samuel, called for her in the asylum room on the second floor. Mrs. Yantis was expecting him, as this was the day she was to rendezvous with the King of Sweden, Oscar II. On the way outside to the firing range, Samuel ushered her into a room near the kitchen.

"Please put these clothes on." Samuel pointed to the buckskin fringed skirt and matching top hanging on a clothes peg next to a barrel of molasses. Kathy quickly changed, with Samuel turning his back, and she was soon wearing the attire she knew well. When she pulled on the long black boots, with spurs, and adorned her curly-blonde head with the cowgirl hat, which was resting on the barrel, her transformation was complete. As sharpshooter Annie Oakley, her authentic identity was at last revealed.

"Mrs. Oakley! I'm so happy you have come." Madeline Olsen, King Oscar's Foreign Secretary, scampered up to Katherine, from out of the shadows of the improvised shooting range, with a Winchester rifle in hand. All four participants were standing between white chalk lines, next to the asylum's vegetable garden, which separated the waving corn stalks and green potato plants, from the rifle range's empty corridor. The shooting path extended 200 yards, ending in a straw-filled, bulls-eye target at the far end.

Katherine accepted the rifle from the secretary and thrust it above her head with both hands. "Thank you. No wind today. That's wonderful weather for my exhibition."

Francis Galton, who was looking at her from the periphery, grasped the elbow of another gentleman, who, to Katherine's limited military knowledge, looked like some sort of naval officer. He had that boat-shaped cap that curled up on the front, and those fancy gilded epaulets, streaming golden spaghetti down his shoulders. He also had a silver banner streaming across his portly chest and a silver sword and scabbard dragging from his waist. They were both heading toward her, so she believed this must be the king.

From the first moment he gazed into her eyes, she could sense his inner lust, pulsing like a sleeping tiger, just beneath his chest. Katherine knew he was going to make a move, but she did not know when. Would he wait for her to show him her marksmanship? No, one would assume not, as he had now wiggled himself over to stand next to her. She could smell the odor of sardines, a brand, which she remembered, was given the name of this horny personage now wagging his gray beard at her: King Oscar.

"How wonderful it is. In this great land, the women can protect themselves against invasion." She watched, as he brought his right hand up to his head, grasped the front of the boat hat, and swiped it upward at first, extended it in a wide arc above his head, and then, simultaneously with his bending torso, he brought that same hat cascading across the soil, until it was swept up, in another wide arc, to his head once more.

The king turned backward toward Mr. Galton and whispered frantically into his ear. Mr. Galton, smiling, stepped toward her and grasped her forearm, gently holding it, between his fingers, as if she were his prized piglet at market.

"The King would very much enjoy speaking to you, in private, before the demonstration. He wants to explain his military philosophy to you concerning snipers. Please, accompany us to my private dining area inside."

Katherine followed the two men, holding the rifle down, beginning to sense a strange presence as she walked. It was as if the asylum were calling her, and it was the first such calling she had experienced. She was going to keep her wits about her, however, as she knew these types could turn a young woman in for any insults made against their noble breeding, either by act, or by word.

"Here we are." Mr. Galton opened the door to the room, and the odor of fresh-brewed tea filled Katherine's nostrils with its steeped grandeur. She remembered mornings with Allan and the children, awakening from pleasant dreams, and her loved ones intently listening to her explain the goal of that day's haunted mansion exploration. "Please, be seated. I shall pour for you both and then be on my way."

She was seated within touching distance, and his knees were aligned toward hers, much the way she suspected a torpedo would be fixed upon a target at sea. The discomfort she felt was not unlike facing a satyr in the Elysian Fields. You knew it was going to happen, but you still believed there might be an escape plan.

"Please, won't you stand up und show me how you address a target?" The pressure inside her was mounting. Katherine's body was radiating its sonorous vibrations outward, attempting to gauge the threat of this man. However, she did as he asked and stood up.

She brought the rifle up, from parade rest, to order arms. Katherine could feel the varnished butt of the rifle's stock, and her left hand moved up to grasp the upper stock beneath the rifle's muzzle. She then moved the rifle upward, toward her cheek, to point, as a standing unit, toward the wall on the other side of the room.

She placed her right eye socket against the black scope and looked into it. From the corner of her eye, she saw that the king had disrobed. He was now standing there, his manhood exposed, smiling back at her with unabashed ardor. At least, the amorous intent was certainly making something stir beneath his stomach.

"Did you know that English composer, Edward Elgar, composed a suite for the lunatics at the Worcester County Lunatic Asylum? Everyone. The staff, the patients, they all felt wonderful after hearing the music. You are like that music to me, my sweet lady. Can't you see? My passion for you holds no bounds! Jawohl!"

Katherine was now looking at the king through the scope of the rifle. All she could hear, however, was the voice that had penetrated her consciousness again. It was the same voice that told her she was Annie Oakley and not that insane woman, Katherine Yantis. When it spoke, she could feel the tribulation it caused, up and down her spine. When she saw this man's penis, it became an onerous object, one that would keep her from her family. It took on the shape of a dagger, a weapon, and she gritted her teeth until they chattered from rage.

"What are you doing, my cooing little dove? We are playing a joke. That gun is not loaded. Come. Make an old man happy. I will reward you with anything you want. I am a doctor. A psychiatrist. I can have you released at once from this asylum. Do you want that?"

She now knew for certain. This man did not have a Swedish accent. It was German. He was an impostor and a rapist. Katherine's forefinger began to twitch around the trigger. As her gaze wandered around his body, from his balding head, to his graying chest hair, and down to that beacon of male inferiority, she heard the voice again. *Shoot him! He will not release you. He is the keeper of the crypt. Where the idiots are imprisoned. Spittle, feces, wails. Shoot him!*

After she pulled the trigger, she sniffed at the odor of the cordite, permeating the air around her, from the bullet's discharge. Her aim was off. Was it an omen of her crumbling persona? She could feel her mind splitting off, becoming other minds, other women, other emotions. A lost world, where an old man did not bleed from his arm, clutching his admiral's sleeve as if he were in control of his pulsing heart. No. He was not in control of any heart. She would always keep that control, until she, one future day, lost it, to unforeseen circumstances.

***

Earlier . . . The handsome young man she dreamed had a name. It was Samuel. He was there to escort her to meet with the other young dreamer named Polly Bedford. But first, he told her she needed to take a magic injection to allow her to see the dreams Polly created. Sarah said we all dream our own versions of reality, so why shouldn't she accept this girl's version?

After Samuel injected her, Jessica began to feel much more relaxed. When he took her hands into his, she almost floated as she stood up. She became very conscious of her eyelids. Blinking became a magical window shade to a new reality, which was burgeoning around her, second by second. The past disappeared, the future did not exist. Only the blinking moment was important, and Jessica followed Samuel out the door and into the asylum.

"Did you know, Samuel, that books are just dreams that we read. The dreamer has written their own dream down, and we can choose to view it, or not, it makes no difference, really. Only your own dream matters."

As she followed Samuel down the winding stairway, Jessica was watching her new dream world enfold around her. She decided Samuel was dreamt by her to keep her company. He seemed kind and attentive, unlike the other women around her who were preoccupied with their own dreams. Some of them were even crying and making nervous movements with their hands, faces, and legs. There was one taking off all her clothing. The other woman, in all-white, was chasing her down, picking up the articles of clothing as she ran after her.

"Will we be there soon, Samuel? These phantoms are frightening me."

"Here we are, Jessica. This is Miss Polly Bedford. Like you, she comes from San Francisco's wealthy area. Her parents had to let her rest here, just as yours allowed you to stay for your own health. Polly? This is Jessica Adkins."

Samuel guided Jessica to the chair next to where Polly was seated on the bed. Polly was drawing again on her pad. She looked up and smiled at Jessica. Dreamers meeting for the first time. Jessica was pleased.

"Why did you kill my friend?" The question was absurd. Jessica knew nothing about this girl's friends.

"I don't understand what you mean. I have never met you before now. I do not know your friends." Jessica's heart began to thrum inside her chest. She should quickly dream this girl back into some semblance of order. She was acting like another Dennis Leary.

"Deidra Watkins kept me safe. She knew how to play Mental Metamorphosis. You are from those others. The ones who would keep me from preventing their atrocities and murders. Get away from me! I want Deidra! I want Deidra!"

Jessica covered her ears. This was not her dream. This girl was insane. Her voice was ripping apart the veil between their separate dreams. Her evil nature was attacking Jessica's sedate reality. Jessica began to sweat, and she picked up a blanket from the nearby bunk and bit into it to stop a scream from erupting. She then realized it was her dream, and this girl was not meant to be inside her world. She was an intruder who needed to be silenced!

"Stop it, Jessica! You're smothering her!" Jessica felt the delicious strength of her arms holding down this girl's body on the mattress. She was squirming and flailing, but to no avail. Soon, she would disappear from Jessica's dream and vanish into her own nightmare.

Jessica Adkins was being carried, and as she looked back at the girl named Polly, who was now sitting up and breathing in deep gasps, her mind became fogged over with a peculiar notion. Dreams were forever meant to be on a collision course, and there was nothing she could do to stop it.

CHAPTER 11: A KILLER ON THE LOOSE

The Women's Section, Jacob's Ladder, Stockton State Insane Asylum, Morning, May 1, 1887.

Clara trusted having her beau, Captain Isaiah Lees, standing guard at the bottom of Jacob's Ladder. However, when she examined their history a bit more closely, it was she who had rescued Isaiah and his partner, Eduard Vanderheiden, from an explosive situation in Chinatown. Nonetheless, the previous evening, when she had slipped out of her bunk and rendezvoused with Isaiah at this same location, his attentive display of affection smoldered her common sense out of the picture, and all she could see was his smiling face above her.

Adeline was up there in the heavens, waiting, and Clara swept the small girl into her arms and swung her about the room. It must have been the residual passion remaining from the night before. When she placed her back on Earth, Clara knew, because she was not returning her smile, that Adeline was full of important information. She could see that the girl's cheeks were flushed, even under the poor lighting, and she was breathing hard.

"Oh my, Mrs. Foltz. Something is happening today, but I have no specific locations to give you. I would not know this much but for my inter-communications with your son and my reading of Mr. Galton's mind."

Clara draped her arm around Adeline's shoulder. "Calm yourself. This is most important to our investigation. My Samuel. Is he inside the asylum? Since when?"

"Since yesterday. He told me Mr. Galton was blackmailing him. Unless Samuel did what Galton instructed, evidence would be given to the police that Polly Bedford testified seeing Samuel murder little Winnie Cotton. Galton also told Samuel that unless he complied I would never get a recommendation for the work I've done here. I don't care about that! I just want to save Samuel. I hope you can help us."

After escorting Adeline over to the two stuffed chairs, in the corner near a wall gaslight, she sat facing her. Clara wanted her mind to be as focused as possible. There could be no untoward mental errors made from this moment forward.

"Have you spoken to Bertha? Where is she and what does she know?" Clara placed her right hand on Adeline's knee and squeezed. "We have suspects now, but I want to add more information to what I have."

Adeline looked toward the ceiling, just the way she approached her channeling posture when contacting the spirit world as a medium. "She is inside a locked room on the second floor. Room 248. Only Samuel has been allowed to talk to her in his duties as Mr. Galton's personal attendant. He told me she was privy to a plan by Galton to use all five of the secret patients in his research experiments concerning heredity. He knows not about what each experiment consists. It is happening today. He does know that."

Clara squeezed Adeline's knee harder. "How does he know it's today?"

"Because he will play an integral part in what will occur."

"Be more specific. This may be the turning point in our investigation. Think carefully, and get every word correct."

"I'll try my best. Although, I do not have your eloquence or emotion. Samuel is going to escort three of these five female patients to their destinies. He did not know their names, nor how to match each name to the specific experiment. Bertha, however, did know the names and what each was going to be doing in the experiment. I was able to channel his conversation with the late Dr. Rooney while Bertha was listening inside the dumbwaiter. Samuel could not match these women to what he had been instructed to do."

"Just give me what you know. You have a photographic memory, so I know it will be quite accurate. Perhaps we can make sense of these details later."

"All right. The first woman's name is Melissa Wilkinson, but you probably know that. Of course, she is now up on murder charges. The second patient is the young Filipina, Sidney Reyes." Adeline's brow furrowed, and she stared off into space. She was channeling her memory from that moment in Francis Galton's mind. "My conjoined twins have established the necessary lustful attraction, and Susanne tells me she should soon have complete control over this Filipina's mind. In phase two, I want to see if that control can lead to murder."

"My God! You're giving me Galton's exact words." Clara was frantically scribbling notes with a stubby pencil upon her small pad. "And the third?"

"Mrs. Angela Thoma. I had my psychic assistant, Miss Quantrill, impersonate a voice from the dead to arouse this woman's sick psyche into a state of suspended disbelief. She can now easily be manipulated by this means, and the same test will be applied to her."

"How interesting. Go on." Clara was rapidly calculating possibilities as she listened. She was torn between hearing Adeline out and rushing downstairs to stop what was most certainly beginning to happen at that very moment.

"The fourth and fifth experiments are being done to Mrs. Katherine Yantis and teenager Jessica Adkins. Yantis believes she is Annie Oakley, the famous sharpshooter. Galton says his Swedish solo triplet, Deandra, shall impersonate King Oscar's personal secretary. At the rendezvous, Mrs. Yantis will be tested to determine if she can kill with a Winchester repeating rifle. As for Miss Adkins, this girl has agreed to meet with Polly Bedford. Galton has a drug he's been testing, and he shall use it on the Adkins girl. With her present psychosis, they can see how far they can extend her dream world. Hopefully, she will enter into homicidal tendencies."

Clara was flummoxed by this challenge. She knew it would be next to impossible to find out the locations of all these so-called experiments at this late hour. All she could hope to do would be to perhaps meet one of the participants during a wild goose chase. Her Samuel was her immediate concern. She knew he was not averse to danger. He had proved that at the Winchester house in San Jose, the year before, when he charged down into the basement to stop the mercury poisoning from happening. Was he now playing along with Galton and company in order to spy for her? That sounded like him.

"Adeline. I want you to find Samuel. He knows where his sister is, and we need to get her out of that room. I want to find out where he was today and what happened. I believe it may be the last chance we have of finding the killer. I'm also sending my team out to possibly disrupt this day's events." Clara hugged the girl tightly.

"You've been doing a wonderful job. We now need to move fast, so be on your way."

The older woman watched the girl dart over to the ladder stairs, reach down, and knock on the trap door three times. This was the signal to Isaiah to let her out. "Oh, and Adeline. I need to tell you one more thing."

"Yes, Mrs. Foltz?" The girl turned toward the voice.

"Don't let Galton read your mind. If he discovers what you know, he will become very suspicious. You don't need to end up in isolation, or, even worse."

"Don't worry. Mum's the word." Clara could see Adeline bring her right hand up to her closed lips and make a twisting motion, pursing her lips tightly together.

As Adeline disappeared down the Jacob's Ladder, Clara glanced around the place where she had made love the night before. Those stacks of rice in burlap bags, where she had reclined, Isaiah towering over her. The long shelf of spices where they had thrown their clothing in a mad rush to become one. She was also picturing what could happen to her children, including her newly adopted daughter, Adeline Quantrill. If Galton and his group were as powerful as she now believed them to be, they might be able to arrest her two children and Adeline, and when they uncovered the fact that they were spying for her and her committee, her entire career as a lawyer and detective would be in jeopardy.

The only chance they had would be to find the killer before he or she murdered again. This would make their efforts, even their spying, more acceptable to the public and to the authorities in the State of California. Clara had already begun a file listing the irregularities during the insanity hearing and the questionable methods being used at the asylum. Now they needed to put the pressure on before their committee's methods were discovered. It seemed she were hoping for the worst possible result, but, in effect, it was the only result that could save them.

***

The Women's Section, Stockton State Insane Asylum, Morning, May 1, 1887.

It was the job of the strong to protect the weak. This was the opposite of what was actually happening. The strong were using the poor, the insane, and the wretched of the Earth in order to establish a dictatorship above them. The wealthy, the strong, and the bigoteds were all conspiring to collect all the riches of the world and use this wealth against them.

Today was the day she had been waiting for. Satan had changed into His original form: The Redeemer Angel for All of the Earth's Downtrodden. As she lifted the mattress, she could picture it all playing out in her mind. Experiments to prove humans were nothing more than victims of their own heredity. Satan had spoken to her about Francis Galton and his work.

She must stop this madness before it took over the consciousness of the public. If Galton succeeded, many more innocents would be locked up, the keys thrown away, and never again would freedom be the vanguard for the future. Only oppression, wars, and misogyny would be accepted to stop the tide of immigrants, hungering for opportunity, needing a chance to start over, wanting to live a life away from hatred and fear. Instead, they would be sailing into a country of madness and destruction!

As she chose the first tool, the poison, she remembered how she had succeeding the time before, with the blade. Satan took it from her in a regal ceremony, in the darkness, as she stood naked and held it out to Him. She wandered while the others slept.

Even a madhouse has a skeleton key. Why would it not? It was very appropriate and kind of the lazy superintendent, Dr. Alfred Rooney. He kept it inside his office, and she had, one day, heard one of the nurses tell another nurse that she could get the drugs by using that key. It opened all the rooms inside the asylum! It was inside a drawer in the wall behind the picture of Jewish Governor Washington Bartlett. Rooney did not bother to lock it, as he was also receiving a share of the proceeds from these clandestine and profitable business transactions. The nurses and attendants who were making money selling drugs to the crazy rich women upstairs called that drawer the "Jewish hideaway."

She had also read about the plans of the experiments by using this key. Again, in the night, she read about the five experiments being planned, written on a document inside a folder on Rooney's desk. Satan had laughed gleefully when she told Him.

The entire asylum was coming alive at last. All the dead souls were being redeemed, and she could feel their jovial presence all around her, as she strolled down the halls, in the evenings. The chill that dispersed and made each room as cold as ice. This icy breathing was the anger from these souls. As every authentic Spiritualist understood: on Earth, Hell was its opposite. Heat was cold. Death was life. Insanity was sane.

Satan watched it all happen, and He told her about it later. The blade was inserted. The poison was administered. The guns were loaded with real bullets. And the hallucinogen was added to the morphine, at the last moment.

Now she could provide her Master with his tools at her leisure. She had the key, she had collected the tools, and she had the powerful will that Galton wished he had. As Satan once said in Milton's grand masterpiece, *Paradise Lost*, "For who can yet believe, though after loss, that all these puissant legions whose exile hath emptied Heav'n shall fail to re-ascend, self-raised, and repossess their native seat?"

The weak shall inherit the Earth, with the help of its grand, original Master, forever changed, forever the Redeemer of Mankind!

***

The Women's Section, First Floor, Stockton State Insane Asylum, Afternoon, May 2, 1887.

After the murder of Matilda Johansen, the wounding of Dr. Emil Kraepelin, and the attempted murder of Polly Bedford, the police were notified by Captain Isaiah Lees. However, in a strange twist of fate, Governor Bartlett intervened, and he gave a direct order to put the Stockton State Insane Asylum on lock-down, until further notice. Isaiah was named in the Western Union telegram as the "official investigator" on the scene, and so he now had privileges that the committee had not been privy to before.

Lees could release any person being held in confinement, which meant Bertha May and Samuel were free to be interviewed, and they had been, and he could also question any staff member, including Francis Galton and his research group. Also, all of Galton's four research patients, and the remaining identical triplets, who had been present at the crime scenes, were now confined inside a locked room for questioning.

Captain Lees had assembled the key officials of the asylum inside the main dining room. Even though that meant the patients were being left unsupervised by doctors, Lees believed it to be prudent at the moment to have "all hands on deck," so to speak, to discuss possible preventative measures that could be taken.

Clara was in full agreement, as she now had enough information at her disposal to re-arrange her list of suspects and begin to narrow their priority. It was a matter of life and death, she believed. Unless Lees established a way to prevent another murder, the entire facility would be a free and open hunting ground for this killer to strike again.

At the main physicians' table, Clara sat next to Captain Lees. To her left, down the line, were Dr. Andrew McFarland, then his granddaughter, Anne, followed by Ah Toy, Elizabeth Packard, and attorney Laura Gordon. To the left of Isaiah Lees were the leading staff members of the asylum, Francis Galton, Dr. Kraepelin, Adeline Quantrill, and Samuel Cortland Foltz. The rest of the table included the four staff physicians and the head nurse, Mrs. Sarah Patterson.

Captain Lees stood up at his seat, looked up and down the table at his audience, and cleared his throat. "Thank you for coming, ladies and gentlemen. As this is an emergency, I want to quickly go over what has happened, and what measures must be taken to ensure there are no more murders committed on these premises. I have been given direct authority by the governor to take steps necessary to ensure the safety of lives, and this is where I must begin. The life of Miss Matilda Johansen has been taken, and her sister, Susanne, is now in surgery, at the Stockton City Hospital, to remove Matilda's corpse from Susanne's body. It is a dangerous procedure, and we hope to have good news in due time. As you can see, Dr. Kraepelin has been patched-up and is doing well, as the bullet passed through his bicep, and the bleeding was stopped in time."

"I want to thank the doctors for that. They saved my life," Dr. Kraepelin said, raising his left hand and pointing to his bandaged right arm.

"Now I want to discuss how we can stop this killer. Clara and I believe he or she is inside the asylum and will strike again. In order to plan a strategy, however, we have several unanswered questions for you. The first is to Mr. Galton. And I want the truth. Did you supply any of your staff with lethal weapons and poisons?"

Francis Galton stood up. His face was beet-red. "Never! My experiments were devised to simulate violence, not realize it. Somebody intervened to replace my harmless weapons with real ones. It began with Mrs. Wilkinson's blade, and it ended with the shooting of my colleague."

"At this point, we are not investigating possible corruption as a committee. We are trying to prevent another murder. Any one of us could become a target, and I want Clara to explain why." Isaiah turned to her, and Clara stood up.

"Thank you, Captain Lees. In order to clear the decks, we must have complete honesty from this point forward. I must be frank. I wanted to expose corruption inside this facility. In point of fact, the murder of Winnifred Cotton was of peripheral importance. Since I knew Francis Galton had special privacy given to him by the governor and Leland Stanford, to conduct research, I needed some way to discover what you were doing. My daughter, Bertha May Foltz, posed as patient Deidra Watkins. In addition, my son, Samuel, and his love, Adeline Quantrill, are also spying for me."

Clara thought Francis Galton would erupt, but he did not. Instead, he smiled, and said, "I knew that. As you may be aware, I have precognizant abilities, as does your Adeline." Galton looked down the row at his blonde-haired assistant and smiled. Adeline did not return the grin. "I am now being honest with you," Galton continued. "I do not want my abilities to become public, however, as it would not be favorable to my academic and research standing. However, as we are all possible murder targets, I want to help as much as I can."

Captain Lees interjected, "I must correct you. You are also suspects. Until I get more answers, everyone on your side of the table, including your patients and research assistants, are under suspicion. The main reason the governor has shut us down is because he wants us to ferret out the killer."

Galton laughed. "Oh really now? And how do you plan to do that, pray tell? Read our minds? Or perhaps you can feel our skulls to ascertain the phrenological basis of our inherited criminality?"

The other doctors at the table also joined in on the laughter.

Clara jumped when Isaiah brought his fist down hard on the table. "Silence! Let Clara speak!"

"You, Mr. Galton, may have telepathic ability, but Adeline, your young assistant can also commune with the spirit world. I am a liberal-minded woman. I am open to all possibilities. There is a real possibility that these circumstances may have a supernatural motive. I am certain you are all aware that before the science of mental health, most societies believed the inflicted person was possessed by some kind of demonic presence, or evil sprit, if you will." Clara looked over at Ah Toy. "Isn't that true, Ah Toy?"

"My culture, and many other cultures around the world, believe this to be the case, even today." Ah Toy smiled. "Of course, exorcism requires the confinement of the person whose body has become possessed."

Again, the physicians, led by Galton, laughed.

"We are not going to go on an evil spirit chase, now are we, Mrs. Foltz? If so, then I shall have to wear my crucifix." Galton flicked his right hand at his shirt collar.

"In order to separate the phenomenal from the practical, we want to investigate further into your experiments, which took place yesterday, the day of the murder. First, I want Dr. McFarland to analyze the contents of the goblet which was seized as evidence. We need to establish the proximate cause of death. If there were a poison in Matilda's drink, then she may have died before she was strangled to death by Sidney Reyes."

"I shall do that as soon as we adjourn, Mrs. Foltz," Dr. McFarland said.

"Next, I want you to also analyze what was in the injection given to Jessica Adkins before she visited patient Polly Bedford. Perhaps Anne can do that?"

Anne McFarland raised her hand. "By all means! My grandfather and I will have the results to you shortly."

Clara smiled. "Good. As for the exchange of weapons in the experiments with Melissa Wilkinson and Katherine Yantis, we are searching for other weapons and ammunition inside this asylum that can match the ones used during the experiments. Finally, we have the fifth, and final experiment. Mrs. Angela Thoma was one of your patients, correct, Mr. Galton?"

"Yes, she was," Galton said.

"Where is she at this moment? We have been unable to locate her, and we've searched everywhere in this building and even outside. Also, we know that she was to also attempt a murder, as Adeline informed us of that fact. How was Mrs. Thoma going to accomplish this?"

"Very well. I gave her a Derringer. It was, of course, unloaded. I simply wanted her to attempt to kill a person she believed was possessed by a demon. I wanted to prove that hereditary homicidal impulses were linked to superstitious beliefs," Galton said.

Clara was furious. "And so, now that we understand there have been at least two purposeful switches made to arm weapons, there is presently a mad woman roaming somewhere inside this asylum with, most likely, another loaded gun?"

Galton was indignant. "I'm afraid I don't know who could have made those switches, and I am also unable to keep track of the hundreds of patients living here. I have been contracted by the State and Leland Stanford to do research, not to be an asylum supervisor. The former superintendent has been murdered, as you know, and there has been no replacement made."

"Your research, as of this moment, has been suspended, Mr. Galton. We now know, thanks to your staff, that there is an armory, of sorts, in one of the store rooms, and we shall be searching it for possible bullets that could have been used in the experiments. Until we complete our investigations, nobody will be armed." Clara's voice was adamant.

"What? Are we supposed to roam these halls without any bloody protection?" Galton and the asylum doctors stood up, and they were all livid.

"Captain Lees will be the only person with a weapon. The only weapon we know that is out there is the single-shot Derringer in the possession of a madwoman, Mrs. Angela Thoma. Let's be on the look-out for her, shall we? I also need a key to the weapon storage room. Since each door seems to have its own key, is there perhaps a master key Captain Lees can use?"

Clara watched as the head nurse, Sarah Patterson, raised her hand. She was frowning, and Clara nodded at her to speak.

"I'm afraid it's been stolen. It was kept in a wall drawer in Dr. Rooney's office. Behind the painting of Governor Bartlett. I went to retrieve it this morning, and it was gone."

It was Isaiah's turn to be livid. "What? You kept a skeleton key for an insane asylum? Now, not only might we have a murderer on the loose, he or she could also have access to every room in this house!"

Clara turned to her beau, and her voice was placating. "This answers a lot of our other questions, Captain Lees. We need to speak of it in private."

Captain Lees gravely nodded, but he was still glowering at the head nurse.

As Clara watched the asylum staff file out of the dining room, she ran over to Adeline and grabbed her arm. "Adeline, stay a moment. You, too, Samuel. I want to ask you some more questions. I may be able to narrow my suspect list down to two people, if I can get the correct answers from you."

CHAPTER 12: EVERYONE CAN DANCE

The Women's Section, First Floor, Stockton State Insane Asylum, Afternoon, May 2, 1887.

Clara wanted to ask Adeline and Samuel about two events they must have witnessed. She also needed to question Adeline's vast mental reserve of knowledge. First, however, she hugged them both closely to her. She then sighed.

"You have been magnificent! I wanted you to know that before I ask you these questions. I wish Bertha were also with us, but you can tell her. First, I know that Samuel accompanied Miss Jessica Adkins when she visited Polly Bedford on the first floor. What exactly happened when you were there?"

Her twenty-year-old was visibly concerned. He kept running his hand through his dark hair as he spoke. "They seemed to be getting on quite well, at first. Then, for no reason that I could ascertain, Miss Adkins picked up a blanket from one of the bunkbeds and began to smother the young girl. I had to pull her off, or she would have, most certainly, killed Polly."

"Can you remember what they said? It's very important. We'll soon be getting the analysis of what was in that injection you gave her, but I need to know exactly what might have been stated to instigate the violence." Clara reached out and held Samuel's hand.

Samuel's eyebrows furrowed in concentration. "Let me see. Just before Jessica attacked her, Polly accused her of killing somebody. Her friend. But she didn't say who it was."

"Perhaps she meant Winnifred Cotton. Go on." Clara's mind was working, making connections.

"Polly then told Jessica she wanted Bertha, or Deidra, to come back to her. She said Deidra played a game with her. I think she called it Mental or Mind Metamorphosis. When she began to scream Deidra's name, Jessica grabbed the blanket and attempted to smother her."

"Thank you. Now, Adeline. How did Polly identify the murderer when she spoke with Bertha that day when we were back at the Hopkins' mansion in San Francisco? What exactly did she call him?" Clara wanted to pinpoint the language used.

Adeline stared off into space. She was channeling the past. "Bertha first stated this, 'It's time to use your mental metamorphosis. If you become his mind, as he is in the act of killing a girl, tell me what you would be thinking and how you could change the reality of murder into something worthwhile and even redeeming.' Polly told her the killer of Winnie Cotton was a demon of some kind. And then, when Bertha had chided her for believing in ghosts, Polly described him thus, 'You would pray there were ghosts, because no human could stop him. When he turned toward me, I saw his face was a continually changing compendium of different people's faces. I fantasized under stress about the possible reasons for this to occur. I may have eaten something horrid or poisonous. Or, supernaturally, I may have been put under a curse of some kind. Could I be an enemy of the government, who needed to be disposed of?' Is this what you wanted, Mrs. Foltz?"

Clara smiled. "Yes. That's exactly what I wanted. You may both leave. Samuel, I want you to hunt for Polly Bedford. Bring the girl to me at once. Also, at five tonight, after dinner, I want you and Bertha to stay with us inside our room. I'll have the staff put in two more bunk beds. I then shall explain to everyone what I believe we now face."

After the children left, Clara summarized what she now had in the way of suspects. Her list had begun with ten. Now, after all that had occurred, she believed there were only two possible murderers. The Cotton parents were out of the picture, as was Leland Stanford. However, since the Cottons were the elite class that Stanford and Galton had vowed to protect, the murder of little Winnifred demonstrated that the murderer was trying to penetrate that exclusive club of genetically superior white families. The killing of the very elite Scandinavian socialite, Matilda Johansen, and the murder of wealthy Superintendent and Eugenics supporter, Dr. Alfred Rooney, proved her theory. Then, when Dr. Emil Kraepelin was shot, and Polly Bedford herself became a target, Clara realized how insane the girl really was.

Polly Bedford believed she was in league with some kind of superior, supernatural entity who would save humanity from those who enslaved lunatics and women. She had staged her own murder, at the hands of Jessica Adkins, in order to trick Clara and her committee. And, now that Clara knew what Polly Bedford had stated, to Bertha, about what the killer looked like, the attorney had reached her conclusion.

The only suspect of the five of Galton's patients who tried to murder Polly Bedford was Jessica Adkins. Now that Clara knew the insane Jessica had been drugged, that meant she was no longer a suspect. Jessica, like the other patients and assistants of Francis Galton, did not have access to the rest of the asylum, especially the downstairs and main storerooms where the armaments and pharmaceuticals were stored. That meant that Claiborne Falcon, whom she suspected might be a Jew, was not a suspect. He and the other identical triplets had not come downstairs at any time. Superintendent Rooney's office was downstairs, and that was the location of the missing master key. That left twelve-year-old daughter of their wealthy neighbors, Polly Bedford.

Clara knew that Polly had described the killer as someone who had tried to cut Winnifred Cotton with a blade of some kind. This person was trying to stop the girl from breeding, so that meant sterilization. At first, Clara had thought Francis Galton and Leland Stanford might be behind such activities. Now, however, Clara understood the logic behind the mad girl's statement. She was attempting to show that the elite were not superior. No, in fact, Polly Bedford, the insane child genius, was trying to discredit and stop Stanford and Galton's effort to incarcerate lunatics by showing that the elite class could be just as vulnerable to evil as any other class.

Clara knew she could not allow this information to be disseminated to the press or even to Polly's family. She also believed that Polly was going to strike again, as she now had the master key to all of the rooms and hidden rooms of this asylum. Clara needed to explain what she believed was going to occur tonight inside the asylum, but she first wanted to hear from Samuel.

As she looked around the vacant dining room, Clara could sense the same ominous presence she had felt on the first day she crossed the threshold of the Stockton State Insane Asylum and heard a woman scream within. When her son burst through the door, she knew.

"She's missing, mother. Polly Bedford cannot be found anywhere," he told her, his chest heaving from running around the asylum.

The Women's Section, First Floor, Stockton State Insane Asylum, Evening, May 2, 1887.

Clara was inside the committee's private room seated on the lower bed. She wanted to tell her group what had occurred and how they needed to proceed. Nobody was missing, thank God, and the three youngsters were also there from upstairs. Two new bunkbeds had been brought in for their new residents, and, except for Samuel, Adeline, and Captain Lees, they all wore their patient's attire of navy blue pullovers. Each person was seated on his or her bed, like children awaiting a bedtime story. Clara knew this would be a grim fairy-tale, and she wanted to unravel it as carefully and logically as she could.

Dr. McFarland and his granddaughter, Anne, had accomplished their analysis of the contents in the goblet and syringe, and Clara's suspicions had been confirmed. She now needed to report the news to her comrades.

"I am very sad to report to you that our killer is a child. Miss Polly Bedford is the only suspect who could have accomplished the switches necessary to cause the violence we now know occurred. The master key to all the rooms has been stolen by her, and this was how she was able to procure the bullets, poison, and drugs she needed." Clara nodded at Samuel, who was on the upper bed near the wall. "Samuel, you became her delivery boy for these items. Matilda Johansen drank from the goblet of the strychnine-poisoned tea that killed her before Sidney Reyes attempted to strangle her. Mrs. Yantis's Winchester was also armed when you escorted her outside to the shooting range, resulting in the wounding of Dr. Kraepelin. Our other missing patient, Angela Thoma, we must assume, also has a loaded Derringer at her disposal. Finally, the injection you gave to Jessica Adkins was a concoction of both morphine and a hallucinogen. Dr. McFarland, would you like to explain the source of the administered drug and what you both have discovered?"

Dr. McFarland was on the bottom bunk and his granddaughter on the top. "When I analyzed the residual contents of the goblet given to Matilda Johansen by Samuel, I discovered that it had also been laced with the hallucinogen of peyote. Working upon an intuitive guess, I learned from Anne that the injection given to Miss Adkins consisted of liquid peyote as well, in its entirety."

Anne McFarland nodded, "Indeed it was. We were so surprised by this that we decided to check this morning's rounds of injections to be made to patients in the Women's Section. Lo and behold, every woman had been given an injection of liquid peyote. This had not occurred on previous days, so we wanted to tell you about it."

Clara was also surprised. "Do you think our Polly did this? If so, why?"

Dr. McFarland cleared his throat. "You are the detective. I do know how this drug has been used by our Native American tribes. For example, just recently, it was discovered that the nations of the Kiowa and Cherokee began using peyote in a ritualized dance called The Ghost Dance. When the European immigrants began killing their members by the thousands, the tribal medicine men, or shamans, believed their hallucinogenic dance would stop the aggression and give their warriors special powers of bravery against the maniacal onslaught of the invaders. And thus, all of the braves would also ingest the drug before going out to battle. As we know, it did not stop the slaughter."

Clara suddenly noticed that Mrs. Packard was not sitting on her reinforced bed. "Has anybody seen Liz?"

"She told me she wanted to search for Polly Bedford," Adeline said. "She said she believed she knew how to cure the child's type of mental illness. I thought you knew."

"I did not! I told all of you in the dining room this morning that I wanted you here at five. She must have not had her hearing trumpet. We now have an old woman out there in an asylum filled with hallucinating mental patients. We must find her before she gets harmed." Clara stood up and rushed over to the door. It was still locked. "Who has the key, dammit?"

Captain Lees walked over to her. He held out the room key. "As the only security officer in this establishment, I have procured all the keys. Except, of course, for the one that matters. The master key, which is now in the possession of our young murderer."

"I don't care about that now." Clara took the key and inserted it into the lock, turned it, and then pushed down on the door latch. As soon as she swung the door open, an ominous sound filled her with dread. Outside the asylum, a raging storm was beginning, and Clara could see the flash of lightening criss-cross along the wall in a dazzling and jagged display of white light, followed immediately by a tremendous boom of thunder, which shook the asylum's foundations. At the other end of the hall, she spotted the ghostly figure of a tall woman in an evening gown. She was singing an operatic aria. Clara listened carefully. It was from *Aida*. The wealthy patients from upstairs were now downstairs.

All the others joined Clara out in the hallway. The rain was pelting the tall windows in sheets, and the lightening and thunder continued, as they walked down the passageway. Isaiah had taken out his Colt-45 revolver, and he was now in front of Clara, leading the way. The gaslights flickered on the walls, and then they went out, leaving the lightening as their sole source of illumination. Clara felt a hand at her elbow. She turned, and it was her best friend, Ah Toy.

"Please. Talk to Adeline. I have some precognition, and I feel we are entering into a confrontation we are powerless to stop."

As they made their way slowly down the hallway, the lightening continuing to flash every few minutes, Clara saw other well-dressed women appearing from rooms along the way, their eyes glowing, as if the lightening had ignited something within their minds. The opera singer kept up her aria, and as they all entered the large dining room, what they saw inside was out of some macabre nightmare.

All the tables had been pushed against the walls. The piano was where the doctors' table used to be, and, between flashes of lightening, Clara observed all the twirling couples out in the middle of the floor. The piano player was one of the well-dressed wealthy women, and she was playing a robust waltz by Strauss. Hundreds of the insane asylum women were dancing, as a group of them had raided the men's section of the asylum and had brought over some dancing hostages. It was clear to Clara, however, that they were all enjoying themselves. The identical Falcone triplets were dancing also, doing pirouettes with wealthy lunatics from the second floor.

The entire staff of seventeen nurses and four doctors were tied-up with rope and gagged with kerchiefs, squirming like worms, piled up in the corner. However, on the riser, where the doctors' table used to sit, Clara saw Francis Galton and his German cohort, Dr. Emil Kraepelin. They were also tied up, standing, their hands behind their backs, but they had no gags. The other five women on the riser each had a weapon. Two of them Clara knew. Liz Packard and Polly Bedford. Mrs. Packard held her ear trumpet against her ear, the better to listen to the music, Clara supposed.

The other three must have been the patients who served as the victims of Francis Galton's experiments. One woman, dressed in fringed buckskin and wearing a cowgirl hat, was pointing her rifle at Mr. Galton. Another female, a shorter Asian, was holding a pistol against Dr. Kraepelin's side. The last woman, the teenager, Jessica Adkins, also had a pistol, which was pointed directly at Captain Lees.

Clara stepped forward. "Stop playing that music!" Clara shouted. The piano player stopped playing, and the dancers became immobile out on the floor, turning as one toward the main riser. There was a dead silence in the dining room as they all listened. "Liz, what happened here? You do realize that Polly is the murderer, don't you?"

The former Illinois asylum resident stepped forward. She looked comfortable in her asylum uniform. She then turned toward Galton and the German and pointed her right index finger at them. "I know you must be an excellent detective, Clara, but I beg to differ. These two men are the murderers. Not only are they responsible for the deaths of Winnifred Cotton, Dr. Rooney, and the attempted murder of one of their own, Dr. Kraepelin, they were also planning to blame it all on Polly Bedford."

"This woman belongs in this madhouse! She instigated this rebellion, and if you don't believe me, ask the doctors and nurses who are gagged over there." It was Francis Galton's turn to point over to the writhing bodies in the corner.

"I must say, Liz, you need to offer us a bit more evidence than finger-pointing. What did you find out?" Clara walked closer to the riser, but when the cowgirl pointed her Winchester and cocked it, she stopped. "Your proof had better be quite good."

"While you were all doing your snooping, I spent each day talking to Polly, and I soon realized she was not suffering from a normal type of depression or obsessive fantasy. I had seen this type of behavior before, but the person who exhibited it was under the influence of a drug." Mrs. Packard pointed toward the girl. "I decided to observe the evening rounds of the doctors, and I saw them giving injections to Polly that were not on the scheduled chart."

Clara again stepped forward, and Mrs. Buckskin pointed at Clara's head. "We know, Liz. Anne McFarland analyzed the contents of the syringe given to Jessica Adkins. It had liquid peyote mixed with the morphine. And the goblet that Matilda Johansen drank also had peyote included with the poison. Polly Bedford was the only person who had access to the poison, drugs and weapons. She stole the master key from Rooney's office. She delivered them all, did she not?"

It was Polly's turn to step forward. "Indeed, it was me, Mrs. Foltz. But I was not in my right mind. Mrs. Packard explained to me how they were doing it. They had been drugging me all along. Even before I was committed to this asylum."

"But why? It makes no earthly sense." Laura Gordon's attorney logic was entering the fray. "The Bedford parents of Polly are on the state's health committee. If Mr. Galton was attempting to seek favor to conduct business, then blaming their daughter for murder would not endear them to him."

"I think I have that scoundrel figured out." Captain Lees holstered his pistol. "If he can control a genius child of the elite, then he could move up. Why not the governor's child? Even the president himself?"

"Right. That's his philosophy. I read about it in the New York magazine. Only the white folks who have the best genes deserve to rule the roost." Dr. McFarland chimed in.

"Wasn't it also because they feared strong women? Perhaps women very similar to my mother." Samuel sidled his way through the dancers to the front of the room near the riser.

Mr. Galton was fuming. "You people have no concept of what it's like to face nature on its own terms. To survive and to serve are the shared rules between humanity and the animal kingdom. I have simply understood my cousin's rules and accepted them. My insight is that there are the same survival of the fittest rules in both the human and animal cultures. The racial statistics are available to rational calculators. The tribal societies were backward, and the races within those societies were brown, yellow and black skinned. The Northern European races, on the other hand, grew stronger racially because of their advanced weapons and tools, which moved them faster along the technological pathway, so they were able to subjugate the less educated and weaker tribal societies. The whites advanced faster because they were genetically superior. They were only coincidentally white. Color had nothing to do with it."

"I am sorry. I still don't understand how Polly's parents are part of this scheme, if that's what it was." Clara was beginning to believe Elizabeth's theory, but she wanted more hard evidence. "How was having a child, who does what Polly supposedly did, a good thing for the racial elite, into which category the Bedfords certainly fit?"

"Galton and Rooney wanted the public, especially the wealthy public, to fear the possibility of racial contamination. Let me bring out the final piece of our little puzzle. Don't worry. Polly and I have discovered that all of this was written down by Galton and Rooney. We have these incriminating documents stored inside Jacob's Ladder." Mrs. Packard motioned to the buckskin woman. The lady stepped down off the riser, Winchester in hand, and walked out of the dining room.

"Clara. If Liz has all this evidence, then we can convict. We can stop this insanity before he can use it inside other asylums," Laura pointed out.

Adeline Quantrill was becoming agitated. Clara noticed her face getting that far-away look once more. This meant she was either telepathically sending or receiving. "Adeline? What information do you have for us?"

The girl stepped forward and took Samuel by his arm. "Mr. Galton has a back-up plan. I couldn't ascertain the details, but he is confident you will fail."

"Look!" Samuel was pointing at the man being escorted, at rifle point, into the dining hall. The buckskin woman was smiling, as if she had captured some wild Indian, who had been intent upon raiding their wagon train on the prairie.

The young man she was pushing toward them was, indeed, dark-skinned, with long, stringy-black hair, multi-colored beads encircling his red shirt, and a red bandana around his forehead. He also wore animal-skin moccasins.

"He looks like Navaho to me," Dr. McFarland pointed out.

"No. He's an Apache. A bit feistier. Galton's people wanted the maximum threat factor for their plan." Mrs. Packard walked over to the young native and stood beside him. "His name is Jacob Windwalker. Since his kind, as well as the Negroes and Chinese, are not allowed to be housed in exclusive insane asylums, like this, Galton and his international cohorts wanted a way to sell their grand plan to governments around the world."

Clara was astounded. "Grand plan? What is that? Certainly you don't mean . . ." The idea that was beginning to fill her consciousness was too horrible to believe.

"Yes, they were going to impregnate Polly after she menstruated. This was their method of showing the elites what would happen if the races became mixed. For, you see, Mrs. Bedford comes from native stock. When Louise Bedford's Sister, Jeanne Forester, overheard Louise tell her husband that Polly could not be interviewed by the police, she was afraid the police would inquire into the family's hereditary lineage. They attempted to cover up Polly's heritage, but I did some fact checking when I saw Polly was being drugged. When you were in San Francisco with the Wilkinson insanity hearing, I journeyed to the Stockton City Hall of Records. Louise Bedford and her husband, Ronald, came to California during the 1850s Gold Rush. Ronald, a prospector, had first met his wife in Kansas. She was a teenage orphan who had been living in a Catholic orphanage. Louise Bedford's mother was a Cheyenne squaw, one of the wives of a Dog Soldier chief named Morning Star. Louise Bedford's mother was captured by a Frenchman who had raided the village, along with his Chippewa allies, and they kidnapped Louise's mother. She was impregnated by the Frenchman, out of wedlock, and Louise was given up for adoption to the Catholic charities."

Dr. McFarland was intrigued. "I know that tribe. The Cheyenne were fierce warriors who were originally peaceful farmers in the Sheyenne River valley. They were forced out by the French into Colorado and Kansas, where they became wandering buffalo hunters. Of course, when the railroads came, the buffalo were shot from those trains, and soon, their herds diminished, until tribes like the Cheyenne had to fight for their survival as a culture."

"That's all very well and good. However, as we now know, people such as Galton and Rooney, and their adherents, have no time for tribal pity. To them, these people are all savages who needed taming and civilization to make them acceptable. The same way we treated the Negros and then the Chinese." Mrs. Packard turned to the young brave. "The Apache tribe is still detested by most settlers in California and Arizona. They raided white wagon trains and towns more than any other tribe. Galton believed when Polly became impregnated by an Apache brave, then our American citizenry would be so shocked that Galton's plans to sterilize women would be accepted more readily."

"Sterilize? How do you know this?" Clara's mind was reeling.

"Yes, it's all written down in their document, in black and white. Come with me. I want to show you something, Clara." Mrs. Packard took Clara's hand. The older woman guided her, along with Polly Bedford, out toward the exit.

"Mother! Be careful." Samuel cried.

"We'll be back shortly," Clara told him, following closely behind the two into the dark hallway.

Liz and Polly still had their pistols, so Clara felt a bit safer. The lightening and thunder cracked, sending a chill down Clara's spine. She had no idea where they were headed, but she had finally begun to realize what Mrs. Packard had uncovered. Clara had been much too conservative with her detection. It had taken a woman who was more experienced with drugs, and the ways of mental asylums, to uncover the final truth.

Clara felt something dripping on her head. She looked up, and it was the ceiling that was fissured and sending down the droplets from the rainstorm outside. Polly and Liz had stopped in the hallway near the Jacob's Ladder access. However, instead of pulling down on the cord to release the ladder up into the storeroom, Polly reached down and pulled away the Persian rug that covered the floor near Dr. Rooney's office. Beneath, as the lightening struck to reveal it, was a metal door. Polly pulled up on a lever inside the door, and it clicked. Grunting, the girl pulled the metal door upward, exposing another set of stairs, going down instead of up.

"Come, Mrs. Foltz. They're down here." Polly scampered down the stairs, as she had obviously done this before. However, Clara saw that it was pitch-dark down those stairs, and she hesitated. As she was about to tell Liz she was not going down there, two wax candles flew up from the darkness and landed at Clara's feet.

"Here are some wooden matches, Clara," Liz said, handing her the box of Indian Chief Fuzees.

Clara lit both candles, and handed one to Mrs. Packard. She followed the old woman as she carefully descended the stairs. The odor of sweat and mould hit Clara immediately, and she could hear the drips from the rain entering this cellar from above.

"Close the hatch, please," Liz told her, and Clara did so. The metal door shut with a thump.

As their candles flickered in the dampness, Clara followed, and her senses were on high alert. In the distance she could hear the sound of human beings. They were groaning and weeping. When they were finally in front of the metal cage, what Clara then saw would haunt her the rest of her life.

Clara, Polly and Liz held their candles up to the cage, and, huddled inside, there must have been fifty or some-odd women, of all ages, races and physical handicaps. Most were dark-skinned, but a few were white, speaking in different foreign languages. Like the lunatics she had met during her stay inside the asylum, they each had a lonely soliloquy, meant to satisfy their inner natures.

However, Clara noted, almost every one of these women was a physical monstrosity. Some had hunchbacks that burst out of their navy-blue uniforms at strange angles, exposing wrinkled bumps, bruises, and hair patches on their discolored skin. Others had pointed heads and were bald; some had the oval, slant-eyed appearance of Mongoloids; and still others were obviously blind, with darting, bloodshot eyes that could not fix upon anything in front of them.

"This is the first group they were going to sterilize. The deformed immigrants, Natives, and Negroes. Galton believed he would gain wide sympathy from the public after he explained why he was doing this, and how much it would save the public coffers." Mrs. Packard's voice was bitter with invective. "I have seen these types of patients before. They require much more care and civility than those upstairs. They can be rehabilitated, however, and some can even perform basic chores and other tasks. The idea that humans, of any physical or mental disability, should be dehumanized with the stigma of permanent sterility, is repugnant to me."

"I understand, Liz. We have other methods to keep these women chaste. If they can be rehabilitated, then why shouldn't they even have the right to procreate? From what I have studied, and from what my daughters, Trella and Bertha, have discovered in their biology courses, hereditary traits are not always passed directly from the parents. Very healthy and normal traits can come from many generations before, sometimes hundreds of years before." Clara pulled her hand back, as one of the women inside attempted to reach her hand through the bars to snuff out the candle.

Mrs. Packard's groan mixed with the imprisoned groans inside the cage. "Galton's theories have no such logic. Mental and physical abnormalities are an anathema to a bigoted person's way of seeing the world. I have fought his kind of thinking my entire life. Like my husband's way of thinking, these bigots have a fixed, incontrovertible rationale, which has no room for more reasonable approaches. They are always looking for the methods which can reap the greatest monetary wealth and a psychologically intimidating power over others. It has always been this way, and it will probably always be this way, unless we can show the public that these very real problems can be handled much differently."

From above them, there was an explosive eruption. It was not the sound of thunder, Clara realized. It was the horrendous ebullition of some kind of bomb going off outside their cellar confines. Polly Bedford was the first to run down the passageway to the stairs, followed by Clara, and, moving much more slowly, Mrs. Packard.

***

Laura, Adeline, and Ah Toy were standing beneath what remained of the Jacob's Ladder storeroom. Burnt paper, splintered wood, and ceiling wax were littered all over the first floor hallway, and there was a gigantic, jagged hole, of about twenty-five feet, directly above them, where the stairs used to be. However, all of the assembled crowd, of about fifteen patients, were looking down at the mangled body of a person lying, burned and bloodied, within the rubble.

"Isaiah? What happened?" Clara screamed.

Lees had his gun out, pointed at Francis Galton and Dr. Emil Kraepelin. "It was Mrs. Angela Thoma. She found the entrance to the stairs, and she went up. This woman, who was singing an aria from *Aida* in the hallway, said she saw Angela before she climbed up into the second-floor hideaway.

"Before she went up, she told me there was an evil spirit up there. She said she needed to kill it to preserve nature's purity." The tall singer began to sob, her shredded evening gown singed black from the explosion.

Captain Lees exhaled. "Galton planted the explosive device up there to protect his written plans. That was his back-up plan. Mrs. Thoma shot at what she perhaps believed to be an evil spirit, and the bomb was triggered. I'm afraid that all of the written evidence of Galton's master plan has been destroyed."

CHAPTER 13: RETURN TO SANITY

The Hopkins Mansion, One Nob Hill, San Francisco, May 4, 1887.

Clara had assembled her group inside the usual meeting place, Mrs. Hopkins' Library. She wanted to explain the aftermath of what occurred during their internment at the Stockton State Insane Asylum. She also wanted to give a sort of bon voyage celebration for Mrs. Elizabeth Ware Packard, who was going on a cruise to Europe, where she would speak to mental health experts in a Paris meeting. Clara believed the ramifications of the California investigation would be changing how patients are treated, but she was also realistic enough to understand these changes would not, most likely, last very long.

As she gazed on either side of the long mahogany table at her guests and family, Clara was thinking about how wonderful it was that her detective business was becoming much more of a cooperative affair. If it had not been for having Mrs. Packard, Dr. McFarland, and his granddaughter, Anne, working along with her usual group of family members, the Stockton Asylum case would have turned out quite differently for all involved. As it was, a freak accident, a "mental metamorphosis," if you will, had changed everything at the last moment. Life was not, sadly, a game that girls played to occupy their minds. No, it was a much more serious affair that allowed obvious scoundrels, like Mr. Francis Galton, to get away, due to circumstance beyond their control.

There were ten of her friends and family at the table, the same number of people who had been on her initial list of suspects in the murder of Winnifred Cotton. To her left, Isaiah Lees sat, his usual, contemplative scowl decorating his handsome face. Whenever she stared hard at him, however, he would look up and give her the smile reserved only for her. Next to him was Dr. Andrew McFarland, and then his granddaughter, Anne. The final three on that side of the table were family members, Adeline Quantrill, who was now officially engaged to her betrothed son, Samuel Cortland, who was beside her. Bertha May, alias Deidra Watkins, was the last person on the end.

On Clara's right were Mrs. Packard, Ah Toy, her best friend, attorney Laura de Force Gordon, Trella Evelyn, and Mrs. Mary Hopkins, the demented, but loving, head of the household. Clara had a surprise for all of them. She waved at her youngest son, David Milton, who knew to bring in the guests, who were waiting in the mansion's foyer.

One by one, each of the five guests entered the Library, and they each sat at the five chairs, two on one side, three on the other, of the long table. Clara's group watched them be seated, and there were smiles on their faces to greet them.

"Ladies and gentlemen. Let me introduce our guests of honor. On our left, Mrs. Melissa "Pepper" Wilkinson, recently discharged from the San Francisco Women's House of Criminal Detention, a free woman. Melissa is also seeing another former patient from Scotland, Mr. Claiborne Falcone, who was able to overcome his own delusion that he was a Jew. Next to her is Mrs. Katherine Yantis. Please notice that Kathy is not wearing her buckskin, as she no longer believes she is Mrs. Annie Oakley, thanks to Liz Packard's counseling. On the right, we have Miss Sidney "Kitty" Reyes, who is now attending the University of California, at Berkeley, majoring in International Studies. Next, we have young Miss Jessica Adkins, who is still an out-patient, but her mental health is improving nicely due to Mrs. Packard's counsel and the promised letters that she will receive from our chief experts here, including Dr. McFarland, myself, and Anne McFarland. Finally, we have young Miss Polly Bedford, who is now free from any mental problems, as she had been drugged most of the time by asylum officials. Please, applaud now, as we shall be adjourning to the dining room for a nice repast with my parents after this meeting." Clara clapped her hands, along with all the others, and their five guests beamed with embarrassment.

"As you may know, our foray into the abyss that was the Stockton Insane Asylum has ended. We were not able to prosecute all the parties involved in the drug sales and experiments being done at the behest of Leland Stanford, and his new private university, but we were able to give enough hard evidence to the courts in order to release Mrs. Wilkinson and to banish Francis Galton and Dr. Emil

Kraepelin back to Great Britain and Germany. Since we could show that Melissa Wilkinson had no knowledge that the weapon she was using was provided from the asylum's armory, she was, therefore, not responsible. In addition, since the person who was murdered, Dr. Alfred Rooney, had ordered the drugging of all patients with the hallucinogen, liquid peyote, Mrs. Wilkinson was not in her right mind at the time of the stabbing. Pepper, would you like to add to what I have just said?" Clara nodded over at the bright-eyed woman wearing a robin's egg blue spring frock.

"I know. I seem to have my speech back. My family now believes I should have it turned back off. However, thanks to Mrs. Foltz, and, most especially to Mrs. Elizabeth Packard, I have my normal wits about me today. After having learned that there are groups wherein I can voice my displeasure with the patriarchal system that is today ravaging female and immigrant rights, I have a normal outlet for my pent-up grievances. We are growing in numbers, every day, and with people like you behind our efforts, I dare say, we shall be victorious!"

"Thank you, Pepper. Your invigoration is very welcome in our Suffrage Movement, and your nickname is well applied, in moderation, of course. I also trust my lawyer friend, Mrs. Gordon, is now aware of how drugs can affect the mental state of a homicidal perpetrator." Clara glanced at Laura, and she was pleased when her friend nodded her head in agreement.

"Mother, how did you not miss the fact that Polly's parents were trying to hide the information that her mother Louisa's side of the family was from native heritage? You need only have contacted me in San Francisco to do such research." Trella Evelyn, ever Clara's antagonist, was again prompting a debate.

"I made a mistake. I have no excuse, other than the fact that we were hard-pressed for time at that moment. Thankfully, however, I had appointed a woman who had such experience, and who filled in for you very nicely. I know, Mrs. Packard and I are not from your generation, Trella, but we do attempt to keep up." Clara smiled at her eldest daughter, and Trella smirked.

"What do you suppose was in that master plan of Francis Galton's? If we had been able to use that as evidence, I dare say, there would be nothing left of this Eugenics controversy," Dr. McFarland pointed out.

"I know. I would assume it was filled with the same bigoted and misogynist declarations that he made in court. Now that the public is aware of the sterilizations he was planning, they are quite angry, especially our suffragists. One would hope our populace is educated enough to see through such bigoted logic, but only time and history will tell," said Clara.

"I want to know, how did Mrs. Packard enlist the aid of the entire community of patients in order to rebel against Galton and his staff?" Anne McFarland asked.

Clara noticed that Liz Packard was not using her ear trumpet. So, she pointed at it, as it was lying in front of the older woman's place at the table. Liz nodded and picked it up, placing it inside her right ear.

"Liz, Anne wants to know how you were able to mount your revolution inside the asylum that night." Clara's voice was a bit louder than her normally feminine and lilting softness.

Obviously deciding that this question was of major importance to the group, Elizabeth Packard stood up to address the assemblage, in the tradition of the elder generation, of whom she was such a noble exemplar. Clara's eyes filled with emotion as she listened to the woman's words. And, as she looked out at the members of her now close-knit group, she could see that their eyes, as well, were tearing up, and she could hear snuffles and sniffs coming from many of them.

"I know you might expect that I had some secret knowledge of how to communicate with the insane mind. I did not. And, I do not have any such knowledge today. I simply spoke to my audience as one would address any fellow human on the planet. I used logic. Plain and simple logic. For, you see, what separates us humans from the animal kingdom is that we can communicate with everyone, despite our language differences, and even despite our mental differences. We do not seek to survive in some violent, tragic display of hatred and warfare, the way Mr. Galton describes his version of reality."

"His version was based on his egotistical outlook," Clara said.

Mrs. Packard nodded. "When I told those patients that the doctors were drugging them without their permission, they immediately knew they had to act. I have seen this response in many other asylums around the world. Humans want to be seen as thinking, moral beings, who can judge what is good for them, on their own, and not by being given chemicals to alter their thinking. I believe, you see, that the mind is one large chemical set, and we must be careful not to pollute it with outside ingredients, which can cause confusion and stress. Observe closely, a child concentrating in a meadow, who watches a butterfly winging its way around her. That child simply wants to behold the beauty of freedom in its natural environment. Mental patients want to also behold freedom, on their own, and they want to be able to work out their own problems, on their own. When I told Dr. Rooney that I work with each person's so-called insane world view, I meant it. Nothing is insane unless it becomes an obsession that keeps us from respecting one another. Most humans, even lunatics, understand that basic human fact. Those who would come between us, as thinking human beings, yearning for individual freedom, and respecting the rights of others, are forever seen as the true villains in our stories. My ladies acted because they wanted their freedom respected. And, if I have anything to say about it, they shall receive it!"

"Mrs. Foltz! There's a messenger here. It's an emergency telegram from Washington D. C." Joseph Hannigan, the butler, stood at the door to the library.

"Bring it forward, please," Clara said, wondering who would write to her from the nation's capitol.

The Western Union boy walked through the Library, glancing warily at the adults assembled therein. He received Clara's signature, and she took the telegram from him.

"Thank you," Clara said, and she read the message.

"I'm afraid it's bad news," she told the group. "It's from Miss Miriam Levine, the Attorney General's assistant. We met her during my first case, the Chinatown murders. She wants me to come to Washington immediately. The current appointee to the Supreme Court, Judge Marshal Owens, has been assassinated. She wants me to defend his assassin, who happens to be a woman."

Ah Toy, Laura, Trella, Bertha, Adeline and Samuel, all stood up in unison. "We will help you pack, mother," Trella told her.

From the back of the room, David Milton, age sixteen, spoke up. "Mother, I wish to help you as well this time."

Clara carefully folded the telegram and placed it inside her dress's top pocket. "Don't worry, we shall decide who assists in due time. Right now, I am going to wire Miss Levine to find out more information. As we know, without adequate information, the truth will never be discovered."

ABOUT THE AUTHOR

James Musgrave's work has been recently featured in *Best New Writing 2011*, Eric Hoffer Book Awards, Hopewell Press, Titusville, N.J. He was semi-finalist in the Black River Chapbook Competition, Fall, 2012. He was also in a Bram Stoker Award Finalist volume of horror fiction, *Beneath the Surface, 13 Shocking Tales of Terror*, Shroud Publishing, San Francisco, CA. His historical mystery series starring Detective Patrick James O'Malley was selected as "featured titles" by the American Library Association's Self-E Program for Independent Authors. The first mystery in that series, *Forevermore*, won the First-Place blue ribbon for Best Historical Mystery, in the Chanticleer International Clue Book Awards, 2013. James lives in San Diego, and is the publisher of EMRE Publishing, LLC.

Sign-up for the Author's Newsletter at emrepublishing.com

Contest and Special Offer

In his third mystery, *The Stockton Insane Asylum Murder*, author James Musgrave recruited five readers to play patients. They each had a specific psychosis being used by the unscrupulous director, and two foreign scientists, who perform inhuman experiments upon them.

Not since Dennis Lehane's *Shutter Island* has there been a thriller so gripping, so horrendously true to its historical roots.

Now, in his sixth Portia of the Pacific volume, Musgrave will again seek out three readers to become suspects in his legal thriller and mystery, this time set in 1888 San Diego. Entitled *Stingaree*, this mystery delves into the lives of the hearty folks buying up real estate and making a lot of money down south, where law and order is in short supply, but greed and murder are not. Suspects will receive a free autographed copy of the novel, and all who enter will receive an early eBook review copy.

Wyatt Earp is arrested for the murder of an itinerant Rabbi Sonenschein, who has been doing some recruiting of his own. The rabbi has a "cult following" in his role as a supposed Kabbalah expert. However, Earp, and his common law wife, Josephine Marcus, also have a money scheme of their own cooking. Attorney detective Clara Foltz, the series heroine, decides to defend Marshal Earp when he is charged with the murder of the rabbi.

This is where you come in. Musgrave will use three readers to supply him with three additional suspects in the plot. *Stingaree* will be extra special, as the eBook will be written using ePub3 technology. It will allow the reader, at a strategic moment in the mystery, to choose which suspect he or she believes is the guilty party.

And, with Musgrave's patented "insert story" feature, the reader can follow the existential trail of that suspect to see if his/her choice is indeed a correct analysis.

If you enjoy mysteries by Arthur Conan Doyle, Agatha Christie, Dennis Lehane, or Margaret Atwood, you will love this new way to experience and participate in a legal thriller and mystery. See how this eBook will also contain a music playlist, an accompanying audio book, and relevant, historically accurate videos about the tumultuous Stingaree gambling and red-light district of San Diego.